"Like Margaret Atwood's
*Handmaid's Tale*, Leni Zumas's
new book describes a future both
frightening and all too possible."
—SEATTLE TIMES

"Zumas's talent is electric. Get ready for a shock." —THE GUARDIAN

"Strange and lovely and luminous. I loved *Red Clocks*
with my whole heart." —KELLY LINK

"This highly absorbing novel imagines a near future of America in which
abortion is illegal in all fifty states. Zumas has a perfectly tuned ear
for the way society relies on a moralizing sentimentalism
to restrict women's lives and enforce conformity."
—NEW YORK TIMES BOOK REVIEW

"Leni Zumas here proves she can do
almost anything. *Red Clocks* is funny,
mordant, poetic, alarming, and
inspiring—not to mention
a way forward for
fiction now."
—MAGGIE NELSON

Praise for Leni Zumas's

# RED CLOCKS

**An Amazon Best Book of the Month**
**A *New York Times* Editors' Choice**
**An Indie Next Pick**

"An enchanting ramble through the myths and mundanities of womanhood...*Red Clocks* ends up feeling like an enjoyable puzzle that is fundamentally unsolvable, some of its pieces playfully misplaced along the way. The fractured narrative leaves us to connect the dots between these disparate characters, all of whom make bleak compromises because they—like so many women throughout history—have so few options available to them." —Joy Press, *Los Angeles Times*

"The story is set in a small Oregon town in a future that Mike Pence can almost see if he stands on his pew...This provocative exploration of female longing, frustration, and determination couldn't be more timely, and yet there's nothing fleeting about it. With *Red Clocks,* Zumas has written a novel that's political without being doctrinaire, that expands the dimensions of our most pressing social debate." —Ron Charles, *Washington Post*

"Intricate and alarming, Leni Zumas's riveting second novel, *Red Clocks,* arrives just in time...Wry and urgent, defiant and stylish, Zumas's braided tale follows the intertwined fates of four women whose lives [the Personhood Amendment] irrevocably alters...Lit up with verbal pyrotechnics and built with an admirably balanced structure, *Red Clocks* is undeniably gorgeously written." —Kathleen Rooney, *Chicago Tribune*

"A lyrical and beautifully observed reflection on women's lives…Highly absorbing…Zumas is a skillful writer, expertly keeping each of her characters in balanced motion, never allowing one to dominate the rest. Her cunning device of not revealing the name of each character in the sections she narrates grants us a multidimensional perspective on all four women, highlighting their roles in one another's stories. It's a beautiful metaphor for the interdependence of women's lives."

—Naomi Alderman, *New York Times Book Review*

"Like Margaret Atwood's *The Handmaid's Tale,* Leni Zumas's new book describes a future both frightening and all too possible…Zumas has a lovely way with a sentence and a sharp understanding of how women can be jealous and supportive of each other in equal measure. The coastal setting is vividly rendered, as is the everyday reality of doctor appointments, dirty dishes, and broken dreams."            —Jeff Baker, *Seattle Times*

"Leni Zumas here proves she can do almost anything. Her tale feels part Melvillean, part Lydia Davis, part Octavia Butler—but really Zumas's vision is entirely her own. *Red Clocks* is funny, mordant, political, poetic, alarming, and inspiring—not to mention a way forward for fiction now."

—Maggie Nelson

"In an alarming peek into a dystopian future, a group of women navigates family and motherhood in an America that has outlawed abortion, in vitro fertilization, and adoption by single women. Each of the interwoven story lines is complex and heartbreaking in its own way, and overall it's a fascinating and unsettling exploration of the limits society can place on women's bodies."            —Samantha Irby, *Marie Claire*

"Intense and beautifully crafted…The dialogue is so quick and multilayered as to take one's breath away…Zumas elucidates, in virtuosic prose, the struggle to be valued running like a power line under every incarnation of feminism. Her talent is electric. Get ready for a shock."

—Katharine Coldiron, *The Guardian*

"A cautionary work of farsighted fiction... A spooky-good novel of ideas about the power of collective resistance against the tyranny of rights and freedoms denied."                    —Lisa Shea, *Elle*

"This is the dystopia that the right wing wants... The characters in *Red Clocks* are nuanced and funny, and the novel itself is as in-your-face yet strangely beautiful as the cover art."    —Maris Kreizman, *Esquire*

"*Red Clocks* asks us to rethink what it really means to be female in a world that's written almost exclusively by men... It is always nice when a novel forces me to revisit the foundation of my values. It's a little bit like rereading your favorite books every decade or so... *Red Clocks* is actually most notable for the brio of its prose—its excellent sense of timing and cadence... Time's a-ticking, this novel seems to say. Wake up."
                                        —Fiona Maazel, *Bookforum*

"Strange and lovely and luminous. I loved *Red Clocks* with my whole heart."           —Kelly Link, author of *Magic for Beginners*

"Zumas's book stands out from the crowd for its thoroughness in revealing the hypocrisy inherent in valuing the lives a woman brings into this world but not the life of the woman herself."    —Kristin Iversen, *Nylon*

"Where a lesser writer might have delivered a shrill, one-sided polemic, Zumas draws us into the intersecting lives of five women in a profound exploration of our attitudes toward motherhood, freedom, and life itself... A page-turning plot is rendered in sentences as gorgeous and wise as poems... Be prepared to dog-ear these pages."
                                        —Dawn Raffel, Oprah.com

"Hilarious, terrifying, and masterful—*Red Clocks* reflects the horror and absurdity of our political landscape with a brilliance that ensures its timelessness. A poignant, wickedly sharp classic."
                                        —Alissa Nutting, author of *Made for Love*

"Zumas's decision to tell the story from four different perspectives is not just a stylistic flourish. Together, they form a raw portrait of the forces of disenfranchisement that women have faced for millennia. What gives *Red Clocks* its lingering pungency is how, despite each character's distinct circumstances, the same features — pregnancy, motherhood, and social expectations — trap and menace them all."

— Mike Mariani, *The Nation*

"Like the best dystopian fiction, *Red Clocks* is so close to reality that it feels almost prophetic; like the best fiction, it's highly inventive, with sharp, stark prose, strong characterizations, and an undercurrent of humor and hope... *Red Clocks* delivers a stark, clear truth about the existential quandary of being a person capable of ceding your body to the gestation of another body. It's an amazing thing to be able to do. It's a monstrous thing to force someone to do. And between these two extremes is where most of us live."

— Megan Burbank, *Portland Mercury*

"Zumas's novel is a reckoning, a warning, and nothing short of a miracle. Don't miss it." — *Ploughshares*

"Shattering...With its strong point of view, the novel, in lesser hands, might have been reduced to agitprop, but Zumas has raised it, instead, to the level of literature, which readers will find deeply moving. The characters are beautifully realized, inviting empathy and understanding; the richly realized plot is compulsively readable; and the theme, with its echoes of Margaret Atwood, is never didactic but invites thought and discussion. The result is powerful and timely." —Michael Cart, Booklist

"Zumas is a lyrical polymath of a writer." — *Kirkus Reviews*

## Also by Leni Zumas

Farewell Navigator

The Listeners

# RED CLOCKS

## A Novel

## LENI ZUMAS

**BACK BAY BOOKS**
LITTLE, BROWN AND COMPANY
NEW YORK  BOSTON  LONDON

Copyright © 2018 by Leni Zumas

Back Bay Books / Little, Brown and Company
Hachette Book Group
1290 Avenue of the Americas, New York, NY 10104
littlebrown.com

Originally published in hardcover by Little, Brown and Company, January 2018
First Back Bay Books trade paperback edition, October 2018

Back Bay Books is an imprint of Little, Brown and Company, a division of Hachette Book Group, Inc. The Back Bay Books name and logo are trademarks of Hachette Book Group, Inc.

The Hachette Speakers Bureau provides a wide range of authors for speaking events. To find out more, go to hachettespeakersbureau.com or call (866) 376-6591.

ISBN 978-0-316-43481-2 (hc) / 978-0-316-43478-2 (pb)
LCCN 2017933411

10 9 8 7 6 5 4 3 2 1

LSC-C

Printed in the United States of America

*for Luca and Nicholas*
per sempre

For nothing was simply one thing. The other
Lighthouse was true too.

*Virginia Woolf*

# RED CLOCKS

Born in 1841 on a Faroese sheep farm,

The polar explorer was raised on a farm near

In the North Atlantic Ocean, between Scotland and Iceland, on an island with more sheep than people, a shepherd's wife gave birth to a child who would grow up to study ice.

Pack ice once posed such a danger to ships that any researcher who knew the personality of this ice could predict its behavior was valuable to the companies and governments that funded polar expeditions.

In 1841, on the Faroe Islands, in a turf-roofed cottage, in a bed that smelled of whale fat, of a mother who had delivered nine children and buried four, the polar explorer Eivør Mínervudottír was born.

# THE BIOGRAPHER

In a room for women whose bodies are broken, Eivør Mínervudottír's biographer waits her turn. She wears sweatpants, is white skinned and freckle cheeked, not young, not old. Before she is called to climb into stirrups and feel her vagina prodded with a wand that makes black pictures, on a screen, of her ovaries and uterus, the biographer sees every wedding ring in the room. Serious rocks, fat bands of glitter. They live on the fingers of women who have leather sofas and solvent husbands but whose cells and tubes and bloods are failing at their animal destiny. This, anyway, is the story the biographer likes. It is a simple, easy story that allows her not to think about what's happening in the women's heads, or in the heads of the husbands who sometimes accompany them.

Nurse Crabby wears a neon-pink wig and a plastic-strap contraption that exposes nearly all of her torso, including a good deal of breast. "Happy Halloween," she explains.

"And to you," says the biographer.

"Let's go suck out some lineage."

"Pardon?"

"Anagram for blood."

"Hmm," says the biographer politely.

Crabby doesn't find the vein straight off. Has to dig, and it hurts. "Where *are* you, mister?" she asks the vein. Months of needlework have streaked and darkened the insides of the biographer's elbows. Luckily long sleeves are common in this part of the world.

"Aunt Flo visited again, did she?" says Crabby.

"Vengefully."

"Well, Roberta, the body's a riddle. Here we go—*got* you." Blood swooshes into the chamber. It will tell them how much follicle-stimulating hormone and estradiol and progesterone the biographer's body is making.

There are good numbers and there are bad. Crabby drops the tube into a rack alongside other little bullets of blood.

Half an hour later, a knock on the exam-room door—a warning, not a request for permission. In comes a man wearing leather trousers, aviator sunglasses, a curly black wig under a porkpie hat.

"I'm the guy from that band," says Dr. Kalbfleisch.

"Wow," says the biographer, bothered by how sexy he's become.

"Shall we take a look?" He settles his leather on a stool in front of her open legs, says "Oops!" and removes the sunglasses. Kalbfleisch played football at an East Coast university and still has the face of a frat boy. He is golden skinned, a poor listener. He smiles while citing bleak statistics. The nurse holds the biographer's file and a pen to write measurements. The doctor will call out how thick the lining, how large the follicles, how many the follicles. Add these numbers to the biographer's age (42) and her level of follicle-stimulating hormone (14.3) and the temperature outside (56) and the number of ants in the square foot of soil directly beneath them (87), and you get the odds. The chance of a child.

Snapping on latex gloves: "Okay, Roberta, let's see what's what."

On a scale of one to ten, with ten being the shrill funk of an elderly cheese and one being no odor at all, how would he rank the smell of the biographer's vagina? How does it compare with the other vaginas barreling through this exam room, day in, day out, years of vaginas, a crowd of vulvic ghosts? Plenty of women don't shower beforehand, or are battling a yeast, or just happen naturally to stink in the nethers. Kalbfleisch has sniffed some ripe tangs in his time.

He slides in the ultrasound wand, dabbed with its neon-blue jelly, and presses it up against her cervix. "Your lining's nice and thin," he says. "Four point five. Right where we want it." On the monitor, the lining of the biographer's uterus is a dash of white chalk in a black swell, hardly enough of a thing, it seems, to measure, but Kalbfleisch is a trained professional in whose expertise she is putting her trust. And her money—so much money that the numbers seem virtual, mythical, details from a story about money rather than money anyone actually has. The biographer, for example, does not have it. She's using credit cards.

The doctor moves to the ovaries, shoving and tilting the wand until he gets an angle he likes. "Here's the right side. Nice bunch of follicles..." The eggs themselves are too small to be seen, even with magnification, but their sacs—black holes on the grayish screen—can be counted.

"Keep our fingers crossed," says Kalbfleisch, easing the wand back out.

*Doctor, is my bunch actually nice?*

He rolls away from her crotch and pulls off his gloves. "For the past several cycles"—looking at her chart, not at her—"you've been taking Clomid to support ovulation."

This she does not need to be told.

"Unfortunately Clomid also causes the uterine lining to shrink, so we advise patients not to take it for long stretches of time. You've already done a long stretch."

*Wait, what?*

She should have looked it up herself.

"So for this round we need to try a different protocol. Another medication that's been known to improve the odds in some elderly pregravid cases."

"Elderly?"

"Just a clinical term." He doesn't glance up from the prescription he's writing. "She'll explain the medication and we'll see you back here on day nine." He hands the file to the nurse, stands, and makes an adjustment to his leather crotch before striding out.

Asshole, in Faroese: *reyvarhol*.

Crabby says, "So you need to fill this today and start taking it tomorrow morning, on an empty stomach. Every morning for ten days. While you're on it, you might notice a foul odor from the discharge from your vagina."

"Great," says the biographer.

"Some women say the smell is quite, um, surprising," she goes on. "Even actually disturbing. But whatever you do, don't douche. That'll introduce chemicals into the canal that if they make their way through the cervix can, you know, compromise the pH of the uterine cavity."

The biographer has never douched in her life, nor does she know anyone who has.

"Questions?" says the nurse.

"What does" — she squints at the prescription — "Ovutran do?"

"It supports ovulation."

"How, though?"

"You'd have to ask the doctor."

She is submitting her area to all kinds of invasion without understanding a fraction of what's being done to it. This seems, suddenly, terrible. How can you raise a child alone if you don't even find out what they're doing to your area?

"I'd like to ask him now," she says.

"He's already with another patient. Best thing to do is call the office."

"But I'm here *in* the office. Can't he — or is there someone else who —"

"Sorry, it's an extra-busy day. Halloween and all."

"Why does Halloween make it busier?"

"It's a holiday."

"Not a *national* holiday. Banks are open and the mail is delivered."

"You will need," says Crabby slowly, carefully, "to call the office."


The biographer cried the first time it failed. She was waiting in line to buy floss, having pledged to improve her dental hygiene now that she was going to be a parent, and her phone rang: one of the nurses, "I'm sorry, sweetie, but your test was negative," the biographer saying thank you, okay, thank you and hitting END before the tears started. Despite the statistics and Kalbfleisch's "This doesn't work for everyone," the biographer had thought it would be easy. Squirt in millions of sperm from a nineteen-year-old biology major, precisely timed to be there waiting when the egg flies out; sperm and egg collide in the warm tunnel — how could fertilization *not* happen? *Don't be stupid anymore,* she wrote in her notebook, under *Immediate action required.*

\*     \*     \*

She drives west on Highway 22 into dark hills dense with hemlock, fir, and spruce. Oregon has the best trees in America, soaring and shaggy winged, alpine sinister. Her tree gratitude mutes her doctor resentment. Two hours from his office, her car crests the cliff road and the church steeple juts into view. The rest of town follows, hunched in rucked hills sloping to the water. Smoke coils from the pub chimney. Fishing nets pile on the shore. In Newville you can watch the sea eat the ground, over and over, unstopping. Millions of abyssal thalassic acres. The sea does not ask permission or wait for instruction. It doesn't suffer from not knowing what on earth, exactly, it is meant to do. Today its walls are high, white lather torn, crashing hard at the sea stacks. "Angry sea," people say, but to the biographer the ascribing of human feeling to a body so inhumanly itself is wrong. The water heaves up for reasons they don't have names for.

*Central Coast Regional H.S. seeks history teacher (U.S./World). Bachelor's degree required. Location: Newville, Oregon, fishing village on quiet ocean harbor, migrating whales. Ivy League–educated principal is committed to creating dynamic, innovative learning environment.*

The biographer applied because of *quiet ocean harbor* and no mention of teaching experience. Her brief interview consisted of the principal, Mr. Fivey, plot-summarizing his favorite seafaring novels and mentioning twice the name of the college he had gone to. He said she could do the teacher-certification course over two summers. For seven years she has lived in the lee of fog-smoked evergreen mountains, thousand-foot cliffs plunging straight down to the sea. It rains and rains and rains. Log trucks stall traffic on the cliff road, locals catch fish or make things for tourists, the pub hangs a list of old shipwrecks, the tsunami siren is tested monthly, and students learn to say "miss" as if they were servants.

She starts class by following her daily plan, but when she sees chins mashing into fists, she decides to abandon it. Tenth-grade global history, the world in forty weeks, with a foolish textbook she is contractually obliged to use, can't be stood without detours. These kids, after all, have not been lost yet. Staring up at her, jaws rimmed with baby fat, they are perched on the brink of not giving a shit. They still give a shit, but not, most of them, for long. She instructs them to close their books, which they are happy to do. They watch her with a new stillness. They will be told a story, can be children again, of whom nothing is asked.

"Boadicea was queen of a Celtic tribe called the Iceni in what is now Norfolk, England. The Romans had invaded a while back and were ruling the land. Her husband died and left his fortune to her and their daughters, but the Romans ignored his will, took the fortune, flogged Boadicea, and raped the daughters."

One kid: "What's 'flog'?"

Another: "Beat the frock out of."

"The Romans had screwed her royally"—somebody laughs softly at this, for which the biographer is grateful—"and in 61 CE she led her people in rebellion. The Iceni fought hard. They forced the Romans all the way back to London. But bear in mind that the Roman soldiers had lots of incentive to win, because if they didn't, they could expect to be cooked on skewers and/or boiled to death, after seeing their own intestines being pulled out of their bodies."

"That rules," says a boy.

"Eventually the Roman forces were too much for the Iceni. Boadicea either poisoned herself to avoid capture or got sick; either way, she died. The win column isn't the point. The point is…" She stops, aware of twenty-four little gazes.

Into the silence the soft laugher ventures: "Don't frock with a woman?"

They like this. They like slogans.

"Well," the biographer says, "*sort* of. But more than that. We also have to consider—"

The bell.

A burst of scraping and sliding, bodies glad to go. "Bye, miss!" "Have a good day, miss."

The soft laugher, Mattie Quarles, idles near the biographer's desk. "So is that where the word 'bodacious' comes from?"

"I wish I could say yes," says the biographer, "but 'bodacious' originated in the nineteenth century, I think. Mix of 'bold' and 'audacious.' Good instinct, though!"

"Thanks, miss."

"You really don't need to call me that," says the biographer for the seven thousandth time.

After school she stops at the Acme, grocery and hardware and drugstore combined. The pharmacist's assistant is a boy—now a young man—she taught in her first year at Central Coast, and she hates the moment each month when he hands her the white bag with the little orange bottle. *I know what this is for,* his eyes say. Even if his eyes don't actually say that, it's hard to look at him. She brings other items to the counter (unsalted peanuts, Q-tips) as if somehow to disguise the fertility medication. The biographer can't recall his name but remembers admiring, in class, seven years ago, his long black lashes—they always looked a little wet.

Waiting on the hard little plastic chair, under elevator music and fluorescent glare, the biographer takes out her notebook. Everything in this notebook must be in list form, and any list is eligible. *Items for next food shop. Kalbfleisch's necktie designs. Countries with most lighthouses per capita.*

She starts a new one: *Accusations from the world.*

1. You're too old.
2. If you can't have a child the natural way, you shouldn't have one at all.
3. Every child needs two parents.
4. Children raised by single mothers are more liable to rape/murder/ drug-take/score low on standardized tests.
5. You're too old.

6. You should've thought of this earlier.
7. You're selfish.
8. You're doing something unnatural.
9. How is that child going to feel when she finds out her father is an anonymous masturbator?
10. Your body is a grizzled husk.
11. You're too old, sad spinster!
12. Are you only doing this because you're lonely?


"Miss? Prescription's ready."

"Thank you." She signs the screen on the counter. "How's your day been?"

Lashes turns up his palms at the ceiling.

"If it makes you feel any better," says the biographer, "this medication is going to make me have a foul-smelling vaginal discharge."

"At least it's for a good cause."

She clears her throat.

"That'll be one hundred fifty-seven dollars and sixty-three cents," he adds.

"Pardon me?"

"I'm really sorry."

"A hundred and fifty-seven dollars? For ten pills?"

"Your insurance doesn't cover it."

"Why the eff not?"

Lashes shakes his head. "I wish I could, like, slip it to you, but they've got cameras on every inch of this bitch."

The polar explorer Eivør Mínervudottír spent many hours, as a child, in the sea-washed lighthouse whose keeper was her uncle.

She knew not to talk while he was making entries in the record book.

Never to strike a match unsupervised.

Red sky at night, sailor's delight.

To keep her head low in the lantern room.

To pee in the pot and leave it, and if she did caca, to wrap it in fish paper for the garbage box.

# THE MENDER

From the halt hen two eggs come down, one cracked, one sound. "Thank you," the mender tells the hen, a Dark Brahma with a red wattle and brindled feathers. Because she limps badly — is not one of the winners — this hen is the mender's favorite. A daily happiness to feed her, save her from foxes and rain.

Sound egg in her pocket, she pours the goats' grain. Hans and Pinka are out rambling but will be home soon. They know she can't protect them if they ramble too far. Three shingles have come off the goat-shed roof; she needs nails. Under the shed there used to sleep a varying hare. Brown in summer, white in winter. He hated carrots and loved apples, whose seeds, poisonous to rabbits, the mender made sure to remove. The hare was so cuddly she didn't care that he stole alfalfa from the goats or strewed poo pellets on her bed when she let him inside. One morning she found his body ripped open, a sack of furry blood. Rage poured up her throat at the fox or coyote, the bobcat, *you took him,* but they were only feeding themselves, *you shouldn't have took him,* prey is scarce in winter, *but he was mine.* She cried while digging. Laid the hare beside her aunt's old cat, two small graves under the madrone.

In the cabin the mender stirs the egg with vinegar and shepherd's purse for the client who's coming later, an over-bleeder. The drink will staunch her clotty, aching flow. She's got no job and no insurance. *I can pay you with batteries,* her note said. Vinegary egg screwed tight in a glass jar and tucked into the mini fridge, beside a foil-wrapped wedge of cheddar. The mender wants the cheese right now, this minute, but cheese is only for Fridays. Black licorice nibs are for Sundays.

*   *   *

She mostly eats from the forest. Watercress and bitter cress, dandelion, plantain. Glasswort and chickweed. Bear grass, delicious when grilled. Burdock root to mash and fry. Miner's lettuce and stinging nettle and, in small quantities, ghost pipe. (She loves the white stalks boiled with lemon and salt, but too much ghost pipe can kill you.) And she gleans from orchards and fields: hazelnuts, apples, cranberries, pears. If she could live off the land alone, without person-made things, she would. She hasn't figured out how yet, but that doesn't mean she won't. Show them how Percivals do.

Her mother was a Percival. Her aunt was a Percival. The mender has been a Percival since age six, when her mother left her father. Which was because her father went away most Friday afternoons and didn't come back until Monday and never said why. "A woman wants to know why," said the mender's mother. "At least give me that, fuckermo. Names and places! Ages and occupations!" They drove west across Oregon's high desert, over the Cascade Mountains, mother smoking and daughter spitting out the window, to the coast, where the mender's aunt ran a shop that sold candles, runes, and tarot packs. On the first night, the mender asked what that noise was and learned it was the ocean. "But when does it stop?" "Never," said her aunt. "It's perpetual, though impermanent." And the mender's mother said, "Pretentious much?"

The mender would take pretentious any day over high.

She lies naked with the cat by the stove's heat, hard steady rain on the roof and the woods black and the foxes quiet, owlets asleep in their nest box. Malky leaps from her lap, paws at the door. "You want to get soaked, little fuckermo?" Gold-splashed eyes watch her solemnly. Gray flanks tremble. "You have a girlfriend you need to meet?" She shakes off the blanket and opens the door, and he flashes out.

\*    \*    \*

Whenever Lola came over, Malky hid; she thought the mender lived in the cabin alone. "Don't you get frightened," said Lola, "all the way up here in the middle of nothing?"

Silly bitch, trees are not nothing. Nor are cats, goats, chickens, owls, foxes, bobcats, black-tailed deer, long-eared bats, red-tailed hawks, dark-eyed juncos, bald-faced hornets, varying hares, mourning cloak butterflies, black vine weevils, and souls fled from their mortal casings.

Alone *human*-wise.

She hasn't heard from Lola since that day of the shouting. No notes left in her mailbox at the P.O., no visits. It was more than shouting. A fight. Lola, in her adorable green dress, was fighting. The mender was not. The mender barely said a word.

Past noon, but the goats aren't home yet. Cramp of worry. Last year they wrecked a campsite near the trail. Not their fault: some dumb tourist left food all over the woods. When the mender found them, the guy was pointing a rifle at Hans. "You better keep them on your property from here on out," he said, "because I love goat stew."

In Europe they once held trials for misbehaving animals. Wasn't just the witches they hanged. A pig was sent to the gallows for eating a child's face, a mule roasted alive for having been penetrated by its human master. For the unnatural act of laying an egg, a rooster was burned at the stake. Bees found guilty of stinging a man to death were suffocated in the hive, their honey destroyed, lest murder honey infect the mouths that ate it.

She with murder honey on her teeth shall bleed salt from where two curves of thigh skin meet. Tasting honey from the body of a bee with devil-face shall start this salty blood. Faces of bees who have done murder do resem-

16

ble those of starving dogs, whose eyes grow more human looking as they starve. *Apis mellifera, Apis diabolus.* If a town be swarmed by bees with devil-face, and those bees do drip honey into open mouths, the body of a woman with honey tooth, bleeding thigh salt, shall be lashed to whatever stake will hold her. The bee swarm shall be gathered in a barrel and dumped upon the fire that eats her. The honey teeth do catch flame first, sparks of blue at the white before the red tongue catches too, and the lips. Bees' bodies when burning do smell of hot marrow; the odor makes onlookers vomit, yet still they look on.

You needed a boat to reach the lighthouse, a quarter mile from shore, and if a storm hit, you slept overnight in a reindeer bag on the watch room's slanted floor.

During storms the polar explorer stood on the lantern gallery, holding its rail as if her life depended on it, because her life did. She loved any circumstance in which survival was not assured. The threat of being swept over the rail woke her from the ~~lethargy~~ sluggery she felt at home chopping rhubarb, cracking puffin eggs, peeling the skin off dead sheep.

# THE DAUGHTER

Grew up in a city born of the terror of the vastness of space, where the streets lie tight in a grid. The men who built Salem, Oregon, were white Methodist missionaries who followed white fur-trade trappers to the Pacific Northwest, and the missionaries were less excited than the trappers by the wildness foaming in every direction. They laid their town in a valley that had been fished, harvested, and winter-camped for centuries by the Kalapuya people, who, in the 1850s, were forced onto reservations by the U.S. government. In the stolen valley the whites huddled and crouched, made everything smaller. Downtown Salem is a box of streets Britishly named: Church and Cottage and Market, Summer and Winter and East.

The daughter knew every tidy inch of her city neighborhood. She is still learning the inches in Newville, where humans are less, nature is more.

She stands in the lantern room of the Gunakadeit Lighthouse, north of town, where she has come after school with the person she hopes to officially call her boyfriend. From here you can see massive cliffs soaring up from the ocean, rust veined, green mossed; giant pines gathering like soldiers along their rim; goblin trees jutting slant from the rock face. You can see silver-white lather smashing at the cliffs' ankles. The harbor and its moored boats and the ocean beyond, a shirred blue prairie stretching to the horizon, cut by bars of green. Far from shore: a black fin.

"Boring up here," says Ephraim.

*Look at the black fin!* she wants to say. *The goblin trees!*

She says, "Yeah," and touches his jaw, specked with new beard. They kiss for a while. She loves it except for the tongue thrusts.

Does the fin belong to a shark? Could it belong to a whale?

She draws back from Ephraim to look at the sea.

"What?"

"Nothing."

Gone.

"Wanna bounce?" he says.

They race down the spiral staircase, boot soles ringing on the stone, and climb into the backseat of his car.

"I think I saw a gray whale. Did you—?"

"Nope," says Ephraim. "But did you know *blue* whales have the biggest cocks of any animal? Eight to ten feet."

"The dinosaurs' were bigger than that."

"Bullshit."

"No, my dad's got this book—" She stops: Ephraim has no father. The daughter's father, though annoying, loves her more than all the world's gold. "Anyway," she says, "here's one: A skeleton asks another skeleton, 'Do you want to hear a joke?' Second skeleton says, 'Only if it's humerus.'"

"Why is that funny?"

"Because—'humerus'? The arm bone?"

"That's a little-kid joke."

Her mom's favorite pun. It's not her fault he didn't know what a humerus was.

"No more *talking*." He goes to kiss her but she dodges, bites his shoulder through the cotton long sleeve, trying to break the skin but also not to. He gets her underpants down so fast it feels professional. Her jeans are already flung to some corner of the car, maybe on the steering wheel, maybe under the front seat, his jeans too, his hat.

She reaches for his penis and circles her palm around the head, like she's polishing.

"Not like that—" Ephraim moves her hand to grip the shaft. Up down up down up down. "Like *that*."

He spits on his hand and wets his penis, guides it into her vagina. He shoves back and forth. It feels okay but not great, definitely not as great as they say it should feel, and it doesn't help that the back of her head keeps slamming against the door handle, but the daughter has also read that it takes some time to get good at sex and to like it, especially for the girl. He has an orgasm with the same jittery moan she found weird at first but is getting used to, and she is relieved that her head has stopped being slammed against the door handle, so she smiles; and Ephraim smiles too; and she flinches at the sticky milk dribbling out of her.

The explorer went to the lighthouse whenever allowed, at first, and once she could handle the boat alone, even when forbidden. Her uncle Bjartur felt bad that her father was dead and so let her come, although she bothered him with her questions; he was a lighthouse keeper, God knows, because he preferred his own company, but this little one, this Eivør, youngest of his favorite sister, he could find it in his chewed heart to let her run up the spiral stairs and dig through his trunk of ships' debris and on drenched tiptoes watch the weather.

# THE WIFE

Between town and home is a long twist of road that hugs the cliffside, climbing and dipping and climbing again.

At the sharpest bend, whose guardrail is measly, the wife's jaw tenses.

What if she took her hands off the wheel and let them go?

The car would jump along the top branches of the shore pines, tearing a fine green wake; flip once before building speed; fly past the rocks and into the water and down forever and—

After the bend, she unclenches.

Almost home.

Second time this week she has pictured it.

Soon as the groceries are in, she'll give herself a few minutes upstairs. It won't kill them to watch a screen.

Why did she buy the grass-fed beef? Six dollars more per pound.

Second time this week.

They say grass-fed has the best fats.

Which might be entirely common. Maybe everyone pictures it, maybe not as often as twice a week but—

A little animal is struggling across the road. Dark, about a foot long.

Possum? Porcupine? Trying to cross.

Maybe it's even healthy to picture it.

Closer: burnt black, scorched to rubber.

Shivering.

Already dead, still trying.

What burned it? Or who?

"You're making us crash!" —from the backseat.

"We're not crashing," says the wife. Her foot is capable and steadfast. They will never crash with her foot on the brake.

Who burned this animal?

Convulsing, trembling, already so dead. Fur singed off. Skin black rubber.

*Who burned you?*

Closer: it's a black plastic bag.

But she can't unsee the shivering thing, burnt and dead and trying.

At the house: unbuckle, untangle, lift, carry, set down.

Unpack, put away.

Peel string cheese.

Distribute string cheese.

Place Bex and John in front of approved cartoon.

Upstairs, the wife closes the sewing-room door. Sits cross-legged on the bed. Fixes her stare on the scuffed white wall.

They are yipping and pipping, her two. They are rolling and polling and slapping and papping, rompling with little fists and heels on the bald carpet.

They are hers, but she can't get inside them.

They can't get back inside her.

They are hurling their fists — Bex fistier, but John brave.

Why did they name him John? Not a family name and almost as dull as the wife's own. Bex had said, "I'm going to call the baby Yarnjee."

Is John brave, or foolish? — he squirms willingly while his sister punches. The wife doesn't say *No hitting* because she doesn't want them to stop, she wants them to get tired.

She remembers why John: because everyone can spell and say it. John because his father hates correcting butchered English pronunciations of his own name. The errors of clerks. John is sometimes *Jean-voyage;* and Ro calls him Pliny the Younger.

In the past hour, the kids have

Rolled and polled.

Eaten leftover popcorn stirred into lemon yogurt.

Asked the wife if they could watch more TV.

Been told no.

Slooped and chooped.

Tipped over the standing lamp.

Broken an eyelash.

Asked the wife why her anus is out in space when it should be in her butt.

Slapped and papped.

Asked the wife what's for dinner.

Been told spaghetti.

Asked the wife what does she think is the best kind of sauce for butt pasta.

The grass-fed beef grows blood in a plastic bag. Does contact with the plastic cancel out its grass-fedness? She shouldn't waste expensive meat in spaghetti sauce. Marinate it tonight? There's a jar of store sauce in the—

"Take your finger out of his nose."

"But he likes it," says Bex.

And broccoli. Those par-baked dinner rolls are delicious, but she isn't going to serve bread with pasta.

Sea-salt-almond chocolate bar stowed in the kitchen drawer, under the maps, please still be there, please still be there.

"Do you like having your sister's finger stuck up your nose?"

John smiles, ducks, and nods.

"When the fuck is dinner?"

*"What?"*

Bex knows her crime; she eyes the wife with a cunning frown. "I mean when the gosh."

"You said something else. Do you even know what it means?"

"It's bad," says Bex.

"Does Mattie ever say that word?"

"Um…"

Which way will her girl's lie go: protect or incriminate?

"I think maybe yes," says Bex dolefully.

Bex loves Mattie, who is the good babysitter, much preferred over Mrs. Costello, the mean. The girl when she lies looks a lot like her father. The hard-sunk eyes the wife once found beguiling are not eyes she would wish upon her daughter. Bex's will have purplish circles before long.

But who cares what the girl looks like, if she is happy?

The world will care.

"To answer your question, dinner is whenever I want it to be."

"When will you want it to be?"

"Don't know," says the wife. "Maybe we just won't have dinner tonight."

Sea-salt-almond. Chocolate. Bar.

Bex frowns again, not cunningly.

The wife kneels on the rug and pulls their bodies against her body, squeezes, nuzzles. "Oh, sprites, don't worry, of course we'll have dinner. I was joking."

"Sometimes you do such bad jokes."

"It's true. I'm sorry. I predict that dinner will happen at six fifteen p.m., Pacific standard time. I predict that it will consist of spaghetti with tomato sauce and broccoli. So what species of sprite are you today?"

John says, "Water."

Bex says, "Wood."

Today's date is marked on the kitchen calendar with a small black *A*. Which stands for "ask."

Ask him again.

From the bay window, whose frame flakes with old paint possibly brimming with lead—she keeps forgetting to arrange to have the kids tested—the wife watches her husband trudge up the drive on short legs in jeans that are too tight, too young for him. He has a horror of dad pants and insists on dressing as he did at nineteen. His messenger bag bangs against one skinny thigh.

"He's home," she calls.

The kids race to greet him. This is a moment she used to love to picture, man home from work and children welcoming him, a perfect moment because it has no past or future—does not care where the man came from or what will happen after he is greeted, cares only for the joyful collision, the *Daddy you're here*.

"Fee fi fo fon, *je sens le sang* of two white middle-class Québécois-American children!" Her sprites scramble all over him. "A'right, a'right, settle down, eh," but he is contented, with John flung over his shoulder and Bex pulling open the satchel to check for vending-machine snacks. She's got his salt tooth. Did she get everything from him? What is in her of the wife?

The nose. She escaped Didier's nose.

"Hi, *meuf*," he says, squatting to set John on the floor.

"How was the day?"

"Usual hell. Actually, not usual. Music teacher got laid off."

*Good.*

"Hello, hell!" says Bex.

"We don't say 'hell,'" says the wife.

*I'm glad she's gone.*

"Daddy—"

"I meant 'heifer,'" says Didier.

"Kids, I want those blocks off the floor. Somebody could trip. Now! But I thought everyone loved the music teacher."

"Budget crisis."

"You mean they're not replacing her?"

He shrugs.

"So there won't be any music classes at all?"

"I must pee."

When he emerges from the bathroom, she is leaning on the banister, listening to Bex boss John into doing all the block gathering.

"We should get a cleaner," says Didier, for the third time this month. "I just counted the number of pubic hairs on the toilet rim."

And soap heel crusted to the sink.

Black dust on the baseboards.

Soft yellow hair balls in every corner.

Sea-salt-almond chocolate bar in the drawer.

"We can't afford one," she says, "unless we stop using Mrs. Costello, and I'm not giving up those eight hours." She looks into his blue-gray eyes, level with hers. She has often wished that Didier were taller. Is her wishing the product of socialization or an evolutionary adaptation from the days when being able to reach more food on a tree was a life-or-death advantage?

"Well," he says, "*somebody* needs to start doing some cleaning. It's like a bus station in there."

She won't be asking him tonight.

She will write the *A* again, on a different day.

"There were twelve, by the way," he says. "I know you have stuff to do, I'm not saying you don't, but could you maybe wash the toilet once in a while? Twelve hairs."

Red sky at morning, sailor take warning.

# THE BIOGRAPHER

Can't see the ocean from her apartment, but she can hear it. Most days between five and six thirty a.m. she sits in the kitchen listening to the waves and working on her study of Eivør Mínervudottír, a nineteenth-century polar hydrologist whose trailblazing research on pack ice was published under a male acquaintance's name. There is no book on Mínervudottír, only passing mentions in other books. The biographer has a mass of notes by now, an outline, some paragraphs. A skein draft—more holes than words. On the kitchen wall she's taped a photo of the shelf in the Salem bookstore where her book will live. The photo reminds her that she is going to finish it.

She opens Mínervudottír's journal, translated from the Danish. *I admit to fearing the attack of a sea bear; and my fingers hurt all the time.* A woman long dead coming to life. But today, staring at the journal, the biographer can't think. Her brain is soapy and throbbing from the new ovary medicine.

She sits in her car, radio on, throat shivering with hints of vomit, until she's late enough for school not to care that her eye–foot–brake reaction time is slowed by the Ovutran. The roads have guardrails. Her forehead pulses hard. She sees a black lace throw itself across the windshield, and blinks it away.

Two years ago the United States Congress ratified the Personhood Amendment, which gives the constitutional right to life, liberty, and property to a fertilized egg at the moment of conception. Abortion is now illegal in all fifty states. Abortion providers can be charged with second-degree murder, abortion seekers with conspiracy to commit murder. In vitro fertilization, too, is federally banned, because the amendment outlaws the transfer of embryos from laboratory to uterus. (The embryos can't give their consent to be moved.)

She was just quietly teaching history when it happened. Woke up one morning to a president-elect she hadn't voted for. This man thought women who miscarried should pay for funerals for the fetal tissue and thought a lab technician who accidentally dropped an embryo during in vitro transfer was guilty of manslaughter. She had heard there was glee on the lawns of her father's Orlando retirement village. Marching in the streets of Portland. In Newville: brackish calm.

Short of sex with some man she wouldn't otherwise want to have sex with, Ovutran and lube-glopped vaginal wands and Dr. Kalbfleisch's golden fingers is the only biological route left. Intrauterine insemination. At her age, not much better than a turkey baster.

She was placed on the adoption wait-list three years ago. In her parent profile she earnestly and meticulously described her job, her apartment, her favorite books, her parents, her brother (drug addiction omitted), and the fierce beauty of Newville. She uploaded a photograph that made her look friendly but responsible, fun loving but stable, easygoing but upper middle class. The coral-pink cardigan she bought to wear in this photo she later threw into the clothing donation bin outside the church.

She was warned, yes, at the outset: birth mothers tend to choose married straight couples, especially if the couple is white. But not all birth mothers choose this way. Anything could happen, she was told. The fact that she was willing to take an older child or a child who needed special care meant the odds were in her favor.

She assumed it would take a while but that it would, eventually, happen.

She thought a foster placement, at least, would come through; and if things went well, that could lead to adoption.

Then the new president moved into the White House.

The Personhood Amendment happened.

One of the ripples in its wake: Public Law 116-72.

On January fifteenth—in less than three months—this law, also known as Every Child Needs Two, takes effect. Its mission: *to restore dignity, strength, and prosperity to American families.* Unmarried persons will be legally prohibited from adopting children. In addition to valid marriage licenses, all adoptions will require approval through a federally regulated agency, rendering private transactions criminal.

Woozy with Ovutran, inching up the steps of Central Coast Regional, the biographer recalls her high school career on the varsity track team. "Keep your legs, Stephens!" the coach would yell when her muscles were about to give out.

She informs the tenth-graders they must scrub their essay drafts clean of the phrase *History tells us.* "A stale rhetorical tic. Means nothing."

"But it does," says Mattie. "History is telling us not to repeat its mistakes."

"We might reach that conclusion from *studying* the past, but history is a concept; it isn't talking to us."

Mattie's cheeks—cold white, blue veined—go red. Not used to correction, she's easily shamed.

Ash raises her hand. "What happened to your arm, miss?"

"What? Oh." The biographer's sleeve is pushed way up above the elbow. She yanks it down. "I gave blood."

"It looks like you gave, like, gallons." Ash rubs her piglet nose. "You should sue the blood bank for defamation."

"Dis*figure*ment," says Mattie.

"You got straight disfigured, miss."

By noon the cloudy throb behind her eyebrows has dialed itself back. In the teachers' lounge she eats maize puffs and watches the French teacher fork pink thumbs out of a Good Ship Chinese takeout box.

"Certain kinds of shrimp produce light," she tells him. "They're like torches bobbing in the water."

How can you raise a child alone when all you're having for lunch is vending-machine maize puffs?

He grunts and chews. "Not these shrimp."

Didier has no particular interest in French but can speak it, the tongue of his Montreal childhood, in his sleep. Like being a teacher of walking or sitting. For this predicament he blames his wife. During his first conversation with the biographer, years ago, over crackers and tube cheese in the lounge, he explained: "She says to me, 'Aside from cooking you have no skills, but at least you can do this, can't you?' — so *ici. Je. Suis.*" The biographer then imagined Susan Korsmo as a huge white crow, shading Didier's life with her great wing.

"Shrimp are sky-high in cholesterol," says Penny, the head English teacher, deseeding grapes at the table.

"This room is where my joy dies," says Didier.

"Boo hoo. Ro, you need nourishment. Here's a banana."

"That's Mr. Fivey's," says the biographer.

"How can anyone be sure?"

"He wrote his name on it."

"Fivey will survive the loss of one fruit," says Penny.

"Ooosh." The biographer holds her temples.

"You okay?"

Thudding back down into the chair: "I just got up too fast."

The PA system sizzles to life, coughs twice. "Attention students and teachers. Attention. This is an emergency announcement."

"Please be a fire drill," says Didier.

"Let us all keep Principal Fivey in our thoughts today. His wife has been admitted to the hospital in critical condition. Principal Fivey will be away from campus until further notice."

"Should she be telling everyone this?" says the biographer.

"I repeat," says the office manager, "Mrs. Fivey is in critical condition at Umpqua General."

"Room number?" yells Didier at the wall-mounted speaker.

The principal's wife always comes to Christmas assembly in skintight cocktail dresses. And every Christmas Didier says: "Mrs. Fivey's gittin sixy."

\*     \*     \*

The biographer drives home to lie on the floor in her underwear.

Her father is calling again. It has been days—weeks?—since she answered.

"How's Florida?"

"I am curious to know your plans for Christmas."

"Months away, Dad."

"But you'll want to book the flight soon. Fares are going to explode. When does school let out?"

"I don't know, the twenty-third?"

"That close to Christmas? Jesus."

"I'll let you know, okay?"

"Any plans for the weekend?"

"Susan and Didier invited me to dinner. You?"

"Might drop by the community center to watch the human rutabagas gum their feed. Unless my back flares up."

"What did the acupuncturist say?"

"*That* was a mistake I won't make twice."

"It works for a lot of people, Dad."

"It's goddamn voodoo. Will you be bringing a date to your friends' dinner?"

"Nope," says the biographer, steeling herself for his next sentence, her face stiff with sadness that he can't help himself.

"About time you found someone, don't you think?"

"I'm fine, Dad."

"Well, I *worry,* kiddo. Don't like the idea of you being all alone."

She could trot out the usual list ("I've got friends, neighbors, colleagues, people from meditation group"), but her okayness with being by herself—ordinary, unheroic okayness—does not need to justify itself to her father. The feeling is hers. She can simply feel okay and not explain it, or apologize for it, or concoct arguments against the argument that she doesn't *truly* feel content and is deluding herself in self-protection.

"Well, Dad," she says, "you're alone too."

Any reference to her mother's death can be relied on to shut him up.


There was Usman for six months in college. Victor for a year in Minneapolis. Liaisons now and again. She is not a long-term person. She likes her own company. Nevertheless, before her first insemination, the biographer forced herself to consult online dating sites. She browsed and bared her teeth. She browsed and felt chest-flatteningly depressed. One night she really did try. Picked the least Christian site and started typing.


What are your three best qualities?

1. Independence
2. Punctuality
3.


Best book you recently read?

*Proceedings of the "Proteus" Court of Inquiry on the Greely Relief Expedition of 1883*


What fascinates you?

1. How cold stops water
2. Patterns ice makes on the fur of a dead sled dog
3. The fact that Eivør Mínervudottír lost two of her fingers to frostbite


But the biographer didn't feel like telling anyone that. Delete, delete, delete. She could say, at least, she had tried. The next day she called for an appointment at a reproductive-medicine clinic in Salem.

Her therapist thought she was moving fast. "You only recently decided to do this," he said, "and already you've chosen a donor?"

Oh, therapist, if only you knew how quickly a donor can be chosen!

You turn on your computer. You click boxes for race, eye color, education, height. A list appears. You read some profiles. You hit PURCHASE.

A woman on the Choosing Single Motherhood discussion board wrote, *I spent more time dead-heading my roses than picking a donor.*

But, as the biographer explained to her therapist, she did *not* choose quickly. She pored. She strained. She sat for hours at her kitchen table, staring at profiles. These men had written essays. Named personal strengths. Recalled moments of childhood jubilance and described favorite traits of grandparents. (For one hundred dollars per ejaculation, they were happy to discuss their grandparents.)

She took notes on dozens and dozens —

Pros:

1. Calls himself "avid reader"
2. "Great cheekbones" (staff)
3. Enjoys "mental challenges and riddles"
4. To future child: "I look forward to hearing from you in eighteen years"

Cons:

1. Handwriting very bad
2. Commercial real-estate appraiser
3. Of own personality: "I'm not too complicated"

— then narrowed it to two. Donor 5546 was a fitness trainer described by sperm-bank staff as "handsome and captivating." Donor 3811 was a biology major with well-written essay answers; the affectionate way he described his aunts made the biographer like him; but what if he wasn't as handsome as the first? Both of their health histories were perfect, or so they claimed. Was the biographer so shallow as to be swayed by handsomeness? But who wants an ugly donor? But 3811 was not necessarily ugly. But was ugly even a problem? What she wanted was good health and a good brain. Donor 5546 claimed to be bursting with health, but she wasn't sure about his brain.

So she bought vials of both. She wouldn't stumble upon 9072, the just-right third, for another couple of months.

"Do you feel undeserving of a romantic partner?" asked the therapist.

"No," said the biographer.

"Are you pessimistic about finding a partner?"

"I don't necessarily *want* a partner."

"Might that attitude be a form of self-protection?"

"You mean am I deluding myself?"

"That's another way to put it."

"If I say yes, then I'm not deluded. And if I say no, it's further evidence of delusion."

"We need to end there," said the therapist.

The polar explorer liked to stand on the turf roof of the two-room cottage and think of her feet being precisely above the head of her mother, who was stirring or cutting or pounding; and how many inches of grass and soil lay between them; and how she was *above,* her mother *below,* reversing the order, flipping the world, with nobody able to tell her it couldn't be flipped.

Then she would be called in to help boil the puffin.

# THE MENDER

Walks home from the library the long way, past the school. The three o'clock bell is big over the harbor, flakes of bronze dropping slow to the water, bell in her mouth, bell in her scabbard. The blue school doors open: boots and scarves and shouts. Part-hid behind a bitter cherry, the mender waits. A string of Aristotle's lanterns — the spiky teeth of sea urchins — hangs on her neck as protection. Last week she stood here an hour until the last child came out and the doors stopped; but the girl she was waiting for did not appear.

The mender herself performed quite poorly at Central Coast Regional, which she left, fifteen years ago, without a diploma. *Fails to meet minimum standards. Acts deliberately uninterested in what goes on in class.* Oh bitches, it was no act. Her brain wasn't even in the room. In class the mender made sure never to talk except to fled souls or a bulb moon blown down into the stomach of the ocean. Her brain cells thrumming in their helmet went off to the forest road, where lay mole mother torn open by owl, her spent babies like red seeds; or to frondlets of sea lawn dragged into mazes by crabs. Her body stayed in the room, but her brain didn't.

They come through the blue doors, little and big, bundled for weather: fishermen's children, shopkeepers' children, waitresses' children. Girls with white cheek paint and black eyelids and crimson lips who are not the girl she is waiting for. The girl she is waiting for doesn't wear makeup, at least not that the mender can tell. She smells smoke. Her aunt Temple's brand. Is Temple close? Has Temple come —? Stupid, stupid, they don't come back. It's the blond weasel, who teaches at the school. His hair and his teeth go in all directions. She has seen him with his daughter and son on the cliff path, pointing at the water.

"Looking for someone?" he says.

She gives him the side-eye.

The blond weasel sucks and blows. "Seems like you are."

"No," she says, and goes.

She shouldn't be seen trying to see the girl. People already think she's unhinged, a forest weirdo, a witch. She is younger than the broomy witches people know from TV, but that doesn't stop them whispering.

Up the cobbly lane to the cliff path. Then back and back into the trees. A Douglas-fir was felled on a hillside, sawn into logs, truck-hauled to a mill. Boards were cut and trimmed, planed true. A man bought the boards and notched them together to make a cabin. Two rooms and a toilet closet. Wood stove. Double sink. A cupboard north and a cupboard south. The lamps and mini fridge run on batteries. Showerhead outside, nailed up. Wintertime she sponge bathes or stinks. The goat shed and chicken coop sit behind the cabin on either side of a dead black hawthorn, lightning split. In its cleft the mender has built nest boxes for the owls, swallows, marbled murrelets, golden-crowned kinglets.

She ought to be more careful. Can't let people see her watching. The yellow-haired, tumble-toothed weasel looked suspicious. It is no crime to watch someone, but humans like to name *these* things normal and *those* things peculiar.

Clementine comes to the mender's door with a picnic cooler and a pain. Her last complaint was vicious burning when she peed; today's pain is new. "Pants off and lie down," says the mender, and Clementine unzips herself, kicks away the jeans. Her thighs are white and very soft, underwear the size of a shoelace. She plumps back on the mender's bed and opens her knees.

A vesicle on Clementine's south lip, the inner fold, white-red in the browny pink: how much does it hurt?

"Oh God, a lot. Sometimes at work I'm like 'Eeesh!' and they think I'm—Anyway, do I have syphilis?"

"No. Plain old cunt wart."

"My vadge isn't having a good year."

The ointment: emulsion of purslane, bishopswort, and devil's claw in sesame oil. She dabs a few drops on the wart, recaps the vial, hands it to Clementine. "Put this on it twice a day." More warts are likely to join it, possibly a lot more, but she doesn't see cause to say this.

After Clementine leaves, the mender misses her, wants back the soft white thighs. She likes her ladies big-sirenic, mermaids of land, pressing and twisting in fleshful bodies.

Out in the shed she pours a scoop of grain and waits for Pinka and Hans to come galloping. Hans nuzzles the mender's crotch, and Pinka lifts a front hoof to be shaken. *Hello, beautifuls.* Their tongues are hard and clean. First time she saw a goat's pupil—rectangular, not round—she felt a stab of recognition. *I know you, strangeness.* They will never be taken from her. They know to behave, now, after that mischief near the trail.

Clementine brought black rockfish as payment. Her brothers are fishermen. The mender lifts it from the cooler, plops it into a bowl, picks up the little knife. She feeds the flesh to Malky and crunches the bones in her own mouth. The eyes she throws into the woods. Malky needs protein for all the hunting he does. Gone for days and comes back thin. Fish bones shouldn't be feared; you just have to chew them right so they won't pierce your throat walls or stomach lining.

"Your science teacher will tell you," said Temple, "fish bones are pure calcium and can't be digested by the human body, but let me assure you, that's not the whole story." One of the things the mender loved best about her aunt was "let me assure you." That and she cooked regular meals. Not once while living with Temple did the mender have to eat sautéed condiments for dinner. Temple became her guardian after the mender's mother left a note saying *Your better off with auntie don't worry I will send letters!* The mender was eight years old and herself not the best speller, but she noticed that the first word of the note was wrong.

Temple said the things she sold in her shop, Goody Hallett's, were props for tourists; but if her niece happened to be interested in the true properties of alchemy, she could teach her. Magic was of two kinds: natural and artificial. Natural magic was no more than a precise knowledge of the secrets of nature. Armed with such knowledge, you could effect marvels that to the ignorant seemed miracles or illusions. A man once cured his father's blindness with the gall bladder of a dragonet fish; the beat of a drum stretched with the skin of a wolf would shatter a drum stretched with the skin of a lamb.

The mender bottled her first tincture soon after her mother left. Per Temple's instructions, she gathered dozens of stalks of flowering mullein, yellow and shaped cheerfully. She picked the flowers and laid them to dry on a towel. Scooped them into a glass jar with chips of garlic, filled the jar with almond oil, left the jar on the sill for a month. Then she strained the oil into six small brown bottles, which she lined up on the kitchen counter—she was already tall enough—and brought Temple to see. Her aunt stood over her, aswirl with red hair, all that long, ropy, sparkling hair, and said, "Well done!" and it was the first time in her life the mender could remember being praised for doing something instead of for not doing it. (Not talking, not crying, not complaining when her mother took six hours to come back from the store.) "Next time your ear hurts," said Temple, "this is what you'll use." The promise of fixing and curing sent hot waves through the mender's belly. Show them how Percivals do.

When she wakes, the cabin is so dark from the rain and the trees, she doesn't know it is morning. But it is, and Malky is scratching, and the door is knocking.

*     *     *

She drinks a tea of horse-flavored ashwagandha. Eats brown bread. The new client wants nothing but water. Her name is Ro Stephens. Face dry and worried, hair dry and dull (feeble blood?), body thin (not perilously). She has lost people, the mender senses. A tiny smell, like a spoonful of smoke.

"I've been trying for a long time with Dr. Kalbfleisch at Hawthorne Reproductive Medicine."

The mender has heard of Kalbfleisch from other clients. One described him as a NILF: Nazi I'd Like to Fuck.

"So you've been taking their medications."

"A shit ton, yes."

"How's your cervical mucus?"

"Fine, I guess?"

"Does it resemble egg whites, near ovulation?"

"For a day or two. But my period's not—that regular. With the medications it gets better, but still it's not, like, clockwork."

She is so worried. And trying to hide the worry. Her face keeps twitching out of its behaving lines, cracking with *What if? What then?* then smoothing, obeying again. Deep down she doesn't believe the mender can help, no matter how much she wants to believe it. This is a person unaccustomed to being helped.

"Let's see your tongue."

White scum over the pink.

"You need to stop drinking milk."

"But I don't—"

"Cream in coffee? Cheese? Yogurt?"

Ro nods.

"Stop all of that."

"I will." But Ro looks like she's thinking *I didn't come here for nutrition tips.*

Eat warm and warming foods. Yams, kidney beans, black beans, bone broth. More red meat: the clock walls need building. Less dairy: the tongue is damp. More green tea: the walls are weakish still. All in the elementals, bitches. Everyone wants charms, but thirty-two years on earth have convinced the mender charms are purely for show. When the body is slow to do something, or galloping too fast toward death, people want wands waved. *Broth? That's it?* The mender teaches them to boil meat bones for days. To simmer seed and stem and dried wrack, strain it, drink it. Womb tea makes a cruel stench.

She pulls down the tea jar from the north cupboard. Shakes some into a brown bag, tapes it closed, hands it to Ro. "Heat this up in a big pot of water. After it boils, turn the heat down and simmer for three hours. Drink a cup every morning and every night. You won't like the taste."

"What's in it?"

"Nothing harmful. Roots and herbs. They'll make your lining lusher and your ovaries stronger."

"*Which* roots and herbs, exactly?"

She's one of those people who think they will understand something if they hear its name, when really they will only hear its name.

"Dried fleeceflower, Himalayan teasel root, wolfberry, shiny bugleweed, Chinese dodder seed, motherwort, dong quai, red peony root, and nut grass rhizome."

The tea tastes (the mender has tried it) like water buried underground for months in a bowl of rotted wood, swum through by worms, spat into by a burrowing vole.

The hair on Ro's upper lip. The irregular bleeding. The scummy tongue. The dryness.

"Has Dr. Kalbfleisch checked you for PCOS?"

"No—what's that?"

"Polycystic ovary syndrome. It affects ovulation, so it could be contributing." Seeing Ro flash with fear, she adds: "A lot of women have it."

"Wouldn't he have mentioned it, though? I've been seeing him for over a year."

"Ask for a test."

Ro has a gentle face — freckled, laugh lined, sad in the mouth corners. But her eyes are angry.

How to make boiled puffin (*mjólkursoðinn lundi*):

1. Skin puffin; rinse.
2. Remove feet and wings; discard.
3. Remove internal organs; set aside for lamb mash.
4. Stuff puffin with raisins and cake dough.
5. Boil in milk and water one hour, or until juices run clear.

# THE DAUGHTER

Is seven weeks late, approximately, more or less.

She stares at the classroom floor, arranging linoleum tiles into groups of seven. One seven. Two seven.

But she doesn't feel pregnant.

Three seven. Four seven.

She would be feeling something by now, five seven, if she was.

Ash passes a note: *Who finer, Xiao or Zakile?*

The daughter writes back: *Ephraim.*

*Not on list, dumblerina.*

"So what are we talking about here?" goes Mr. Zakile. "We've got whiteness. The white whale. How come it's white?"

Ash goes, "God made it white?"

Six seven.

"Well, okay, that wasn't really what I was..." Mr. Zakile paws through his notes, likely ripped whole from online, searching in those cut-and-pasted sentences for the brain he wasn't born with.

*Of all divers,* said Captain Ahab, *thou hast dived the deepest.*

*Has moved amid this world's foundations.*

The daughter wants to float down into the murderous hold of this frigate Earth.

*Hast seen enough to split the planets.*

Seven seven.

*And not one syllable is thine.*

She's been late before. Everyone has. The anorexics, for instance, miss periods constantly, as starving shuts down the blood; or if you haven't been eating enough iron; or if you're smoking too much. The daughter smoked three-quarters of a pack yesterday. Ash's sister, Clementine, says tweaker girls have sex fearlessly because meth prevents conception.

Last year one of the seniors threw herself down the gym stairs, but even after she broke a rib she was still pregnant, and Ro/Miss said in class she hoped they understood who was to blame for this rib: the monsters in Congress who passed the Personhood Amendment and the walking lobotomies on the Supreme Court who reversed *Roe v. Wade*. "Two short years ago," she said—or, actually, shouted—"abortion was legal in this country, but now we have to resort to throwing ourselves down the stairs."

And, of course: Yasmine.

The self-scraper. The mutilator.

Yasmine, who was the first person the daughter became blood sisters with (second grade).

Yasmine, who was the first person the daughter ever kissed (fourth grade).

Yasmine, who made him use a condom but got pregnant anyway.

The daughter wishes she could talk to her mom about it. Get told "Seven weeks late is nothing, pigeon!"

In most areas, her mom is sensible and knowledgeable—

"My poo is furry!"

"Don't worry. It's from that green cleanse you did. It's mucoid plaque sloughing off the intestinal walls."

—but not in all areas.

Can you tell me what color eyes my grandmother had?

What color hair my grandfather had?

Were my great-aunts all deaf?

My great-great-uncles all lunatics?

Do I come from a long line of mathematicians?

Were their teeth as crooked as my teeth?

No, you can't tell me, and neither can Dad, and neither can the agency.

It was a closed adoption. Zero trace.

*Are you mine?*

\*   \*   \*

Ephraim doesn't have an orgasm, he stops after a couple of minutes, says he isn't feeling it. Shifts his weight off her. The first thing she feels is relief. The second is fear. No male teenager ever passes up the chance for intercourse, according to her mom, who last year gave her A Talk that included, thank God, no anatomical details but did feature warnings about the sex-enslaved minds of boys. Yet here is Ephraim, sixteen going on seventeen, passing up a chance. Or stopping mid-chance.

"Did I, like, do something wrong?" she says quietly.

"Unh-unh. I'm just way tired." He yawns, as though to prove it. Pushes back his blond-streaked hair. "We're doing two-a-days for soccer. Hand me my hat?"

She loves this hat, which makes him look like a gorgeous detective.

But her own clothes: Black wool leggings. Red tube skirt. White glitter-paste long sleeve. Purple loop scarf. A pathetic outfit; no wonder he stopped.

"Want me to drop you at Ash's?"

"Yeah, thanks." She waits for him to say something about the next time, make a plan, allude to their future together, even just *You coming to our game Friday?* They get to Ash's and he hasn't. She says, "So…"

"See you, September girl," he says, and kisses, more like bites, her mouth.

In Ash's bathroom she drops the purple scarf in the trash and covers it with a handful of smushed toilet paper.

Eivør Mínervudottír's family lived on fish, potatoes, fermented mutton, milk-boiled puffin, and pilot whale. Her favorite food was the *fastelavnsbolle*, a sweet Shrovetide bun. ~~In 1771 the Swedish king ate fourteen *fastelavnsboller* with lobster and champagne, then promptly died of indigestion.~~

# THE WIFE

Bex won't wear a raincoat. They will be in the *car* mostly and she doesn't *care* if her hair gets wet between the car and the store and she *hates* how the plastic feels on her *neck*.

"Fine, get wet" is Didier's answer, but the wife isn't having it. It's pouring. Bex will wear a raincoat. "Put. It. On," she bellows.

"No!" screams the girl.

"Yes."

"No!"

"Bex, nobody is getting in the car until you put it on."

"Daddy said I don't have to."

"Do you see how hard it's raining out there?"

"Rain is good for my skin."

"No, it's not," says the wife.

"Jesus, let's *go*," says Didier.

"Please back me up on this."

"I would if I agreed with you, but we've been standing here for ten goddamn minutes. It's ridiculous."

"Enforcing rules is ridiculous?"

"I didn't know we had a *rule* about—"

"Well, we do," says the wife. "Bex? Do you want to keep holding everyone up, or are you ready to act like a six-year-old and wear your raincoat?"

"I'm not a six-year-old," she says, arms crossed. "I'm a little babykins. I need my diaper changed."

The wife slaps the raincoat across Bex's shoulders, yanks the hood into place, and ties the strings under her chin. Lifts up the girl's rigid body and carries her out to the car.

*   *   *

Her husband's hands sit on the wheel at ten and two, a habit that in their courting days shocked the wife: he had played in bands, done drugs, punched his father in the face at age fourteen. Yet he steered—steers—like a grandma.

She is glad not to be driving. No decisions to be made at the bend in the road.

Little animal black and twitching, burnt to death but not quite dead.

A scrap of tire struggling its way across.

Little animal, plastic bag.

But maybe it wasn't a plastic bag.

Maybe her first sight was correct.

Somebody lit it on fire, some bad kid, bad adult. Newville is not lacking in badness—

*but it's beautiful here and your family's been coming here for generations and the sea air's full of negative ions. They boost the mood, remember?*

Bex is chattering again by the time they reach the store.

Where's the doll section.

John's so lazy.

Somebody's mom came to class who's a dental hygienist and said even the nub of an adult tooth growing in still needs to be brushed.

"Perfects at two o'clock," hisses Didier, elbowing the wife's elbow.

Not them. Not today.

"Shell!" squeals Bex. "Oh my God, *Shelly!*"

The girls embrace dramatically, as though bumping into each other in the town where they both live were the most amazing surprise.

Bex: "Your dress is so pretty."

Shell: "Thanks. My mom made it."

"Hey, friends!" chirps Jessica Perfect. "Good to see you!"

"You too." The wife leans in for an air-kiss. "Brought the whole crew, huh?"

Shell's tanned, slender siblings stand in a row behind their tanned, slender parents.

"Yep, it's one of those days."

*Those days* at the Perfects' are probably a little different from *those days* on the hill.

On top of making dresses, Jessica knits sweaters out of local Shetland wool for all four children.

Cans jam from the wild berries they pick.

Home-cooks their wheat-free, dairy-free meals.

Chicken nuggets and string cheese never cross her threshold.

Her husband is a nutritionist who once lectured Didier on the importance of soaking nuts overnight.

"Blake." Didier nods.

"How's it hangin, buddy?"

"Long and strong," says her husband, with only a flicker of a smile.

"Look at *this* guy! He's getting so big! How old are you now?" Blake leans down toward John, who squirms in the shopping cart, shoving his face into Didier's stomach.

"Three and a half," says the wife.

"Wow. Time just *passes,* doesn't it?"

"I know," says Jessica, "and it's been forever since we had you over! We need to do that. It's hard to find a good night with the kids so busy after school. We've got soccer, cross-country, violin—gosh, what am I missing?"

The oldest child says, "My gifted-and-talented class?"

"That's right, my love. *This* one"—she nuzzles the boy's head—"tested off the charts last year, so he qualifies for an accelerated math and language-arts program. You guys aren't vegetarian, are you? We've been getting the most heavenly beef from our friends down the road. Their cows are grass-fed, no antibiotics whatsoever, just pure happy beef."

"You mean happy before they're slaughtered," says Didier, "or once they turn into food?"

She doesn't bat an eye. "So when you guys come over, I'll make steaks, and the chard will be ready soon. Gosh, we've got *acres* of it this year. Fortunately the kids love chard."

Still raining hard on the way home. Wipers furious.

"Shooting?" says Didier.

"Too quick," says the wife. "What's a very slow poison?"

"Hemlock, I think," he says, taking a hand off the wheel to caress the back of her neck. "No, wait—starvation! Hoist them on their own, like, whatevers."

"Petards," she says.

"What is a petard, anyway?"

"Can't remember. But I vote for starvation."

" 'I notice you've got some unsoaked nuts on the premises, and I'm a little concerned. Frankly I wouldn't dream of feeding my children an unsoaked nut.' "

"What are you guys talking about?" says Bex.

"A TV show we saw," says Didier, "called *The World's Smallest Petard*. You would like it, Bexy. There's an episode where every time a person farts, you can actually see the fart—there's these little brown clouds trailing behind the characters."

Bex giggles.

The wife moves his hand from her neck down to her thigh and closes her eyes, smiling. He squeezes her jeaned flesh.

She remembers what she loves.

Not the fart jokes, but the sweetness. The solidarity against the Perfects of this world.

She will ask him tomorrow.

In the car-window fog she draws an *A*.

It was bad, yes, the last time he refused. She promised herself she wouldn't ask again.

But the kids adore him.

And he really is sweet sometimes.

*I got the name of a person in Salem,* she will say, *who's supposed to be fantastic, not that expensive, does late appointments. We can get Mattie to sit—*

And she has seen herself driving off the cliff road with the kids in the car.

When the polar explorer turned six, she was shown the best way to hold the knife and how to make a slice across the lamb's throat—just one, they don't feel it, do it hard, watch your brother. But when she had the knife, and her mother was squatting beside her with the little wriggler, she didn't want to. Eivør was ordered twice to cut it and twice she said *"Nei, Mamma."*

Her mother put a hand over hers and drew the knife under the lamb's face; its face fell off; Eivør fell with it, screaming; and her mother hoisted the animal above a washtub to bleed.

Eivør was beaten on her thighs with a leather strap used for hanging slit lambs in the drying shed. And she ate no *ræst kjøt* that Christmas or *sker-pikjøt* that spring, apart from the occasional secret bite her brother Gunni saved in his shoe.

# THE BIOGRAPHER

Doesn't know for a fact that Gunni saved pieces of fermented lamb in his shoe when Eivør wasn't allowed to have any, but she writes it in her book, because her own brother used to hide cookies in his napkin when their mother told the biographer she didn't need more dessert unless she wanted to get chubby. Archie would leave the cookies in his drawer for her to retrieve. Each time she opened the drawer and saw the grease-darkened napkin tucked among socks, a flame of happiness lit in her throat.

She wrote the first sentences of *Mínervudottír: A Life* ten years ago, when she was working at a café in Minneapolis and trying to help Archie get clean. When she wasn't driving him to meetings or outpatient appointments, she was dropping leafy greens into smoothies he didn't drink. She was checking his pupils for pinnedness, his drawers for needles, her own wallet for missing cash. Sometimes he would ask to read the manuscript. He liked the part where the polar explorer watches men drive whales to their deaths in a shallow cove.

As a hater of tradition, Archie would have applauded her solo pregnancy efforts. Would have tried to get his friends to supply sperm for free. (One dose of semen from Athena Cryobank costs eight hundred dollars.)

She has not told her father about the efforts.

She closes her computer and sets Mínervudottír's journal on a pile of books about nineteenth-century Arctic expeditions. Rolls her head toward one shoulder, then the other. Is a stiff neck another sign of polycystic ovary syndrome? She has researched PCOS online, a little, as much as she can stand. The pregnancy statistics aren't good.

But Gin Percival might not know what she's talking about. She didn't even graduate from high school, according to Penny, who was already teaching at Central Coast when Gin dropped out. The visit to her did not go badly, or particularly well. She liked Gin Percival fine. She came away with a bag of gruesome tea.

Speaking of: the biographer gets out the saucepan. While the tea heats, she braces for the flavor of a human mouth unbrushed for many moons and debates whether to change for dinner. It's only Didier and Susan and the kids; but these sweatpants, truth be told, have not been washed in a while.

Her white mug is streaked tan inside. Are her teeth this stained? Probably almost. Years of frequent coffee. Long hiatuses from dentistry. Could poor mouth hygiene be a cause of PCOS? Inflammation leaking from the gums into the bloodstream, a slow poison, her hormones dizzy and ineffectual?

If she *does* have PCOS, maybe Gin Percival can give her another concoction—to lower her testosterone levels, repair her blood. Her cells will jump to work, plumping and fluffing and densing, her FSH numbers will drop into the single digits, Nurse Crabby will call with her bloodwork results and say, "Wow! Just, wow!" and even Fleischy will give a golden nod of amazement. They'll shoot in the sperm of the rock climber or the personal trainer or the biology student or Kalbfleisch himself, and the biographer, at last, will conceive.

It's got to be mostly hokum, of course. Tree bark and frog's spit and spells. Mash up a few berries and seeds and call it a solution.

But what if it works? Thousands of years in the making, fine-tuned by women in the dark creases of history, helping each other.

And at this point, what else can she do?

*You could stop trying so hard.*

*You could love your life as it is.*


The Korsmos' place, horror-movie handsome on its hill, would make the biographer jealous if she were a house wanter, which she is not, as houses make her think of being stuck neck-deep in a mortgage; but she admires its lead-glazed panes and the ocellated trim work vining its porch. It was built by Susan's great-grandfather as a summer place. In winter they duct-tape the windows and stuff sweaters under the doors.

Didier smokes on the porch steps, yellow hair poking like hay from under his beanie. He is sunk-eyed and snaggletoothed yet manages somehow—the biographer can't figure out how—to be fetching. *Beau-laid.* He raises one beautiful-ugly palm in greeting.

"ROOOOOO!" yells Bex, running at the biographer across the lawn.

"Pipe the fuck down," says her father. He squashes the cigarette on his bootheel, tosses it into a large brown bush, and ambles over to lift the girl into the air. "Bexy, remember that 'fuck' goes in the special box. You hungry, Robitussin? Also, we invited Pete."

"I'm elated. What's the special box?"

"The box of words we never say to Mommy," says Bex.

"Or even near Mommy." Didier sets the girl down, and she scurries back toward the house. "I see you didn't bring anything, which is awesome."

"What?"

"My wife adheres to the twentieth-century belief that civilized people arrive with small gifts or contributions to an invited meal. And once again this proves her wrong because you're civilized but, as usual, you brought zilch."

The biographer foresees the wince, the disapproval filed away. Susan keeps track to the grave.

Pliny the Younger stomps behind while Bex gives the biographer yet another tour of her room. She is very proud of her room. The purple walls are thick with fairies, leopards, alphabets, and Pinocchio noses. When her brother dares to move a rabbit from the bed, Bex slaps his hand; he yowls; the biographer says, "I don't think you're supposed to do that."

"It was only a *soft* hit," says the girl. "See, I have one shelf for the monster and one shelf for the fish. Here's a squirrel mummy."

The biographer peers. "Is that a real squirrel?"

"Yeah, but it died. Which is, like, when…" Bex sighs, twists her hands together, and looks up at the biographer. "What is death?"

"Oh, you know," says the biographer.

Blond-brown, endearing, demanding, sometimes quite irritating—how eerily they resemble Susan and Didier. It's much more than the coloring: they are *shaped* like their parents, Bex with Didier's shadowy eye sockets, John with Susan's elfin chin—small faces imprinted by two traceable lineages. They are the products of desire: sexual, yes, but more importantly (in the age of contraception, at least) they come from the desire to recur. Give me the chance to repeat myself. Give me a life lived again, and bigger. Give me a self to take care of, and better. Again, please, again! We're wired, it's said, to want repeating. To want seed and soil, egg and shell, or so it's said. Give me a bucket and give me a bell. Give me a cow with her udders a-swell. Give me the calf—long eyes, long tongue—who clamps the teat and sucks.

Downstairs she trips on a plastic truck and slams elbow first into a side table. The floor is choked with toys. She kicks a blue train against the wall.

"They live in squalor," says Pete Xiao.

"I may have sprained my elbow."

"That aside, how are you?" Pete came to Central Coast Regional two years ago, to teach math, and announced he'd only be here for one year because he wasn't built for a hinterland. This year, too, is meant to be his last; and next year will undoubtedly be his last.

"Swell," she says. Swollen. The Ovutran bloats.

They gather in the dining room, which Susan's forebears rigged up in style: fat oak ceiling beams, hand-carved wall panels, built-in credenza. The little black roast is sliced and served. Munchings and slurpings.

"This year's parents," says Pete, "are even more racist than last year's. One guy goes, 'I'm glad my child is finally studying math with someone of your persuasion.'"

"Calm your yard, Pete-moss," says Didier.

"I have a yard?"

"It's in your pants, nestled like a teeny mouse."

"How very white of you to change the subject away from model-minority stereotypes."

"Hey, Roosevelt, are you using only white sperm donors out of racism?"

"Didier, *God,*" says Susan.

"White is the state color of Oregon," says Pete.

"The kid is already going to feel weird about his paternity situation," says the biographer, "and I don't want to add to the confusion."

"Once you have that kid, you won't be able to take a dump by yourself. And you'll become even less cool than you are now. As they say, 'Heroin never hurt my music collection, but parenthood sure has!'"

"No one says that," says Susan, reaching for another roll.

"I once did a research paper," says Didier, "on the history of words for penis, and 'yard' was a preferred term until a couple of centuries ago."

"Was that considered a research topic at your wattle-and-daub college?" says Pete.

"Not wattle and daub," says Susan, "so much as frosted glass block and drive-through window."

"What's wattle and daub?" says Bex.

Didier scratches his neck. "Even if it *had* been a community college, which it was not, so what? I mean, literally, *meuf,* why would it matter?"

Pete shouts, "Why does everyone say 'literally' so much these days?"

"'When I lay with my bouncing Nell,'" recites Didier, "'I gave her an inch, but she took an Ell: But…it was damnable hard, When I gave her an inch, she'd want more than a Yard.' Ell meant the minge, by the way."

"Yet he can't remember the name of the kids' pediatrician," says Susan.

Didier gives his wife a long look, rises from the table, heads for the kitchen.

He returns with a butter dish.

"We don't need butter," says Susan. "Why did you get out the butter?"

"Because," he says, "I want to put some butter on my potatoes. They happen to be a little *dry*."

"Daddy," says Bex, "your face just looked like a butt." Giggles. "Don't be a buttinski, you buttinski!"

"Use your NPR voice, *chouchou*," says Didier.

"I hate NPR!"

"What Daddy means is you need to speak more quietly, or you're leaving the table."

Bex whispers something to her brother, then counts to three. "AAAAAAHHHHHH!" they roar.

"That's it," snaps Susan. "You're done. Leave the table."

"But John's not done! If you don't feed us it's, um, it's *child abuse*."

"Where did you hear that term?"

"Jesus," says Didier, "she prolly got it from TV. Relax."

Susan closes her eyes. For a few seconds, nothing moves. Then her eyes open and her voice comes out placid: "Let's go, sprites, time for bath. Say good night!"

Pete and Didier keep opening beers and ignoring the biographer. Their conversation topics include European soccer, artisanal whiskey, famous drug overdoses, and a multiplayer video game whose name sounds like "They Mask Us." Then Didier, suddenly remembering her, says: "Instead of driving a million miles to Salem, why don't you just go to the witch? I saw her the other day, waiting outside the school. At least I think it was her, although she looks less witchy than most of the girls at Central Coast."

"She's not a *witch*. She's—" Tall, pale, heavy browed. Eyes wide and pond-green. Black cloth pinned around her neck. "Unusual."

"Still," says Didier, "worth a try?"

"Nah. She'd give me a bowl of tree bark. And I'm already in massive debt." The biographer isn't sure why she's lying. She's not ashamed of her visit to Gin Percival.

"All the more reason to avoid single motherhood," says Didier.

Is she ashamed?

"So only couples in massive debt"—she raises her voice—"should have kids?"

"No, I just mean you have no idea how hard it's going to be."

"Actually I do," she says.

"You very much don't. Look, I'm the *product* of a single mother."

"Exactly."

"What?"

"You turned out fine," says the biographer.

"You're human evidence," adds Pete.

"Wait'll it's four a.m.," says Didier, "and the kid's puking and shitting and screaming and you can't decide if you should take him to the emergency room and there's no one to help you decide."

"Why would I need someone to help me decide?"

"Okay, what about when the kid has a guitar performance in assembly and you can't be there because of work and everyone laughs at him for crying?"

The biographer does the tiny violin.

Didier pats his shirt pocket. "Hell are my smokes? Pete, do you—?"

"I got you, brah." They head out together.

She thinks to start clearing the table—this would be a good thing to do, a courteous and helpful thing—but stays in her chair.

Susan, in the doorway: "They're finally down." Her narrow face, edged by blond waves, pulses with anger. At her kids for not settling faster? At her husband for doing nothing? She goes to hover behind a chair, surveying the mess of the table. Even angry she is shining, every piece of dining-room light caught and smeared across her cheeks.

The males clomp back in, smelling of smoke and cold, Didier laughing, "Which is what I told the ninth-graders!"

"Classic," says Pete.

Susan reaches for plates. The biographer gets up and hefts the roast pan.

"Thanks," says Susan, to the pan.

"I'll wash."

"No, it's fine. Can you get the strawberries out of the fridge? And the cream."

The biographer rinses, pats, and de-tops.

"I bought those specially for you," says Susan.

"In case I need some folic acid?"

"Are you—?"

"Another insemination next week."

"Well, distract yourself if you can. Go to the movies."

"The movies," repeats the biographer. Susan has a knack for commiserating with suffering she hasn't suffered. Which doesn't feel like compassion or empathy, but why not? Here is a friend trying to connect over a trouble. But the effort itself is insulting, the biographer decides. The first time Susan got pregnant, it wasn't planned. The second time (she told the biographer) they'd only just started trying again; she must be one of those Fertile Myrtles; she'd expected it to take longer, but lo and behold. If she told Susan about seeing the witch, Susan would act supportive and serious, then laugh about it behind the biographer's back. With Didier. Oh, poor Ro—first she's buying sperm online, now she's tramping into the forest to consult a homeless woman. Oh, poor Ro—why does she keep trying? She has no idea how hard it's going to be.

On her teacher's salary she will die holding notices from credit-card agencies, whereas Susan and Didier, who also live on a teacher's salary, are debt-free, as far as she knows, and pay no rent. Bex and John no doubt have trust funds set up by Susan's parents, fattening and fattening.

"The comparing mind is a despairing mind," says the meditation teacher.

Well, the biographer will figure out how to send her baby who does not exist yet to college. If the baby chooses to go to college, that is. She won't push the baby. The biographer herself liked college, but who's to say what the baby will like? Might decide to be a fisherperson and stay right here on the coast and eat dinner with the biographer every night, not out of obligation but out of wanting to. They will linger at the table and tell each other how the day went. The biographer won't be teaching by that point, only writing, having published *Mínervudottír: A Life* to critical acclaim and now working on a comprehensive history of female Arctic explorers; and the baby, tired from hours on the fishing boat but still paying attention, will ask the biographer intelligent questions about menstruating at eighty degrees below zero.

As a girl, I loved (but why?) to watch the *grindadráp*. It was a death dance. I couldn't stop looking. To smell the bonfires lit on the cliffs, calling men to the hunt. To see the boats herd the pod into the cove, the whales thrashing faster as they panic. Men and boys wade into the water with knives to cut their spinal cords. They touch the whale's eye to make sure it is dead. And the water foams up red.

# THE MENDER

Malky's been gone three days. Long for him—she doesn't like it. The sun is dropping. Killers in the woods. Malky is a killer himself but no match for coyotes and foxes and red-tailed hawks. Every creature, prey to someone. The girl rides away from school in the car of a boy in an old-fashioned hat. (Does he believe the hat looks *good*?) Hat boy walks hips first, boom swagger swagger, pirate-like.

Not that the mender can warn her. She has been keeping away from town for fear the girl will catch her watching.

She wipes down the sink, the oak countertop. Tidies the seed drawer. Sets clean jars by a basket of eyeless onions.

Boom swagger boom.

A pirate slept off his dreadful deeds at a tavern on Cape Cod. He met the local beauty, not yet sixteen. Maria Hallett fell hard for this bandit. Then Black Sam Bellamy sailed away. She was packed with child. Child died the same night born—hid in a barn, choked on a piece of straw.

Or so went the story. Little did they know. The farmer's wife who raised the child told no one but her diary.

Goody Hallett was imprisoned. Or banned from the village. Became a recluse. Lived in a shack by a poverty grass. Waited on the cliffs for Black Sam Bellamy in her best red shoes. Rode the backs of whales, tied lanterns to their flukes, lured ships to crash on the shoals. Got a reputation: witch.

*       *       *

Black Sam was the Robin Hood of pirates. They rob the poor under the cover of law, he said, and we plunder the rich under the protection of our own courage. In 1717, after some Caribbean plundering, Captain Bellamy rode back up the Atlantic with his gang of buccaneers. Their stolen ship, *Whydah,* sailed into the worst nor'easter in Cape Cod history. Ship went to pieces. Dead pirates all over the beach. Black Sam's body was never recovered.

In 1984 the remains of *Whydah* were found off the coast of Wellfleet, Massachusetts. That same year Temple Percival bought a foreclosed tackle shop in Newville, Oregon, and arranged on the shelves some spooky trinkets and called it Goody Hallett's.

Now Temple's fingernails live in a jar on the cabin shelf. Lashes in a glassine packet. Head hair and pubic hair in separate paper cartons—both almost gone. The rest of her body in the chest freezer behind the feed trough in the goat shed.

Scratching on the doorstep. Malky slinks in without greeting or apology. She tries to sound stern: "Don't ever stay out that long again, fuckermo." He purrs tetchily, demanding supper. She gets a plate of salmon from the mini fridge. It is happiness to see his pink tongue lapping. Merry, merry king of the woods is he.

Two short knocks. Stop. Two more. Stop. One. Malky, who knows this knock, goes on eating.
    "Is it you?"
    "It's me."
    She opens the door but stays on the threshold. Cotter is her only human friend, the kindest person she knows; doesn't mean she wants him in the cabin.
    "New client," he says, holding up a white envelope. His poor pimpled cheeks are worse than usual. Toxins trying to exit. They should be leaving through the liver but are leaving through the skin.

The mender pockets the envelope. "You talk to this one?"

"Works at the pulp mill in Wenport. Ten weeks along."

"Okay, thanks." She needs to replenish coltsfoot and fleabane. Check her supply of pennyroyal. "Good night."

Cotter rubs his black wool cap. "You all right? You need anything?"

"I'm fine. Good night!"

"One more thing, Ginny—" He pulls off the cap, palms his forehead. "People are saying you brought the dead man's fingers back."

The mender nods.

"I'm just telling you," says Cotter.

She wants to sit by the stove with Malky in her lap and nothing in her head. No vigilance, no fear. "I'm tired."

Cotter sighs. "Get to bed early, then." He turns, is taken by the woods.

Cotter works at the P.O. Whatever people are talking about, he hears. But she knew before he told her. She's been getting notes in her post box. From fishermen, or fishermen's wives, frightened by the seaweed plague.

A lace of dried dead man's fingers does hang in a window of her cabin. Did Clementine report this to her fishermen brothers? Fishermen hate dead man's fingers for fouling hulls in the harbor, fastening to oysters and carrying them away.

*U think its funny? Its our LIVING.*

She adds pine branches to the stove. Where is Malky? "Come here, little mo." He can't be persuaded onto her lap, even though he knows how much she's missed him.

*Cunt, quit hexing the water.*

Her own cat does not obey her; why should seaweed?

Why could I stand to see the whales killed,
but not the lambs?

# THE DAUGHTER

She thought it would go a different way. She thought the way it would go would not include taking the east stairwell to lunch and seeing Ephraim's hand in the shirt of Nouri Withers, whose eyes were shut and fluttering.

The daughter makes no sound. She creeps back up the stairs.

But she can't breathe.

*Breathe, dumblerina.*

She sits on the landing, spreading her rib cage to make room for air.

*Breathe, ignorant white girl.*

Still has to finish the day. Get through Latin and math. Go pick up her new retainer.

Nouri Withers? Maybe if you like tangled hair and black eye shadow and nail polish made from otter dung.

She has never missed Yasmine more than exactly right now.

Yasmine, lover of strawberries, queen of whipped cream.

Singer of hymns and smoker of weed.

Who'd say: *Forget that Transylvanian slut.*

Who'd say: *Are you even going to remember his ass in five years?*

Yasmine, who was smarter than the daughter but who got worse grades because of her "attitude."

Yasmine came out of the bathroom and held up the pee stick.

A month earlier the federal abortion ban had gone into effect.

The daughter was thinking: we need to get you to Canada. They hadn't closed the border to abortion seekers yet. The Pink Wall was still just an idea.

A year and a half later the Canadian border patrol arrests American seekers and returns them to the States for prosecution. "Let's spend the taxpayers' money to criminalize vulnerable women, shall we?" said Ro/Miss in class, and somebody said, "But if they're breaking the law, they *are* criminals," and Ro/Miss said, "Laws aren't natural phenomena. They have particular and often horrific histories. Ever heard of the Nuremberg Laws? Ever heard of Jim Crow?"

Yasmine would have liked Ro/Miss, who talks about history in a way that makes it memorable and who wears the clothes of a kid: brown cords, green hoodies, sneakers.

A tuft of cells inside her, multiplying. Half Ephraim, half her.

*You can't be sure.*

She carries the test around unopened in her satchel.

If she *is*—

She might not be. Her body feels pretty much like it always does.

But if she is, what the hell is she going to do?

*Don't borrow worry.* —Mom

*Stay in your lane.* —Dad

After all, she might not be.

In math Nouri Withers taps her steel-toed boot against the chair leg, from excitement probably; she's thinking of her next time with Ephraim. Where will they go? What will they do? *What have they already done?* Ash isn't there to comfort her; the daughter has no friends in this room; it's calculus, all eleventh- and twelfth-graders except for her. The tenth-graders think she's a snob because she moved here from Salem and takes AP classes and her dad's not a fisherman and she once said it was dumb to call the teachers "miss." To prove her lack of snobbery, she says "miss" now too.

After class Mr. Xiao pulls her aside for "a word." She is already shaky from the combination of eight weeks late plus Ephraim's hand up Nouri's shirt; the prospect of a reprimand from her second-favorite teacher makes her eyes water.

"Whoa, whoa! You're not in trouble. Jesus, Quarles, it's *cool*."

She dabs her eyes. "Sorry."

"Everything all right?"

"My period." Men teachers don't touch that excuse.

"Okay, well, I've got some good news for you. Do you know about the Oregon Math Academy?"

The daughter nods.

As if she shook her head, Mr. Xiao explains: "It's a weeklong residential program in Eugene. The most prestigious and competitive academic camp in the state. Nobody from Central Coast has ever been selected. And I'm nominating you for it."

She hears the words, but no feeling follows. "Thank you so much."

"I think your chances are good. You're bright, you're female, and as a little bonus, I went to undergrad with one of their admissions guys." He waits for her to look impressed.

The Matilda Quarles of last year—of last *month*—would be euphoric right now. Would be dying to get home and tell her parents.

"The deadline is January fifteenth," adds Mr. Xiao, who is not good at noticing how people feel unless they're crying or yelling and so believes the daughter is just as happy as she should be.

"I look forward to applying," she says.


She knows quite a lot, in fact, about the Oregon Math Academy. She has wanted to go since the seventh grade. She and Yasmine planned to apply together. In eighth grade Yasmine scored highest in their school on the math section of the state exam; the daughter was two points behind her.

Going to the academy would help her get into colleges with top marine-biology departments.

Her parents would be over the moon.

The academy happens in April, over spring break.

If she's three months pregnant now, she'll be eight months pregnant then.

How to make *skerpikjøt* ("sharp meat"):

1. Hang lamb's hind legs and saddle in drying shed (October).
2. Cut down saddle and eat as *ræst kjøt* ("semi-dried meat") (Christmastime).
3. Cut down legs and carve for serving (April).

# THE WIFE

Herd crumbs into palm.

Spray table.

Wipe down table.

Rinse cups and bowls.

Place cups and bowls in dishwasher.

Open bill for Didier's dentist co-pay.

Open bill for plumber, who did not even fix the dripping tap.

Open overdue notice for John's trip to the ER, where all they did was give him an antinausea pill yet somehow it cost six hundred dollars.

Write check for dentist co-pay because it's only $49.84.

Slide plumber and hospital into folder labeled PAY NEXT MONTH.

Start a list on the back of an envelope: *Why we should go to counseling*.

Think of what to put first — not the strongest reason, nor the weakest.

In law school they teach you to end any litany on the most convincing item and bury in the middle the weakest.

Last spring, Didier's answer was five variations on "Because I don't want to."

At eleven a.m., the violet sedan pulls up.

Mrs. Costello bothers John less than she bothers Bex, and sweet John never complains on Tuesdays and Thursdays when the sedan deposits Mrs. Costello and her knitting bag. The wife is always ready with purse on shoulder, keys in hand. Four hours, twice a week, belong to her alone.

"There's fish sticks in the freezer, and baby carrots, and I got more PG Tips for you—"

"We'll be splendid," Mrs. Costello mournfully says.

And John lets her pet his blond head — John, who is nicer than the rest of the hill dwellers, who will snuggle against Mrs. Costello even though she smells like old-person teeth. Bex was an accident, but it took ten months of trying to conceive John; the wife had begun to despair; she cried every morning after Didier left for school; then, finally, it worked. And John came murmuring into the world, leaking what looked like milk. Little white drops kept forming on his nipples. Witches' milk.

The wife has until two forty-five, pickup time for Bex.

What should she do until pickup?

She isn't impressed with the first-grade teacher. Homework is a sheet of fill-in-the-blanks or some tame question they have to answer using a computer encyclopedia.

Does not want to shop or otherwise errand; the kids might as well be with her for that.

But what does she expect from a rural school district that can't afford music classes.

Does not like to stay at home, hidden from John, because she's home all the bleeding time.

The nearest private school is an hour away and Catholic and, though less expensive than the average private, still too expensive for the Korsmos. The wife's parents have nothing more to give them. Didier's mother is a part-time bartender, and his father he hasn't seen since he was fourteen.

She chooses the library. She was once a good researcher, at ease in the stacks, fetching, piling, skimming, choosing.

The rain is letting up.

The wife had her own carrel at the law library with its thirty-foot windows, black mirrors at night.

On a low stool by the newspaper rack is Temple Percival's niece, stinking of onion, twigs in her hair. That stool is her favorite.

The wife smiles, as she always does.

Guilty for finding her repulsive.

But she *is* repulsive.

Temple Percival once gave the wife a tarot reading, at her store: "The castle will fall."

At one of the two blond-wood tables, she spreads the paper before her.

"Excuse me, but are you done with the sports section?"

Armpits and aftershave. She turns. He teaches at the high school. What's his—

"Oh, hi," he says. "You're Didier's wife, yeah?"

"Susan. I think we met at the summer picnic. How are you?" It hurts her neck to look up at him, he's so long.

"*Sweaty.* I apologize." He pulls out the chair beside her. "The kids are taking bubble tests so I'm free until soccer practice, and I ill-advisedly went for a run."

"What do you teach?"

"English. For my sins." He is big, everything about him big: neck, forearms, shoulders, head, damp shining sprouts of black hair. A dimple when he smiles.

"Sorry, but I forgot your—"

"Bryan Zakile."

"Of course! My husband says you're, um, a great teacher."

"Didier's a good guy—kids love him."

"So he's always telling me," she says.

He fingers the corner of the newspaper. "I take it you're not reading the sports?"

"Can't say I'm a fan."

"Frivolous shit, I agree. But it keeps men's lizard cortexes occupied." The wife watches Bryan Zakile not take his eyes off her. In a lower voice: "So what *are* you a fan of?"

"Um," she says. "Various things."


They go two doors down to Cone Wolf. Over single-scoop chocolates she learns a few facts about Bryan.

He played Division I college soccer and was invited to try out for the U.S. Olympic team, but a knee injury put paid to that.

He has traveled in South America.

He is starting his third year at the high school, where he got the job because the principal is married to his second cousin.

"Mrs. Fivey's your cousin? How is she—?"

"Talking and moving around. Still in the hospital, but going home soon."

"Oh, that's good. Didier said they had to induce a coma?"

"She banged her head hella hard on those stairs. Got swelling on the brain. They couldn't wake her up until the swelling went down."

"How did she fall—do you know?"

Bryan shrugs. He licks his spoon, throws it on the counter, crosses his arms. "*That* was satisfying."

The wife did not find her teensy little marble of a scoop satisfying. "Delectable," she says, and blushes. The shop clock says 2:38. "I have to go pick up my daughter."

"How old?"—the first question he has asked her since the library.

"Six. I also have a three-year-old son."

"Wow, you're a busy woman."

The wife sees how he must see her. Shower-bunned blond hair. Drapey scarf to hide stomach. Black yoga pants. Mom clogs.

Over the course of human evolution, did men learn to be attracted to skinny women because they were not visibly pregnant? Did voluptuousness signal that a body was already ensuring the survival of another man's genetic material?

When Bex climbs into the booster seat, she's on a verge. The wife has come to fear this particular after-school look: reddened, scrunched. "Shell is so stupid."

"What happened?"

"I hate her."

"Seat belt, please. Did you and Shell fight?"

"I don't *fight*, Momplee. It's against the rules."

"I mean argue?" The wife turns off the ignition. The cars behind them in the pickup line will just have to go around.

The girl takes a long, shuddering breath. "She said I stole her bag of pennies and I didn't."

"What bag of pennies?"

"She had pennies in a bag which she wasn't supposed to because you can't bring money to school but she did and she couldn't find them and said I stole them. And I *didn't!*"

"Of course you didn't."

She might have.

She is her father's daughter.

The wife and Didier make fun of Ro's sperm donors, but what about Didier's genes, which may have deposited in Bex a puerile interest in drugs and a willingness to embezzle cash from a doughnut shop?

Two sets of instructions battle it out in the girl: well-shaped brown eyes vs. sunken blue-gray ones, orderly teeth vs. huge and crooked, solid SAT scores vs. never took the SAT.

When she got pregnant with Bex, at thirty, the wife felt as though she were sliding under a closing garage door.

Why did "thirty" loom like an expiration date?

She and Didier hadn't planned it; they weren't married; they'd been dating for seven months. But the wife felt old. It was August, her last year of law school was about to start, the home pregnancy test made a cross. *This is what I want, this!*—law school was nothing to this.

"She said I did steal," says Bex, "and so she isn't friends with me anymore."

"Give Shell some time to cool off."

"But what if she *never* cools off?"

"I think she will," says the wife. "Also, we need to talk about your research project! Have you decided on a topic yet?"

A small smile. "It's narrow to two."

"Oh, you narrowed it down?" The wife starts the ignition, flips her turn signal. Throat stab: she forgot to get any new books for Bex at the library.

"Wood sprite or ghost pepper, the hottest pepper known to man."

"Those are good choices, sweetpea."

"Shell's mom has ghost pepper from India at their house. They have seventy-three different spices in their spice cabinet."

"Oh, they don't have that many."

"Yes, they do—we counted. How many spices do *we* have, Momplee?"

"No idea."

In the rearview, some cow is waving at her to get moving.

The wife will take her sweet time.

If she constructs a solid argument, he'll be convinced.

*But then you'd actually have to go to counseling with him.*

Which might work!

Which would be the whole point.

To feel okay again. Even good.

To stop her throat from hurting when Bex asks "Do you and Daddy love each other?"

To stop reading online articles about the maladaptive coping mechanisms of kids from broken homes.

To stop *brokenhomebrokenhomebrokenhome* from reeling in her head.

To stop staring at the guardrails.

I brought aboard with me a sack of *sker-pikjøt,* which the Canadian sailors were interested to try. They called its taste "harrowing." I explained that if the lamb is dried during an unusually wet or warm season, it may ferment to the point of decay.

# THE BIOGRAPHER

The biographer loves Penny at school, sharing snacks in the teachers' lounge, but she loves her best on Sunday nights, when they watch Masterpiece mysteries in her little house with its rose-dotted wallpaper and stone fireplace and wool rugs, rain pattering on the oriel windows.

Penny hands her a napkin, a fork, and a plate of shepherd's pie. "Tap water or limeade?"

"Limeade. But isn't it time?"

"Oh damn!" Penny hurries to the television. (She is always losing her clicker.) Settles with her own plate next to the biographer, tucks a napkin into the collar of her turquoise sweater. "Let's see what skills you've got for us, Sergeant Hathaway." The opening credits begin, theme song swelling over shots of Oxford's dreaming spires, a weak English sun turning Cotswold limestone the color of apricots. Penny intones, "Who will die tonight?"

"You should write mysteries instead of bra rippers," says the biographer.

"But I prefer the beating heart. Did I tell you I'm going to a romance writers' convention? They have agents you can pitch to."

"How much do they charge you for that privilege?"

"Well, they charge plenty. And why shouldn't they? The agents are being flown all the way from New York."

"Can I read your pitch?"

"Honey, I have it memorized. '*Rapture on Black Sand* opens at the end of World War I. Euphrosyne Farrell is a young Irish nurse so gutted by her sweetheart's death at the Somme that she emigrates to New York City. After becoming engaged to a middle-aged widower, she finds herself drawn to Renzo, the widower's nephew, whose magnetic Neapolitan eyes prove irresistible.'"

"Where does black sand come in?" asks the biographer.

"Euphrosyne and Renzo make love for the first time in a small cove on Long Island."

"But wouldn't it be more interesting and, um, maybe less clichéd if she got engaged to the nephew, then found his *uncle* irresistible?"

"Lord no! This isn't *Little Women*. Renzo's a Brooklyn stallion and his britches are strained to bursting."

Penny is a teacher of English and an inventor, she says, of entertainments. "They're a hoot," she answered when the biographer once ventured to ask why she wanted to write soap operas valorizing romantic love as the sole telos of a female life. Penny has written nine of them, all waiting for cover art showing bulge-groined men relieving bulge-chested women of their bodices. She intends to be a published author by her seventieth birthday. Three years to make it happen.

"Okay," she says, "here's Detective Sergeant Hathaway. Can't *buy* cheekbones like that."

Inspector Lewis and DS Hathaway trade jokes across a sheeted corpse; enjoy beers at The Lamb & Flag; and chase a murderous puppeteer through a faculty drinks party, leaving a wake of Oxford dons agape.

Then a large rosy meat bursts onto the screen. "It's never too early to reserve joy. Call today for your Christmas ham!" Having lost all of its government funding, because the current administration won't sanction the liberal bias of baking shows and mountaineering documentaries, PBS now airs long blocks of advertising. A spot for control-top hose ("Mom, you look extra beautiful tonight—is it your hair?" "No, my Tummy Tamers!") makes the biographer's nose sting.

"Hey, you're crying!" says Penny, returning from the kitchen with glasses of limeade.

"Am not."

Penny presses a napkin to the biographer's cheek.

"It's this new elderly-ovary medication," sobs the biographer.

"Blow your nose," says Penny. "Just use the napkin; I can wash it. Do the commercials with children make you—"

"No." The biographer blows and wipes, shoves the napkin between her knees. "They make me think about my mom."

In-breath.

Who would pity her daughter for these solo efforts, this manless life. Out-breath.

But her mother, who went from father's house to college dorm to husband's house without a single day lived on her own, never knew the pleasures of solitude.

"What does your therapist say?" asks Penny.

"I quit seeing him."

"Was that such a smart move?"

"Poison is a woman's weapon," a grim lady tells Lewis and Hathaway. " 'I love the old way best, the simple way of poison, where we too are strong as men.' "

"Medea!" shouts the biographer.

"We should get you on a game show," says Penny.

Five thirty a.m., the air cold and gritty with salt. She can't face the drive to her day-nine egg-check appointment without coffee, even though caffeine is on Hawthorne Reproductive Medicine's *What to Avoid* handout. Teeth on her mug, she steers up the hill, under towering balsam fir and Sitka spruce, away from her town. Newville gets ninety-eight inches of rain a year. The inland fields are quaggy, hard to farm. Cliff roads dangerous in winter. Storms so bad they sink boats and tear roofs from houses. The biographer likes these problems because they keep people away — the people who might otherwise move here, that is, not the tourists, who cruise in on dry summer asphalt and don't give a sea onion about farming.

A billboard on Highway 22 is a stick drawing of a skirt-wearing person with a balloon for a stomach, accompanied by:

WON'T STOP ONE,
WON'T START ONE.
CANADA UPHOLDS U.S. LAW!

\*    \*    \*

American intelligence agencies must have some nice dirt on the Canadian prime minister. Otherwise, why agree to the Pink Wall? The border control can detain any woman or girl they "reasonably" suspect of crossing into Canada for the purpose of ending a pregnancy. Seekers are returned (by police escort) to their state of residence, where the district attorney can prosecute them for attempting a termination. Healthcare providers in Canada are also barred from offering in vitro fertilization to U.S. citizens.

Unveiling these terms at a press conference last year, the Canadian prime minister said: "Geography has made us neighbors. History has made us friends. Economics has made us partners. And necessity has made us allies. Those whom nature hath so joined together, let no man put asunder."

Kalbfleisch calls her ultrasound "encouraging." The biographer has five follicles measuring twelve and thirteen, plus a gaggle of smallers. "You'll be ready for insemination right on schedule, I suspect. Day fourteen. Which is…" He leans back, waits for the nurse to open the calendar and count off the squares with her finger. "Wednesday. Do we have at least a couple of vials here?" As usual, he doesn't look at her, even when asking a direct question.

Four, in fact, are sitting in the clinic's frozen storage, tiny bottles of ejaculate from the scrota of a college sophomore majoring in biology (3811) and a rock-climbing enthusiast who described his sister as "extremely beautiful" (9072). She also owns some semen from 5546, the personal trainer who baked a cake for sperm-bank staff; but his remaining vials are still at the bank in Los Angeles.

"Start the OPKs tomorrow or the next day," says Kalbfleisch. "Fingers crossed." He rubs foaming sanitizer into his hands.

"By the way." She sits up on the exam table, covers her crotch with a paper sheet. "Do you think I might have polycystic ovary syndrome?"

Kalbfleisch stops mid-rub. A golden frown. "Why do you ask?"

"A friend told me about it. I don't have *all* of the symptoms, but—"

"Roberta, were you looking online?" He sighs. "You can diagnose yourself with anything and everything online. First of all, the majority of women with PCOS are overweight, and you are not."

"Okay, so you don't—"

"Although." He is looking at her, but not in the eye. More in the mouth. "You do have excessive facial hair. And, come to think of it, excessive body hair. Which is a symptom."

*Come to think of it?* "But, um, how does that account for genetics? Certain ethnic groups are naturally hairier. My mom's grandmothers both had mustaches."

"I can't speak to that," says Kalbfleisch. "I'm not an anthropologist. I do know that hirsutism is a sign of PCOS."

Wouldn't that be human biology, in which all physicians are trained, and not anthropology?

"When you come in on—" He glances at the nurse.

"Wednesday," she says.

"—I'll take a closer look at your ovaries, and we'll include a testosterone check with your bloodwork."

"If I have PCOS, what does that mean?"

"That the odds of your conceiving via intrauterine insemination are exceedingly low."

To justify being late to work, sometimes as often as twice a week, she scatters crumbs of mortal illness. Principal Fivey is annoyed—has broached the subject of unpaid leave. But he hasn't been around much since his wife went into the hospital.

Taking fresh blue books from the supply closet, the biographer asks the office manager how Mrs. Fivey is doing.

"Poor thing's still in very critical condition."

Is "critical" an adjective that can take an intensifying premodifier? "What happened, exactly?"

"Took a nasty tumble down the stairs."

"What stairs?"—picturing the *Exorcist* steps, the biographer's favorite ten minutes of a family trip to Washington, DC.

"At home, I think? We're circulating a card."

Mrs. Fivey always looks good in her Christmas costumes. Garish, true, but good. Also: why garish? Probably only because the biographer grew up in suburban Minnesota. A saying of her mother's was "Don't take your clothes off before they do." The muddy grammar always bothered the biographer. Should she not take her clothes off before the men removed their *own* clothes? Or should she keep her clothes on until the men took them off for her?

"Here's the card," says the manager. "And can you write something personal? Most people have only been signing their names."

"I don't—"

"Sheesh, I'll tell you what to say: 'Heartfelt hopes for a speedy recovery.' Is that so hard?"

"Hard? No. But my hopes are not heartfelt."

The two long jowls on the manager's face shake a little, as though in a breeze. "You don't want her to get better?"

"I do in my mind. Not in my heart."

In her mind she wants Mrs. Fivey to walk out of the hospital. In her heart she wants her brother to be alive again. In a place that is neither mind nor heart, or both at once, she wants an ashy line down the center of a round belly; she wants nausea. Susan's marks of motherhood: spider veins at the knee backs, loose stomach skin, lowered breasts. Affronts to vanity worn as badges of the ultimate accomplishment.

But why does she want them, really? Because Susan has them? Because the Salem bookstore manager has them? Because she always vaguely assumed she would have them herself? Or does the desire come from some creaturely place, pre-civilized, some biological throb that floods her bloodways with the message *Make more of yourself!* To repeat, not to improve. It doesn't matter to the ancient throb if she does good works in this short life—if she publishes, for instance, a magnificent book on Eivør Mínervudottír that would give people pleasure and knowledge. The throb simply wants another human machine that can, in turn, make another.

Sperm, in Faroese: *sáð*.

Three donors walk into a bar.

"What can I get you?" says the bartender.

Donor 5546, dumb and cocky and hot, says: "Whiskey."

Donor 3811, looking up the weather on his phone, says: "Hold on."

Donor 9072, who notices the bartender has his own glass going, says: "Whatever you're drinking."

Bartender points to 5546 and says: "You're a little too hot."

And to 3811: "You're a little too cold."

And to 9072: "But you're just right."

True to 9072's humble nature, he blushes, only deepening the bartender's sense that this man would make a first-class provider of genetic material. Throughout the evening, 9072 is sociable and composed, at ease with self and others. Meanwhile, 5546 hits on four different women before last call, and 3811 stays on a stool, swiping through his phone, aloof and alone.

The least confident of the four women takes 5546 to her house, where they have unprotected sex, and she happens to be ovulating, but because his sperm are too weak to puncture her egg, she doesn't get pregnant.

Donor 3811 leaves after two beers, without talking to any humans.

Donor 9072 strikes up a conversation with the most confident of the four women hit on by 5546. She is drawn to 9072's good health and good brain. They discuss his rock-climbing skills and his beautiful sister. He walks the woman to her car, where she tells him she wants to have sex, but he shakes his head politely.

"I'm a sperm donor," he explains, "and my sperm are exceptionally vigorous, which means I'm likely to impregnate whatever body receives them, whether through intercourse or intrauterine insemination. So I can't go around having a lot of sex. If too many children are conceived from my loin butter, especially in the same geographical area, some of them might meet each other and fall in love. Which would be bad."

The woman understands, and they part as friends.

But how can you raise a child alone when you can't resist twelve ounces of coffee?

When you've been known to eat peanut butter on a spoon for dinner?

When you often go to bed without brushing your teeth?

Ab ovo. The twin eggs of Leda, impregnated by Zeus in swan form: one hatched into Helen, who would launch ships. Start from the beginning. Except there is no beginning. Can the biographer remember first thinking, feeling, or deciding she wanted to be someone's mother? The original moment of longing to let a bulb of lichen grow in her until it came out human? The longing is widely endorsed. Legislators, aunts, and advertisers approve. Which makes the longing, she thinks, a little suspicious.

Babies once were abstractions. They were *Maybe I do, but not now.* The biographer used to sneer at talk of biological deadlines, believing the topic of baby craziness to be crap for lifestyle magazines. Women who worried about ticking clocks were the same women who traded salmon-loaf recipes and asked their husbands to clean the gutters. She was not and never would be one of them.

Then, suddenly, she was one of them. Not the gutters, but the clock.

The narwhal's blotchy hide has been likened to the skin of a drowned mariner. Its stomach has five rooms. It can hold its breath under the ice for outrageous lengths. And the male horn, of course—much could be said.

# THE MENDER

Would kill to never make another trip to the Acme, yet her needs can't be met entirely by the forest, orchards, fields, or clients who trade with fish and batteries. For certain essentials she must use green cash. But the store lights hurt the mender's eyes. And the floors are so hard. And she notices—because even though the teachers at Central Coast Regional called her stupid, she is not stupid—that people stare at her in the Acme. They take their children's hands.

She is here for ginger, sesame oil, Band-Aids, thread, and a box of black licorice nibs. Passing the butcher counter, she is sickened to see the machine-pressed slices, the loaves of meat. Oils from the tissues of pig and cow and lamb glisten on the air. She has a long walk in front of her, in the rain, and night is coming. She speeds up toward the candy aisle, where her nibs—

"I know what you did"—a low snarl, nearly unhearable.

The mender keeps on.

Louder: "Dolores Fivey almost *died*."

She keeps on, staring at the end of the aisle, where she will turn right.

Loudest: "She was in the ICU! Do you care? Do you even *care?*"—voice lifting to the vast fluorescent beds, but the mender won't look, she won't grace them with a look.

"Find everything okay today?" says the cashier.

The mender nods, staring down.

"Cool necklace, by the way."

She always wears her Aristotle's lanterns to town.

Lola didn't almost die. It would have been in the newspaper at the library.

*Ignore them*, says Temple from the freezer. *People will believe any old crap.*

\*     \*     \*

Her cloak is sopping by the time she reaches home. Wool socks squelch in her sandals. In the goat shed, pouring grain, nuzzled by the snouts of her beautifuls, she tells Temple: "I hate them all." Runs her hand over the lid of the chest freezer, listening, though she knows Temple won't come back.

Salem, Massachusetts, 1692: a "witch cake" was baked with rye flour and urine from girls said to have been stricken by spells. This fragrant cake was fed to a dog. When the dog ate it, the witch would suffer—so went the folk wisdom—and her yelps of agony would incriminate her.

"How did they get the girls' urine?" the young mender wanted to know.

"Unimportant," said Temple. "The important thing is that people will believe any old crap. Never forget that, okay? Any. Old. Crap."

The mender misses her aunt every day.

It's not true that she hates them all, but it makes her feel better to say it.

She doesn't hate the girl she watches for.

And she doesn't hate Lola. She misses the compliments—"You have the coolest eyes I ever saw." The sugar packets and shakers of salt Lola stole from restaurants for the mender. She misses Lola's finger in her slit, Lola's plump tits in her mouth.

No visits or notes in over a month. The mender has considered going back to the big sandstone house, when the husband's at work, to bring her a spray of fawn lily. But Lola might get confused again.

She had come to the cabin for help with a burn. The mender knew she was lying about how she got the burn.

*   *   *

She adds wood to the stove. Eats a cold white stalk of ghost pipe. Steps out of her wet clothes, stands naked by the stove until she is dry.

Who was that yelling in the Acme? What has Lola been telling people?

The last time, Lola wore a green dress, shoulders bare. The scar was knitting well, less puckery, but it would be on her forearm the rest of her life. Into the marked skin the mender rubbed elderflower oil infused with lemon, lavender, and fenugreek.

"That feels so good," said Lola.

"Okay," said the mender, wiping her hands on an old washcloth. Packed bottle and washcloth into her rucksack. "See you."

"But you just got here!"

The mender blinked at the flowered couch, bag of golf clubs, family photos running up the long staircase. Through the cork soles of her sandals she felt the wall-to-wall teeming with carpet-beetle larvae.

"He won't be back until five. We could...?" Little plucked eyebrow twitched coaxingly. "I haven't seen you for two whole weeks," added Lola, coming closer. "I *missed* you. I have this friend in Santa Fe" — nudging the mender's toe with her shiny black boot — "who sells handmade piñon kokopellis. We could go there for a while. He'd never find—"

"I won't leave my animals."

Clumsily stroking the mender's biceps: "Maybe I could stay with you, then?"

Jab of heat in her throat. "You can't stay."

"Why not?" Lola stepped back, frowning. "I thought you liked me, Gin."

Humans always want more.

"I like you," said the mender.

"But—" A panicky smile. "Hold on, are you...?"

"It's just," began the mender.

Devil flowers danced on the couch, jumping, blurring.

"What? *What?*"

But some feelings aren't fastened to words.

"It—isn't—I don't—" The mender's tongue was an oily toe.

"Can't you talk? Can't you even *say a sentence?*" Lola slid her hands up and down her thighs, bunching the green dress, smoothing it, bunching again. "You know everyone thinks you're crazy, right?"

"I'm not crazy."

"You're *bat*shit," hissed Lola.

The mender took the scar oil from her sack and set it on the coffee table. "You can keep the whole bottle. No charge."

Lola said, "Get the fuck out of my house."

She couldn't understand—and the mender wasn't good at helping her understand—how much the mender likes to be alone. Human-wise.

Sea-washed lighthouse built with:

Aberdeen granite
salt-tolerant poplar
hydraulic lime

Bells and sledgehammer = fog signal

# THE DAUGHTER

Please be bloody. Please be a gush of dark mucus, black-strung red.

Pulls down her underwear.

White as cake.

"Where's the goddamn table leaf?" shouts her dad, stomping downstairs.

The Salem cousins come for dinner in an hour.

She fishes under the sink for the box of tampons and tugs out what's hidden under the Regulars and Super Pluses.

"Shut up," she tells the shiny blond infant on the box.

Thighs planted on the toilet, she tears the plastic sheath off the pee stick.

*There is a loving home out there for every baby who comes into the world.*

She doesn't weep or hyperventilate or text Ash a photo of the plus sign blazing on the stick. She wraps the test box and its contents in a brown paper bag, which she tucks into a rain boot at the back of her closet. She gets dressed.

The witch has a treatment, if it's early enough. And she doesn't charge money. Ash's sister's friend, who got an abortion from the witch last year, said it only works before a certain week in the pregnancy. The witch uses wild herbs that won't incriminate you if you're caught with them, because the police can't tell what they are. And the daughter doesn't plan to be caught.

Yasmine could have gone to Canada for an abortion, because the Pink Wall didn't exist yet. Or she could have given the baby to someone else.

Yasmine asked what it felt like to be adopted.

The daughter said, "Normal."

Which was true and not true.

*   *   *

Yasmine knew the daughter was curious about her bio mother.

Maybe she

Was too young.
Was too old — didn't have the energy.
Already had six kids.
Knew she was about to die of cancer.
Was a tweaker.
Just didn't feel like dealing.

It was a closed adoption. There is no way to find her, aside from a private detective the daughter can't afford yet.

So she dreams.

About her bio mother getting famous for developing a cure for paralysis and being on the cover of a magazine in the checkout line, where the daughter instantly recognizes her face.

About her bio mother finding *her*. The daughter comes down the school steps, the three o'clock bell is ringing, and a woman in sunglasses rushes up, shouting, "Are you mine?"

About her bio grandmother, who maybe loved to bake. She sees the ramekins her bio grandmother used for custard. A set of six, white-rimmed blue, one chipped. Her bio mother maybe always chose to eat from the chipped one.

The ramekins are smashed at the bottom of a well in the yard of the house where they all died, grandmother and grandfather and cousins and her bio mother, who was still weak from giving birth, overwhelmed with sadness, resolved to go the next day to the agency and get her baby back — she had a forty-eight-hour window; it had only been thirty hours; she would go the next day; now she just needed a little rest, but what was that smell? It was smoke, because fire, because malfunctioning space heater, but nobody was paying attention because drunk, and her bio mother, though not drunk, was too exhausted from the pain of labor to call out a warning; so they died.

An aunt, arriving later to pick through the rubble, threw all non-valuables into the well. If this well existed—if the daughter could find it—she'd climb down a rope and save the pieces of white ramekin, the spoons and knives, tin canisters of love notes, steel lockets packed with hair. That hair would have the DNA of her bio mother, sealed safe from fire and from damp.

Sixteen years ago abortion was legal in every state.

Why did she spend nine months growing the daughter if she was just going to give her up?

The Salem cousins yammer in the hall. Upon seeing the daughter, Aunt Bernadette goes, "What is it about these teenagers dressing so *unemployably?*" and Dad laughs. Mom, not laughing, tells Aunt Bernadette: "Mattie can wear whatever she wants. Last time I checked, this was America."

Mom and daughter escape to the kitchen.

"Would you wash the potatoes?"

The daughter dumps them into a colander, starts scrubbing under the faucet.

"By the way…" There's a forced-cheerful note in her voice. "I got a call from Susan Korsmo."

"Yeah?" says the daughter, scrubbing harder.

"It was an odd conversation, frankly."

"Oh really?"

"She expressed some concerns."

"About what?" Thank God for you, potato dirt. So much scrubbing you require.

"Well, I told her it was ridiculous, but she sounded—I don't know, adamant. Although she tends to sound adamant most of the time."

There is no way Mrs. K. could know. No way.

"Matilda, look at me."

She turns off the faucet, wipes her hands on her jeans. "So what was she adamant about?"

Mom's face is papery, punched in. "She says you were vomiting at her house. When you babysat last week. She heard you in the bathroom."

*No.*

"And she thinks you have an eating disorder."

Yes!

"This is funny to you?" says Mom.

"It's—no—because she's so wrong."

"Is she?"

The daughter reaches her arms around Mom's neck, presses a cheek into her shoulder. "I ate a bad burrito at school and threw up. Mrs. K. has too much time on her hands, so she—"

"Creates a crisis where there is none," whispers Mom. Then she draws back, cups the daughter's chin in her fingers. "You're sure, pigeon? You'd tell me if something was up?"

"I swear to you, I do not have an eating disorder."

"Thank Christ." Tears in her eyes.

The daughter is lucky to have this mother, even if she's already sixty, even if she makes jokes about pulling a mussel at a seafood disco. A young mom like Ephraim's might have said "Bulimia? I've taught you well!"

For reasons she can't figure out, the daughter almost never dreams of her bio father.

She takes an extra-big spoonful of mashed potatoes. Looks at Mom, points to the plate, winks, hates how hard Mom is smiling. She breathes through her mouth when passed the bowl of brussels sprouts, the vegetable whose odor, when cooked, most closely resembles human wind.

The Salem cousins blather and blither. "Well, what do the illegals expect, a red carpet?" Blahblahblahblah. "And then they refuse to learn English—" Blahblahblahblah. "So then why should I have to take three years of Spanish?" Blahblahblahblahblah. The invaders all look like xeroxes of each other, their beefiness repeating itself, reheating itself. Whereas the daughter is tall, and Dad is short. The daughter is pale, and Mom is sallow.

This clump of cells would have turned out tall, though maybe not pale. Ephraim tans brown in the summer.

Gravy has dried on the daughter's sleeve. She hates this shirt anyway. Maybe she'll give it to Aunt Bernadette, who hates it even more.

Mom and Dad can never know.

*What if your bio mother had chosen to terminate?*

"Matilda, your turn."

"Pass," says the daughter.

*Think of all the happy adopted families that wouldn't exist!*

Never, ever know.

"Oh, you!"

"Don't be a poop at the party."

"I can't think of any jokes," she says.

"Very funny!"

"What is it with these kids pretending to be so miserable?"

Yasmine said she'd die before telling her parents.

jumps down the sky (lightning)

sheep groaning (what narwhals sound like)

a smell grew

sea struck, ice bound

causing regret where it did not exist before

# THE WIFE

Didier hums "You Are My Sunshine" and trims fat off raw breasts. He worked in kitchens for years, scorns recipes, is good with a knife. A decent restaurant job would pay better than teaching at Central Coast Regional, but he swore off food and bev because he'd miss the kids' childhoods. The wife sees a calendar of vacant blue evenings, Didier away cooking, children in bed, herself alone and accountable to no one.

"—the tinfoil?"

"What?"

"Foil, woman!" Didier trots over to snatch it. His mood is merry; he's happiest when cooking, a dish towel slung over his shoulder. Happiest, yet he rarely cooks.

"What else?" she says.

"I'm good here. Go relax."

"Really? Okay." She rubs at a smear of old yogurt on the stovetop. "Should I do a salad?"

"You should sit down."

She watches him chop, one hand herding the olives and the other bringing down the knife, fast, accurate. Eyes don't waver from the olives. Shoulders don't slump. Happy and confident, yet most of the meals fall to her, the one who "has time."

"By the way, why is Mattie still here?"

"She's putting them to bed."

Didier sets down the knife and looks at her. "We're paying twelve dollars an hour to keep our kids at home while we're at home?"

"Well, I would like, for once, to have dinner with you alone. Without the kids underfoot."

"Just saying, it's a luxury, whereas a cleaning service—"

"You mean like living rent-free is a luxury?"

He scrapes the olives off the cutting board into a bowl and lifts his beer bottle. "Is that gonna be held over my head for a*nother* six years?"

"How about, regardless, it's saving us a lot of money?"

"That's like saying 'Be grateful you live in purgatory, because it's cheaper than—'"

"Newville is hardly purgatory," says the wife. The yogurt is stubborn; she licks her finger and rubs again. "I saw this thing on the road. A burnt little animal. I thought some kid had set it on fire. It was trying to get across to the other side."

"As in the great hereafter?"

"Of the road. It was burnt within an inch of its life, but it was still moving—which felt so, I don't know, brave?—and I wanted to help it, but it was already dead."

Her husband slaps the breasts onto a foiled baking sheet. "I've never understood that saying, 'within an inch of its life.' Like there was some danger right *next* to its life but not quite touching it?"

"This little animal. It's weird. I can't stop thinking about it."

"Where's the salt?"

"I think it was a possum. It was like it wasn't accepting death—or didn't even realize death was near. It *kept going.*"

"There you are, Salty McSalterton." He dusts the chicken, slides the pan into the oven. "You know what's so messed up about Ro's sperm donors?"

The wife closes her eyes. "What?"

"They can totally lie on the application. All four grandparents died of cirrhosis, but dude claims they're alive and healthy? Nobody's checking. I'm surprised that somebody as neurotic as Ro isn't worried."

"She's not neurotic." But it pleases her to hear him say it.

"You don't work with her." He sets the timer. "She's in full denial mode. Doesn't realize what a nightmare it's going to be. By herself? It's a nightmare even where there's two of you."

"Didier, I want to go to counseling."

He wipes his hands, hard, on a kitchen towel. "So go."

"*Couples* counseling."

"Told you before"—reaching for his beer—"I'm not a therapy person. Sorry."

"What does that even mean?"

"Means that I don't respond well to being blamed for things that aren't my fault."

Oh God, not his father again.

"I found someone in Salem," she says, "who's highly recommended, and they do late-afternoon appointments—"

"Did you not hear me, Susan?"

"Just because you had an incompetent therapist in Montreal thirty years ago? That's a *great* reason not to try to save—" She stops. Licks her finger again, scratches at the yogurt on the stove.

"What? Save what?"

"Can you please just *consider* it? One session?"

"Why are people in the States obsessed with therapy? There's other ways to solve problems."

"Such as?"

"Such as hiring a cleaning service."

"Oh, *okay.*"

"Since you clearly don't want to do it yourself. Which"—he holds up a palm, nodding—"I *get.* I don't feel like cleaning either, especially after being at work all day."

"I'd much rather be at work all day," she says, wondering, as the words settle in the air, if this is true.

"Then get a job. No one's stopping you. Or go back to law school."

"I wish it were that easy."

"Seems pretty easy to me." He is paper-toweling translucent pink shreds of raw chicken off the cutting board. "Honestly, Susan? Things aren't that bad. I mean, yes, some things could be better. But I'm not gonna drive ninety miles to talk about how I should've bought you better presents on your birthday."

*Or any presents.*

"But what about the kids?" she says. "They sense things—Bex asks—"

"The kids are fine."

She takes a long breath. "Are you saying they wouldn't benefit from our relationship improving?"

"It's kind of interesting that you don't give a fuck about *my* benefit. That douchebag brainwashed my mom, and she never stopped blaming me. Me, who was basically a child."

"I know it wasn't your fault he left, but—"

"The therapist didn't even care why I hit him. Said it was 'immaterial.' Really, dude?"

"You broke your dad's nose."

"Well, he did a lot worse to me. Which is my point. The goal of therapy is to make you feel like dog shit in the name of insight. I'm gonna pay two hundred bucks an hour to feel like dog shit?"

"Mrs. Korsmo?" A small voice from the hall.

"Yes?"

"Sorry to bother you," calls Mattie, "but John scratched Bex's arm, and she's pretty upset about it."

"Did he break the skin?" shouts the wife.

"No, but—"

"Then can you please just deal with it?"

Mattie appears in the doorway, nervous. "Bex says she needs you."

"Well, she doesn't. Tell her I'll be up to check on her later."

"I'll go," says Didier. "Take the chicken out when it buzzes."

"But we weren't finished," says the wife.

He follows Mattie toward the stairs.

The wife shoves the chicken-stained cutting board into the dishwasher. Picks olives off the countertop. Wipes stray salt into her palm.

She washes her hands.

Switches the timer off but keeps the oven on.

Ignites a burner on the gas stovetop to high.

Reaches in with a pot holder for a breast, which she drops onto the burner's high open flame. It flares and spits and sizzles, the whole breast blue with fire.

Darkening, bubbling.

Charred and rubbery.

Little animal, burnt black.

Her mother's hand over hers on the knife.

The lamb's face coming off.

Upon tasting a new batch of *skerpikjøt,* her mother boasted she could name the very hillside on which the lamb had grazed. No one believed her, but it was wiser, with this mother, to applaud the sensitivity of her tongue.

This mother informed the explorer only two days before the wedding that she was to marry a man she'd never set eyes on, a widowed salmoner aged fifty-two. Eivør was old to be unmarried—nineteen.

# THE BIOGRAPHER

Good Ship Chinese is full of teachers, thanks to a federal mandate that doubled the number of standardized tests in public schools. Only half the staff are needed to proctor this afternoon's exams.

The bleached-blond waitress pours their waters and says, "I'll give you a minute." A hairy mole clings to her cheek.

Didier reaches to pinch something from the biographer's collar. "You had oatmeal for breakfast."

She bats his hand away. He kicks her under the table. In front of Susan she doesn't touch Didier. Doesn't want her thinking *Does she want my husband?* because the biographer doesn't, and if she did, all the more reason not to arouse suspicion. Susan once told the biographer how the music teacher had flirted her tiny ass off with Didier at the summer picnic, and Bex, drawing at the kitchen table, said, "Did she put her tiny ass back on?" and Susan said, "I wish you'd be seen and not heard for once in your life." The biographer was pleased to know that Susan could be an unskillful parent.

"How goes your saga," says Pete, "of the lady adventurer?"

"Almost finished."

"I have no doubt." He flaps his placemat vigorously, airing himself. "Everyone needs a good hobby."

"It's not a hobby," she says.

"The hair coming out of that mole," says Didier, "has got to be three inches long."

"Of course it's a hobby," says Pete. "You do it on weekends or vacations. The act of doing it brings you amusement but no profit or gain."

"You guys want to order? I can flag down the hair taxi."

"So if something doesn't make money," says the biographer, "it's automatically relegated to hobby?"

The waitress returns. Her sprouting hair—quite long, quite black—for a moment mesmerizes all of them. The biographer, who bleaches her own upper lip every few weeks, warms with fellow feeling. She and Pete order Golden Lily platters, Didier the Emperor's Consolation.

Didier leans forward to say, low: "Why don't she just bleeding yank that thing out, eh?"

There is an egg bracing to burst out of its sac into the wet fallopian warmth. Today the ovulation predictor kit showed no smiley face; she'll test again tomorrow. Back to Kalbfleisch for sperm, once she gets the smiley face.

"Pour me some more tea, Roanoke?"

She moves the teapot six inches toward him.

"I said *pour,* woman! Can I get a ride home, by the way? I left Susan the car today."

"How were you planning on getting home if I didn't drive you?"

Didier grins, *beau-laid.* "I knew you'd drive me."

Bryan Zakile saunters over to their table and bellows, "*These* three are clearly up to no good! Want to hear my fortune? 'You will leave a trail of gratitude.'"

"'In bed,'" adds Didier.

"You said it, not me."

"Not I," mutters the biographer.

Bryan flinches. "Thank you, grammar Schutzstaffel."

She drags her fork through the Golden Lilies. "I'm not the one who teaches English."

"He don't really teach English either," says Didier. "His subject is the beautiful game."

"If only that knee had held up," says Pete, "we'd be watching Bryan on telly. Who'd you be playing for? Barça? Man United?"

"Hilarious, Peter, but I was All-Conference for three years at Maryland."

"That is tre*mend*ously impressive."

The biographer smiles at Pete. Surprised, he smiles back.

Sometimes he reminds her of her brother.

\* \* \*

She can't use the ovulation predictor test when she wakes up, because first morning urine isn't optimal for detecting the surge of luteinizing hormone that augurs the egg's release. She has to wait four hours to let enough urine accumulate in her bladder, and in these four hours she can't drink too many fluids, lest she dilute the urine and skew the results. Instead of coffee, she toasts a frozen waffle and gnaws it unbuttered at the kitchen table. She stares at the bookstore photograph. The shelf where her book will go.

Between first and second periods, in a stall of the staff bathroom, the biographer inserts a fresh pee-catching tab into the plastic wand of the ovulation predictor kit and squats over the toilet. The instructions say you don't need to absorb the whole stream, only five seconds' worth, which is good because the opening spray goes wide of the stick. She has to keep moving the stick around under herself to find it. Count to five. Rest the stick on some toilet paper on the metal tampon receptacle, angled just so, to allow the caught pee to wend its way through the stick into whatever mechanism tests it for luteinizing hormone. Which takes a minute or longer.

She wipes her wet hands, pulls up her jeans, sits back down on the toilet. During this minute or longer, while the digital display blinks—it will turn into an empty circle or a smiley-faced circle—the biographer sings the egg-coaxing song. "I may be alone, I may be a crone, but fuck you, I can still ovulate!"

She checks: still blinking.

Woman who is thin and ugly. Withered old woman. Cruel and ugly old woman. Witch-like woman. Stock character in fairy tale. Woman over forty. From the Old Northern French *caroigne* ("carrion" or "cantankerous woman") and from the Middle Dutch *croonje* ("old ewe").

Still blinking.

Through the bathroom wall come shrieks of girls whose ovaries are young and juicy, crammed with eggs.

Still blinking.

What is the total number of human eggs in this building right now?

Still blinking.

How many of the human eggs in this building right now will get sperm pricked, cracked open, to produce another human?

She checks: smiley face!

Bloom of delight in her ribs.

*I may be forty-two, but I can still fucking ovulate.*

"Hello, yes, I'm calling because I got my LH surge today—Okay, sure…" Holding, holding. "Yes, hi, this is Roberta Stephens…Yes, right…And I surged today…Yeah…And I'm using donor sperm so I wanted to—Okay, sure…" Holding, holding, bell shrilling; that was the second bell; she's late for her own class. "Okay…Yes, I've got more than one donor in storage, but I'd like you to use number 9072."

Donor semen is frozen shortly after collection and thawed shortly before insemination. In between, millions of sperm lie arrested, aslant, their genetic material paused. Tomorrow morning, before she arrives, the clinic staff will thaw a vial of 9072 (Rock Climber Beautiful Sister) and spin its contents in a centrifuge to separate sperm from seminal fluid, wash the swimmers clean of prostaglandins and debris.

"See you at seven!" she tells the nurse, so excited her throat hurts.

Tomorrow at seven. At seven tomorrow. Tomorrow, in Salem, on a leafy little upmarket street, at the hands of a former tight end, the biographer will be inseminated.

If it is possible for you to come to me, little one, let you come to me.

If it is not possible, let you not come, and let me not be shattered.

She can hardly sleep. Is holding a jar of some sort of face cream that contains opiates, and is going to cook it and shoot it, and is hunting in her mother's bathroom for cotton. She needs to hide the gear from her mother. But she also *is* her mother, and the person with the jar is Archie. "What happened to the cotton balls?" he asks. "All gone. Use a filter." "But I'm out of cigarettes!" says Archie. "Maybe I have some," says the biographer.

She wakes before the alarm. Glass of water, her brother's old green parka, her mother's bike-lock key on a chain around her neck. The biographer is an atheist, but she doesn't rule out helpful ghosts.

"Archie's the charmer," said their mother. "You're the wise one."

She leaves her apartment building in the briny dark, sea crashing, car freezing. No other cars on the cliff road. Her headlights sweep the rock wall, the fir tops, the black ocean flecked with silver, same road and water the baby will see one day.

7:12 a.m.: Signs in at the front desk. Takes her place among the silent, rock-fingered women.

7:58 a.m.: Nurse Jolly leads her to an exam room, where she strips below the waist and climbs under the paper sheet. Her heart is going twice as fast. Do quickened beats affect fertilization? In last night's dream, she— as Archie—planned to shoot up into her chest, left-hand side, because she'd been told a "heart direct" made the pleasure immense.

8:49 a.m.: Kalbfleisch stands beside the biographer's spread legs and stir- ruped feet and shows her a vial. "Is this the correct donor?" She squints: 9072 from Athena Cryobank. Yes. "The count on this vial was quite good," he says. "Thirteen point three million moving sperm."

"Remind me what the average is?"

"We want the count to be at least five million."

He inserts a speculum into the biographer's vagina. It does not exactly hurt—more of a serious pressure—then he opens her cervix, and the pres- sure turns teeth clenching. A plastic catheter is guided through the specu- lum into the biographer's uterus. The nurse hands Kalbfleisch the syringe of washed semen, an inch of pale yellow. He injects it into the catheter, depositing the semen at the top of her uterus, near the fallopian tubes.

The whole thing takes less than a minute.

He snaps off his gloves and says "Good luck" and goes.

"Rest for a bit, hon," says Nurse Jolly. "You want any water?"

"No thanks, but thank you."

In-breath.

She is so, so scared.

Out-breath.

Either this has to work or she has to be matched with a bio mother in the next two months. After January fifteenth, when Every Child Needs Two goes into effect, no adopted kid will have to suffer from a single woman's lack of time, her low self-esteem, her inferior earning power. Every adopted kid will now reap the rewards of growing up in a two-parent home. Fewer single mothers, say the congressmen, will mean fewer criminals and addicts and welfare recipients. Fewer pomegranate farmers. Fewer talk-show hosts. Fewer cure inventors. Fewer presidents of the United States.

In-breath.

*Keep your legs, Stephens.*

Out-breath.

She lies perfectly still.

In high school she ran for hours every day of track season—had muscles then, had stamina. She competed in the four hundred and the eight hundred, and though not a star, she was decent, even won a few meets her senior year. Archie, tenth-grader, pressed himself against the chain-link fence and cheered. Her parents sat in the bleachers and cheered. Her mother made celebratory dinners with the biographer's favorite foods: green-chile scrambled eggs, peanut-butter pie. How she loved the laden table, the lamps, the spring-night crickets, Mama before she got sick, Archie in his skull T-shirt balancing a spoonful of pie on his head. In the beam of their attention she was tired and proud, a warrior who had slung her arrow into every heel she aimed for.

\*     \*     \*

If it is possible for you to come to me, let you come to me, and I will name you Archie.

In the car, she opens the ziplock of pineapple chunks, whose bromelain is supposed to encourage a fertilized egg to implant itself in the uterine wall. It will be five days before the egg is ready to implant, but eating pineapple comforts the biographer. Its sweetness is strong and good against the bitter, spitty fear.

Five days. Two months. Forty-two years. She hates the calendar.

Please let it work this time.

She doesn't move her pelvis the whole drive home. Lifts her toes carefully on the brake and accelerator, no thigh muscle. "Hell, you could go to the gym today if you wanted," said Kalbfleisch after the first insemination, to underscore how much it didn't matter what the biographer's body did after a few minutes of lying still on the exam table; but the biographer's body is going to stay as quiet as it can.

It has to work this time.

She will sit behind her desk in class without thigh movement or pelvic commotion of any kind; and the eggs will float in the tube waters unjarred, open, amenable; and one sperm-struck egg will welcome a single invading spermatozoon into itself, ready to meld and to split. From one cell, two. From two, four. From four, eight. An eight-celled blastocyst has a chance.

I spent eighteen months in my husband's house before a storm sank his boat and him with it.

That in eighteen months I had not been gotten with child brought shame to my mother.

The red morn I left for Aberdeen, she said, "Go on, get that broken *fisa* away from us."

# THE DAUGHTER

Her parents aren't religious. Their reasons are pragmatic, they say. Logical. So many people *want* to adopt. Why should people be deprived of babies they will nourish, cherish, rain love down upon, just because other people don't feel like being pregnant for a few months? When the Personhood Amendment passed, her father said it was about time the country came to its senses. He had no truck with the wackos who bombed clinics, and he thought it was going a little too far to make women pay for funerals for their miscarried fetuses; but, he said, there was a loving home out there for every baby who came into the world.

Her eighth-grade social-studies class held a mock debate on abortion. The daughter prepared bullet points for the pro-choice team. Her father proofread her work, as usual; but instead of his usual "This is top-notch!" he sat down beside her, rested a hand on her shoulder, and said he was concerned about the implications of her argument.

"What if your bio mother had chosen to terminate?"

"Well, *she* didn't, but other people should be able to."

"Think of all the happy adopted families that wouldn't exist."

"But Dad, a lot of women would still give their babies up for adoption."

"But what about the women who didn't?"

"Why can't everyone just decide for themselves?"

"When someone decides to murder a fellow human with a gun, we put them in jail, don't we?"

"Not if they're a cop."

"Think of all the families waiting for a child. Think of me and your mom, how long we waited."

"But—"

"An embryo is a living being."

"So is a dandelion."

"Well, I can't imagine the world without you, pigeon, and neither can your mother."

She doesn't want them to imagine the world without her.

Ash offers a ride home, but the daughter says no, her dad is coming; retirement means he's so bored he can pick her up anytime. It is cold, dim skied, the grass on the soccer field stiff and silver. The team has an away game today. She hasn't told Ephraim. What if he's like "Is it even mine?" Or "You made your bed; now lie in it." They passed each other last week in the cafeteria, and Ephraim in the old-school hat she once adored said, "Hey," and she said, "Hey, how are you?" but he kept moving and her non-rhetorical question was rhetorical. He was probably on his way to put his hand up Nouri Withers's shirt.

Her bio mother could have been young too. She could have been headed to medical school, then to a neurochemistry doctorate program, then to her own research lab in California. (What if she's close, at this very moment, to finding a cure for paralysis?) Keeping the daughter would have meant forfeiting her med-school scholarship.

She doesn't want the kid to wonder why he wasn't kept.

And she doesn't want to wonder what happened to him. Was he given to parents like hers or parents who scream and are bigots and don't take him to the doctor enough?

She jumps at the tsunami siren—will never get used to that nerve-scraping howl.

"Only a test, my love," says Dad.

She turns up the car radio.

"How was school?"

"Fine."

"Finished the academy application yet?"

"Almost."

"Mom's making fish tacos."

She swallows down a little spurt of vomit. "Awesome."

*"Earlier today,"* goes the radio, *"twelve sperm whales ran aground a half mile south of Gunakadeit Point. The cause of the beaching has not yet been determined."*

"Oh my God." She turns it up.

*"Eleven of the whales are dead, says the sheriff's office, though it remains unclear—"*

"Remember the stranding of '79?" says Dad. "Forty-one sperms on the beach near Florence. My pop drove out to photograph them up close. He said they made—"

"Little clicking sounds while they died." She knows the gruesome details, because Dad likes to repeat them. He's told her many times that a whale can be killed by the pressure of its own flesh. Out of water, the animal's bulk is too heavy for its rib cage—the ribs break; the internal organs are crushed. And heat hurts whales. Greenpeacers brought in bedsheets to soak with seawater and throw over them; it didn't help.

But that was 1979. Hasn't somebody by now figured out a way to get them back into the ocean?

"Can we go down there, Dad?"

"They don't need the public meddling in—"

"But one is still alive."

"Are you going to roll it back down to the water yourself? Don't turn this into a morbid preoccupation."

"The heart of a sperm whale weighs almost three hundred pounds."

"How do—?"

"Me and Yasmine once made a list of how much different animals' hearts weigh."

"Yasmine and I." Dad gets tense at the mention of her. "Don't worry too much about the whales, okay, pigeon? Otherwise those lovely eyebrows might get tangled up in one another, never to untangle."

"They're not lovely, they're thick."

"Which is what makes them lovely!"

"You're not objective." She wants a cigarette but will content herself with a licorice nib, for now.

Ash isn't into the idea. So tired, etc. But she is convincible. The daughter crawls out her bedroom window onto the roof, rappels down the trellis, stands still a full minute in the porch shadow in case any noises were heard. A block away is the blue mailbox, their meeting place, where she smokes and waits.

Yasmine once asked her why white people are so obsessed with saving whales.

The beach is crowded with people shouting, dogs yapping, cameras popping, rain raining. A TV crew has aimed screeching lights on the whales, a row of twelve, their pewter-gray hides slashed with chalky white. They look like stone buses. The one at the very end is slowly lifting and dropping its flukes. Each time a fluke hits the sand, the daughter's thighs tremble.

Humans pose for photos in front of the dead.

A guy has clambered onto a massive gray tail. "Snap me!" he shouts. "Snap me!"

"Get the hell down."

"Move back, folks!"

"Did the dead man's fingers have anything to do with this?"

"Who do I talk to about reserving some of the teeth? For scrimshaw?"

"Sir, get down from there immediately."

"Were they poisoned by the seaweed?"

"Move aside, move aside."

A woman with gloves and a long knife—a scientist?—squats by the first whale in the row. Will she carve off a slice of blubber to test for disease? A madness, maybe, has infected their spines and driven them onto land, all twelve fevered with death wish. Maybe the infection can pass to humans. Newville will be quarantined.

"You need to leave, girls," says a cop not much older than they are. "We're clearing the beach. And put out that cigarette."

"Why isn't anyone putting them back in the water?" says the daughter.

The cop peers at her. "A, they're dead. B, you realize how much these goddamn things weigh?"

"But one of them *isn't* dead!"

"Go home, okay?"

She and Ash walk past the enormous bodies—one spray-painted with an orange question mark, another sprayed with OUR FAULT!—to the last breathing whale. Its flukes lie still. Blood pools on the sand by its head. The mouth is open, drenched red. The beaky lower jaw, illogically small for such a huge skull, is sown with teeth. The daughter touches one: a banana of bone.

*Has moved amid this world's foundations.*

"Now your hand is infected," says Ash.

She wipes it on her jeans.

The whale's eye, wedged between wrinkled lips of skin, is open and black and quivering. *Hast seen enough to split the planets.* She kneels down. Leans her cheek against the gray body. Dry, scarred leather.

"It'll be okay," she says.

Can't hear any clicking sounds.

Where are the machines? The cables, the levers?

A whale is a house in the ocean.

A womb for a person.

Whale song is heard from sea floor to star, from Icy Strait Point to Península Valdés.

"Ash, give me your hoodie."

"I'm cold."

"*Give* it." The daughter runs down to the waves and douses Ash's hoodie and her own. Runs back to throw them, dripping, onto the whale's head. The only song she can think of is "I've Been Working on the Rail-

126

road." She's in the midst of chanting "Someone's in the kitchen with Dinah" when she hears a gunshot.

Then screams.

Everyone is clustering around something up the beach.

It wasn't a gun; it was a whale. Exploding. The gray belly, split wide, leaks slimy bundles of pink intestine and purple organ meat. Fat shreds of flesh flap in the wind. "Get it off! Get it off!" yells a boy, pawing at ropes of innards stuck to his chest.

And the stink—God!—rancid blast of farts, fish rot, and sewage. The daughter pulls her shirt up over her mouth.

Black-red liquid foams at her feet.

The scientist is explaining to the cop that she'd been trying to collect samples of subcutaneous adipose tissue and visceral adipose tissue. When she sank her knife into the whale, it burst.

"Methane gas builds up in the carcass," she says. "This one must have been the first to die, possibly days ago. If he was their leader and died at sea, and his body floated to shore, the other whales would have followed. They're loyal to a fault."

"Ma'am, you can't just go around chopping up corpses," says the cop.

"This magnificent creature isn't anyone's property," says the scientist. "I intend to analyze the tissue and figure out how they ended up here."

"What lab are you with, ma'am? My captain said the OIMB guys weren't going to be here until—"

"I'm an independent researcher. But *this*"—she holds up two clear plastic bags of red flesh—"I know what to do with."

The daughter heads back to her whale.

His eye is no longer moving.

*Thou saw'st the murdered mate when tossed by pirates from the midnight deck.*

She presses the eye with her fingertip.

It is clammy and springy, like a hard-cooked egg.

How to make *tvøst og spik*:

1. Prepare pilot-whale meat in one of the following ways: boil fresh, fry fresh, store in dry salt, store in brine, or cut into long strips (*grindalikkja*) and hang to dry.
2. Prepare pilot-whale blubber by boiling, salting, or drying. (Do not fry.)
3. Serve meat and blubber together with boiled and salted potatoes. In some Faroese homes, dried fish is also included on the *tvøst og spik* plate.

# THE MENDER

Cotter reports that Lola fell down the stairs. Was in a little coma. Better now.

New clients are supposed to leave a note at the P.O., but Lola just showed up one day, drenched. "I heard of you from my friend." The mender brought her inside, gave her a towel, inspected the red smear on her forearm.

"Is it going to scar?"

"Yes," said the mender. She pressed fresh-bruised leaves of houseleek to the damaged skin, waited, blinked at Lola's breasts, those plump puddings, then wrapped the arm with a poultice of leek juice and lard. "How did this happen?"

"It was stupid," said Lola. "I was making dinner and I caught my arm on a hot pan."

Her husband also snapped her finger bone. Left a six-colored bruise on her jaw.

Two more warts on Clementine's fig.

Clementine says, "This is kind of extremely humiliating?"

"Just a body doing what it does."

"But they're so *nasty*."

"Lots of people get them," says the mender, and she holds a compress of crushed, wet lupine seeds against the vulva. White lupine is also good for bringing down blood—a missed period, a uterus unhappily full— and for calling worms to the surface of the skin. Summers, the mender burns its seeds in stone cups to fend off gnats.

"Stick out your tongue."

Scalloped at the edges, as usual.

"Still eating pizza?"

Clementine cutely scrunches her mouth. "Not *that* much."

"Stop all dairy. Too much dampness in you."

"Hey, would you ever consider waxing your eyebrows?"

"Why?"

"I mean, not that you *need* to, because big brows are making a comeback, but a friend of mine at Snippity Doo Dah does great sugar waxes, if you ever—"

"No," says the mender. If she has such a friend, why not deal with the two-inch hair dangling from that mole? It is a misfit hair, discordant with her bleached curls and fake nails.

The mender spoons a mash of mugwort and ginger into Clementine's belly button; lays a fresh slice of ginger across the mash; holds a burning moxa stick over the ginger until she complains of the heat; and tapes the belly button with two Band-Aids to keep the mash in place for a day at least, better two.

Clementine pulls her shirt down. "Thanks for all your help, Gin." Takes small white boxes from her backpack. "Hope you like fried rice and garlic shrimp. Don't worry, it's not customer leftovers—"

"I'm not worried," says the mender.

Or hungry enough for Chinese food. Once Clementine is gone she drizzles half a slice of brown bread with sesame oil. Every Thursday Cotter leaves a loaf he baked himself, wrapped in a towel, on her cabin step.

Some supermarket breads are made with human hair dissolved in acid, part of a dough conditioner that accelerates industrial processing. The mender does not eat bread from the supermarket, and she has her own supply of hair, which instead of dissolving in acid she grinds into her mixtures. She keeps head hair in a separate box from pubic, as they're good for different things—pubic has more iron, head more magnesium and selenium. The mender's supply came from one person and is dwindling.

\*　　\*　　\*

Long red head hairs can be used in mixtures. Brown pubic hairs can be used. But there are some hairs that can't be. The stray whiskers under the arms; the little breath of brown on the upper lip. Those hairs are iced onto the skin of the body in the freezer.

What does the girl's hair taste like, her shining flat dark hair? The girl doesn't slick or shellac it. Long enough to get caught in her satchel strap, the mender noticed when she saw her come through the blue school doors, the girl had to tug and rearrange, she was annoyed for a second, a flip of heat on her cheeks, then she forgot her hair, the mender saw, because she was looking for someone, but the someone wasn't among the burst of kids. The girl kept walking, alone, and the mender almost followed.

The brown bread is dry, because today is Tuesday.

Aunt Temple died on a Tuesday, eight winters ago.

Before Temple, when her mother forgot to buy food, the mender cooked ketchup, mustard, and mayonnaise into a hot crust.

Before Temple, she put herself to bed.

Before Temple, she took a lot of aspirin, because regular doctors were too expensive and the ER staff knew the mender's mother only too well.

Before Temple, she had never been to the movies.

She had those wild red braids and wore billowy purple pants and wasn't married. She laughed in a shrieky way. Her shop was named after a witch who lived in Massachusetts three centuries ago. The people of Newville called Temple a witch too, but they didn't mean it the same way they mean it about the mender.

*       *       *

When she was young, Goody Hallett loved a pirate who forsook her. Legend has it she killed their baby on the night of its birth, suffocated the thing in a barn, then was imprisoned and lost her mind and lured ships to crash on the Cape Cod rocks. In truth, said Temple, she gave the child in secret to a farmer's wife. The wife kept a diary, which preserved the fact.

The baby is the mender's great-great-great-great-great-great-great-grandfather.

The innermost chamber of her left ear notices powderpost beetles scratching in the roof joists, laying their eggs in the seams of the wood.

"Never forget," said Temple, "that you descend from Black Sam Bellamy and Maria Hallett."

But the mender would never tie a lantern to a whale. Like sailors and fishermen, she hates to swim.

The red morn betoken'd wreck to the seaman and sorrow to the shepherds, woe unto the birds, gusts and foul flaws to herdmen and to herds.

# THE WIFE

Screaming screaming screaming. No stop no stop no stop.

"TURN!"

John wants her to play the record again; she will not do it. The whole morning has been records: yell scream yell scream, throw self on floor, starfish arms and legs "TURN!" no stop no.

"Mommy turn it Mommy turn it Mommy turn it Mommy…"

She has reasoned, she has implored, she has ignored, she has worried her eardrums will be actually damaged; and now she says, "Shut the *fuck* up," which makes no difference to John, still screaming and starfishing, but Didier yells from the dining room, "Don't say that to him!"

"Either come and deal with him yourself," calls the wife, "or fuck off."

Her husband stomps in, lifts the dustcover, sets the needle on the record, unleashes a bouncy guitar.

John goes quiet, wetly heaving.

*"We are the dinosaurs, marching, marching.*

*"We are the dinosaurs. Whaddaya think of that?"*

"The lesson he just learned," says the wife, "is that if he screams long enough, he'll get what he wants."

"Well, good. It's a hard world."

*"We are the dinosaurs, marching, marching.*

*"We are the dinosaurs. We make the earth flat!"*

"Could you take him for a walk?" says the wife.

"It's raining," says Didier.

"His raincoat's on the banister."

"He doesn't look like he wants to go for a walk."

"Please do this one tiny thing," she says.

"I really don't feel like it."

"I'm never alone."

"Well, me neither. I'm with those *trous du cul* all day, five days a week."

"Didier"—slowly, carefully—"will you please take him out. Bex will be back in an hour, and I'll make lunch, but until then, I would like to be alone."

"I'd like to be alone too," he says, but heads for the banister. "Come on, *Jean-voyage*."

Herd crumbs into palm.

Spray table.

Wipe down table.

Rinse cups and bowls.

Put cups and bowls in dishwasher.

Soak quinoa in bowl of water.

Rinse and chop red bell peppers.

Put strips in fridge.

Rinse quinoa in sieve.

Put clean, uncooked quinoa in fridge.

Pour water from quinoa soaking into pot of ficus tree.

Spray mist onto snake-like arms of Medusa's head plant.

Pull clothes out of dryer in basement.

Fold clothes.

Stack clothes in hamper.

Leave hamper at bottom of stairs to second floor.

Write *laundry detergent* on list in wallet.

*Plip, plip, plip,* says the kitchen tap.

Nobody on this hill even likes quinoa.

She pulls the kids' plastic pumpkins down off the high shelf.

Over a month since Halloween. She told them the candy ran out.

In the empty kitchen or the sewing room, she eats sugar nobody knows about.

She allows herself, now, three coconut crunches. And one almond smushie. And one packet of candy corn.

*This is what you're missing, Ro! Ramming stale candy stolen from your own children down your throat.*

How can the wife hope that Ro doesn't get pregnant? Doesn't publish her book on the ice scientist?

*Plip, plip, plip.*

As if Ro's not having a kid or a book would make the wife's life any better.

As if the wife's having a job would make Ro's any worse.

The rivalry is so shameful she can't look at it.

It flickers and hangs.

It waits.

So cold in this house.

She takes off her sweater and pushes it between the back door and the kitchen floor, which is, she notices, sandy with crumbs.

She goes for the broom but ends up with her phone.

Saturday morning: her mother will be puttering, cleaning, paging through magazines.

They see each other, of course, make visits—Thanksgiving is next week—but that's not the same as having her here, in pinches, on spurs of moments. A hundred miles is too far for an unplanned pinch.

She is thirty-seven years old and pines for her mother.

But won't she be thrilled, thirty years hence, to learn that Bex and John are pining for her?

She can see John's little face bigger but still with its translucent emotions, clean feelings surging and waning, her tidal boy. He will always want her.

Bex has too strong an instinct for self-reliance; she'll be fine on her own.

"Hi, Mom," says the wife. "What's your weather?"

"Drizzling. Yours?"

"Oh, um—just gray."

"Sweetpea…?"

"The sprites are good," says the wife.

"Susan, what's going on?"

"Bex's class is doing the *Mayflower,* and John is obsessed by dinosaur songs."

"With you, I meant."

"Nothing," she says.

"What time do you want us on Thursday?" says her mother. "I'm bringing candied yams. I think they'll be a hit."

Everyone on this hill hates yams.

"Come as early as you feel like. I love you, Mom."

*Plip, plip, plip.*

Shell's perfect mother will drop Bex off in fifteen minutes, and the girl will be full of praise for the fun she has with that family, the plucking of wild berries, the baking of homemade berry pie sweetened only with Grade B maple syrup because refined sugar is toxic.

Then she'll want help with her worksheet. *Write down the weather for each day of the week. Was it sunny? Was it foggy? Was the ocean cheerful or angry?*

At the rim of sleep, she dreams of how Bryan would fuck her, the big thick plunge of him, the brawny thrusting, he's a shoving leopard, lord, he does not tire, all that soccer, those extra-long muscles to drive the blood heartward—

*"Meuf."* A pinch in the rib meat.

"Nnnnnhhhh."

Didier's breath on her neck. "It bugged me what you said today. To John."

"Nnnnnhhhh."

"Bugged me a lot."

"Are you joking?" she whispers. "You say 'fuck' in front of them all the time. I say it once?"

"But I never tell them to shut up. I don't want you talking to them like that."

"Too bad you don't get to decide," says the wife.

\*    \*    \*

The next morning she walks out back, feet bare on the cold, wet grass, past the lavender bushes and the garage and the tire swing. Opens her phone and dials.

"Hello?"

"Hi, Bryan, it's Susan." Air, silence. "Didier's wife?"

"Yeah, yeah, of course. How are you?"

"Fine! I, ah, got your number from the school directory and was calling to—say hi." *What?*

"Well, hi there," says Bryan.

"Also, I wanted to invite you to Thanksgiving dinner at our place. If you don't have plans. Ro will be there. She's sort of an orphan. I mean not technically but—And my parents, which isn't—I mean—" *Cease talking. You must cease talking.*

"That's really nice," he says, "but actually I do have plans."

"Oh! Well, I thought I'd ask."

"Mmm."

"Anyway." She coughs.

"Yeah," he says.

"But you and I should have coffee sometime," she says.

Air, silence.

Eventually he says, "I'd like that."

anchor
candle
drift
fast
frazil
grease
nilas
old
pack
pancake
rafted
young

# THE BIOGRAPHER

She breaks it to her father quickly, on the drive to school. He doesn't bother to conceal his displeasure. "Another Christmas by myself?"

"I'm sorry, Dad. I have so little time off, and it takes a whole day to fly—"

"I never should've moved."

"You hated Minnesota."

"Give me a blizzard any day over this humid netherworld."

The crease above her pubic bone feels vaguely bloated—or sore— different from period cramps, but the same family of sensation. It's been almost a week since the insemination; she will take a pregnancy test in eight days. Are these signs of implantation? Has a blastocyst burrowed into the red wall? Does it cling and grow with all its might? Are its chromosomes XX or XY?

"Am I ever going to see you again?" says her father.

He won't fly, on account of his back. He would send her money for a plane ticket if she asked, but he can't afford it any more than the biographer can. His income is fixed and small. "I may not have cash to leave you," he likes to say, "but you can sell my coin collection. Worth thousands!"

"You will, Dad."

"I *worry*, kiddo."

"No need! I'm fine."

"But who knows," he says, "how many more trips around the sun *I've* got?"

The boys in ninth-grade history make spitballs and ask, "Miss, in the olden days, when you were young, did they have spitballs?"

The eleventh-graders are enjoying the fruits of someone's research on archaic terms for "penis." When Ephraim yells "Bilbo!" the biographer stares him down, but he stares right back. Usually she has no issues with discipline; this outburst makes her feel like a failure.

Well, she *is* a failure. She and her uterus fail, fail, fail.

Ephraim: "Prepuce!"

The biographer: "That just means foreskin, my friend."

Giggles. Haws. *You said foreskin.*

The biographer and her ovaries fail, fail, fail.

"Baldpate friar!"

But there have been twinges — sharp little aches. Something feels like it's happening down there. Maybe *not* fail, finally? Thousands of bodies succeed every day; why not the body of a biographer from Minnesota whose favorite garment is the sweatpant?

"Nouri," she says, "you can wait to put on lipstick until after class."

"I'm not putting on, I'm refreshing."

Nouri Withers loves books about famous murders and writes the best sentences of any child the biographer has taught. Her sentences need to be typed into a search program to make sure they're not plagiarized.

"You can refresh later."

"But my lips look janky *now.*"

"Agreed!" shouts Ephraim, long legged and fidgety, who thinks himself dashing in his vintage trilby hat. A boy who moves through the world unafraid. If he weren't so fearless and handsome and good at soccer, he might have been forced to grow in more interesting directions. The only thing interesting about Ephraim, as far as the biographer can tell, is his name.

The biographer decides she will shout too. "Have you ever considered, people, how much time has been stolen from the lives of girls and women due to agonizing over their appearance?"

A few faces smile, uneasy.

Even louder: "How many minutes, hours, months, even actual *years,* of their lives do girls and women waste in agonizing? And how many billions of dollars of corporate profit are made as a result?"

Nouri, open mouthed, sets down her lipstick. It stands on the desk like a crimson finger.

"A *lot* of billions, miss?"

These kids must think she's a joke.

"The institution began," she tells the tenth-graders, "as a fiscal arrangement in which the father's household transferred land, money, and livestock to the husband's household, attached to the body of the daughter-bride. Its economic foundations have in recent centuries become shrouded by—some might even say smothered by—the veil of romantic love."

"Are you married, miss?" says Ash.

"Shut up," someone says.

"Nope," says the biographer.

"Why not?" says Ash.

"Shut up!" shouts Mattie.

Silence crackles. Even the half-asleep kids are suddenly alert.

Mattie says, more quietly, "Why did they *die?*"

From the next desk, Ash rubs her shoulder. "You mean the whales?"

"The independent researcher said their sonar could've broken. High-decibel submarine signals can make whales go deaf." Mattie cups her lunar cheeks.

"My dad said it's the witch's fault," says the son of the local navy hero, "because she lured the dead man's fingers back to Newville and they messed up the water."

Shouts and cries: "Yeah, the seaweed poisoned the whales!" "That's so dumb." "But there's been more dead whiting in the nets too—"

"Hold on, people!" says the biographer. "Maybe your dad was joking?"

"My Gramma Costello said the same thing," says Ash, "and the last time she told a joke was 1973."

"Also my dad is not dumb," says the hero's son.

The biographer contemplates digressions into marine biology and the history of witch persecution in Kingdom and States United, but she needs to end class five minutes early to get to her clinic appointment. Kalbfleisch is insisting that she come in to discuss the PCOS test results. A two-hour drive to receive what is probably—almost certainly—going to be bad news.

"There's a Buddhist temple," she says, "on a small island in Japan that used to hold requiems for whales killed by whalers. They prayed for the whales' souls. They also had a tomb for whale fetuses taken from their mothers' bodies during flensing. They would give a posthumous name to every fetus they buried, and they kept a necrology that listed the mothers' dates of capture." She pauses, scanning the room. "Do you see where I'm going with this?"

"Field trip to Japan!"

"Did the ones on the beach have any fetuses inside them?"

"Did you know a 'tus' is a male fetus?"

"We do a requiem," says Mattie. "But first we need to name them."

Good girl. Even when distraught, she pays attention.

"Okay," says the biographer, "there are twenty-four of you. Pair off. Each pair names a whale. You have three minutes. Then we'll reconvene for a recitation and a moment of silence."

"But the temple guys named the *fetuses*, not the grown-ups. You changed the ritual."

"So I did, Ash. Get to work."

She opens her notebook.

Things to do with baby:

1.  Take train to Alaska
2.  Burrow in blankets
3.  Gorge on dried mango
4.  Tell stories about the Great Sperm-Whale Stranding
5.  Put toes in waves on year's shortest day

Her students christen a Moby-Dick, two Mikes, a Spermy, for God's sake. But then whales are not exotic to these kids. The coastline near Newville is known as the whale-watching capital of the American West. For decades the local economies have depended on injections from tourists eager to see a breaching, lunging, slapping, spraying, spy-hopping colossus. They pay to watch from the decks of boats and through high-powered spotting scopes from the Gunakadeit Lighthouse; or to swim with guides, in wet suits, in the whales' feeding grounds.

The biographer is closing her backpack, thinking ahead to the traffic on 22—she can miss the worst of it if she hurries—when Mattie comes to the desk. "Can I talk to you about something?"

"Of course. I mean not right *now,* because I have a doctor's appointment, but tomorrow?" If she gets out of the parking lot in three minutes, she'll be on the cliff road in seven.

"Tomorrow's Thanksgiving."

"Monday, then."

The girl nods, staring at her hands.

"I know the whales are upsetting," says the biographer, "but—"

"It's not about that."

"Have a good weekend, Mattie." Parka zipped, pack shouldered, she bolts.

She read about the stranding in the paper but has hardly thought of it since. Barnacly, fat-lidded blocks of beast—they only feel real in her book, when young Eivør watches them die in the *grindadráp.*

"How late is Dr. Kalbfleisch running?" she asks the front-desk nurse. "I've been here almost an hour."

"He's a popular guy," says the nurse.

"Could you give me a general idea?"

"It's the day before a holiday," she says.

"And?"

"Sorry?"

"Why should that make a difference?"

The nurse pretends to read something on her computer screen. "I have no way of knowing how much longer the doctor will be. If you need to reschedule, I am happy to help you with that."

"Gee, thanks," says the biographer, and returns to her fawn-colored chair. She touches the bike-lock key on her neck. Her mother rode her bike every morning, shine or rain, until she went to the doctor about shoulder pain and learned she had lung cancer.

Accusations from the world:

13. Preferring one's own company is pathological.
14. Human beings were designed for companionship.
15. Why didn't you try harder to find a mate?
16. Married people live longer, healthier lives.
17. Do you think anyone actually believes that you're happy on your own?
18. It's creepy that you relate so much to lighthouse keepers.

Kalbfleisch wears a necktie of chuckling chipmunks. "Have a seat, Roberta."

"That's your best tie yet," she says.

"As you know, I was concerned about the possibility of you having polycystic ovary syndrome. After seeing some evidence of ovarian enlargement and polycystism, we checked your testosterone levels, and I'm afraid the results confirm that you do, in fact, suffer from PCOS."

Of course.

But she will be calm and resilient. She will be a problem solver.

"Okay, which means?"

"Which means that some or many of your follicles aren't maturing properly, and therefore ovulation is significantly compromised. Even when the OPK detects an LH surge, for instance, it's very possible no egg will appear. Let's cross our fingers for your current cycle. When do you come back for the pregnancy blood test?"

"Wednesday," she says, recruiting her facial muscles into a smile. *Problem solver.* "And if it's negative, I'll use a different donor for the next cycle. Someone with more reported pregnancies than—"

"Roberta." Kalbfleisch leans forward and looks her, for once, in the eye. "There won't be a next cycle."

"What?"

"Given your age, your FSH levels, and now this diagnosis, the chance of conception via IUI is little to none."

"But if there's a chance, at least—"

"By 'little to none,' I mean more like 'none.'"

Taut pain at the back of her mouth. "Oh."

"I'm sorry. It wouldn't be ethical for me to continue the inseminations when the statistics just don't bear it out."

*Do not cry in front of this man. Do not cry in front of this man.*

He adds, "But let's, well, let's keep our hopes up for this cycle, okay? You never know. I've seen miracles."

She doesn't cry until the parking lot.

On the dark highway, she works the calendar.

She will take the pregnancy test, her last ever, on the first day of December.

If positive—!

If negative, she'll have six and a half weeks before January fifteenth.

Before January fifteenth, she could still be picked from the catalog, chosen by a biological mother, phoned by the caseworker: *Ms. Stephens, I've got some good news!*

On January fifteenth, the Every Child Needs Two law will restore dignity, strength, and prosperity to American families.

In the lobby of her apartment building, she checks the mailbox. A reminder card from the dentist; a catalog of long skirts and floaty tops for women of a certain age; and an envelope from Hawthorne Reproductive Medicine, which she rips open. THIS IS A BILL, it says, to the tune of $936.85.

*Very possible no egg will appear.*

In her kitchen, on a cookie sheet, she sets fire to the bill and watches the flames until the smoke alarm goes off. *WANH! WANH! WANH! WANH!*

"Shut up, shut up—"
*WANH! WANH! WANH!*
Drags a chair toward the shrieks
*WANH! WANH!*
and climbs on
*WANH! WANH!*
and punches the alarm with her fist ("Shut the *shit* up") until its plastic cover splits in two.

I took my broken *fisa* to Aberdeen. Worked as a mangler in a shipyard laundry.

# THE DAUGHTER

The three o'clock bell is still clanging when she heads up Lupatia Street toward the cliff path. In her pocket are directions to the witch's house, which Ash managed to pry from her sister.

The heart of a guinea pig weighs three ounces.

Of a giraffe, twenty-six pounds.

*Yasmine, I've been adding to our list.*

Where is Yasmine, at this very moment?

The daughter can hear the thumping of her own aorta as she crunches over needles and rocks and leaves, following what she prays is the right path. She left the road by the blue CAMPING 4 MI. sign, followed the hiking trail to the brown GUNAKADEIT STATE FOREST sign, then turned onto a smaller trail—but what if there's more than one brown state forest sign?

"You just drink some wild herbs," explained Ash's sister.

Her body will be clean again.

But it will be a crime.

Half Ephraim, half her.

Less of a crime than crossing into Canada for it.

But they could still lock her up in Bolt River Youth Correctional Facility.

And it might hurt.

Less than it would hurt at a termination house, where they use rusty—

The daughter walks faster. Her neck is sweating, thighs stinging, ribs loud with cramp.

Ash refused to come with. If they were caught, the police might think she was seeking one too, and she'd be charged with conspiracy to commit murder, and she's already sixteen, and at sixteen you can be prosecuted as an adult.

The daughter gets it. But Yasmine would have come with.

*    *    *

A cabin appears, a plain little log square, windows lit, smoke drifting from the chimney. Ash's sister said to look for chickens and goats as proof it was the witch's place and not a rapist's. Although rapists could have goats and chickens. The daughter sees what might be a coop but no chickens around—are they sleeping?—and a shed, in which (she sidles up to check) are two little goats, one black, one gray. They watch her with robot eyes. "Shhh," she says, though they haven't made a sound. Chimney puffing, lights on, the witch is home; so why is the daughter dawdling by these goats? But what if the witch hates unannounced visitors, what if she has guns? It's legal to shoot someone if you say they were invading.

Going up the cabin steps, the daughter takes long breaths like Mom taught her to do at gymnastics meets, when she was still short enough for gymnastics.

Mom would understand this whole situation better than Dad would.

Not that the daughter is ever going to tell her.

Knock, knock.

The person who opens the door isn't old. Is even almost pretty. Big green eyes, dark hair in coils around pale cheeks. Her outfit—velvet choker and coarse sack dress—is Victorian prostitute meets Cro-Magnon. Is this even the witch?

The person frowns and stares.

"Hello," says the daughter.

Is it the witch's servant, or the witch's younger sister?

"*You.*" The person crosses her arms over her chest, begins to scratch her sack-covered shoulders. The fingernails make a whispering sound.

"I'm sorry to disturb you, but I'm looking for... I don't know if you're... Gin Percival?"

"Why?" She stares sideways at the daughter. More like an animal than a human.

"I need some gynecological help?"

"How did you come here?"

153

"I heard about you from Clementine?"

"Clementine." Still frowning, but now smiling too: a face pulled two ways.

"She said to tell you the, um, wart is gone?"

"Okay." The person stands back. The daughter steps in. The room is warm and smells of wood; its rafters are strung with tiny white lights, shelves packed with jars and bottles and books. There is an old-fashioned stove. No cauldron.

"I'm Mattie — Matilda."

"My name is Gin Percival."

"Nice to meet you."

The witch's throat makes a long, low gurgle. Her big eyebrows are twitching. It might be true that she's crazy.

"Sit."

"Thank you." The daughter takes a chair.

"What kind of help?"

"I need the termination herbs."

"You're pregnant and don't want to be?"

She nods.

Gin Percival stretches a hand across her forehead, as though shielding her eyes. Gives a hard, short laugh.

"I'm not here undercover," adds Mattie. "And nobody followed me." That she knows of.

"How old are you?"

"Almost sixteen."

"When's your birthday?"

"February."

"When in February?"

"The fifteenth. I'm an Aquarius."

Gin paces around the small room, fingers interlaced on top of her head. "Oh-two-one-five. You'll be sixteen."

"Do you not —" The daughter coughs, to bury her nervousness. "Is the jail sentence worse if the seeker is a minor?"

She stops pacing. Lowers her hands to her sack-smocked sides. "That has nothing to do with anything. Want some water?"

"No thanks. I'm sorry I didn't make an appointment."

"How many weeks are you?"

"I'm not *totally* sure but I think eleven or twelve? My period was supposed to come midway through September. Ish."

"Then you're around fourteen. End of first trimester. You have to include the two weeks before conception."

"But I still have time, right?"

Those *eyebrows*. Frantic brown caterpillars. Maybe because she lives by herself she has no idea how her eyebrows behave? No mirrors in the cabin that the daughter can see.

"For the kind of treatments I do? Barely. But yes. You sure you want to?"

*What if your bio mother had chosen to terminate?*

"Will it—" The daughter looks at the bare planks under her feet. "Hurt a lot?"

"Not a lot. You'll drink a bad-tasting tea, then later you'll bleed. You'll have to stay home for a day at least. Better two. Do your, uh, parents know?"

*Think of me and your mom, how long we waited.*

The daughter shakes her head. "But I can go to my friend's—Whoa! Hello!" A gray thing has leapt into her lap, a purring accordion.

"That's Malky."

"Hi, Malky." She sort of hates cats, but she wants this cat to like her and for the witch to notice that he likes her. "Friendly little guy," she adds.

"He's not friendly," says Gin. "Get on the bed. I need to look at you. Jeans and underpants off." She goes to the sink to wash.

The daughter undresses. Gin has put nothing over the bed she presumably sleeps in, no fresh towel or sheet. Cat hairs all over the brown blanket.

"Lie back," says Gin, kneeling. She smells a little like sour milk. She places both hands on the daughter's belly and starts a gentle pressure. The hands move methodically, rubbing, pushing. Above her pubic bone they pause for a while. As if listening.

Then she unscrews a jar and thumbs out a scoop of clear jelly. "I'm going to put two of my fingers into your vagina. Okay with you?"

"Yeah." The daughter shuts her eyes, concentrates on the goal of her visit.

The fingers aren't in there more than a few seconds, and it doesn't hurt. Still —

Gin washes her hands again, returns to sit on the edge of the bed. Stares at the daughter. "Your teeth are very straight," she says.

"Braces," says the daughter, not sure why Gin feels the need to point this out. "I still wear a retainer."

"You grew up in Newville?"

"Salem."

"Moved here when?"

"Last year."

Gin touches the skin above the daughter's right hip. "How'd this scar happen?"

"Fell off my bike."

"And this mole?" — pressing the apple-shaped one on her left thigh. "When did it appear?"

"I had it when I was born, I think."

Gin's finger circles the mole. Her eyebrows have quit moving, but the eyes themselves, staring moleward, are shining with tears.

It's weird that she is feeling the mole for this long.

The daughter says, loudly, "Does it look cancerous or something?"

"Nope," says Gin, getting to her feet. "You can put your clothes on." She takes something down from a shelf. The termination herbs?

Offering the jar: "Horehound candy."

"Uh, sure." The brown nub, minty and licoricey, sticks to the daughter's molars. "By the way, my gums have been bleeding when I brush my teeth. Could I have scurvy?"

"Scurvy is only on boats. Your body's making more blood now — that's why." Gin frowns, taps her cheek with one finger. "I can end the pregnancy, but not today. I need to restock some supplies."

"So, like, tomorrow?"

"Longer. I'll leave a note at the P.O."

*Longer?* Spasm of fear in her ribs.

"But I don't have a box at the P.O."

"Cotter will know about it. Ask him in two, three days."

"The guy with the acne?"

"Yes. And the tea will taste terrible."

The damn cat is back on her lap. She pets it. "Like kombucha?"

"A different bad. A stronger." Gin Percival smiles. Her teeth are yellow and not very straight. She isn't pretty, the daughter decides, but she is bold looking. A person uninterested in being pleasing to other persons. In this way she reminds the daughter of Ro/Miss. "Better leave now—dark's coming. You know how to go?"

Follow the track to the hiking trail, then to the cliff path, then down to Lupatia, where she will call Dad to pick her up from studying at the library. Returning home clumped as ever. She isn't stupid, but she has been stupid. Why did she think it would get taken care of today?

"I better show you." Gin is pulling on a dirt-colored sweater. The cat springs off the daughter's lap.

"You don't have to."

"Easy to get lost. I'll take you as far as the trail."

"Are you sure?"

"I'm sure, Mattie Matilda."

Among the different names for polar ice, the name I like best is "pack."

It reminds of dogs and wolves. Things that hunt.

To be chased by ice, and torn apart.

# THE MENDER

The mender lied. She is well stocked with fleabane and pennyroyal, has plenty of coltsfoot. But she wanted time to think. Time, at least, to abide with the idea of reaching into a body she made to unmake a future body.

When she saw the girl outside the library, months ago, it was like looking in a mirror, not at herself but at her whole family shoved together in one face. The agency had guaranteed that the baby would be placed at least seventy-five miles away, yet here she was, dancing out of the Newville library, face full of the mender's mother and aunt.

The girl is a mirror, repeating, folding time in half. When the mender had the same problem, she didn't solve it how Temple told her to. Terminations were lawful then, but the mender wanted to know how it felt to grow a human, with her own blood and minerals, in her own red clock.

Grow, but not keep.

The girl's parents have kept her well. Her breath smells sweet, and her hair is lustrous, her tongue salmon-pink, her eyeballs moist. The moon-colored skin she comes by naturally, and, of course, the height.

At the hiking trail they say goodbye. She waits until Mattie Matilda has disappeared down the trail, one minute, in the purpling air, two minutes, below the blatting owls, three minutes, upon the frost-veined ground— then follows: she'll make sure no demons touch this girl. She steps like a cat, unheard, on soil alive with blind hexapods, who ingest fungi and roots. Malky recognized the girl from her oils; he went right into her lap because underneath the lip gloss and deodorant he smelled the oils of a Percival.

\*   \*   \*

From the fir shadows the mender watches her reach the cliff path and go left, in the direction of town and people. The mender goes right, toward the sea, night seeping through holes in her sweater. Closer and closer to the cliff's edge. The shark field is resting. Stripe of moon on the flat water. Out by the horizon, a black fin. And the lighthouse. House has light so ship won't crash. Light has beam so sea won't swallow. Ship has watchers, wary squinters, men in raincoats scared of dying. Light will tell them *Don't come here;* light will steer them other ways on water black and full of bones these men don't want their bones to meet. Bad luck on ships to mention lawyers, rabbits, pigs, and churches. Don't say "drown" on ships; say "spoil."

On Parent Conference Day the teacher said, "But where's your mother?" and the mender said, "She took a ship."

But really she left in a taxi, paid for with cash stolen from the till at Goody Hallett's. And the mender, eight years old, waited by the hour. The day. The winter. Then Temple drove them to Salem and got legal guardianship.

Eight winters ago she found Temple's body flopped at the base of a silver fir, and will never be sure of the reason. Heart attack? Stroke? Out to gather miner's lettuce, her aunt had been gone so long the mender started to worry. Went looking. There she was. Her skin was bluish, but otherwise she seemed asleep.

Goody Hallett's was closed by then, because not enough tourists were buying candles and tarot packs. Temple had sold the building. They had moved from the apartment above the shop to a cabin in the forest, and Temple had told the mender, who since leaving high school had kept to herself in the library and on the cliffs: "Time for you to get to work."

The mender did not want anyone taking the body away. She couldn't give her aunt to a funeral home to be gutted and waxed; and the ground was hard; and Temple had never liked fire. So the mender clipped off her nails and her hair and her lashes, shaved the skin from each fingertip, and put her body in the chest freezer, under salmon and ice.

Last winter the mender turned thirty-two: two times sixteen (the age of the girl come February) and half of sixty-four. Sixty-four is the number of demons in the *Dictionnaire Infernal*. Of squares on a chessboard. Sixty-four is the square of eight, which is the number of regeneration and resurrection: beginning again, again.

How can she sleep when she keeps seeing the girl's face?

She used to go months, years, not thinking about it. Then something (the smell of cherries, the word "soon") would remind her. Then she would forget again, let the little fish slip away. But after seeing that face outside the library, she couldn't stop thinking. Wondering if she really was. *Are you?*

She is.

"Malky, come here."

She cuts a piece from Cotter's loaf, offers the first bite to the cat. She presses a drop of black spruce oil to the corner of the ball of her right foot.

And sleeps.

The wood is knocking, Malky's hissing, and every chicken in the family is squawking its throat off. She stands, stuporish. Clears her throat. Farts.

Her door is knocking. Malky goes from hiss to howl.

"Quiet, mo," toeing him away from the threshold.
    Men in blue uniforms. A black haired, a blond.

"What," she says.

The black haired says, "I'm Officer Withers and this is Officer Smith. Are you Gin Percival?"

Did they see her watching? Will she be accused of stalking? Did the girl, on meeting her, remember seeing her in the trees by the school and tell her parents?

She only wanted to look at her face. Hear her voice. See how she turned out.

"Gin Percival," says the black haired, "I'm placing you under arrest for medical malpractice."

The mender gapes.

"Does she not speak English?" says the blond.

The black haired clears his throat. "You have the right to remain silent. Anything you say can and will be used against you in a court of law. You have the right to speak to an attorney and to have an attorney present during questioning. If you cannot afford an attorney, one will be appointed for you. Do you understand these rights as they have been read to you?"

She waits on a bench near the desk of the blond policeman. They have given her a package of elf crackers, water in a wax cup.

Who will pour grain for Pinka and Hans? Carry the halt hen to shelter? Set out fish for Malky? And what if they open—

"I want to call someone," says the mender.

"You already had your call," says the blond policeman.

"No, I didn't."

He yells over his shoulder, "Jack, did this one get a phone call?"

"I have no idea," someone the mender can't see yells back.

"Go ahead, I guess," says the blond.

She stands at the desk with her fingers on the plastic receiver.

"Go ahead, ma'am."

She hasn't used a phone since Temple was alive.

"I forgot the number," she says.

How many salmons has she thawed recently? How many are still in the freezer? How many bags of ice?

"All your contacts are on your cell, am I right?" says the policeman. "Common predicament."

"I need the number for the P.O."

"The one in Newville?"

She smiles, because a nod would shake the tears out of her eyes and down her face.

The ice that would chase me is called by the Inupiat *ivu* and by the Europeans "ice shove," and it never gives warning. It gallops to shore from the outer sea, a heave of water caught and stropped into an iron tidal wave. But I would be faster than *ivu*. I would change into a snow deer and outrun it.

# THE WIFE

Walks the children down Lupatia Street, killing time. The wind is fast and blue and sharp with late November.

In front of Cone Wolf, she thinks of Bryan's dimple.

Bryan's thighs.

The way he looked at her.

"Morning, Susan!" says the passing librarian.

"Morning."

Goody Hallett's is gone, Snippity Doo Dah is new, but otherwise the shops and pub and library and church have sat here, in the salt wind, for decades.

Is the wife going to die in Newville?

As they cross Lupatia, a bicycle whips past so close her arm hairs crackle.

"Watch the fuck out!" yells the rider, slowing and turning to look at the wife. "It's bad enough you chose to procreate on a dying planet."

"Dick," she calls after him.

Admittedly she was not in the crosswalk.

Admittedly she has added more people to this steaming pile.

Warm, silky new smell of Bex's neck.

Her rapturous mouth on the wife's nipple to bring down the milk tingling in the ducts.

How John slept on her chest with measureless trust.

This planet may be choking to death, bleeding from every hole, but still she would choose them, every time.

"Momplee, is there school tomorrow?"

"Yes, sweetpea." She signals, brakes, turns off the paved road.

"Why?"

"Because tomorrow's Monday."

Up the hill beneath a waving roof of red alder and madrone.

*You and I should have coffee sometime.*

They could meet in Wenport. For coffee.

She used to pass through Wenport on those endless drives to get Bex to nap—infant Bex who never wanted to close her eyes—when Didier was teaching and the wife didn't know how to make her baby fall asleep.

The air in Wenport stinks like eggs, from the pulp mill.

She and Bryan could have sex in the backseat of this car.

Maybe not in the backseat; Bryan's too big.

A motel. Pay in cash.

The trees give way to an open slope, patchy with salt grass and lavender. The dirt driveway. The house.

"We're home, baby bones!" Bex tells John, who will be scarred for life because the wife told him to shut the fuck up. John, whom she'd give her own life not to scar.

Unbuckle, untangle, lift, set down.

She drops the car keys on the hall table. Her husband is prostrate on the living-room couch.

"Your shift now," she says. "I'm going for a walk."

"What about lunch?"

"I ate with the kids in town."

"But I haven't eaten."

"So—eat."

"I was waiting for you," he says. "There's nothing in the house."

"Untrue."

"What am I supposed to have, then?"

The wife starts for the kitchen, then stops. "Actually, it's not my job to figure out what you're having for lunch."

"Could you at least make a suggestion? There's like absolutely *rien* in the fridge."

"I suggest you put the kids back in the car, drive somewhere, and buy something."

"I'm exhausted," he says.

The wife kicks off her flats and puts on sneakers, yanks the laces. The clock has started on her alone time.

"Daddy, I'll cook you a cake if you want."

"I'd love a *space* cake."

"What are the ingredients of that?" says Bex.

Didier throws the wife the look, polished by years of use, that casts her as a prudish shrew and him as a guilty but unrepentant fourteen-year-old. "On second thought, Bex, would you fix me a sammie? Butter and brown sugar?"

"One sammie, upcoming!" The girl hops away.

"See you in an hour and fifty-seven minutes," says the wife.

Walks down the hill into the hushed green gloom.

Warmer in the woods than in the house. If Didier made more money, they could afford to renovate the drafty mess, but he never will, so they won't.

*Why don't you make some money, then?* screams Ro.

*Why don't you go back to law school?* screams the wife's younger self.

She shouldn't have dropped out.

Of course she should have.

What if she hadn't?

Her program wasn't top tier, but it was respectable. Two years in, she went drinking with a friend from her cohort. At last call the friend said she knew an all-night doughnut shop.

If the friend had not known the doughnut shop, or if the friend had been tired, or if the friend had never existed, the wife would have finished the program and sat for the bar and been hired by a firm and maybe, yes, still have had time to make children.

But maybe not. And anyway, those children, if she'd had time to make them, would not be Bex and John.

This fact outlasts all other facts.

*   *   *

The wife steps on a hand, soft and rubbery.

A dead hand on the floor of the woods.

A hand torn from its owner, left loose.

A dead hand is also a mushroom.

A black plastic bag is also an animal.

You can't believe your eyes.

She convinced herself at the time it was a bag because she didn't want it to be a writhing animal.

*I wanted to help it, but it was already dead.*

How do you help a cinder, half-alive?

Run over it fast to stop the burning.


She could stop being married to Didier.

Put John in daycare and finish the law degree.

With what money?

Put John in daycare and get a job at Cone Wolf.

Or at Central Coast Regional, where someone with a BA and no experience can teach history, and someone with a glorified-community-college degree and no experience can teach French.

She could stop being Didier's wife.

In therapy the kids will blame her for their broken childhoods and the maladaptive coping mechanisms that have ruined their adulthoods.

Their therapists will say, *Do you think you can ever forgive her?*

First a mangler in the shipyard laundry, then a maid in the house of the shipyard director. Brewed tea for the butler and cook, learned English, overheard the lessons given to the director's oldest son. Jars of creatures to pin and dissect. A volcano built of papier-mâché. Maritime navigation demonstrated with an astrolabe.

The polar explorer asked to sit in the schoolroom with them.
The young tutor agreed and wanted nothing in return.
The young tutor agreed but wanted half her monthly pay in return.
The young tutor agreed but wanted sex in return.
The young tutor, Harry Rattray, agreed if she promised to walk with him on Sundays through the purple crocus in Aberdeen's newly opened Victoria Park.

# THE BIOGRAPHER

Drives for two hours to give the clinic her blood. They will measure its HCG levels and call with the results. She did not test at home beforehand, as she typically does. She wants to make everything about this last-ever pregnancy test different, so that its result can be different too.

If this cycle fails, she isn't having a biological child.

To adopt from China, your body-mass index must be under 35, your annual household income over eighty thousand. Dollars.

To adopt from Russia, your annual household income must be at least a hundred thousand. Dollars.

To adopt from the United States — as of January 15 — you must be married.

*Are you married, miss?*

When her first caseworker at the adoption agency said "You do realize, I hope, that a child is not a replacement for a romantic partner?" the biographer almost walked out of the interview. She did not walk out, because she wanted to get onto their wait-list. That night she threw a potted cactus against her refrigerator.

The last time she had sex was almost two years ago, with Jupiter from meditation group. "Your cunt smells yummy," he said, extending the first syllable of "yummy" into a ghastly warble. Wiped semen from the dark swirls of his belly hair and said, "You sure you're not getting attached?"

"Scout's honor," said the biographer.

"Not that attachment is always a bad thing," said Jupiter, "but I don't really see us having that. I think we connect well sexually and intellectually, but not emotionally or spiritually."

"I'm getting a Klondike bar," said the biographer, rolling off the bed. "Want one?"

"Unless you're secretly using me for *this*." He held up five glistening fingers. "Are you having a *Torschlusspanik* moment?"

"I do not speak German."

"'Gate-closing panic.' The fear of diminishing opportunities as one ages. Like when women worry about getting too old to —"

"Do you want a Klondike bar or not?"

"Not," said Jupiter, and she could feel him wondering, *now that he thought about it,* if it might be true. Afraid of withering on her own vine, had she decided to steal his vegan cum?

She bit hard into the frozen chocolate, which sparkled along her tooth nerves, and he said: "Those things are so bad for you."

Though she mentions no sex in her notebooks, it's possible that Eivør Mínervudottír slept with lots of men. Lots of women. Who can say what she got up to with the other maids in Aberdeen, or with her shipmates on ocean voyages?

Also possible: she spent her whole life (apart from or including the eighteen-month marriage) without sex. Out of necessity. Out of choice.

But how many people have sailed to the Arctic Circle, slept in tents bolted to ice floes, watched a man's skin peel off from eating the toxic liver of a polar bear?

In the clinic waiting room, under the vexing tinkle of the adult-contemporary station, the biographer does a pump of hand sanitizer. The news murmurs on a wall-mounted flat-screen and a few faces watch it and nobody talks.

"What are you in for today?"

She looks up: a blond-pigtailed woman is smiling from the chair opposite. "A pregnancy test."

"Wow! So this could be it!"

"Unlikely," says the biographer. But, yes, in fact, it could be. If this cycle works, the eleventh-hour victory will be a story to tell the baby. *You showed up just in time.* She notes that the woman wears a simple band, no rocky engagement ring. "What about you?"

"Day nine check," says the woman. "This is my second cycle. My hubby says we should adopt, but I—I don't know. It's—" Eyes fill, shimmer.

The word "hubby" cancels out the lack of a diamond.

"At least you *can* adopt," says the biographer, louder than she meant to.

The woman nods, unperturbed. Maybe she's never heard of Every Child Needs Two; or forgot about it promptly after hearing it, because the law did not apply to her.

Compare and despair.

The biographer unbuttons her sleeve, hoists it, makes a fist. Nurse Crabby swabs the bruised skin. Archie was proud of his track marks and would neglect on purpose to wear long sleeves.

The nurse has trouble, as usual, finding a vein. "They're way buried."

"The one closer to the elbow usually works better—?"

"First let's see what we can get over here."

The biographer's car crests the cliff and the ocean spreads below. Vast dark luminous perilous sea, floors white with sailors' bones, tides stronger than any human effort. Sea stacks sleep like tiny mountains in the waves. She loves the sheer fact of how many millions of creatures the water holds— microscopic and gargantuan, alive and long dead.

In eyeshot of such a sea, one can pretend things are fine. Notice only the cares within reach. Coyotes on Lupatia Street. Fund-raising for light-house repairs. It's why the biographer liked this country of pointed firs, at first: how easily here she could forget the hurtling world. She could almost stop seeing the blue lips of her brother, the gray jaw of her mother in the hospital bed.

*　　*　　*

While the biographer was hiding out in a rainy Arcadia, they closed the women's health clinics that couldn't afford mandated renovations.

They prohibited second-trimester abortions.

They required women to wait ten days before the procedure and to complete a lengthy online tutorial on fetal pain thresholds and celebrities whose mothers had planned to abort them.

They started talking about this thing called the Personhood Amendment, which for years had been a fringe idea, a farce.

At her kitchen table she eats a bowl of pineapple chunks.

Sips water.

Waits for the call.

When Congress proposed the Twenty-Eighth Amendment to the U.S. Constitution and it was sent to the states for a vote, the biographer wrote emails to her representatives. Marched in protests in Salem and Portland. Donated to Planned Parenthood. But she wasn't all that worried. It had to be political theater, she thought, a flexing of muscle by the conservative-controlled House and Senate in league with a fetus-loving new president.

Thirty-nine states voted to ratify. A three-quarters majority. The biographer watched the computer screen splashed with this news, thought of the signs at the rallies (KEEP YOUR ROSARIES OFF MY OVARIES! THINK OUTSIDE MY BOX!) and the online petitions, the celebrity op-eds. She couldn't believe the Personhood Amendment had become real with all these citizens so against it.

Which (the disbelief) was stupid. She knew—it was her job as a teacher of history to know—how many horrors are legitimated in public daylight, against the will of most of the people.

With abortion illegal, said the congressmen, more babies would be available to adopt. It wasn't hurting anyone, they said, to ban IVF, because the people with faulty uteri and busted sperm could simply adopt all those extra babies.

Which isn't the way it turned out.

She finishes the pineapple.

Swallows the rest of the water.

Tells her ovaries: *For your patience, for your eggs, I thank you.*

Tells her uterus: *May you be happy.*

Her blood: *May you be safe.*

Her brain: *May you be free from suffering.*

Her phone rings.

"Hello, Roberta." Kalbfleisch himself is calling. Usually a nurse does.

"Hello, Doctor."

Is he calling himself because the news is different this time?

She stands with her back pressed against the refrigerator. Please please please please please please please.

Firs shake and shiver on the hill.

"I'm sorry," he says, "but your test came back negative."

"Oh," she says.

"I know this is disappointing."

"Yeah," she says.

"The odds just weren't, you know, in our favor." The doctor clears his golden throat. "I'm curious whether — Well, have you — Let me put it this way: do you travel much?"

"Florida sometimes, to see my dad."

"International travel."

Take a vacation to console herself?

*Screw. You.*

Wait.

No.

He's saying something else.

"So you recommend," she says haltingly, "in light of my — *difficulties,* that I should go — somewhere where IVF is legal?"

"I am *not* recommending that," he says.

"But you just said —"

"I am not giving you any advice that is against the law and for which I could lose my medical license."

Has she, without realizing it, been talking to a human being?

"Do you understand me, Roberta?"

"I think so."

"Okay then."

"Thank you for—"

"Happy holidays."

"You too." She presses END.

Fingers the tea towel draped on the oven handle.

Watches the fir-fledged hill, the deep green waving.

Maybe he genuinely, sincerely believes she has the money for "international travel."

*Get in the shower,* she tells herself.

Too sad to take a shower.

She wanted to study sea ice, which

begins as a cold crystal soup

Harry Rattray, the Scottish tutor, knew nothing about

forms a swaying crust ~~strong enough to hold up a puffin~~ thicker than the
height of a man

can block, trap, gouge, or

                    outright crush
                    a ship

                                        too sad

# THE DAUGHTER

While they take their quiz, Ro/Miss is doing a weird thing with her fingers on the sides of her face. Rubbing in a sort of violent way. Her eyes are closed. Bad headache? The daughter doesn't agree with Dad that Ro/Miss is a radical leftist; she's just smart. A smart spinster. If the daughter were to say that word in front of Ro/Miss, she'd get a sermon: *What does the word "spinster" do that "bachelor" doesn't do? Why do they carry different associations? These are language acts, people!*

The witch is a spinster too. She is bold and cold and wouldn't be agitated by the Nouri Witherses of this world. In the daughter's shoes, instead of fretting over some little melancholy jelly Ephraim prefers, Gin Percival would either quit caring or take revenge. Devise a potion that made Nouri's fingertips numb for the rest of her life, so that if she went blind in old age, she couldn't read braille.

Except she can't make potions in jail.

"Everyone finished?" goes Ro/Miss. "If not, too bad."

She hurt the principal's wife, according to the newspaper.

"Ash, stop writing. *Now.* Give me that paper."

Except she didn't seem like a person who would hurt anyone.

Do they provide tampons in jail? Gin Percival might not have brought any with her. And what if they give her the wrong size? A Slender when she needs a Super Plus?

Yasmine coached the daughter on the phone when she lost a tampon inside herself. Explained how to find the muscles that would expel it. "Pretend you're stopping yourself from peeing."

Pack ice could block, trap, gouge, or outright crush a three-hundred-fifty-ton ship. Mínervudottír wanted to acquaint herself with this brute.

# THE MENDER

She is come from walking on the bottom of the sea. There the tiny eyeless and the footless walked with she. Ran with she the finned and flattened, sailed with she the lungless; swayed with she the fantom grasses, lantern fishes, wolf eels. To the north bathed viperfish, who did not even see she; to the south flew goblin sharks, who did not even eat she. Toed a wolf eel, thumbed a skate, fingered the sucker of a cockeyed squid.

And back again, on waking, to the concrete bed.

Like the cell of any hive.

"Here's your tray," says the day guard, who has six fingers on her off hand. Hyperdactylia is a sign of the visionary. "And you got a letter."
    On white paper, in pencil:

Dear Ginny,

Everything will be all right. I'm feeding the animals. And I took care of the other thing. I hope you like this kind of chocolate.

                                                                    C.

So polite, Cotter. "I'm going to put it in now, okay?" he said, the first time they had sex. Polite till the cows come home. In, and in, and in. Her scabbard hurt after.

She had been curious to try. They did it five times, on four different days, on a blanket on the floor of Cotter's parents' basement, until she decided she didn't want to do it anymore.

*    *    *

Cotter was sad but still walked her home from school, and they didn't talk much, sometimes not at all. Her scabbard stopped hurting. They listened to the *scroof* and *bap* of their shoes on the sidewalk. The tsunami siren went off so loud the mender fell to her knees—"Will we drown?" She hated to swim, was frightened of sharks. "No, it's just a test," he said, and crouched to hug her.

Cotter was not her future husband, even though, back then, he sort of wanted to be. Scottish virgins used to douse charred peat with cow piss and hang it in their doorways, and whatever color the piss-moss was, next morning, would equal the color of their future husbands' hair.

Has Mattie Matilda solved her problem by now? Or is the little fish still inside?

"The letter says chocolate," she tells the guard.

"You're not allowed to have the chocolate."

"But it was sent to me."

"You're in jail, Stretch. Nothing here is yours."

"At least tell me what *kind* it was?" she yells at the guard's back.

The other guards are eating the chocolate, she knows. Smearing it all over their faces.

They took away her Aristotle's lanterns too. Her neckcloth.

"If we go to trial, it will help if you look as mainstream as you can," said the lawyer. "Studies have shown that juries are influenced by grooming and attire."

Her grooming won't change one inch of itself. She won't let him bring her any department-store clothes. Her aunt yells from the freezer: *Show those fuckshits how Percivals do!* The mender has been refusing the instant mashed potato and pork nuggets; she eats her own nails and the brickling skin around them. The lawyer has promised to bring better food. He said, "I'll have you out by Christmas."

\*    \*    \*

Christmas, her favorite criminal. Stockings are hanged, trees chopped, geese shot, children threatened with coal.

Christmas is next week.

Medical malpractice: who'll believe forest weirdo over school principal? Naturally that prick became a principal—plenty of little ones to boss around. Wasn't enough for him to boss Lola. "You divorce me at your age, you'll never get another man, it's just numbers, babe, you're at the wrong end of the numbers," she told the mender he'd said.

They think the mender harmed her grievously. Think she waved her broom at the moon and saved her own menstrual blood in a cat skull and dipped a live toad in the blood and tore off one of the toad's legs and stuffed it into Lola's butthole.

Nobody knows why the dead man's fingers—poisonous to ships' hulls and oysters and fishermen's paychecks—have come back to Newville. Nobody knows, so they've decided that it's the mender's fault. She hexed the seaweed. Called it to shore with her special weed-hexing whistle. And her reason? What reason, bitches?

Some things are true; some are not.
   That Lola fell down the stairs, hard.
   That she fell down so hard her brain swelled up.
   That she fell down because she drank a "potion."
   That the "potion" she drank before falling down was directly responsible for the falling down.
   That the providing of the "potion" counts as medical malpractice.
   That the newspaper headline says POTION COMMOTION.
   That the oil she gave Lola was for calming her scar.
   That the oil was topical, not meant to be swallowed.

That, even if swallowed, elderflower, lemon, lavender, and fenugreek don't make people fall down.

That nobody will believe forest weirdo over school principal.

"Percival!"—a guard through the screen box. "Get dressed. Your lawyer's here."

The lawyer wears a suit, like last time. As if to make himself more real. As if, in a suit, he will appear forceful and real and not the plump weird trembler he is. Among humans, the mender prefers the weird and the trembling, so she likes him.

From his briefcase he produces two boxes of licorice nibs. "As requested."

The mender breaks one open. Crams her mouth thick with the black taste, holds the box out to him.

"Mmh. I don't eat those." He pulls out a bottle of hand sanitizer and squirts a palmful. "So your friend Cotter's been checking on the animals and says everyone is fine."

"Did he make sure the goats aren't going up to the trail?"

The lawyer nods. Scratches the back of his neck. "So I'm afraid I have some tough news."

Mattie Matilda?

Went to a term house—*died?*

"The prosecutor's office has appended a charge," says the lawyer.

"Appended?"

"Added. They're bringing a new charge against you."

"What charge?"

"Conspiracy to commit murder."

Silver cold burn in her belly.

"Because fertilized eggs are now classified as persons," he says, "intentionally destroying an embryo or fetus constitutes second-degree murder. Or, if you're in Oregon, 'murder' rather than 'aggravated murder.'"

"What did the music teacher tell you?"

"Who?"

"The—"

"Stop talking," he barks.

She looks at him sidelong.

"Ms. Percival, it is much better if you don't tell me whatever you were about to tell me. Understood? The charge is being added by Dolores Fivey's attorney. Mrs. Fivey claims you consented to terminate a pregnancy of hers. Any truth to that?"

"No."

"All right, good." He fusses in his briefcase for a notepad and pen. "Did she ever mention being pregnant? Or that she was seeking an abortion?"

That clock never had a kernel in it.

"Lola's lying," says the mender.

"Why would she lie?"

"Get a doctor to look at her. Womb's been silent."

The lawyer looks up from his pad. "Not a talkative womb?"

He is helping her when she has no money to pay him, so she fakes a laugh. "She was never pregnant."

"Well, she can testify that she *believed* she was." He reaches under his suit sleeve to rub a forearm, then applies more hand sanitizer. "Per our last conversation, I haven't been able to find any evidence that implicates Mr. Fivey in domestic violence. No hospital records, no police reports, no concerned friends or doctors. Zero."

"But he snapped her finger bone," she says, "and burned her arm and punched her in the jaw."

"Without any corroborating evidence, we can't present this information in court."

*I am descended from a pirate. From a pirate. I am—*

"Ms. Percival, I want you to understand that conspiracy to commit murder carries a mandatory minimum prison term of ninety months."

Seven years, six months.

"And that's the *minimum*. They could add more at sentencing."

"But I didn't," she says.

"I believe you," says the lawyer. "And I'm going to make the jury believe you. But we need to go over every single detail of your acquaintance with Mrs. Fivey."

He wants to know what Lola paid for the scar treatments. If the prosecution can prove that money or goods changed hands, then the jury might plausibly leap to believing that the money or goods were prepayment for a termination. By accepting the compensation, the mender conspired to commit murder.

"This is the narrative they'll build for the jury," says the lawyer. "We need to hack away at it. Anything that can throw this narrative into doubt, we'll use."

"I can't remember," says the mender. Telling about the sex would make it worse. The world's oldest method of payment.

In seven years and six months the chickens and goats will be dead, Malky will have forgotten her, and the powderpost beetles will have eaten the roof clean off.

The skin on the explorer's hands grew hard from housemaid duties.

She grew bored of the ~~payments sex~~ walks with Harry Rattray, the Scottish tutor, in Victoria Park.

# THE WIFE

The high school auditorium, muggy and tinseled.

*"All of the other reindeer. Used to laugh and call him names."*

"Santa?" asks John.

"Soon."

"Santa doesn't *come* to holiday assembly," corrects Bex, hell-bent on accuracy.

Didier, on the other side of John: "Pipe down, *chouchous.*"

The wife glances around for Bryan. Pauses at the silver-sequined breasts of Dolores Fivey, which seem smaller, like the rest of her, shrunk down in those long weeks at the hospital. Not so sixy anymore. Penny, yawning. Pete, checking his phone. Ro, sagged down in her seat, looking enraged.

*"As they shouted out with glee, 'Rudolph the Red-Nosed Reindeer, you'll go down in history!'"*

Applause, bowing, then Bryan strides onstage in a Grinch-green sports jacket. She can't see his dimple from here.

"Thank you, choir!" he booms. More applause. "And thanks to all of you for joining us at our, ah, seasonal celebration."

Didier leans over John to whisper: "That man is dumb as a melon in a sock."

"May everyone's holidays be merry and bright," says Bryan. Where will he be having Christmas dinner? He must eat like a shire horse, big as he is.

Outside the auditorium she stands with Didier and Pete, postponing the moment when she must snap the kids into their seats, drive back up the hill, unbuckle them, rinse apples, spread almond butter onto whole-grain bread, pour cups of milk from cows who eat wild grasses only.

Pete: "That record didn't come out until 1981."

Didier: "Excuse me, but it was 1980, exactly two months after he hanged himself."

Yet he can't remember to give the kids their fluoride supplement.

"And exactly a hundred years," adds the wife, "after our house was built."

"I bet Chinese laborers hammered every nail in it," says Pete, "for criminally low wages. My people got *fucked* in Oregon. Railroad workers especially, but also the miners. Ever heard of the Hells Canyon Massacre?"

"No," says the wife.

"Well, you should look it up."

Pete's scorn for her is always just barely concealed. Pampered white lady who doesn't have a job, lives on family property—what does she *do* all day? Whereas Didier regales him with stories of his trasherjack childhood in Montreal public housing and is revered.

Her phone vibrates: an unknown number. She prepares her telemarketer line: *Remove me from your call list immediately.*

"Susan MacInnes?" The name she had for thirty years. "It's Edward Tilghman. From law school?"

"Of course, Edward—I remember."

"Well, I should hope so." He hasn't lost his primness, or his nasal congestion. Book-smart and life-dumb Edward.

"How are you?"

"Tolerable," says Edward. "But here's the thing: I'm in your village."

She looks around, as though he might be watching from the auditorium steps.

"I'm representing a client in the area, and I wanted you to know I'm in town. It would be somewhat awkward if we just bumped into each other."

"Do you have a place to stay?" she says.

Edward would be a clean houseguest but a finicky one; he'd want extra blankets and would remark on the drafts, the dripping taps.

"The Narwhal," he says.

"Well, you're more than welcome to—"

"Thank you. I'm already ensconced."

She has followed his career, a little. He was an excellent student, could have gotten hired in a minute at a white-shoe firm. But he works at the public defender's office in Salem. Must earn practically nothing.

"You should come for dinner one of these nights."

When he sees her he'll think *She's blown up a bit. Used to be a slender thing, and now*—although it happens, he'll think, *after they reproduce. Fat hardens.*

"Mmh. That's a thought." That was one of his trademarks, she recalls: soft grunting.

There have been reports of bedbugs at the Narwhal.

"So . . . ?" but she realizes he has hung up.

Didier bumps his shoulder against hers. "Who that?"

"Guy from law school."

"Not Chad the Impaler, I hope."

"Just a nerd I worked on the law review with."

True to form, her husband asks nothing further.

John whimpers, yanking on her hand. She didn't remember to bring the porcupine book or the bag of grapes. And there are streaks of her own feces in the upstairs toilet. She's grown afraid of the toilet brush, damp and rusted in its cup.

Bryan is surrounded by eager, jostling boys; they must be his players. Isn't the season over?—but of course they wouldn't stop adoring him when the season ends.

Ro, too, is thronged by students. She has wiped the rage off her face and is gesturing theatrically, making them laugh. They love her—and why not? She's a good person. The wife would like to be a good person, a person who'll be happy if Ro gets pregnant or adopts a baby, who will not hope that she doesn't.

When Ro sees the wife's children, is she jealous? What if she never conceives? Can't adopt? What will be her life's pull light then? When the wife goes down a street, John in the stroller and Bex holding her hand, purpose is written all over them. These little animals were hatched by the wife, are being fed and cleaned and sheltered and loved by the wife, on their way to becoming persons in their own right. The wife *made persons.* No need to otherwise justify what she is doing on the planet.

Huge brown eyes, sunlit hair, perfect little chins. *All small children are cute. You know that, right?*—D.'s reliable smashing of her happiness. Okay, yes, kids are built adorable so they won't be abandoned to die before they can survive on their own; but it is also true that some kids are more adorable than others. *Jambon sur les yeux,* Didier likes to say. You've got ham over your eyes.

Lifting, settling, buckling.

Specks of rain on the windshield.

Soon, the sea.

"Starving!" calls Bex.

"Almost home," says the wife.

Almost to the sharpest bend, whose guardrail is measly. Hands off the wheel. They would plow through the branches, fly past the rocks, tear open the water.

The newspapers tomorrow: MOTHER AND CHILDREN PERISH IN CLIFF TRAGEDY.

"Momplee," says Bex, "do reindeer sleep?"

As they approach the bend, she eases her foot off the accelerator.

Didier was once jealous of Chad, the third-year student she'd gone out with a few times before meeting her husband.

If she were ever to tell him *I slept with Bryan,* would he spring into action, agree to counseling, fight to get her back? Or would he say, without looking up from the screen, *Congratulations*?

She is too chickenshit to leave her marriage.

She wants Didier to leave it first.

In the summer of 1868, aged twenty-seven, Mínervudottír left Aberdeen, taking with her an extra month's salary (the shipyard director's wife liked her) and, shoved deep in her suitcase, four silver candlesticks.

Went to London.

Sold the candlesticks.

Obtained a reader's ticket to the British Museum Reading Room, which required no membership fee.

Bought a notebook with a brown leather cover.

This notebook filled with facts.

# THE DAUGHTER

Behind the Dumpsters she lights her first cigarette of the day, which is normally the best one but they haven't been tasting right lately. Soft chemical bloom on the roof of her mouth.

Why do some walruses in Washington, DC, who've never met the daughter care what she does with the clump? They don't seem bothered that baby wolves are shot to death from helicopters. Those babies were already breathing on their own, running and sleeping and eating on their own, whereas the clump is not even a baby yet. Couldn't survive two seconds outside the daughter.

The walruses are to blame for Yasmine.

Who sang at church.

Whose church was African Methodist Episcopal. Whenever the daughter went to services with the Salters after sleepovers, she felt strange.

Yasmine said: "Well, Matts, I feel strange all the time."

*Ignorant white girl.*

It starts to rain. The daughter lights a second cigarette and decides to skip math, even if it means annoying Mr. Xiao, whom she does not want to annoy and who'll say, next time he sees her, *What the hell, Quarles?* Nouri Withers will be in math, and who needs a glimpse of that mess. She closes her eyes, sucking, rain pittering on her lashes.

"Trying to get cancer?" Ro/Miss is standing right in front of her.

"No." The daughter grinds the cigarette under her boot.

"Pick that up, please."

The daughter tucks it into her peacoat pocket to avoid the inelegance of walking over to the Dumpster and struggling to lift its crusty lid. Her peacoat is going to reek of dead cigarette.

"Tell me what's going on, Mattie."

"Nothing."

"You've never gotten a B minus on a quiz before."

"I studied the wrong chapter."

"Are you still upset about the whales?"

The daughter spits out a laugh. Looks across the soccer field at the jagged evergreens, the sky darkening behind them.

"You can talk to me, you know. I'll help if I can."

"You can't," says the daughter.

"Try me," says Ro/Miss.

*I'm too scared to go to Canada because of the Pink Wall but the witch went to jail and I need a plan and I don't have a plan and what would you do if you were me?*

But what if it's in her teaching contract—mandatory reporting of child abuse and, in her case, child murder?

The daughter is not a murderer.

They're only cells, multiplying.

No face yet. No dreams or opinions.

*You didn't have a face once either.*

Ro/Miss reports her, and Principal Fivey kicks her out of Central Coast Regional.

Math Academy not thrilled about that.

Colleges not thrilled about that.

Mom and Dad least thrilled of all.

"I have class in a minute," she says, "and Mr. Xiao said he's going to rip the next person who's late a new turd cutter."

"Emotional health takes priority. I'll handle Mr. Xiao."

Maybe she can.

"It's nothing," says the daughter.

"*Try* me."

Ro/Miss wouldn't care if it's in her contract. She's fiercer than that.

The daughter says, still watching the trees: "I'm pregs?"

"Oh Jesus—"

"But I'm taking care of it."

"In what way?" snaps Ro/Miss, engine-red, freckles pulsing like brown stars.

She's *angry?*

"It's being dealt with," says the daughter.

"How can you be smoking?"

How can she be angry?

"It doesn't matter."

"Oh really?"

"The smoke won't—"

"What do you plan to do, Mattie?"

"Terminate," says the daughter.

Ro/Miss frowns.

"It's just an embryo, miss. It can't make an offer on a house, even though it has the legal right to."

Not even the littlest twist of a smile at hearing herself quoted. "What happens if you get caught?"

This is not the Ro/Miss she loves.

"I won't get caught," says the daughter, buttoning her peacoat. The rain is coming down harder.

"But what if you do?"

"I *won't.*"

What happened to the Ro/Miss who says we have better things to do with our lives than throw ourselves down the stairs?

"You know they'll charge you with a felony? Which means juvenile detention until you're eighteen, then—"

"I know, miss."

She would be sent to Bolt River.

Who is this monstrous imposter?

Ro/Miss pushes back her parka hood and starts raking all ten fingers through her hair, scalp to ends, scalp to ends, like an actor playing a mental-hospital patient.

"I got the name of a termination house," lies the daughter. "It's supposed to be good."

Raking, raking, scalp to ends. "Are you kidding?"

"Um, no?"

"Term houses charge a shit ton," says Ro/Miss, "and take shortcuts because nobody, obviously, is regulating them. They use out-of-date equipment, don't disinfect between patients, administer anesthesia without" — the first bell rings — "training." The fingers stop, mid-rake.

"Please don't tell my parents or Mr. Fivey?"

Tears in Ro/Miss's eyes. As if this moment needed to get any worse.

"Are you going to tell them?" bleats the daughter. "Please don't!"

It is weird to be scared of a person you've always been the opposite of scared of.

Ro/Miss pulls her hood back up. Tightens the drawstrings around her scrunched, streaming face. "I won't." She wipes her eyes with a parka sleeve. "This is just — This is really, I don't know —"

"It's okay," says the daughter, touching her elbow.

The elbow stays against her hand.

Ro/Miss blinks and shudders.

They stand hand to elbow for what feels like a long time. They are both getting soaked and the daughter's arm starts to hurt.

The second bell rings.

She says, "I have math?" and unhands the elbow.

"Sure. Yes." Sniffles. "But Mattie...?"

The daughter waits.

The teacher shakes her head.

They walk together along the soccer field, not talking, and up the steps, not talking, and through the blue doors.

She shouted "Help" in three languages.

Slit lambs hung in the shed, throats red.

# THE BIOGRAPHER

There are four oranges in a bowl on her table. She throws them one at a time at the kitchen wall. Two bounce, one splits, one splatters. Opens the fridge: soft cheese, broccoli, chocolate pudding. Flings the cheese and pudding out the window into the neighboring yard, hears no splat because the wind is up. Recalls that chocolate is fatal to dogs. Has never seen a dog in that yard.

Words I hate:

33. hubby
34. sammie
35. diagnosis
36. pregs

She will leave the oranges where they are. Head off soon to this goddamn eve of Christmas Eve dinner.

Mattie will head off soon to her abortion.

That's one more married couple ahead of the biographer on the waitlist who's not getting a baby.

Which is not Mattie's problem.

She rubs her cold forearms.

Her veins are buried. Archie's were collapsed.

A friend of Archie's wore black wire-and-mesh wings to his funeral.

The biographer once watched, on television, a church group chanting "Hurray!" outside the funeral of a politician's wife who had used IVF to acquire two children and thereby had summoned (said the church's press release) her own death by cancer. She and her husband coveted things that were not theirs, they reared up in fury, decided to show God who was boss, and meddled in matters of the womb. The politician's wife was now a resident of hell. Flee her example.

The biographer's ex-therapist asked, "Are you claiming not to need a romantic relationship in order to shield yourself from disappointment and rejection?"

"Would you ask that question of a male client?"

"You're not a male client."

"But would you?"

"Maybe, sure." He folded spotty hands on a baggy corduroy lap. "I am simply wondering to what extent your campaign to have a baby is a defense against the pain of being alone."

"Did you say *campaign?*"

"I'm recalling the period when you were sleeping with—Zeus, was it?"

"Jupiter," she said.

"*Jupiter,* and you told me that you'd just as soon support the death penalty as have a relationship with him. And yet you were fucking him." He said "fucking" with a relish that disturbed the biographer even more than "campaign." "There's of course also the issue of your brother, who abandoned you in rather a gruesome fashion."

The biographer never set foot in his office again.

Things I have failed at:

1. Finishing book
2. Having baby
3. Keeping brother alive

She starts dialing Susan, to cancel. Then thinks about being alone all night, smelling the broken oranges.

Bex meets her on the porch steps. "You're not dressed up," accuses the girl, herself stuffed into a burgundy pinafore and black patent leathers. "It's Christmas Eve eve!"

"Sorry," says the biographer, clenching her fists.

"I made popcorn for the reindeer." Bex points to a salad bowl on the lawn.

In Mínervudottír's day, sleeping bags were made from reindeer hides, the hairy skin good for warming wrecked men huddled on bergs.

"For my Christmas I asked for a kitten, but my mom says Santa can't bring a kitten, which is a lie because a girl in my class got one for Hanukkah."

The biographer sits beside her on the damp step. "Well, Santa doesn't deliver Hanukkah presents, only Christmas presents."

"Why?"

"Because that's how it works."

"But I want a Hanukkah present," says Bex, fingering a burgundy button.

"You're not Jewish."

"I want to switch to Jewish. Also, what's a cunt?"

The biographer leans to examine the eye-shaped pattern carved into the railing. "Um, have you asked your mom?"

"No, because it goes in the special box."

"Did you ask your dad?"

"He said let's talk about it later. Look it up on your phone."

"My phone can't look things up; it's too old. 'Cunt' is just another word for vagina."

In Faroese: *fisa*.

"Okay," says Bex, taking her hand.

The tinsel has been hung halfheartedly; the eggnog resembles a bodily fluid; Susan looks as though she'd rather be anywhere else. They've been invited to gather because it's what you do, and Susan is a person who does what you do. At the teachers' picnic last summer she said to a fellow mother, "You don't truly become an adult until you have kids." The fellow mother said, "Totally." The biographer, standing nearby with a mustard-glopped hot dog, said, "Seriously?" but this went unheard. Susan is an expert in adulthood. Kid things, cooking things, knowing which fork to use for fish in a high-end restaurant things. And the Korsmos live in what is basically a mansion, even if it was built as a summer home, because a summer home in the 1880s was fancier than today's average winter home. Susan's parents own it, but the deed will doubtless come to her.

*You don't even want a house,* the biographer reminds herself.

Didier is bent over an open oven, squirting pan juices on a sizzling hunk of meat. "Get ready for some fine damn beef," he greets the biographer. John comes barreling toward the oven, but his father yanks him up in time ("No scorched babies on my watch") and sets him down ("Go find your porcupine book"), and he scampers away. "You know, I wanted to name that kid Mick. I should've argued harder. John Korsmo is a real-estate agent, but Mick Korsmo is a badass."

"Except," says the biographer, "that pretty much every one-syllable word that rhymes with Mick has a negative, lewd, or derogatory connotation. Ick. Sick. Lick. Prick."

"Wow," says Didier.

"Kick. Brick. Trick—"

"Why is brick negative, eh?" he says. "Unless it's a brick of heroin, although that, to some people, would be very positive indeed."

Straw.

Camel.

She's really in no mood.

"Didier, is there any particular reason you mention heroin so much?"

He frowns. "Do I?"

*Keep your legs, Stephens.*

"Well, yes, actually, and somebody important to me died from it, so I would appreciate it if you'd stop glamorizing it when I'm around."

"Oh. Sorry." He frets an oily strand of blond hair between his fingers. Purple lids hood blue-gray eyes. *Beau-laid.* "A boyfriend?"

Her face pounds with heat. "Somebody important," she says.

"Such as a boyfriend?"

"So we have a deal?" she says. "No more romanticizing?"

"Okay, but hold on, eh — I need to hear more."

"Another time."

"I'll get it out of you eventually," he says. "I'll huff, and I'll puff, and I'll blow your story down!"

Didier hapless. Penny yawning. Bex whining about kittens. Mattie's luck. The semeny eggnog. The cysts on her ovaries. Her dad eating soft vegetables at Ambrosia Ridge Retirement Village. Susan believing the biographer is not yet an adult. Every Child Needs Two coming true in three weeks.

They've tucked into Didier's roast when a late-arriving guest is ushered in, a pudgy white guy with a shaved head. "Everyone," says Susan, "this is Edward Tilghman. We were in law school together. By the way, you didn't need to dress up."

"I didn't," he says, brushing rain off his suit jacket. "These are my work clothes."

"Edward has a client in town," explains Susan.

The guest settles in between Penny and the biographer, takes a sip of water, and shakes out his napkin.

Something warm and moist hits the biographer under her left eye. She finds it in her lap: a slice of meat.

Another wet little slap — Bex is hit too.

"Cunt!" says the girl.

"Goddammit, John," says Didier, "if you can't sit at the table without throwing food, you're not going to sit at the table."

Susan stares at her husband. "Why does she know that word?"

"How should I know?"

Bex sings, "Cunty McGee was a happy little cunt."

"Goodness," says Edward.

"Not a nice word, Bexy —" But Didier is laughing.

"Does it go in the special box?" she asks.

"What special box?"

"*Nothing,* Momplee."

"Mommy," cries John, "a boy and a fish is friends."

Penny asks, "Whom are you representing, Edward?"

"He can't divulge," says Susan.

"Their *names* aren't confidential," says Edward. "This isn't Alcoholics Anonymous," and Susan takes the shock of correction square in the face.

"But the fact of representation," she insists, "is privileged in some jurisdictions—"

"A woman named Gin Percival." Edward helps himself to a plop of parsnip.

"The witch!" says Didier. "She's been doling out the wrong kind of family planning."

"Ucchh, shut *up,*" says Susan.

"Momplee, that's rude and you should say sorry."

"I think Daddy should say sorry. For being an idiot."

Didier is watching Susan with an expression the biographer has never seen on him before.

Penny stands up and claps. "Time for all children who live in this house to prepare a welcome letter for Mr. Claus! All children of the house, please come with me to the letter-writing station."

"We have to be excused first," says Bex.

"You're frigging excused," says Susan.

The kids follow Penny to the living room, and Susan carries plates to the kitchen. Didier, wordless, heads out to smoke.

The biographer feels bad that Gin Percival is in jail, but not as bad as she should. Gin can't help her anymore, and the biographer can't be sympathetic right now.

Unless a pregnant woman or girl decides, in the next three weeks, that she'd actually really love for her baby to be raised by a single mother on a high school teacher's salary, then the biographer will be removed from the agency's list. *To restore dignity, strength, and prosperity to American families.*

She can remain on the fostering list; but ECN2 stipulates that in single-parent homes, foster placement cannot lead to permanent legal adoption.

She sneezes, wipes her nose on the pink linen napkin.

Edward leans away from her and says, "Could you please cover your mouth?"

"I did cover my mouth."

He moves three chairs away.

"Really?" says the biographer.

"Sorry, but my immune system isn't strong and I can't afford to get sick right now."

The biographer pushes the tip of her napkin up one nostril.

In-breath.

She wants to go home, where no one can see her.

Out-breath.

Sneak out now without saying goodbye.

In-breath.

Susan would hold a grudge for such rudeness.

Out-breath.

But what if—

What if, instead—

Mattie gave her the baby?

What if she just gave it to her?

But that's insane.

*Demento dementarium.*

What if Mattie said, *Yes, okay, here—for you. Take care of him. Take care. I'll see you later, miss. I'm off to my life. Tell him about me one day.*

What if she asked, and Mattie said yes?

She would never ask, obviously.

Unethical. Malfeasant. Pathetic.

But what if?

Ice fog = pogonip
Ice crystal = frazil
Ice feathers = rime

# THE WIFE

What joy to walk naked after a shower and hear your labia clap. To rise from the toilet and hear your labia clap.

The stretching and loosening is permanent, no matter what miracles they tell you Kegels can work. Kegels can't fix the lips. The wife's college roommate got the surgery after her third child. "Flappy no more!" reported the roommate in a mass email. The wife remembers thinking how odd to announce your labiaplasty to seventy-nine people—the addresses weren't hidden—but odder still were the replies. "Tell your javiva congrats." "Bet your man is lurving it!"

She buttons her jeans, flushes the toilet, returns to her children, slumped on the sofa. Didier is hiding upstairs, pretending to write lesson plans.

Bex moans: "I'm so bored."

"Then play with your Christmas presents."

"I played with everything."

"Have you read all the books Grammy gave you?"

"Yes." She is facedown on the Turkish carpet, snow-angeling.

"I doubt that." The wife watches John start to remove, one by one, the blocks she just put away.

"Where's Ro?"

"At her own house. John, leave those in the basket, please—"

"Why are you sleeping in the sewing room and not with Daddy?" Still facedown, but the girl has stopped moving, is waiting hard for the answer.

"Daddy snores."

"So do you."

"No, I do not." The wife grabs two blocks from John, bangs them into the basket with their fellows.

"Also, if you have another baby—"

"I'm not having another baby."

"But if you do have another baby, will you get a purple nurple again? And will your hair fall out and your breasts die?"

"They didn't *die*. They changed shape when John stopped nursing."

"Went flat," says Bex.

*Just wait until you get here, sweetpea.*

"I'm not going to hit you," she whispers.

She has never hit her sprites, and never will.

Fifteen minutes later she's alone in the car, going fast. The road is wet and dreamy with fog, but she is a good driver; her foot is steadfast and capable.

Inside the Acme she slows, lingers over her selections. In the chocolate department she has her preferred brands and flavors, the organic rainforest companies, the mints and the sea-salt-almonds; but sometimes she likes to mix it up with a hazelnut-coriander or a black-pepper-fennel-cardamom.

She sets six bars (three cardamoms, three mints) and a family-size of soft-batch chocolate-chip cookies on the conveyor belt, along with an unneeded pack of kitchen sponges.

"Looks like you're in for a fun night," says the cashier.

"It's for my daughter's class," says the wife.

"Right," says the cashier.

On the way home she pulls into the scenic overlook parking lot, whose guardrail is sturdy.

Dials Bryan.

Gets his growly message: "You know what to do and when to do it."

"Hey there," she chirps, "hope you had a good Christmas. Checking to see if you wanted to have that coffee sometime. Oh, and this is Susan. Okay, well, call me! Thanks!"

What will Bryan make of her clapping labia?

The cardamoms go in the kitchen drawer, under the maps.

The mints stay in the torn lining of her purse.

The soft batches were eaten in the eight minutes between the scenic overlook and home.

She spots husband and children through the window, tumbling in the brown grass behind the garage. He has given them a snack, at least, even if he didn't clean it up.

Herd crumbs into palm.

Spray table.

Wipe down table.

Rinse cups and bowls.

Set cups and bowls in dishwasher.

Throw empty family-size soft-batch cookie box into recycling.

If she leaves first, she breaks her family.

Knot up recycling and take out to blue bin.

Pour compost pail rinse water into pot of ficus tree.

Spray mist onto green snake arms of Medusa's head.

If she sleeps with Bryan, it won't be a relationship.

Stack books.

Push fairy costumes into trunk.

Only sex.

Ignore black dust on baseboards.

Intercourse with a shire horse.

Ignore soft yellow hair balls in every corner.

Ignore beds of children, but make own.

That little red motel on 22 —

While making own bed find sock of husband in covers.

Sniff sock; be surprised that sock does not smell bad.

Run rag through dust on dresser.

She will leave the credit-card statement open on the dining-room table.

In downstairs bathroom, ignore soap heel crusted to sink.

Except that Didier wouldn't bother reading the charges.

Lift toilet seat.

Count three pubic hairs.

Slam seat back down.

Then she will just tell him, flat-out.

And he will leave first.

When London was colder, "frost fairs" were held upon the Thames. Fire pits and puppet stages, caged lions and gingerbread booths, were dragged onto the ice; there were sled races, pigs turning on spits, fortune-tellers, bull-baiters. One could see flounder and porpoise trapped mid-swim in the glass river. But not since 1814 has the ice been solid enough to withstand this revelry. I came to London too late.

# THE MENDER

The jail washes its blankets with so much bleach she has to shove them in the opposite corner of the cell. She sleeps in her clothes, the mattress thin, she pretends it's the forest floor. When she wakes, her chest hurts and her nostrils are full of chemicals. The walls are still gray.

She draws the outside inside her head. Sky full of water. Clouds full of mountains. Shark field full of bones. Stoves full of trees. Trees full of smoke. Smoke full of winter. Sea full of seaweed. Fishes full of fishes.

In here they bring her nuggets and colas, but no fishes.

The bitches are squirrely. They are sending letters. They want advice remotely. Give them recipes, they demand. What about the ointments for their figs? The stinky teas for their bloods? Oh, bitches. Please can the mender provide the name of a pharmacy that carries the ingredients? No, she can't, because the pharmacy is the phorest. It is pherns, phunghi, phauna. It is hairs from dead Temple, ground up.

Mattie Matilda has not written to her. Term-house procedure gone wrong. Untrained scrapers. Dirty gear. If the girl started to hemorrhage, they would've been too nervous to take her to the hospital.

"Breakfast," calls the day guard.
"Don't want it," says the mender, not sure if she is saying this out loud.
The guard has unlocked the cell door, stands holding a tray. "Cereal and sausage."
"Poison." When she eats cereal, her scabbard gets yeasty; and truly anything could be in that sausage.

"Your trial starts next week, Stretch. I'd advise you to eat."

Can she see into next week, this guard with the sixth finger on her off hand? Can she see the mender fainting from hunger on the stand?

"Well, it's here if you change your mind." Clunks the tray down on the floor, and the little milk box jumps.

Squeeze the lemon. Grind dried lavender and fenugreek seeds in a mortar. Unscrew the jar of elderflower oil.

Then Lola's husband gets ahold of the bottle. Pours in the crushed-up drug. Makes her drink it, or she drinks willingly. Washes it all down with Scotch.

Ninety months is two thousand, seven hundred thirty-nine days. All those days in a cell like this one. Her nostril walls will turn white from bleach. Hans and Pinka and the halt hen will die. Malky will forget her.

To quit shaking, she reminds herself: *You are a Percival. Descended from a pirate.*

25 January 1875

Dear Captain Holm,

Allow me to offer my services on the upcoming voyage of *Oreius* from Copenhagen to the Polar North. I am a hydrologist with significant expertise in the behavior of pack ice. It would be my honor to assist in your collecting of magnetic and meteorological data.

Though a Scotsman by birth, I speak and write fluent Danish.

I am, Sir,
Your most obedient servant,
HARRY M. RATTRAY

# THE BIOGRAPHER

You can't just say to a person, "Would you give me your baby, please?"

*Allow me to offer my services.*

Eivør Mínervudottír did things she wasn't supposed to. Took plunges.

"It doesn't work for everyone," said Dr. Kalbfleisch at their first appointment. "And you're well over forty."

Woman who is thin and ugly. Cruel and ugly old woman. Witch-like woman. Mínervudottír was forty-three when she died; the biographer turns forty-three in April. Crones to the bone.

"You need to cultivate acceptance," said the meditation teacher. "Maybe motherhood isn't your path."

Acceptance, thinks the biographer, is the ability to see what is. But also to see what is possible.

She puts on her running shoes. Her gloves. Dark out: she'll keep to the lit streets. She jogs up the hill, focusing, as her track coach taught her, on the balls of the feet pressing at the asphalt, press and release, press and release. Her breath is stiff. Sweat tingles in her armpits and at the top of her butt. She's too out of shape for running to feel good, but it feels correct, a corrective—slam the blood through every vein, unseat the sediment, flush the channels, ask the heart to do more.

She cuts over to Lupatia and back down toward the ocean. Passes Good Ship Chinese and the church. If she turned left here, she would end up, after a zigzag or two, on Mattie's block. She stops. Leans against the trunk of a madrone, panting. On the family trip to the nation's capital she raced her brother up the *Exorcist* steps and won. Archie said, "Only because you're older." Dad yelled, "Come the hell back down."

*Mattie, can I ask you something?*

The biographer doesn't know when the average person eats dinner, but she guesses by eight p.m. most dinners in Newville are done.

When Mama made a whole chicken, she claimed one drumstick for herself, and Dad and Archie fought for the other, and the biographer was the good child who ate breast.

*Mattie, if I paid for all your checkups and vitamins, would you—*

Her feet turn left.

*If I drove you to all the appointments, would you—*

She is not really doing this.

It can't hurt to ask, can it?

But how would she even get the words out?

The biographer's baby will be the good child always, even when he scribbles with permanent marker on the walls. Even when he throws his drumstick out the window into the neighbor's yard.

Bike-lock key at her throat, gloved fingers fisted tight against the cold. Her fingers ache, but not as much as the fingers of Eivør Mínervudottír once ached. All the plunges that woman took—gigantic plunges—the biographer can take one too.

She starts to sprint.


Dear baby,


You have one live grandparent. He moved to Orlando after your grandmother died. Your uncle is gone, so you're out of luck on the cousin front. As cousin stand-ins you will have Bex and Pliny the Younger.


Dear baby,


I love you already. Can't wait for you to get here. Your hometown is one of the most beautiful places I've ever known. Full of ocean and cliffs and mountains and the best trees in America. You'll see for yourself, unless you are born blind, in which case I will love you even harder.

The Quarles house is gray shingled, flanked by shore pines. Lights are on behind the curtained windows. You are not really doing this. But she is. Climbing the wooden steps to a wooden deck heavy with ceramic bowls of wintering dirt. She is. Going to convince her. She is. Whispering the sentences of her prepared speech. As she brings a finger to the doorbell, it occurs to her that a logical outcome of this plan is that she'll be fired from Central Coast Regional.

*Mattie, I will take the baby on a train to Alaska.*

*Row a boat with the baby to the Gunakadeit Light.*

Her finger hovers over the white plastic button, heart thumping frantic in her ears, rain spitting on her forehead. *Keep your legs, Stephens.*

She plunges.

Not until the steamship *Oreius* had rounded the Jutland Peninsula into the North Sea did the captain understand a woman was aboard.

He told the explorer, "We have no choice but to bear you."

# THE BIOGRAPHER

Eight seconds after she presses the bell, Mattie's mother opens the door, smiling. "Miss Stephens?"

"Sorry to drop by unannounced."

"No, please, come in."

Photos of the girl overwhelm the living room—on walls, on tables, on bookshelves, their daughter's every year, it seems, well captured. "We go a little wild with the pictures," says Mrs. Quarles, noticing the biographer notice.

"You have a fabulous child, so why not?"

"I doubt Matilda would agree. She says the number of pictures is, quote, demented. Can I get you something to drink?"

"Oh no, please, I'm not staying long, I—needed to—" Breathe. "Before Christmas Mattie asked me for more comments on an essay draft, but things were so busy that—Well, now that the holidays are over, I want to give her the feedback."

"That's unusual," says Mrs. Quarles.

"When a student puts in the extra effort that she does, I'm willing to do some extra too."

"But she's not here."

"Oh?"

"She's at the conference."

The biographer is clearly meant to understand what Mrs. Quarles means by *the conference*. "Oh?"

"You knew she was going, didn't you?"

"To the—conference?"

"She told us you *nominated* her."

"Of course. I must have mixed up the dates."

"I have to say," says Mrs. Quarles, "she didn't give us many details about this thing."

"What did she tell you?"

"That it's a Cascadia history conference for high school students, and only one student from any given school is nominated to attend."

"That's right," says the biographer.

"Not as prestigious as the Math Academy, she said, but it will still look good on her applications."

Damp swoosh down the biographer's throat, into her ribs.

Is the baby gone?

Her mouth is full of bits from the planned speech—chewy clichés. *I can give it a good home. I mean her. Or him. You've got your whole life ahead of you.*

"Yes," mutters the biographer, "it'll be impressive."

"And they're all staying at the same hotel in Vancouver? Is there adult supervision?"

The biographer stands up. "I'm pretty sure they have supervision, yes. Sorry to interrupt your evening."

"You're *pretty* sure, or you're sure? Mattie hasn't been answering my calls. And I can't find anything about the conference online."

"That's because of its, um, principles? The people who run it are committed to students spending less time on computers, so they work only on paper, through the mail."

Mattie's mother is an intelligent woman, yet she appears to accept this.


The biographer walks slowly back to her apartment.

Archer Stephens may not be getting a namesake.

Her brother's blue lips on the kitchen floor.

The gravelly whine in his voice when he said he wasn't high.

"Yes, you are."

"I'm not."

"You are!"

"Jesus, I'm not—you're so paranoid."

But his pupils were the barest dots in the pale green; mouth ajar; tongue slow. She knew the signs, was becoming something of an expert;

and yet, and still, Archie's denials undid her. Dad said, "You're being duped!"—he was never much help, aside from the time he put up five grand for bail. She said, "I'm not paranoid; you're pinned!" and Archie said, "Because it's *sunny,* my friend." Possibly it was not sunny at all, but the biographer wanted to believe him. Her Archie, her dear one, no matter how buried, was still in there.

Shut up, she tells her monkey mind. Please shut up, you picker of nits, presser of bruises, counter of losses, fearer of failures, collector of grievances future and past.

At the kitchen table she opens her notebook to the *For which I am grateful* page. Adds to the list:

28. Two working legs
29. Two working hands
30. Two working eyes
31. The ocean
32. Penny on Sunday nights
33. Didier in the teachers' lounge
34.

But fuck this shitty list. She's sick of being grateful. Why the fuck should she be grateful? She is *angry*—at the amendment laws, the agencies, Dr. Kalbfleisch, her ovaries, the married couples, the term-house procedures. At Mattie for getting pregnant at the drop of a trilby. At Archie for dying. At their mother for dying. At Roberta Louise Stephens for trying so hard.

Rips the gratitude list out of her notebook, lights it in the sink with a match. She hasn't yet fixed the smoke alarm.

Mattie told her mother the conference was in Vancouver. She could have said Portland or Seattle.

By now she will have reached the border. If she manages to get across, manages to find the clinic, manages to produce a convincing Canadian ID, the abortion will happen tomorrow.

She might not get across, of course.

She might be stopped.

*Don't hope she's stopped, you monstress.*

But she does.

I have been lifted off the earth to sit on the ocean with men whose lives are nothing like mine yet whose waking dreams are identical: clumsy suits of caribou hide, our fingers numb, the flame-red gash of sunrise. If wrecked in this vessel, we wreck together.

# THE DAUGHTER

Stares out a rain-lashed bus window at Washington State. Trees and trees and trees. A wet meadow or two. For the hundredth time she opens her passport. Date of expiration still valid. She is merely traveling, which is not a crime.

According to the online forums, you should carry evidence of your purpose in Canada. She and Ash created an email account for Delphine Gray — a sweet person but not the best speller — and sent several messages to the daughter. *Can't wait to see u Mattie, girl your going to love Raincouver, we will check out all the sites!*

For the clinic, she has a British Columbia driver's license bought from Clementine's boyfriend. Ash is lucky to have an older sister to advise her, giant brothers to defend her. A big rowdy fish-scented gang.

She keeps her bag on the aisle seat so that no friendly passenger can inquire about her destination. Rolls a licorice nib on her tongue. The sugar and chemicals ride her veins to the clump. Half Ephraim, half her.

She went to Vancouver once with Yasmine's family. Mrs. Salter, who represented Portland (District 43) in the Oregon State Legislature, was giving a speech on housing rights. The daughter remembers a city in a bowl of mountains and dark silver water. Bored at the hotel, she and Yas started their list of cardiac weights. The heart of a Canada goose weighs seven ounces. Of a caribou, seven pounds.

The bus judders to a halt. The daughter opens her eyes. Dark-green forest, steel-colored sky, a chain of tollbooths crowned with red maple leaves.

"Everyone off," shouts the driver. "Take all belongings with you and remove your suitcases from the luggage compartment."

A woman calls, "Can I leave a sweater to save my seat?"

"No, ma'am, you may not."

"What is this," she says, "the Soviet Union?"

The passengers are herded through the icy air into a low wooden building next to the tollbooths. Pale young men in olive-green uniforms sit behind the desks. A muscular dog led by an officer trots across the linoleum, nails clicking.

Do they have pregnancy-sniffing dogs?

Seekers are transported back in Canadian police cars, or buses—the daughter isn't sure. When they arrive in their home states, they are charged with conspiracy to commit murder.

An officer scans her passport. "What's your destination in Canada?"

"Vancouver."

"Reason for your trip?"

"Visiting a friend."

"For what purpose?"

"Vacation," says the daughter.

The officer looks at the passport again. Looks at her forehead, then at her chest. "You're how old, miss?"

"Almost sixteen. My birthday's in February."

"And you're traveling alone to Vancouver—for a vacation?"

Her face is getting hot. "My friend lives there. She used to go to my school in Oregon but moved to Canada a few years ago and I'm visiting her."

*Don't offer too many details,* say the forums.

"What's your friend's name and address?"

"Delphine Gray. She's picking me up from the bus station."

"You don't know her address?"

"Sorry, yes, I do. Four-six-one-eight Laburnum Street, Vancouver."

"Phone number?"

"We always talk online, so I don't—I don't need her number. It's so much cheaper to talk online. But I have an email from her printed out, if you want to see it?"

"Why did you print out her email?"

"It has her address on it."

"You said she was picking you up from the bus station."

"I know, but just in case? Like if I need to take a cab."

"Wait here, okay?" says the officer.

You can't say it was rape or incest—nobody cares how it got into you.

The daughter watches the Soviet sweater woman and her husband pass their check. A middle-aged white couple breezes through after them. Older Asian woman: breeze. Younger black guy: less of a breeze. They ask him extra questions, which he answers in a flat, irritated voice. But he, too, finally heads back outside.

"Matilda Quarles?" says an officer with frizzy blond curls. "Would you come with me?"

"Where?"

"Just come with me, please."

"My bus is leaving in a minute."

"I understand that. You need to come with me."

"But what if I miss my bus?"

The officer crosses her big arms. "Do we have a problem here?"

"No, ma'am."

Meant to be slitting lambs and hanging them to drain over washtubs.

Instead: riding a ship to gather facts in the boreal wilderness.

# THE MENDER

Was disappointed to learn the girl's name—such a well-behaved name. The mender's own is no better. People have asked, over the years, Is it actually Virginia? Jennifer? No, just Gin. Are you named for a relative? No, for the alcohol. Oh, how funny, but really, where does it come from? But really it came from the alcohol, her mother's preferred.

The mender would have named the girl Temple Jr.

She doesn't remember the pain but knows there was pain; and Temple saying "Over soon, over soon" while she rocked the mender; and eating cherries Temple had dug the pits out of; and her stomach feeling spongy and collapsed. She doesn't remember the baby. They kept it elsewhere in the hospital. Every two hours the nurses brought in a manual pump to express colostrum, then milk, from her engorged breasts. The agency woman came with papers to sign.

People used to believe that new roses were born from the cinders of burnt roses, new frogs from rotting dead ones. Which is no stranger than believing the mender gave Lola a potion that made her fall down the stairs, or that the mender's mother is out there, somewhere, alive.

When the mender was a baby, her mother stayed clean. "She never used drugs while she was breastfeeding," said Temple. "Which doesn't exactly warrant a medal, but—you were important to her. Don't forget that, okay?"

A bad mother who was sometimes not bad. Who could still be out there, living off flowers in a tower, yarn in a barn.

Mother and mender and girl: descended from Goody Hallett of Eastham, Massachusetts, who tied lanterns to the flukes of whales.

A "lead" is the finger of open water between floes of sea ice. I have a theory: the shape and texture of a lead can foretell its behavior. How likely it is to freeze shut or open wider.

# THE WIFE

On her way to meet Bryan, the tsunami siren goes off. She pulls over on the cliff road. The wail, forlorn and animal, lifts and crests, swings down and up and over again. A haunted wolf. Once a month it goes for three minutes, followed by chimes (all clear) or a piercing blast (evacuate). If an earthquake blows up the sea, a sucking wall of water will come at them, and minutes will matter.

The sprites are on the hill, higher than any wave could reach, playing camping with their father.

The ocean is a green pane. Pillars of rock shaped like chimneys, seals, and haystacks rise from the water.

She hears the chimes. Safe, sound.

She could be caught: a text sent to the wrong phone.

Or she could confess. Watch her husband's face when she says *I slept with Bryan.*

She keeps the house and he gets an apartment in town, carpools to school with Ro. The apartment will have a second bedroom for the sprites, who'll stay with him on weekends. During the week things won't be much different, no help with bath and bedtime as usual; same with the mornings, when she alone handles the boiling of oatmeal and dressing of bodies and brushing of teeth. But the weekends—the wife will have those to herself.

Or Didier could stay in the house, for now. The drafts and dripping taps and ugly wallpaper. The house has been in her family for generations; she read her first chapter book in its dining room, got her first period in its bathroom, watched Bex take her first steps on its porch. But for a while now she's been letting it go.

Too chickenshit to leave first, she will blow up her life instead.

*       *       *

Wenport is a dreary townlet adjacent to a pulp mill, and no one from Newville goes there except to buy drugs. Sometimes the wife asks herself which of her children is more likely to buy drugs one day, and the answer is always: Didier.

She parks right in front of the coffee shop. It wouldn't be Didier himself spotting the car, of course — he is crouched in a tent of blankets in the living room, being fed marshmallows fakely cooked on a fake fire — but Ro? Pete Xiao? Mrs. Costello?

*I thought I saw Susan's car the other day…*

*Was Susan in Wenport with Bryan Zakile?*

The coffee shop is too warm. The wife slips off her jacket and sweat darts to her cheeks. It is three minutes after two. The only other customers are two trench-coated boys playing cards.

"Can I getcha?" says the barista.

Almond pastries glisten under the glass.

"Tall skim latte, please," says the wife.

"For your info, ma'am, we are an independent business with no ties to multinational corporations. I.e., a mermaid-free zone."

"What?" The wife has one eye on the door, one eye on the boys. They could be Didier's students. Or Bryan's.

"You need to order a *small*," says the barista.

"Then can I have a small skim latte. And a water."

"Water is self-serve."

She settles at the table farthest from the boys, facing the door. Ten minutes after two.

One boy cries, "Your griffin spell doesn't frighten me, sir!"

Seventeen minutes after. No texts or missed calls.

At twenty after, she will leave.

At twenty after, she finishes all the water in her cup.

She will leave in one minute.

At 2:24, Bryan appears. Not in a hurry at all. "Well, *hi* there," he says. "How's your day going?"

"Great, yours?"

While he's at the counter, the wife, facing the door, hears him ask the barista if she knows where the word "cappuccino" comes from; and she hears the barista giggle and say, "Um, Italy?" and Bryan say, "Well, for starters."

When he sits down across from her, she remembers that his face is not beautiful, despite the dimple. A fair to middling face. But the body that follows—

"Your hair looks awesome," he says.

"Oh—thanks!"

Slurping milk foam: "Get it cut?"

"Ah, no, actually. So how were your holidays?"

"Good, good. Went to see my folks in La Jolla. Nice to be in civilization again."

"Do you find this area uncivilized?"

He shrugs. Napkins the foam off his lip.

"Or too remote?"

"How do you mean?"

"Well, in terms of, I don't know—"

Bryan smiles. "Do you mean is it hard to meet women?"

"Or whatever. Yes."

"Not to sound conceited?—but that's never been a problem of mine."

"I'm sure it hasn't."

He pushes one fist slowly down the length of his thigh. "*Are* you?"

"What?"

"Sure. That it hasn't."

A clod of dried mascara falls off the lashes of her right eye, landing on her forearm.

"Look," says Bryan, "the way I see it, the scarcity model is a bunch of crap. When people are worried about not finding anyone, they pick the first person who comes along."

She flicks the mascara away. Her mouth is so dry.

"That's what happened to one of my cousins," he continues. "Married a total dick because she didn't think she could do better. And maybe she *couldn't* have, but, hey, I'd take lonely over beaten to a paste."

"Beaten?"

"Like I said, he's a dick."

"But that's—?"

"We all wish she would leave him. They don't have any kids."

"Even if they did."

"Well, maybe. Although children really need both parents at home."

The wife can see and hear and feel but is no longer thinking.

She wants to feel the thigh sitting two inches from her knee. Feel the fingers resting on the thigh.

Long, hard fingers.

Long, hard thigh.

"What about you, Susan? Do you find Newville remote?"

"I find it..." She twists her mouth to one side, which Didier used to say was sexy. "Boring."

"I wonder what we could do to make it less boring."

"I wonder."

"I can think of a few things."

"Can you?" Wet flare in her pit.

"I can."

"For instance?"

"Well..." Bryan leans forward, elbows on table, and holds his face in his palms. The wife leans in too, but the angle is awkward with her legs crossed. He stares at her. She stares back. Something is about to happen. He is going to kiss her right here, amid griffins and steam, twelve miles away from the house on the hill. She is going to blow up her life.

"Mini-golf team!" he says, grinning so wide she can see the black fillings in his teeth.

"What?"

"It's a thing now, competitive mini golf. There's a place right off 22. They run teams of four. I'm thinking you, me, Didier, and Xiao. You can actually win decent money."

As though a giant hand had released its grip, the wife sags in her chair. "I suck at golf," she says.

"Come now!"

"Get Ro to be on your team."

"The grammar police? *No gracias.*"

He does not want her.

Why did she think he wanted her?

"Hey," says Bryan, "let's share an original sin amen bun. They're fantastic here."

Black fillings all over his mouth.

"Why the hell not," says the wife.

In November of 1875, in the Arctic Ocean north of Siberia, pack ice started closing in on *Oreius*. The belts of open water grew farther apart; the leads shrank to black ribbons. Mínervudottír saw that the straighter leads seemed to stay open longer than the wavy, eel-shaped ones: was there something about the irregular margins that sped the knitting of the ice?

She suggested as much to the captain, who said, "And will you be pointing out the snow fairies too?"

# THE BIOGRAPHER

Notices today how large Mr. Fivey's desk is. He grips its burnished surface with his hands wide apart, as a mogul might. Hanging behind him are the Ivy League diploma and several photos of Mrs. Fivey, which prompt the biographer to say: "I'm glad your wife is doing so much better."

"That's nice, Ro. But let's get down to the marrow. Since the school year began, you have been late no less than fourteen times."

*No fewer.*

"And absent five times."

"Four, actually."

"Tomato, tomahto—it's become a problem. These kids aren't going to teach themselves. Instead of learning history they're memorizing the anti-meth posters in study hall. I'd like to know how you intend to solve this problem."

"Well," says the biographer.

"Unless you'd prefer not to teach here at all?"

She uncrosses and recrosses her legs. "I do want to teach here. Very much. The thing is, I've been having some health issues, which—"

"Whatever it is, Ro, it can't go on. Either take a medical leave, quit, or get to work on time." His saliva lands on her face.

Has he gotten more dickish because his wife was in a coma? Or because Gin Percival's trial starts soon? Fivey will have to sit in the courtroom and hear how his wife allegedly sought an abortion from the witch, though she wasn't allegedly pregnant in the first place. And how his wife allegedly had an affair with Cotter at the P.O. And how her breasts are allegedly real. Even the biographer, whose finger is not on the pulse, has heard these rumors.

"I won't be late again," she says.

"No, you won't, because I'm giving you an official warning. One more violation and you'll need to call your union rep."

"We don't have a union."

"It's an expression. I don't mean to be a hard-ass," he adds. "You're good at your job, when you're around."

Fivey is a bush-league fish in a bush-league pond.

And these kids *are* going to teach themselves.

She's only here to give them some nudges and clues. She is here to tell them they don't have to get married or buy a house or read the list of shipwrecks at the pub every Saturday night.

Ten days until Every Child Needs Two comes true.

She should have asked Mattie sooner.

Plunged faster.

When told, last year, of the biographer's desire for a child, the meditation teacher suggested that she get a dog.

With a knife she stirs cream into her third cup of coffee. She inherited the family silverware, which Dad was not interested in carrying to Ambrosia Ridge, but most of the spoons had to be thrown away. The same spoons that had once entered the mouths of the biographer and Archie freighted with ice cream or pudding or soup were later used to heat the heroin and water that was sucked through a shred of cotton into a needle that went into Archie's skin. The charred spoons were useful to stumble upon (under beds, in creases of couches) when the biographer needed to confront him with irrefutable, unarguable evidence—though he did, in fact, to her amazement, sometimes argue.

"Ever heard of a dishwasher? They mess up spoons."

Or "That's probably been there for two years; it's not a current event, my friend."

Archie was a dumb fuck.

And her favorite person of all.

She will name her kid after him, if she ever has a kid.

Why does she even want one?

How can she tell her students to reject the myth that their happiness depends on having a mate if she believes the same myth about having a child?

Why isn't she glad, as Eivør Mínervudottír was glad, to be free?

She sips coffee. Drums her heel to the throbbing clank of the kitchen radiator. Opens her notebook. Writes on a new page: *Reasons I am envious of Susan*. It embarrasses her to write the word "envious," but a good researcher can't be stopped by ugly data.

1. Convenient/free source of sperm
2. Has two

The biographer's family once looked like the Korsmos—mother father sister brother, a foursquare American family. They had a weedy yard, a house. The biographer doesn't want a house, but she wants a kid. She can't explain why. She can only say *Because I do*.

Which doesn't seem like a good enough reason for all of this suffering effort.

Maybe she has flat-out been programmed by marketing. Awash in images of mother and child, mama bear and baby bear, she learned, without knowing she was learning it, to desire them.

Maybe there are better things she could be doing with the life she already has.

She glances down at the pasty insides of her elbows: the tracks are fading. Resemblance to Archie evaporating. Weeks since her last blood draw, since she last laid eyes on Kalbfleisch's indifferent golden cheeks.

Reasons I ~~am envious of~~ hate Susan:

1. Convenient/free source of sperm
2. Has two
3. Doesn't pay rent

4. Told me to distract self at movies
5. Has two
6. Said you don't truly become an adult until, etc.
7. Has two

A less envious, less hateful person would not be hoping that Mattie Quarles was arrested at the Canadian border.

The ice is a solid floor around our ship. No amount of chopping and sawing and hacking cracks its grip. The rudder hangs useless. *Oreius* is beset.

# THE DAUGHTER

Follows the officer into a closet room with a brown table, brown chairs, and no windows. Sits down before being asked. The officer stays standing, hands on hips. "Can you tell me the real reason for your visit?"

"Going to see a friend in Vancouver."

"I said the real reason."

The door is closed.

Nobody knows she's here, aside from Ash, and what the hell is Ash going to do?

"That is the real reason, ma'am."

"We see a lot of girls like you trying to cross. Problem is, Canada has an official agreement with the United States. We've agreed to stop you from breaking *your* country's laws in *our* country."

"But I'm not breaking—"

"The nice thing about pregnancy tests? Results in one minute."

"I don't know what you're talking about, ma'am."

"Section 10.31 of the Canadian Border Services Agency Regulations states: 'If an unaccompanied minor registers a positive result on a FIRST RESPONSE Rapid Result Pregnancy Test, and cannot verify a legitimate personal or professional purpose in a Canadian province, she shall be taken into custody and returned to U.S. law enforcement officials.'"

"But I *can* verify my purpose. My friend Delphine?" The daughter opens her satchel and pulls out the email.

The officer glances at it. "Seriously?" Hands the page back.

The daughter presses her thighs together.

"This is what's going to happen, Matilda. I'm going to give you a cup, and you're going to go down the hall to the bathroom and urinate in the cup."

"You can't randomly drug-test me. That's illegal."

"Nice try."

The daughter decides to look this woman in the eye. "I can—I can pay you."

"For what?"

"For letting me get back on the bus."

"You mean a *bribe?*"

"No. Just—" Her mouth is quivering. "Ma'am, please?"

"Hey, you know who loves being called ma'am?"

"Who?"

"Nobody."

"I have a hundred dollars," says the daughter. She can sleep in the bus station and eat when she's back in Oregon.

"Keep it, eh?" The officer takes a plastic-wrapped cup from her jacket pocket and plunks it on the brown table. "Ready to pee, or do you need water?"

"Water," says the daughter, because it means delay.


Yasmine said she didn't intend to be anyone's stereotype. Black teen mother slurping welfare off the backs of hardworking citizens, etc.


And Mrs. Salter was the only woman of color in the Oregon State Legislature. She didn't intend to jeopardize her mother's career.


She gave herself a homemade abortion.


Blond Frizzy comes back without any water, followed by a man officer, blue eyed and in charge. He smiles at the daughter. "I'll take it from here, Alice."

"I was almost—"

"Why don't you go on your lunch?"

The subordinate officer does a long blink at the daughter. Wrinkles her mouth. "You betcha." And leaves.

"How are you today, Miss Quarles?" says the guy, propping one black boot on a chair. His crotch is at eye level.

She shrugs, too scared to be polite.

"So you're visiting the True North for pleasure? For fun?"

She nods.

"You know, we may be nice up here, but we still don't enjoy being lied to."

"I'm not—"

"Your face is *very* expressive. It betrays a lot."

Fear pricks up along her arms, across her chest.

"Some folks have unreadable faces. They're the tough ones, you know? The ones you second-guess yourself with. Not you, Miss Quarles. But"—he lifts up the propped foot, bangs it down on the floor—"I'm not going to arrest you."

"You're not?"

"I've got two daughters aboot your age. Let's say I've got a soft spot."

"That's—wow. Thank you."

"You'll need to go back where you came from, though. Next bus south gets here in three and a half hours. I will personally ensure that you're on it. If you don't already have a return ticket, you can pay the driver."

*Back?* Soft gray hole in her throat.

"Your photo and driver's license," says the guy, "will be distributed to every border patrol office in Canada, so don't even think aboot trying to cross again."

You can't tell from looking (scarves, big sweaters), but her stomach is thicker and harder. Soon it will be too late.

"I want you to learn a lesson from this. Don't repeat your mistakes. Like I tell my daughters: be the cow they have to buy."

"Sorry?"

"Don't be the free milk."

In the chilly waiting room, she eats chocolate-covered peanuts from the machine.

Mom has called twice to ask about the conference. Listening to her messages ("So proud of you, pigeon!") makes the daughter's nose run.

The daughter is ashamed to be ashamed of Mom when cashiers say "You and your grandma find everything you were looking for?"

This is the worst day of her life.

Second worst: when her father mistook Representative Salter for the school bus driver.

Is the failure of this trip a sign? She has tried twice now. Maybe she should just stay pregnant. Skip the Math Academy and push it out and give it to some couple with gray hair and good hearts. It's the legal way. The safe way. *Think of all the happy adopted families that wouldn't exist.*

She could skip the Math Academy and push it out and quit Central Coast Regional. Finish high school online. Let her mom help her wash and dress and feed it. When the daughter tries to picture herself as a mother, she sees the wall of trees by the soccer field, swaying and faceless.

She doesn't want to skip the Math Academy.

(She kicks Nouri's gothsickle ass at calculus.)

Or to push it out.

She doesn't want to wonder; and she would.

The kid too — *Why wasn't I kept?*

Was his mother too young? Too old? Too hot? Too cold?

She doesn't want him wondering, or herself wondering.

*Are you mine?*

And she doesn't want to worry she'll be found.

*Selfish.*

But she has a self. Why not use it?

*Oreius* would be trapped in the ice for seven months.

# THE WIFE

Thanks Mrs. Costello for coming early. Kisses John's perfect ear. Gets on the road.

Twice almost turns the car around.

She hasn't been inside a courtroom since law school. This one is sultry with rain drippings raised to a boil by the heaters. At the front table sit Edward and Gin Percival. The wife can't see their faces. Fluorescent light bounces off Edward's shaved head. No sign of Mrs. Fivey, but Mr. is in the front row, checking his watch. Eight forty-five a.m.

The wife takes a seat against the back wall. In the jury box are seven women, five men, middle-aged and elderly, all white. Edward should have asked for a bench trial. Temple's niece won't make a good impression on any jury around here.

"Gin Percival," says the gnomish judge, "you will stand while the charges against you are read."

She gets to her feet. Dark hair in a bun, orange jumpsuit loose at her waist. She's gotten thinner since the wife last saw her, on the low metal stool at the library.

The bailiff intones:

"One misdemeanor count of Medical Malpractice by Commission against Sarah Dolores Fivey.

"One felony count of Conspiracy to Commit Murder in acceding to terminate the pregnancy of Sarah Dolores Fivey."

How much time could she get? The wife can't recall anything about sentence lengths.

She can recall reading aloud "manslaughter" as "man's laughter," and Edward being the only person in class to agree it was funny.

Unable to see Mr. Fivey's face, she pictures its mortification. Everyone knows his business now. The principal's wife and her backwoods abortion. No matter how this case turns out, the Fiveys will leave tarnished.

From the prosecution table rises a slender red-haired attorney in a pin-striped suit. She takes her time strolling to the jury box, palms together at her throat as though in prayer. She looks younger than the wife.

"Fellow Oregonians, you've heard the charges against Gin Percival. Your job is simple: to decide whether there is sufficient evidence to convict Ms. Percival of these crimes. During the course of this trial, you'll be shown a vast array of facts that establish her guilt on both counts. Listen to the facts. Base your verdict on the facts. I know that the facts will lead you to conclude beyond a reasonable doubt that Gin Percival is guilty of the crimes she's been charged with."

"Vast array"—lazy phrase. Repetition of "crimes," "charge," "guilt," and "facts"—predictable move. Edward can take her.

He clears his throat. "Thank you, Judge Stoughton, and thank you, members of the jury—you're performing an important civic duty." He pauses to scratch the back of his neck, under the collar. "Mmh. My counterpart has told you that your job is simple, and I would agree. But I beg to differ with her assertion that the evidence will clearly show you much of anything. Because there is virtually no evidence. You will be presented with hearsay, speculation, and circumstantial evidence, but no *direct* evidence. And your job, which is, indeed, simple, is to see that there is not enough evidence to convict my client beyond a reasonable doubt of these spurious charges."

His sentences are too long. He should have said "bogus" instead of "spurious." This is rural Oregon.

"Thank you, and I look forward to working with you over the coming days." He sits, wipes his face with a handkerchief.

Gin Percival keeps staring at the wall. Will Edward dare to put her on the stand? By all accounts—and from what the wife has smelled at the library—she's a bit unhinged.

Has the wife become a person who believes all accounts?

Sort of, yes, she has.

She has been too tired to care.

The Personhood Amendment, the overturning of *Roe v. Wade,* the calls for abortion providers to face the death penalty—the person she planned to be would care about this mess, would bother to be furious.

Too tired to be furious.

The past future Susan MacInnes could have been a battling litigator who brought milestone cases to the higher courts. Edward is battling; he has marched into the mess. The wife can hardly bring herself to read about the case.

*Bring yourself.*

At the library, Gin Percival's hair sometimes had twigs in it, and she gave off an oniony scent. The wife felt repelled by her animal dishevelment; yet she is coming to see the value in being repellent.

Bryan was a pitiful diversion, an excuse. This is an inside job.

Whatever frees Gin Percival to leave her hair twiggy and wear shapeless sack dresses and smell unwashed—the wife wants that.

Two days, two nights every week to herself.

*Tell Didier you are leaving.*

Before having kids, she envisioned motherhood as a jubilant merging. She never thought she would long to spend time away from them. It is hideous to admit she can't bear the merging 24-7. Same guilt that's kept her from putting John in daycare: she doesn't want it to be true that she wants to be apart.

The judge says, "Prosecution may call its first witness."

Mrs. Costello, never one to put much faith in science, believes Gin Percival cursed the waters, charmed the tides, and brought the seaweed back. Half of these jurors may think the same. And if a witch can charm the tides, what else is she capable of?

The pin-striped suit stands up. "Your Honor, we call Dolores Fivey."

In law school, the wife excelled at trial performance. She used to get rounds of applause. But here in the gallery, watching the judicial choreography, she feels no desire to go back to law school. If she puts John in daycare it will be for other reasons, as yet unknown.

What is the flavor of human meat? The men in Franklin's expedition, lost in the Canadian Arctic, turned to cannibalism, according to Inuit reports.

# THE MENDER

Lola's tits aren't so fat anymore, they look drained, cells collapsing like houses of butter. She's wearing them thrust up hell-for-leather, but they are ghosts of their former selves. Butter ghosts. She sits in the box in her push-up bra and a blue suit with long sleeves to hide the scar—less of a scar (thanks to the mender) than it would have been.

"Mrs. Fivey," says the prosecutor, "please tell us how you came to be acquainted with the accused."

The lawyer leaps up. "Objection. Your Honor, I ask that the prosecution refer to Ms. Percival using the less inflammatory term 'defendant.'"

Drowning in his robes, the walnut-faced judge says, "Sustained."

"How did you meet the defendant?"

Lola won't stop staring at her hands. The mender loves those hands, small and graceful, the nails filed square. They held the mender's ass timidly at first; then not timidly. They found their way into her wet scabbard.

"Mrs. Fivey?"

In a frightened voice: "I went to her for medical treatment."

"Even though the acc—sorry, *defendant* is not a medical doctor? Or any kind of doctor, in fact? Even though she does not even have a high school diploma?"

"Objection," says the lawyer. "The prosecution is testifying."

"Withdrawn. Why did you seek medical treatment from the, ah, defendant?"

"I needed," says Lola, then stops.

"Mrs. Fivey?" says the prosecutor. "What did you need?"

"Medical treatment."

"Yes, that's been established. What specific treatment was it?"

Lola shrugs. Twists her hands on the rail of the witness box.

"Mrs. Fivey?"

"You will answer the question, Mrs. Fivey," says the judge.

"A termination."

"A termination of what?"

"Of..."

"Please speak up, Mrs. Fivey."

"Of a pregnancy? I thought I was pregnant but I wasn't."

In exchange for testifying, the lawyer explained, Lola gets immunity. Won't be charged with conspiring to murder.

"And did Ms. Percival agree to provide an abortion?"

She looks at the prosecutor with her beautiful, painted-on eyes. Then back down at her hands. "Yeah, she did."

Lola has reason to lie. She's a cornered animal. The life she saves will be her own.

There is nobody to contradict her but the mender herself, who is a forest weirdo, a seaweed-hexing kook.

This predicament is not new. The mender is one of many. They aren't allowed to burn her, at least, though they can send her to a room for ninety months. Officials of the Spanish Inquisition roasted them alive. If the witch was lactating, her breasts exploded when the fire grew high.

The blacksmith harpooned a polar bear. Cook made stew from the liver and heart. I did not take a portion, though it was agony to smell the rich broth. After supper the sailors grew sluggish—slept poorly—by morning, the skin around their mouths was peeling. The skin on their hands, bellies, and thighs began to slough away. They did not believe me that vitamin A occurs at toxic levels in polar-bear livers. They are saying I cursed the stew.

# THE DAUGHTER

Doesn't need to be convinced. What's one absence? She has always been the good girl. Spotless record. Besides, she can't think—her eyes keep closing. She wants to sleep for a year.

"Cool," says Ash. "I've never seen a testimony before."

When the Quarles family moved to Newville, Ash was the only person willing to hang out with the daughter. She warned her that Good Ship uses ghost pepper (which can numb your lips permanently) in its hot and sour soup. She took her to the lighthouse. She taught her to find creatures in the tide pools—ass-mouthed anemones, ribbed limpets whose shells fit into dents in the rock called home scars.

They drive north in slashing sleet. Order mochas at the drive-through espresso hut. Lick the quaking towers of whip.

"New scarf?"

"Christmas," says the daughter.

"The purple one looked better."

Yasmine wouldn't like Ash much; but she is all the daughter has.

She lights a cigarette. Everything out the window is gray, the sky and the cliffs and the water, the cold curtains of rain. The cops at the hospital kept asking "How did she do it? What did she use?" and the daughter couldn't answer.

"So, um, I have a question," she says.

Ash holds out two fingers. The daughter puts her cigarette between them.

"Can you ask your sister for the number of a term house?"

Ash exhales, hands the cigarette back. "No way."

"But the ones online, you can't tell if they're real or traps. Can't you just *ask*?"

"Fuck no. Clementine wouldn't tell me, anyhow."

"She might, if she knew I didn't—have much time left?"

"Yeah, but no. Too dangerous. Clem knows a girl who got such a bad infection at this place in Seattle she had to get emergency surgery and almost died."

"Was she arrested?"

"Of course." Ash reaches for the cigarette again. "But her dad hired this famous lawyer. The girl told my sister the term house was sickening. She saw a plastic bucket of another girl's stuff just sitting there. A *clear* plastic bucket."

Hot spike in the daughter's ribs. Taste of pennies on her teeth.

Yasmine didn't die either. But she lost so much blood she needed transfusions. All night the daughter and her parents waited at the ER with Mrs. Salter, who rocked back and forth in her pink ski jacket. The lights squeaked. The daughter had to pee horribly but wanted to be there when the doctor brought news.

Yasmine's uterus was so badly damaged it had to be removed.

The cops came while she was still in the hospital.

The witch wears an orange prisoner suit, not the stitched sack, and her hair looks brushed, which in the forest cabin it did not. Good thing she can't see Gin Percival's face, in case the face looks scared. The daughter, scared all the time now, wants there to be people who aren't.

Clementine is scheduled to testify as a character witness. The rest of Ash's family thinks Gin Percival contaminated the waters. More fish are turning up dead in the nets, and the dead man's fingers are messing up the hulls of boats.

"Please silence your electronic devices," says the little judge.

At this moment Ro/Miss is taking attendance and doing the bit where she repeats the names of the missing ("Quarles…? Quarles…? *Quarles…?*") in reference to an old movie the daughter hasn't seen.

"Doctor," says the lemon-mouthed prosecutor, "before we adjourned yesterday you said Dolores Fivey suffered a grade-three mild traumatic brain injury as the result of falling down a flight of stairs of twelve vertical feet, which—"

"Objection," says Gin Percival's lawyer, bald and round. "The doctor has already testified to these details; I can't imagine why we need to hear them again."

"Withdrawn. Can you please tell the court the results of a tox screen administered to Mrs. Fivey shortly after her arrival at Umpqua General Hospital?"

"Sure can," says the doctor. "We found alcohol and colarozam in her system."

"As you know, terminating a pregnancy is a felony."

Her clothes are too tight. The room is too hot.

*A plastic bucket of another girl's stuff.*

"Objection."

"Can cause dizziness and falling."

"When mixed with alcohol."

"When mixed with lemon, lavender, fenugreek, and elderflower oil."

"A felony."

"Seeking a termination."

"A felony."

She needs to find a bathroom—

"Dizzy, disoriented, prone to stumbling."

"When Dolores Fivey was admitted."

"Standard procedure."

Websites say nausea is only first trimester—

"And what were the results of."

"Women of childbearing age."

The daughter needs a bathroom. Can't think. Too hot.

Colarozam.

*A plastic bucket.*

The shunning of a boar.

Claimed to believe.

When mixed with alcohol.

A boar shun.

So tight this hoodie this room too hot —

Ash's mocha breath on her cheek: "Girl, are you okay?"

"What."

"You're sweating like a freak. Let's get some water."

"Bathroom."

"Hush," says Ash, and shoves her down the slippery bench toward the door.

Mínervudottír saw a narwhal come to breathe at one of the holes cut in the ice near the ship, for quick water in case a fire broke out. He was soon joined by others, their helical tusks spearing the air. The sailors watched the fire holes too and would shout "Unicorn!" when a whale appeared.

# THE BIOGRAPHER

From narwhals she moves to notes on the Greely Expedition. In August of 1881 the American explorer Adolphus Greely and his team of twenty-five men and forty-two dogs arrived at Lady Franklin Bay, west of Greenland. They were to gather astronomical and magnetic data from the Arctic Circle and to attain a new "Farthest North" record.

The second summer, the expedition waited on the supply ship that was scheduled to bring food and letters. It never appeared. (*Neptune* had been blocked by ice.)

The third summer: no ship. (*Proteus* had been crushed by ice.)

Between 1882 and 1884, several vessels went in search of Greely and his crew—at first to restock them, then to save them.

Each time she types the word "ice," the biographer thinks *trial*.

Boots. Parka. Gloves. Rain has rinsed the frost from her windshield. Instead of driving down the hill toward school, she drives up: toward the cliff road and highway, the county seat. If Fivey tries to fire her, she'll hire Edward to contest it.

She has been in a courtroom twice before, in Minnesota, for Archie's possession charges. "How can you tell when a lawyer's lying?" he turned to whisper. "When he opens his mouth," she said, dismayed by how obvious the joke was.

Fiveys at the front; Cotter from the P.O. behind them; Susan in a middle row; Mattie and Ash at the very back. Mattie looks haggard and dazed. Having never needed to terminate a pregnancy, the biographer doesn't know how long it takes to recover. A hard little glass splinter in her hopes the girl is miserable.

The new laws turn the girl into a criminal, Gin Percival into a criminal, the biographer herself—had she asked for Mattie's baby, forged its birth certificate—into a criminal.

If not for her comparing mind and covetous heart, the biographer could feel compassion for her fellow criminals.

Instead she feels a splinter of glass.

In the witness box Gin Percival sits absolutely still. Expression flat as a knife.

PROSECUTOR: Ms. Percival, on Monday we heard sworn testimony from Dolores Fivey that you caused significant injuries to her. That you gave her a powerful drug that you claimed would terminate her pregnancy but which resulted in her falling down a flight of stairs and—

EDWARD: Objection. Is there a *question* hidden in there?

PROSECUTOR: Withdrawn. Did you administer a mixture of colarozam, fenugreek, lavender, lemon, and elderflower oil to Dolores Fivey?

GIN: No.

PROSECUTOR: I'll remind you that you are under oath, Ms. Percival. A bottle containing traces of those ingredients was found in Mrs. Fivey's home, with your fingerprints all over it.

GIN: That was my bottle. Oil for scars. Only the last four things. Not the first thing.

PROSECUTOR: Sorry, Ms. Percival, you're not making much sense.

EDWARD: Objection.

JUDGE: Sustained.

PROSECUTOR: Ms. Percival, tell me: are you a witch?

EDWARD: Objection!

PROSECUTOR: It's a reasonable question, Your Honor. Goes to the defendant's proficiency with herbal medicines and to her state of mind. If she self-identifies, even if delusionally, as a health-care provider—

JUDGE: I will allow it.

PROSECUTOR: Are you a witch?

GIN: [Silent]

PROSECUTOR: How long have you identified as a witch?

GIN: [Silent]

JUDGE: The defendant will answer.

GIN: If you knew about the *real* powers, if you knew, you'd be—

EDWARD: Your Honor, I request a short recess.

PROSECUTOR: Your Honor, I demand to finish my line of questioning.

JUDGE: "Demand"? You are in no position to demand anything here, Ms. Checkley. We will adjourn for thirty minutes.

Accused witches in the seventeenth century were dunked in rivers or ponds. The innocent drowned. The guilty floated, surviving to be tortured or killed some other way.

*This isn't 1693!* the biographer wants to yell.

She shakes her head.

*Don't just shake your head.*

While she hid out in Newville, they closed the clinics and defunded Planned Parenthood and amended the Constitution. She watched on her computer screen.

*Don't just sit there watching.*

While she hid out in her book, imagining the nineteenth-century deaths of Nordic pilot whales, twelve sperm whales perished, for reasons unknown, on the Oregon coast.

She looks for Mattie, but she and Ash and their coats are gone.

"Hey, Ro," calls Susan from the aisle.

"Hi," says the biographer, engrossed in her ancient flip phone, which can't even go online. She doesn't want to talk to Susan the non-criminal, the good adult.

Out in the marble-floored hallway she sees Mattie come out of the women's bathroom and head for the exit.

"Wait!" The biographer jogs after her.

Mattie doesn't stop. "Ash is getting the car."

Snow is flurrying down. On the courthouse steps they stand blinking at the little wet stars.

"How are you feeling?" says the biographer. "How was the procedure?"

The girl pulls on blue mittens. "I have to go."

"Wait, okay? I'm not going to tell anyone. Pretend I don't work at school."

"You do work at school."

"Did you go to Vancouver?"

Mattie's lips are purplish in the snow light. Her eyes are lake-green. "Didn't happen."

"Why not?"

"The Pink Wall."

*You mean*—The biographer gleams inside. "But why—did they not arrest you?"

"One was going to. Then I thought another one was about to, like, sexually assault me in exchange for letting me go. But he actually just let me go."

The baby is not gone?

The splinter is thrilled.

"Were you scared?"

Mattie wipes snow from her upper lip. "Yeah. But honestly?" Inhales a shredded breath. "I'm more scared now."

I will take the baby on a train to Alaska.

Row a boat with the baby to the Gunakadeit Light.

*Ask her.*

"Did they notify your parents?"

"No." A stricken look. "And you won't either, right?"

"Scout's honor."

"I better go—there's Ash."

*Ask her now.*

But the biographer is halted, held mute.

She pats Mattie's shoulder.

The baby will see the black ocean flecked with silver.

I will eat dinner with the baby every night.

*FUCKING. ASK. HER.*

Her mouth can't make those words.

"Well, if you need anything, let me know?"

"Thanks, miss."

The girl descends the steps, blue scarf rippling behind; and the biographer sees blue-swaddled babies shot from cannons across the Canadian border, then tossed back, still wrapped and cooing, onto American soil.

The significance of ~~Eivør Mínervudottír's research was~~

~~Mínervudottír was important because~~

Was she important?

From the Latin: to be of consequence; weigh. To carry in, to bring in.

She brought in:

1. Refusal to submit to cottage life
2. Measurements of ice chlorides and Arctic sea temperatures
3. Metric analyses of ice responses to wind speed and tide speed
4. A theory of refreezing predictors in sea-ice leads, invaluable for navigating ice-choked waters

And thus helped to bring in:

1. Shipping and trade through the Northeast Passage, once considered impenetrable
2. More ways for white pirates to steal from the not-white, the not-rich, or the not-human
3. Oil, gas, and mineral drilling in the Arctic
4. The shrinking of the ice

Mínervudottír may have felt free; but she was a cog in a land-snatching, resource-sucking, climate-fucking imperialist machine.

~~Wasn't she?~~

~~Was she?~~

## LENI ZUMAS

I DON'T KNOW
WHAT I AM
EVEN SAYING
ABOUT THIS PERSON THERE IS NOT
A SINGLE KNOWN PHOTOGRAPH OF

or why I couldn't bring
myself to ask for

my lips aren't working

# THE WIFE

Labiaplasty surgeons earn up to $250,000 per month.

A little animal—possum? porcupine?—tries to cross the cliff road.

Sooty, burnt, charred to rubber.

Shivering, trying to cross.

Already so dead.

After federal and state taxes, social security, retirement, and health insurance, Didier brings home $2,573 per month. They don't have rent or mortgage payments, but it's still not enough.

*Clap, clap,* say the labia.

If the wife were a better budgeter, it would be enough. If she were more organized.

The wife has been letting the house "go."

And letting herself "go."

We'll go if you let us.

Wife and house run away together, hand in door. Hand in dormer window.

*I'd take lonely over beaten to a paste.*

She pictures Bryan's cousin, whoever she is, in a shack in the woods, hurled against a moldy particleboard wall. The husband is long bearded, wild haired. He rarely comes out of the woods or lets his wife come out. They drive to town once a month for supplies. On these trips Bryan's cousin wears sunglasses and a wide-brimmed hat.

Why does Bryan stand by and let it happen? Shouldn't he run into those woods and find the shack and put a stop to the beatings? Shouldn't he and the mother he visits in La Jolla, if they care so much, call the police?

Can't think of Bryan without broiling with shame.

"Mommy."

"Yes, sprite?"

"Cold," he says, her dear boy who isn't interested in saying much, who is so different from his chattery sister.

"Let's go put on a sweater," hoisting him onto her hip.

After they separate, will Didier buy pot gumdrops and leave them out on the coffee table for the children to find?

*You need to tell him.*

Upstairs, she finds a blue wool pullover.

Can pot be overdosed on?

"No!" shouts John.

"I forgot, you hate this one — sorry." She pulls off the blue wool and picks a red cotton, less itchy, from the drawer.

Will he remember to give them their vitamin D?

*Tell him.*


Downstairs the wife sits at the dining room table with her eyes closed.

"Momplee!"

"Don't yell, Bex."

"Then pay attention."

"What?"

"I *said*, what will you get Daddy for Valentine's Day?"

"That's over a month away."

"I know but I already know which cards I'm giving to people. The turtle ones, remember, that we saw?"

"Well, I'm not going to get Daddy anything."

"Why?"

"It's not a holiday we celebrate."

"But it's the day of love."

"Not for us," says the wife.

"Do you love Daddy?"

"Of course I do, Bex."

"Then why don't you celebrate it?"

"Because it's silly."

"Oh." The girl looks at her interlaced fingers and is thinking of the turtle cards, signed and sealed in small white envelopes, one for each classmate.

"I meant for grown-ups," adds the wife. "Not for kids—it's great for kids."

"Okay," says Bex, wandering off.

Two days and nights of solitude every week. The house to herself.

*But first you need to tell him.*

She'll feel so much better from the solitude that she will teach John to like foods other than buttered spaghetti and chicken nuggets. She'll bake those barley walnut muffins Bex eats at the Perfects'. She will start cleaning again, keep the rooms scrubbed and dusted, wipe the toilet rims weekly, buy a dehumidifier for the attic, make an appointment to test the kids' bloodstreams for lead.

Or she won't be living in this house at all: she will rent an apartment that requires virtually no cleaning.

Maybe the apartment will be in Salem.

*After you tell him.*

"Daddy's here!" shrieks Bex, galloping onto the porch.

"Daddy," sniffles John.

"Fee fi fo fon," calls Didier.

*Children need two parents at home. Every child needs two.*

So say the legislators and the commercials and Bryan, the child-free boy whose aim in life is to win money at competitive mini golf.

Jessica Perfect will have a field day. *Oh my God, did you hear? The Korsmos are separating. I feel so bad for the kids—*they're *the ones who really pay.*

The wife's mother, never a Didier fan, is going to say: *I saw this coming a mile away.*

She rummages in the kitchen drawer to see how many chocolate bars she has left.

"Momplee?"

Two.

"Yeah?"

"I lost my homework sheet."

"Look in your room."

"Incinerate! All homework sheets!" sings Didier.

Last summer at the teachers' picnic Ro asked her why she'd taken Korsmo, and the wife said, "Because I wanted us all to have the same last name."

"But why?"

*"Because."*

"It's the twenty-first century."

"I'm not going to sit here and justify my choices to you," said the wife.

"Why not?"

"Because I don't need to."

Ro kept her teeth on the bone. "How come nobody's allowed to criticize a woman's decision to give up her name for a man's name? Just because it's her *choice?* I can think of some other bad choices that—"

"Shut up, please," said the wife, and that was the beginning of the end of her friendship with Ro.

On the kitchen calendar, in Saturday's square, she writes a *T.*

*Tell him.*

She can't cheat her way out.

She can't wait her way out, head in the sand.

She has to say it herself.

"Momplee?"

"Jesus, Bex—it must be in your room. Have you checked under the bed?"

"Not about that," says the girl.

"Then *what?*" The wife stands holding the ballpoint pen with which she has just written herself a reminder to inform her husband she is leaving him. She wants to ram the pen into her own neck.

"Am I fat?"

"No!"

Voice wobbly: "I weigh eight pounds more than Shell."

"Oh, sweetpea." She kneels down on the kitchen floor, gathering Bex into her lap. "You're exactly the right size for *you*. Who cares how much Shell weighs? You're beautiful and perfect just the way you are."

The wife fails, as a parent, on so many fronts.

"You're my perfect darling gorgeous girl."

But she will do this one thing right.

I hate the chewy lard meat called pemmican; and I admit to fearing the attack of a sea bear; and my fingers hurt all the time; but I prefer immurement in these spectral wastes to a seat at the warmest hearth.

# THE MENDER

A witch who says no to her lover and no to the law must be suffocated in a cell of the hive. She who says no to her lover and no to the law shall bleed salt from the face. Two eyes of salt in the face of a witch who says no to her lover and no to the law shall be seen by policemen who come to the cabin. Faces of witches who say no do resemble those of owls tied by leashes to stakes. *Venefica mellifera, Venefica diabolus.* If a town be plagued by a witch who says *No, I won't stop mending* and who says *No, you can't hide in my house,* and the lover Lola does feel sorrow and shame, and the hard-fisted husband of Lola does discover the betrayal of his wife, and the lover Lola, to save her own life, tells a lie about the witch, the witch's body shall be lashed to a stake. Her owl teeth shall catch flame first, sparks of blue at the white before the red tongue catches too. A witch's body when burning does smell of blistered milk; the odor makes onlookers vomit, yet still they look on.

My fingers hurt so much I am always humming.

Boatswain says he will punch my mouth if I
don't stop.

# THE BIOGRAPHER

The adoption caseworker's cubicle is festooned with evergreen boughs and reindeer cards on a string. She wears peppermint barrettes in her hair. "How was your Yuletide?"

"Fine," says the biographer. "I made this appointment because— Sorry, how was *your* Yuletide?"

"Super fun. We went up to my sister's in Scappoose. I drank way too much spiked nog, of course, but when in Rome!"

This caseworker is the biographer's fourth; turnover is high at the agency. She is straight out of college and has a tiny attention span and thinks "Fer sher" is an appropriate response to an emotionally charged disclosure. But she's better than the one who asked the biographer if she knew that a child is not a replacement for a romantic partner.

"Next week is January fifteenth. I am here to quite literally beg you to get me matched before then."

It takes the caseworker a few frowning seconds to grasp the date's significance. "I understand your concern," she says. "Let's see what's been happening in your file." She types, waits, stares. The screen is hidden from the biographer. "Okay. Since you last updated your profile, on September second, your landing page has received six views and zero Tell Me More clicks."

"Six? Jesus."

"It's difficult for some birth mothers to get past the age. You're older than some of their own parents, which—"

"Okay, yeah, thanks, I know. But you guys said if I played up my teaching career, and the fact that I'm about to finish a book, I'd have more hits?"

"I thought it would help, fer sher. We notice, though, that status and income associated with occupation can make a difference, which for you would not necessarily be great? Compounded with the singleness."

"What if you only showed them one profile?"

"What do you mean?"

"The next birth mother. You could show her my profile and no one else's. Those married people on the wait-list, they've got plenty of time ahead of them, but I only have a week left."

The caseworker smiles. "What you're suggesting is unethical."

"It's *very* ethical, actually. You'd be bending the rules in a minor, temporary way to create an opportunity for someone who is worthy but otherwise wouldn't have a snowball's chance. You'd be making a moral choice. Think of all the change makers throughout history who—"

"I'm not one of your students, Ms. Stephens."

"What? Sorry. I wasn't trying to lecture you."

"Well, you kind of were."

"I apologize. It would just be such a microscopic drop in the—"

"A drop I could lose my job over."

"What if..." The biographer has no idea how to phrase this, so she grabs language from the movies. "What if I made it worth your while?"

"What does that mean?"

"If I offered you an *incentive* to take the risk."

"Sorry, what?"

"As in, a financial incentive."

Light of no understanding on the caseworker's face.

"What if I gave you, personally, a thousand dollars," whispers the biographer, naming a sum she could realistically borrow. Her father, Penny, Didier—

"Oh my God, are you bribing me? This is my first bribe! I'm the only person in the office who hasn't been offered one. Until today."

Heartened by the lack of outrage, the biographer says, "Congratulations?"

"That's wild. I mean, of course I can't take it, but thank you."

"Why not? Nobody would find out. I give you cash, you show my profile to a birth mother before the fifteenth, I get matched with a baby, you get on with your life."

"Ms. Stephens, I totally sympathize with your situation, but I can't take part in an illegal transaction."

"You *can,* you just don't want to." The biographer is trying to breathe normally, but her lungs feel damp and fibrous, like rained-on wood. "Please? It would — it would change my life. I would never tell anyone. I'd lie on the stand if it went to court." Wrong thing to say: the caseworker's eyes crinkle up. "Which it *wouldn't,* of course, it never would, nobody will find out, I don't know why I said that but I guess it was to emphasize how much this would mean to me, and to the baby, who would have a good home with me, a really good home."

The black silver, flecked with ocean.

On a train to the Gunakadeit Light.

"Please?" she says. *"Please?"*

*Breathe, Stephens.*

"My supervisor's out today," says the caseworker, slowly, carefully, "but would you like me to have her call you?"

"Can she give me an extension on the deadline?"

"Every Child Needs Two is a federal law. Even if *we* made exceptions for unmarried applicants, the adoptions wouldn't be valid. Which would create more misery for all involved." She adds, "But you can stay on the fostering wait-list, fer sher."

The biographer's sodden lungs fight to take a full breath.

She drives back to Newville, gasping.

On the beach the wind drives hair into her eyes. She hurls a sneaker at a low-flying gull. Curses her aim. Retrieves her shoe. Jumps on an old log. The beach is a good place for rage: the sky and sea can take it. Her screams are absorbed by the booming waves, the heaped fields of oyster cloud. Because this is Oregon in January, nobody human is around to hear.

Doctor reported his medicine chest stolen. It was found in the snow a few yards from the tents, missing its morphine and opium pills. An able seaman was blamed for the theft, and shot dead.

# THE DAUGHTER

"The jury's going to convict," says Dad.

"Are you now a fortune-teller?" says the daughter.

"She completely lost it on the stand, I hear. Looks as if she'll go to prison for a good little bit."

"Why are you *cheerful* about it?" She is extra seasick tonight.

"It's only fair she pay her debt."

Sipping water to mute the queasiness: "What if she didn't do what they said she did? What if—"

"More rice, Mattie?"

"It's like you're accepting whatever the news says. You weren't even at the trial."

"Your mother asked if you would like more rice."

"No thank you."

Mom, still holding the bowl: "You sure, pigeon?"

"Has Miss Stephens been telling you this woman is innocent? It's not her place to bring politics into the classroom, and if she is, then—"

"I can think of my own ideas. Miss Stephens didn't say shit."

"Language?" says Mom.

"Tons of injustices happen in broad daylight," adds the daughter, "when ordinary citizens are aware but do nothing."

"For instance," says Dad.

"The bystander effect. Nobody helping a crime victim when other people are around because everyone thinks someone else is going to do it."

"Fair enough. What else?"

Her father has trained her to give more than one example in any debate; and that numbers not ending in zero are more convincing in a negotiation, because they sound less arbitrary.

"For instance," she says, "the whole world knows about the pilot-whale slaughter in the Faroe Islands, but nobody's been able to—"

"People have every right to practice their own cultural rituals." He saws at his little pink pork chop. "The Faroese have been hunting whales that way for centuries."

"Pilot whales are technically dolphins. Oceanic dolphins."

"I don't know about that."

"Well, Dad, I do, and they are."

"Point is, they eat what they kill, and they only kill as much as they can eat. The haul is shared out fairly among the community."

"Good for them," mutters the daughter.

"Are you coming down with something?" says Mom. "You look—"

"I'm *fine*."

"I don't want you stressing out about the Math Academy," she says. "If you get in, you get in. If not, you try again next year."

"No reason she shouldn't get in this year," says Dad.

"May I be excused," says the daughter.


She has to get her body clean. Stop being seasick. Stop the blue veins from branching across her tightening breasts. *Don't be the free milk.*


Terribly she misses Yasmine.


Bolt River Youth Correctional Facility is a medium-security state prison for females twelve to twenty years old.

Number of letters, cards, and care packages the daughter mailed to Bolt River the first year Yasmine was inside: sixty-four.

Number of words she heard back from Yasmine: zero.

Whenever she phoned the front office, she was told, "The offender is refusing your call."

Yasmine's mother said, "I've got no idea, Matts. I simply don't."

After a year, the daughter stopped trying.

The frostbitten skin, which at first itched intolerably, has gone waxen and lifeless. Black-purple blisters seep rank-smelling pus. The doctor offered to cut the fingers off, but without morphine or opium, he said, it will be the worst pain I've ever known. I declined the offer.

# THE WIFE

Puts away clean clothes while the girls play Amelia Earhart on Bex's bed. Didier is at the pub with Pete, home by dinnertime. Dinner will be taco casserole, and Shell is going to ask whether the beans were home soaked or from a can.

"What's that sound!"

"Oh no, the plane's running out of gas!"

"My only choice is to fall into the sea!"

"I'm falling! *Flump.*"

*"Flump."*

In a non-game voice Shell says, "Gross, why is there dust all over your floor?"

Bex looks at the floor, then up at the wife.

"My mom says," adds Shell, "that a clean house is the only house worth living in."

*That's enough, Perfect. That is enough.*

"I guess your mom doesn't know much about dust," says the wife. "Because if she did, then she'd know that dust has pollen fibers, which are very good for you."

Bex smiles.

"How are they good for you?" says Shell.

This wallpaper is horrendous. Dark purple flowers on a brown ground. It shouldn't be the first thing her girl sees every morning.

"When you breathe them in, they create more white blood cells in your body, which keep you from getting sick. Dust is *extremely* nutritious."

By dinnertime her husband hasn't appeared, so she serves the kids their casserole, slides the dish back into a two-hundred-degree oven, hustles Shell out to Blake Perfect's car, gives Bex and John a bath, tries to recall when Didier last gave them a bath. While she's reading about the little fur family (*Warm as toast, smaller than most*) the front door slams and voices thud in the hall.

"Will Daddy come say good night?"

"I don't know. That's up to him."

"Well, can you *tell* him to?"


Downstairs she sees he has managed to find the casserole, which is piled, all of it, onto his and Pete's plates. "This is hella good," says Pete by way of greeting, slurping a forkful.

"Yeah it is," says Didier. "Did you use more salsa than usual?"

"So there's none left? I didn't have any."

"I figured you ate with the kids."

"I waited for you."

Didier looks down at his plate. "Want the rest of mine?"

"I'll make a sandwich."

She slathers cream cheese on whole wheat, adds cucumber slices and salt. A virtuous sandwich. A sandwich that might need to be supplemented, later on, by soft-batch chocolate-chip cookies.

Soft-batch—scenic overlook—Bryan Zakile—

Something nips at the edge of her mind.

She looks over at the ficus, which, though brittle, is still alive (didn't she water it yesterday?), and the Medusa's head plant, always chancy in winter, snaky green arms quick to rot without enough sun.

Something Bryan told her.

"I'm literally stunned," Pete is saying, probably about a school matter the wife can't be part of.

"I thought you hated it," she says, "when people say 'literally.'"

Shark-eyed glare. "I was referring to people's misuse and overuse of the term. In this case, I *am* literally stunned."

"By what?"

"The news of my colleague acquiring a literary agent for her flaming piece of hogswaddle."

The wife's face aches. "Ro got an agent?" She will sell the story of the polar explorer, be paid, be reviewed, maybe even become—

"No, Penny Dreadful."

"Good for her," says the relieved, disgusting wife.

"And bad for literature," says Pete.

Something is chewing now on her brain. Some hook, some link, two things she is meant to connect.

Bryan—the cookies—the Medusa's head—

"I need to go smoke."

"Sorry if I'm *boring* you, Didier," says Pete, "but I happen to think it's important to critique the hegemony of commercial publishing. Otherwise, they've got us where they want us."

"Who?"

"The corporate tastemakers. The romance–industrial complex. Dance, puppet, dance!"

"Go tell the kids good night," says the wife.

"I will, right after—"

"By the time you finish that, they'll be asleep."

Didier throws the unlit cigarette on the counter and heads for the stairs.

In the bathroom she pees, wipes, stands, but does not pull up her underwear. She gazes past her sucked-in stomach at the shaggy hillock. How many individual hairs are on this mound? More than a hundred, or less? She pinches one and yanks it out. It hurts a little. She pulls another. Hurts. And a third. A fourth, a fifth. The wife lifts the seat and lays the hairs, one by one, on the toilet rim.

What is nipping at her mind?

Something about Bryan.

Going after him was a coward's move.

She needs to figure out how she got to be such a coward.

But it's more than Bryan.

But what?

*　　*　　*

She looks at the kitchen calendar, where *T* has been written and crossed out, written and crossed out, written and crossed out.

Stands at the sink, scrubbing the casserole dish.

Didier and Pete come back in from their cigarettes.

"Want a beer, Peetle-juice?"

Little animal burnt black, trying to cross. Rubber and shivering.

"Can you believe she's never heard of them?"

"Dude, the sum total of Ro's musical knowledge would fit into Bryan Zakile's jockstrap."

Rubber and shivering.

"Do they make those in extra-small?"

Strapped jock. Jock of Bryan. Balls. Family jewels. Father. Mother. Cousin. *Cousin*—

"He actually uses a kids' size."

*They don't have any kids, so why not leave?*

Cousin beaten to a paste.

Oh no.

The wife drops the casserole dish. It clatters at the bottom of the sink.

Where is her phone—where is—"Where's my *phone?*" Furiously shaking water off her hands.

"Right here on the table," says Didier. "Jesus."

She snatches it up and hurries into the dark dining room, dialing.

He picks up on the first ring. "Susan?"

Blood beats hard in her neck. "Listen, Edward"—talking faster than she ever talks—"you need to interview a new witness, his name's Bryan Zakile, he told me firsthand that his cousin's husband hits her, and his cousin is Dolores Fivey. I think he could—"

"Hold on," says Edward.

She is light-headed. Can't find her breath.

"Did he witness the hitting himself?"

"Okay, *second*hand, but—"

"Also known as hearsay," he says.

"Which is admissible if it constitutes materially exculpatory evidence, and if corroborating circumstances clearly support the hearsay's trustworthiness."

"Damn, Susan. After seven years?"

Splashing glow in her chest. She rushes on: "It would introduce some compelling *doubt,* at least—"

"Hold it. Mmh."

Silence, while he thinks.

Her whole body is throbbing. This matters.

Edward says, "It would corroborate Ms. Percival's claim that Mrs. Fivey disclosed her husband's physical abuse. Which would in turn suggest a motive for Mrs. Fivey to lie about the—mmh."

"You should talk to Bryan tonight," she says. "I'll text you his number."

"Wait a minute. You said, 'He told me his cousin's husband hits her.' Most people have more than one cousin."

"He didn't specify, but it *is* Mrs. Fivey, Edward. It has to be."

"When did he give you this information?"

"A couple of weeks ago."

"And you're only telling me now?"

The glow cools. "I didn't—connect them."

"Mmh. I don't know that any of this will make a difference. But give me his number. Good night."

She sends the text and sits, twitching and exhilarated, in her grandmother's chair in the dark.

Upon *Oreius*'s return to Copenhagen, in the summer of 1876, the gangrenous ring finger and pinky on Eivør Mínervudottír's left hand were amputated. Her notebook does not brood long on the loss: "Two taken, under anesthesia. I have eight others."

With her right hand she wrote up the *Oreius* data. Even before she had finished a draft of the article, she knew her title: "On the Contours and Tendencies of Arctic Sea Ice."

# THE MENDER

Keeps asking for different blankets, but they say work with what you have, Stretch. She hasn't been sleeping. Her throat hurts. She misses Temple, who would burn the bleachy blankets and boil a throat syrup of marshmallow root and say *Show them you're not afraid.*

Except she is.

There is one man on the jury whose eyes are alive. He looks at the mender like she's a person. He smiled when Clementine told the courtroom "Gin Percival saved my vagina." The other eleven watch her like she's batshit.

Kook. *People like to throw around labels.*

Kooky. *Don't let them define you.*

Kookaburra. *You are exactly yourself, that's who.*

*Temple, wish you weren't gone.*

The lawyer is excited today. His face is moving faster. He's brought licorice nibs and lettuce, a brown loaf from Cotter, butter in a ziplock. He explains about the new witness he's calling—Lola's cousin—who doesn't want to testify, so must be considered hostile.

"He'll just lie," says the mender, ripping bread with her teeth.

"Not if I approach him the right way." He takes the butter-smeared hunk she hands him and sets it on the metal bench, too polite to say no. "And if he says what I think he's going to say, then we recall Dolores Fivey to the stand."

"Also me? I could tell them what she told me. After he broke her finger he said she better start taking calcium supplements."

"You—" The lawyer smiles. "Not you."

"Why?"

"You are so much your own person, Gin. And some people on the jury may feel...unnerved by that? People tend to be more comfortable with speech and behavior that does what they already expect it to do. Yours doesn't, and I respect that it doesn't. But I have to think about the jury's perceptions."

She side-eyes him. Being fake? Talking down? With this lawyer, not easy to tell.

Clementine waves at her from the gallery. Cotter's there too, and the pissed-off blond lady from the library who doesn't lower her voice when talking to the librarian.

The mender can't remember seeing Lola's cousin ever before. He looks like your basic man in a suit, dark hair cruelly combed.

"Mr. Zakile," says her lawyer, "it is true you were a soccer star in college?"

The cousin's mouth opens in surprise. "I don't know about 'star,' but yeah, I made a contribution."

"More than a contribution, I would say! According to the University of Maryland student newspaper, *The Diamondback,* you earned All-Conference honors with your 'exquisite ball control and panther-like aggressiveness.'"

"Objection," says the prosecutor. "Where is Mr. Tilghman going with this?"

"Your Honor, I'm establishing context and background for this witness. Mr. Zakile, the *Washington Post* described you as 'a revelation' in a win over Georgetown, during which you scored three goals."

Hesitant smile from the cousin. "That was a great game."

"Plainly, then, Central Coast Regional was fortunate to hire you as their boys' soccer coach. I'm told you are an effective coach—would you agree?"

"We went fourteen and four last season. I'm proud of my guys."

"Your Honor, *what?*" says the prosecutor.

The mender watches her lawyer lead Bryan Zakile to water. As the story of his own awesomeness—as athlete, coach, English teacher, and citizen of the world—unfolds, the witness grows animated. Talkative. Of course he loves his family. Of course he wants to tell the truth as an example to his students. Of course he has no reason to slander Mr. Fivey. On the contrary (as her lawyer meekly points out) he has a motive to *protect* him, even if that would require lying, because Mr. Fivey has the power to fire him. At least, he *had* the power. Now, of course, Mr. Fivey cannot fire him, no matter what Bryan says on the stand. That would look biased, wouldn't it? That would look, frankly, *actionable*. So if Bryan had the freedom, as he now does, to tell the whole truth and nothing but the truth—the freedom to act as befits a man of his character—what would he tell us about his cousin Lola's relationship with her husband?

19 February 1878

Dear Miss Mínervudottír,

I am in receipt of your submission, "On the Contours and Tendencies of Arctic Sea Ice," a paper which, it is patently clear, you did not write. Notwithstanding the stirring discoveries it contains, unless its true author is acknowledged, the Royal Society cannot publish it.

Yours Sincerely,
SIR GEORGE GABRIEL STOKES
Physical Sciences Secretary
The Royal Society of London
for Improving Natural
Knowledge

# THE BIOGRAPHER

At two forty p.m. on January fifteenth she waits, sweating and trembling, outside the door of eighth-period Latin.

It will need to be a home birth, to circumvent hospital records. Mattie is young and strong and shouldn't be in any danger. The biographer can drive her to the ER if something goes awry. She'll find a midwife to help them. They will doctor the birth certificate.

The girl will have all summer to recover.

The biographer will handle Mr. and Mrs. Quarles somehow.

Mattie emerges, knotting the blue scarf at her throat. Her cheeks are fuller, but you can't otherwise tell—scarves and big sweatshirts and winter coats do a fine job of hiding her.

"Quick word?" says the biographer.

Too cold for a walk. They duck into the music room, used for storage ever since the music program was canceled. Posters of tubas and flutes hang over broken chairs, reams of copy paper.

"Are you checking to see if I'm all right?" says Mattie.

"Well, are you?"

"It smells like ham in here."

The biographer only smells her own watery dread.

"Nothing has changed," says Mattie, "since you asked me the other day."

The biographer opens her mouth.

*Give it to me.*

Air moves lightly on her tongue and teeth. Dries her lips. "Mattie?"

"Yeah, miss?"

"I want to help you."

"Then don't tell anyone, okay? Not even Mr. Korsmo. I know you're pals."

She prepares to shape the words: *Pay for your vitamins. Drive you to every checkup. If you give it to me.*

The girl coughs, swallows a curd of phlegm. "By the way, I made an appointment at a—a place in Portland. I need to do it soon because I'm almost twenty-one weeks."

Twenty-one weeks means nineteen left. Four and a half months.

Only four and a half months, Mattie!

"That far along," says the biographer, "the procedure could be dangerous." The glass splinter is choosing these words. "A lot of term houses have no idea what they're doing. They just want to make money."

"I don't care," says Mattie.

"I've heard of—" The biographer's whole self is a splinter. "Fatal errors."

"I don't care! Even if the place is foul and they have other girls' stuff in the buckets, I don't care, I want this to be *over*." Hands in fists, she starts hitting herself on either side of the head, bam bam bam bam bam bam bam, until the biographer pulls her arms, gently, down.

"I'm just saying"—holding Mattie's wrists—"you have other choices."

You can wait four and a half short months.

"Choices?" A new edge in her voice.

"Well, like adoption."

"Don't want to do that." Mattie jerks out of her grasp, turns away.

"Why not?" *Give it to me.*

"Just don't."

"But why?" *Give it to me. I've been waiting.*

"You always tell us"—the girl's voice flicks up into a whine—"that we make our own roads and we don't have to justify or explain them to anyone."

"I do say that," says the biographer.

Mattie glares.

"However, I'd like to make sure you've thought this through."

The girl slumps down against a green filing cabinet. Holds her head in both hands, knees up to her chest, rocking a little. "I just want it out of my body. I want to stop being *infiltrated*. God, please get this out of my body. Make this stop." Rocking, rocking.

She is terrified, realizes the biographer.

"And I don't want to put someone on the planet," whispers Mattie, "who I'll always wonder about my whole life. Like where *is* the someone? Are they okay?"

"What if you knew who was raising them?" The biographer sees a vast, sunny cliff top, blue sky and blue ocean beyond; and Mattie in a flowered dress, shielding her eyes; and the biographer crouching beside the baby, saying, "There's your Aunt Mattie!" and the baby toddling toward her.

"I just *can't*," rasps the girl. "I'm sorry."

Horror thuds in the biographer's chest: she has made her apologize for something that needs no apology.

Mattie is a kid, light boned and soft cheeked. She can't even legally drive.

Four and a half months.

Of swelling and aching and burning and straining and worrying and waiting and feeling her body burst its banks. Of hiding from the stares in town, the questions at school. Of seeing the faces, each day, of her parents as they watch the grandchild who won't be their grandchild be grown. Having to wonder, later on, where is the someone she grew.

The glass splinter says: *Who gives a fuck?*

Mattie says: "Would you go with me?"

To the checkups and the prenatal yoga.

To the store for dark leafy greens.

To the clean, comfortable birthing bed set up in the biographer's apartment, when it's time.

For a dazzling instant she has her baby, who will be tall and dark haired, good at soccer and math. She will take the baby on a rowboat to the lighthouse, on a train to Alaska, practice math problems with the baby on a soccer field. She will love the baby so much.

Except that's not, of course, what Mattie means.

Down her spine, an itching wire.

If the biographer were to admit her own *Torschlusspanik* motives, clarify that the baby would be for her, Mattie might end up agreeing. She wants to please—to be pleasing. She wants to make her favorite teacher happy.

The biographer would be asking something of her that she doesn't believe should be asked of anyone. Deepest convictions, trampled.

Yet here she is, about to tell a sniffly child to give her what she's growing.

The glass splinter says: *This is your last chance.*

*Plunge.*

The biographer says: "Okay."

Mattie looks up, green eyes red and spilling. "You'll go with me?"

"I will." She feels like vomiting.

"I'm sorry to—There's nobody who—Ash won't—"

"I get it, Mattie."

"Thank you," she says. Then: "Is there more than one girls' juvenile correctional facility in Oregon, do you know?"

"Are you—" But of course she's scared. The biographer pats, clumsily, the top of Mattie's head. "We'll be all right."

*We will?* They could both get arrested. The biographer could become a headline. SHIFTY SCHOOLMARM IS ABORTER'S ACCOMPLICE. She feels a rush of raw love for those who are caught, and for those who know they could be.

The girl stands up, shoulders her satchel, adjusts her scarf. Won't meet the biographer's eye. "I'll see you tomorrow?" And she is out the door.

Seed and soil. Egg and shell.

A plug of bile is bobbing at the foot of her throat.

"The key to happiness is hopelessness," says the meditation teacher.

Like a shark: keep moving.

The biographer walks up to a poster for the music club (WHY ARE PIRATES SUCH GOOD SINGERS? THEY CAN HIT THE HIGH Cs!) and claws it off the wall and rips it in half.

The explorer wrote to the tutor, Harry Rattray, who still worked for the shipyard director in Aberdeen:

> After many weeks of reflection on my difficulties with the Royal Society I have taken the painful decision to request that you publish my findings under your own name. Otherwise the world will never know them.

# THE MENDER

Cousin Bryan's testimony, while damning of Mr. Fivey, only matters if Lola corroborates it. When the lawyer explains this to the mender, warning that it may have been a pointless detour, she smiles and says: "Not for Lola."

"How do you mean?"

"Other people know now," she says. "Outside her family. She's free."

The lawyer thoughtfully pets the clean pink skin over his skull. Murmurs, "There we go."

Today Lola isn't wearing as much eye makeup, so her face looks farther away.

"Mrs. Fivey," says the lawyer, "thank you for coming back to the stand."

"Well, I was subpoenaed." But she's looking at the lawyer. Last time she only looked at her hands.

"You heard the testimony of your cousin, Bryan Zakile. I want to ask you, Mrs. Fivey—"

"I prefer Lola?"

Yes, her family members have witnessed arguments between her and her husband. Yes, these arguments can get heated. No, her cousin was not wrong when he described an altercation on Thanksgiving that involved her husband clapping his hand across her mouth in an extremely forceful manner. He was not wrong when he testified that her mandible had been bruised by her husband. Or that, on another occasion, she confided to him that her phalanx had been snapped by her husband. And, yes, the scar on her right forearm was caused when her husband held a hot skillet against the skin. She did not report any of these incidents because it takes two to tango. She's not perfect either. A few family members have expressed concern, yes, but as her mother says, you don't go into other people's marriages uninvited.

When Mr. Fivey found the scar oil in Lola's purse, he pestered her until she admitted going to Ms. Percival about the burn. Hadn't that been a better idea than going to Umpqua General, where they might ask questions? Mr. Fivey didn't agree. He saw a bonkers witchy-woo too deranged to graduate from high school who had no business ministering to his wife.

Lola went to pack her suitcase. She planned to drive to New Mexico (she has a friend there who makes piñon kokopellis) to think things over.

Mr. Fivey came into the bedroom with a glass of vodka and the bottle of scar oil. He had crushed up (she learned later) several tabs of colorozam and mixed them into the oil. He handed her the oil and said, "Drink." When she said no, he slapped her. She drank. And chased the oil with the vodka. And got so wasted that on her way to the kitchen, she fell down the stairs.

She was not—nor did she believe she was—pregnant when she consulted Ms. Percival. That was the last thing on her mind.

Has she ever been pregnant?

Once, thirteen years ago, before she met her husband. She would prefer not to talk about that.

Why is she recanting her previous testimony?

This question makes her quiet. The judge has to remind her she is obliged to answer.

Finally Lola says, "Because I'm done doing his laundry."

They wait in the transition room while the jury deliberates. The lawyer's assistant brings in a box of chocolate-covered blueberries and says, "Fortitude?"

The mender tastes: delicious.

Lola didn't say: *I'm recanting because it wouldn't be fair to make Gin Percival spend seven years in prison.* Barely mentioned Gin Percival at all.

The lawyer is scratching, as usual: wrists, ears, the back of his neck.

"Eczema?" says the mender.

"Bedbugs," he says. "Courtesy of the Narwhal Inn. My apartment in Salem now has them too. I'm on my second fumigation."

"I know some good banishments. If I get out—"

*"When."* He lifts his arms to air out the drenched pits.

"Where will Lola go?" she asks. "She can't stay at home."

"Her attorney said she's already moved to her parents'. The question remains, where will *Mr.* Fivey be staying?"

The mender eats the last blueberry. "You mean, which cell?"

When the jury foreman rises, she shuts her eyes.

"Ladiesanjinnelminnuv."

"Haveyoureached."

"Have yeronner."

"Whatsayyou?"

*Stop shaking. You're a Percival.*

"We find the defendant—"

*Descended from a pirate.*

"—not guilty on both counts."

A whoop from the audience. She is shaking too hard to look, but it sounded like the voice of the pissed-off library lady.

She takes the lawyer's damp hand.

In the first fairy tale Uncle taught me, a glass splinter in the eye would make all the world ugly and bad. I have such a splinter now. I see Harry's name on my paper in *Philosophical Transactions of the Royal Society of London* and curl with rage. It is mine but no one knows. They know the facts imparted, which have more value than my small self; yet with this splinter lodged in me, I can't rest. I would like to run up to Sir George Gabriel Stokes at the Royal Society and show him my finger stumps and say, "I gave these in exchange for my facts."

# THE DAUGHTER

Friday night she scours the Math Academy website, rereading the seminar descriptions and inserting her own face into photos of nerds laughing around tables. If she even gets in. The application was hard. All the nominees will have top grades and test scores, said Mr. Xiao: "You have to stand out. Make yourself come alive in the essay answers."

*How do you see mathematics figuring into your future?*
~~My future will include~~
~~Math will be important in my future because~~
~~In my future, I see~~
~~I notice there is a pun in this question~~

If she gets in, she plans to take the seminar on recursion. Self-similar structures. Variability through repetition. Fractals. Chaos theory.

Think about fractals, not about suction and sloshing tubes and the termhouse door smashed open by a cop's battering ram.

She won't be sixteen for almost a month; she wouldn't be tried as an adult. But even non-adults can be sent away.

When Yasmine operated on her own clump, most termination houses didn't exist yet. It was right after the federal ban had gone into effect. To help the ban take hold, the attorney general ordered district attorneys nationwide to go after the harshest possible sentences for seekers. Send a message. Girls as young as thirteen were incarcerated for three to five years. Even the daughter of Erica Salter, member of the Oregon House of Representatives, was locked up in Bolt River Youth Correctional Facility. A message had to be sent.

*　　*　　*

A day before the self-operation, Yasmine said nobody could know she'd been pregnant, and if the daughter told anyone, she wouldn't speak to her ever again.

"I'm not giving them another reason to think I'm not smart."

"Why would anyone think you're not smart?"

"Is that a joke?"

"No," said the daughter.

"You are a very ignorant white girl," said Yasmine.

She counts every tile in the upstairs bathroom so she won't think about it.

Saturday morning she reminds Mom that after the aquarium she'll spend the night at Ash's—see you tomorrow. Yes, she packed her retainer.

When Ash delivers her to the church parking lot, it seems Ro/Miss is not in the greatest mood. Cold faced, quiet. The daughter offers money for gas and Ro/Miss rolls her eyes. How will they find topics for conversation? Thankfully Ro/Miss turns the radio on. The daughter sinks down in the seat as they drive through town: what would it look like, a student in a teacher's car? Think about Newville gossip, not about the procedure.

Passing a logged hillside, gashed and barren, the stumps like headstones, the daughter sees the shining fir floors in her house. Smells smoke on herself. Chimneylina. One day she'll quit, after she's gotten her marine-biology degree and is working in cetacean situations. Her future will include a study of whale-harming toxins dumped by humans into the sea. A trip to the Faroe Islands to disrupt the slaughter of pilot whales, who are technically dolphins. A trip to a Japanese temple that sings requiems for the whales' souls, gives names to the fetuses inside the captured mothers.

She digs both thumbs into her belly, house of the tufting, clumping, unnamed infiltrator. Please let them not leave it sitting around in a bucket.

The motto of the Royal Society of London: NULLIUS IN VERBA. Take nobody's word for it.

# THE BIOGRAPHER

Mattie's directions bring them to a quiet narrow street in southeast Portland. Flat-roofed ranch homes, yellow lawns. The house they want is hidden by vine-clogged chain link and a live oak dangling with metal figurines. The front door can't be seen through the bushes. The fence gate is padlocked.

"Let's go around back." The biographer trudges ahead, up the gravel driveway. Between the garage and the house is a high wooden gate, locked as well.

"Did I mess up?" says Mattie. "I double-checked the address five times."

"Let's knock, at least."

Before either of them can, the gate opens. "I saw you on the security cameras," says a young woman with long-tailed cat eyeliner, ink-swirled arms. "You're Delphine?"

"Yeah," says Mattie. "And this is my—"

"Mom," blurts the biographer. They'll take better care of her if the mother is watching.

Mattie stares red-faced at the ground.

"I'm L. Let's get into the van." The woman nods at the garage.

"Van?" they say together.

"We don't do the procedures here at headquarters. We use temporary sites that keep changing. For safety reasons. And I need to ask you to wear masks during the drive."

The biographer laughs. "Are you serious?"

L. drags up the garage's roll door. "Yeah, we take the surveillance state and male-supremacist legislation pretty seriously. Call us crazy."

"No, it's fine," says Mattie.

"Seat belts, please. Then I'll give you the masks. Did you lock your car?"

"Aye, aye!" says the biographer.

Mattie turns from the passenger seat to give her a little frown, and the world is flipped, the order reversed.

The cotton eye mask feels absurd. The van's windows are tinted dark already. But the biographer wishes not to embarrass Mattie further.

"In your phone intake," says L., "you estimated you'd be about twenty-one weeks by now?" The van rattles over a speed bump. "Under optimal conditions, a late second-trimester abortion would require a minimum of two days, to dilate your cervix adequately before the evacuation, but these are not optimal conditions."

A bedside manner almost as delightful as Kalbfleisch's.

L. goes over a few more things—ultrasound, sedative, anesthesia. The biographer scarcely listens: she would really love to be elsewhere. The best she can do is be a body near Mattie, a body able to drive her home. At the word "speculum" she flinches, feeling the many specula Kalbfleisch slid into her. She counts her in-breaths, counts her out-breaths.

Mattie has no questions for L.

Cash only. Pay after. No forms to sign, for obvious reasons, but they do keep confidential patient records, using aliases.

"Delphine, your name for our files will be Ida."

"Okay," says Mattie.

"Hey, Mom," calls L., "any questions back there?"

"Not right now," says the biographer.

They take off their masks and step out of the van into the overgrown backyard of a bungalow. The sky is high and quiet. L.'s hands on their backs, hurrying them. Next to the screen door hangs a piece of wood painted with black letters: POLYPHONTE COLLECTIVE. The biographer strains to summon her Greek mythology. Polyphonte—Aphrodite—Artemis?

L. opens three locks with three keys and ushers them into a bright, purple-walled kitchen that smells like chili. Books, spice jars, pots of cactus, a boardful of yellow peppers in mid-chop.

"Upstairs," says their ferrywoman.

A bedroom's bed has been replaced by an exam table whose stirrups wear red knitted socks. Next to it stands an ultrasound machine. For an eerie beat the biographer thinks it is she who will climb on the table, press her heels into the stirrups, wait for the blue-lubed wand to read the shapes inside her. *You will feel a slight pressure.*

"This is Delphine and her mom," announces L.

"I'm Dr. V.," says a small, beautiful woman in a green medical smock. "I'm gonna take care of you, okay?" She looks South Asian and sounds like the ladies from Queens who live at Dad's retirement village. "Let's get started with your vitals."

"Have you done many of these before?" asks the biographer.

Dr. V. wipes back a strand of silver-black hair. "Thousands." Wraps a blood-pressure cuff around Mattie's biceps. "I worked at Planned Parenthood for almost twenty years. Until the day they shut it down."

Mattie says, "You can go now, um, Mom."

Their providers are skilled. They do not charge a shit ton.

She wants Mattie to be happy. To be safe. To be free from suffering.

Also: she can't stand her.

She hates her for getting to experience the twenty-one weeks of pregnancy she'll never get to experience herself.

There are millions of things the biographer will never do that she doesn't pity herself for missing. (Climbing a mountain, cracking a code, attending her own wedding.) So why *this* thing?

She came prepared to wait, brought a stack of tests to grade, but faced with the prospect of all day in this room of wicker couches and zebra pillows, hot bean smell blowing in from the kitchen, the biographer feels itchy. She wanders into a front hallway, where posters and pamphlets describe the other services offered by the Polyphonte Collective. Sliding-scale mental-health counseling. Sliding-scale legal services for women who are unhoused, undocumented, battered, addicted. Free childcare during court appearances. Cop watching at protests. This house must be their headquarters. It was the first address, in fact, that was a decoy.

The largest poster says:

REPEAL THE 28TH AMENDMENT!

SIT IN / RISE UP FOR REPRODUCTIVE RIGHTS

FEATURED SPEAKERS:

REP. ERICA SALTER (D-PORTLAND)

& DOCTORS FROM WOMEN ON WAVES

MAY 1, OREGON STATE CAPITOL

Up through the gummy darkness in her chest, through the self-pity and resentment, poke thin stalks of gratitude. The Polyphontes aren't just shaking their heads.

She starts to read blue books, pen in hand. *The events that led up to the American Revolutionary War included.* What about events on the second floor? Is Mattie scared? *Three main causes of the war were.* Should the biographer go and check? *The colonists really hated taxes—and still do!*

From the coffee table she picks up a graphic novel about women in the Cretan resistance during World War II. Dark-eyed schoolgirls and crones in cartridge belts lug packs of ammunition up craggy mountainsides. They shoot at German parachutists as they land. They don't just sit there watching.

The biographer falls asleep with her face in a zebra pillow.

Dr. V. shakes her awake. "Time to go, Mom."
"Who?"
"Delphine's fine. All went well. You can be on your way."
The future baby, the kid-to-be, her own—

*It was never yours.*

"L. will drive you back to your car. The sooner you're gone, the safer everyone is. Let's see—she'll be loopy for a bit, from the painkillers. Bleeding is expected, including clots. She can take ibuprofen for cramps. No alcohol, tampons, or sex for at least a week. She's Rh-positive, luckily, and won't need an immune globulin shot. She should be doing a course of antibiotics, but the Collective can't afford them and we certainly can't write scripts—so keep an eye out, okay? Any fever above a hundred, take her straight to the ER. Is this your bag?" Dr. V. passes the biographer her backpack and gestures to the door. "They're waiting."

In the kitchen Mattie sits bundled in her peacoat, drinking a glass of water. She looks sleepy and bleary and younger. Seeing the biographer, she grins wide. "Well," she says, her relief unmistakable, "*that* happened."

L. can't drop them off fast enough. The midnight street makes chirring sounds. Are they being surveilled from a parked car?

"You hungry?" The biographer helps Mattie negotiate the seat belt.

"Nix nought nein."

It comes to her: Polyphonte was one of Artemis's virgin followers. Punished by Aphrodite for—something.

No cars follow them out.

The police probably don't even know the Collective exists.

Unless she's being stupid. Naively ascribing common decency to people in power, as she did before the Personhood Amendment showed all of its teeth.

Aphrodite made Polyphonte fall in love with a bear.

WE NEED COP WATCHERS ON MAY 1ST, said a flyer in the front hall. PLEASE VOLUNTEER!

*Don't be stupid anymore,* she once wrote in her notebook, under *Immediate action required.*

By the time they get to Newville, it will be almost three a.m.

After giving birth to twin bear sons, Polyphonte was turned into an owl.

Is this even the right road?

"Miss?" comes a drowsy little voice.

"Yeah?" She thought this road was taking them to the highway access ramp, but it just keeps going, ramplessly.

"I'm sorry but I have to go to the bathroom."

"Can you hold it for a little while?" The biographer strains to read a sign, faint in the dark. Could there be *one* goddamn streetlight in this city?

"Well it's actually kind of an emergency unless it's another feeling from the, you know, and I don't actually need to but it *feels* like I do?"

Please don't let them be lost. Her phone knows nothing.

The Canadian government is funding a new search mission for Lt. Adolphus Greely and his men. Their survival is not assured: resupply ships have failed to reach the expedition two years in a row. A steam-powered icebreaker named *Khione* leaves from Newfoundland in two months. I will be on that boat, I promise you.

# THE DAUGHTER

The heart of a Canada goose weighs seven ounces. Of a caribou, seven pounds.

The daughter's own heart weighs nothing. Not tonight, at least—no blood in it. All her upper blood is down, replacing what's gone. She's got on a pad and thick sweatpants, and has spread a towel across Ro/Miss's bed. The towel is beige, but a stained towel seems easier to pardon than a sheet. The pad is a little blood diaper. At home there's a picture of her baby self getting changed, fat legs in the air, and Mom, wipe in hand, making a face at the camera.

*Are you mine?*

The daughter is emptying.

She saw no bucket.

It feels weird to be in a teacher's bedroom. Like eavesdropping. This room doesn't give much away, though. No posters or stereo. The only thing on the wall is an old-fashioned map—the kind with dragons drawn in the waves—of the North Pole. On the dresser, two framed photos: her parents, must be, then a younger Ro/Miss next to a handsome guy in a skull T-shirt. Boyfriend? Ex-fiancé?

Saltines and a peeled orange on the bedside table; but her mouth doesn't want anything in it, not even a cigarette. She can't decide what to call this feeling. It isn't sadness. More like a wilting. A deflation. The skin of a balloon after all the air except a breath or two has seeped out.

Zero weeks, zero days.

A soft knock. Ro/Miss's face in the door crack. "How're you feeling?"

"Crampy."

"Want more ibuprofen?"

"Sure you don't mind me taking your bed?"

"My couch is so comfortable." Ro/Miss shakes two caplets onto her palm; the daughter swallows them waterless. "You ready to sleep? It's *really* late."

"What do you call a time-traveling flower shop?"

Ro/Miss raises one eyebrow.

"Back to the Fuchsia," says the daughter.

"Time to sleep?"

"I have an idea for an invention," says the daughter. "Which might not work but would be so incredible if it did. Want to hear it?"

Ro/Miss folds her arms across her chest. "Sure."

"Okay, so, you know how the world is going to run out of energy unless we stop burning oil and make more wind farms?"

"Well, among other things."

"So my idea is to harness whales. You could make very light but strong harnesses, like out of steel thread, and hook them up to super-long steel reins. The reins would be attached to turbines, which would be on their own floating platforms, capturing the energy. There would also be generators on the platforms to convert the energy to electricity."

"That's . . . huh."

The daughter winces at a pinch of dark heat above her pubic bone. "I haven't worked out the details yet. The point is, the whales won't be killed if they're making energy. They'll be treasured."

"Not by Big Coal or Big Oil, but yeah—interesting."

"You think it's dumb."

"Nope, I do not. I think you should probably go to sleep, my dear."

She doesn't want her to leave.

"Would you read to me first?"

Ro/Miss sighs. "What should I read?"

"Anything. Except not poetry or self-help."

"I'll have you know there is not a single self-help book in this house! Okay, that's not true; there might be a few." She tugs the blanket up higher, to the daughter's shoulders. "Warm enough?"

She nods.

Ro/Miss goes out, comes back. Turns the overhead light off and bed-side lamp on. "Close your eyes."

All the News down in Newville sleep deep by the sea.

*Your name for our files will be Ida.*

Throat clearing. Paper rustling. "'As a girl, I loved (but why?) to watch the *grindadráp*. It was a death dance. I couldn't stop looking. To smell the bonfires lit on the cliffs calling men to the hunt. To see the boats herd the pod into the cove, the whales thrashing faster as they panic. Men and boys wade into the water with knives to cut their spinal cords. They touch the whale's eye to make sure it is dead. And the water...'"

Who is this water—girl—Ida—knife—

"'...foams up red.'"

She sleeps.

Off the coast of Greenland they saw the Crimson Cliffs: enormous shoulders of red-stained snow.

"God's blood," said the blacksmith.

"Algae," corrected Mínervudottír.

# THE WIFE

Early to the pub, she stands at the wall reading names of sunk ships. *Antelope. Fearless. Phoebe Fay.*

Please let her stop being a coward.

*Pilots Bride. Gem. Perpetua.*

Please let her children not be scarred.

*Onward. Czarina. Chinook.*

Didier arrives from school, believing their purpose is beer and fried-fish sandwiches. The wife suggests they wait for the after-work crowd to thin. In the little park behind the church, they walk between flower beds thrusting with young stems. Early buds in a warm February. The soil is black and soft from yesterday's rain.

She is a selfish coward.

"Up for darts tonight?" says Didier. "You had an off night last time, true, but—"

"We need to talk about something." She stops walking. *Say it, Susan.*

"Do you have cash for Costello?"

"I think—" *Say it.*

"Because I have none. We can stop on the way home."

"I think we should take a break."

"Huh?"

"From each other."

He narrows his eyes.

"Like a separation," she adds.

"Why?"

"Because it's not"—no breath in her lungs—"good anymore."

Too frightened to look at his face, she concentrates on the blue leather toes of her clogs.

"Susan, I'm looking for the joke with a microscope."

She shakes her head.

"We have stuff that could improve, okay, but everyone does. We can work on it."

"You didn't *want* to work on it," she says.

"You mean the therapy? But that's—"

"It's better this way, anyway."

"Why?" he says softly.

"I'm sorry," says the wife.

Didier's face has gone rubbery. Eyes tight in their shadowed sockets. She sees how he will look as an old man.

He takes out his cigarettes.

"If you keep squinting like that," says the wife, "your eyes might get stuck."

"And if you keep eating like that, your ass might get stuck. In every door."

"I'm going to my parents' tomorrow," she says. "You can stay in the house, for now."

"Oh really? I can stay? In that broke-down bourgeois firetrap?"

But he will. That's the thing. He will judge and dismiss, he will scorn and rage; yet out of sheer laziness, he will stay.

Sucking on his cigarette: "We don't have to decide now."

"Didier."

"Let's talk about it tomorrow, yeah?" On the last word his voice quavers.

"Nothing will be different tomorrow."

She has no plan.

For telling the kids, for making a custody schedule, for finding a job.

Her mother said on the phone this morning, "You've at least opened your own bank account, I hope?" and the wife had to lie.

The only idea in her sore, stalled brain has been: *Tell him.*

He stamps out the cigarette on the gravel path. "You know what I won't miss?"

*Me.*

"Your shitty cooking."

"And I won't miss having three children," says the wife.

"Fuck you, Susan."

The wife kneels on the path.

Rent a car. Open a bank account. Bring yourself to care.

She reaches for the black earth.

Her body yearns, inexplicably, to taste it.

Brings a handful to her lips. The minerals sizzle on her tongue, rich with the gists of flower and bone.

"Hell are you doing?" says Didier.

Bright minerals. Powdered feathers. Ancient shells.

"Jesus, *stop* that!"

She keeps tasting. The soil is bark and needle and flecks of brain, little animal burnt and dead.

Goodbye, shipwrecks.

Goodbye, house.

Goodbye, wife.

Greely's men shot the rest of the sled dogs. They had kept alive their favorites as long as they could; but there was no food. The starving animals had already eaten their leather harnesses. They killed first the one called King, a rascal and a gentleman. His brothers waiting in the dogloo knew they, too, would be killed. Badger, Scruffles, Cricket, Howler, Odysseus, Samson—a bullet for each. The youngest sailor cried, and by the time they reached his meager beard, the tears were buttons of ice. When the Greely expedition was rescued, in June of 1884, this youngest sailor would be dead of

# THE BIOGRAPHER

Knocks cup and cup tips and coffee runs across table onto floor.

When the youngest sailor died, of starvation and exposure, his ship-mates probably ate him. She can only speculate. *I am inserting the speculum into your vagina; you will feel a slight pressure.* After the return to civilization of its six survivors, rumors arose that the Greely expedition had practiced cannibalism. The coffin of one of its dead, a Frederick Kis-lingbury, was exhumed. The body had no skin on it; the arms and legs were attached by ligaments alone. Greely claimed they had carved up Kis-lingbury for bait in shrimp and fish traps, not for themselves.

She paper-towels her brown spill.

Susan once told her she shouldn't be so quick to claim that Mínervu-dottír's life was more meaningful for having left the Faroe Islands. "That's the predictable narrative," said Susan. "But couldn't she have had an equally meaningful life if she'd stayed?"

"Depends what you mean by 'meaningful,'" said the biographer. "I don't see how gutting fish and washing six kids' underwear by hand is equal to doing research in the Arctic Circle."

"Why not?"

"One is repetitive and mindless, and the other is thrilling, coura-geous, and beneficial to the lives of many people."

"If she'd raised six kids," said Susan, "she would've been beneficial to *their* lives."

Mínervudottír had no wool-capped, lamb-fed children to grow.

And Susan has no book. No law career. No job, in fact, at all.

The biographer, strictly speaking, has no book either. Her kitchen table is loaded with overdue library loans about whale hunts and ice—she has read the translation of Mínervudottír's journals a dozen times—yet her manuscript has more holes than words. She wants to tell the story of a woman the world should have known about long before this; so why can't she get done telling it?

The biographer eats the dry rim off a blueberry muffin she found at the back of the teachers' lounge fridge. Forces herself to say: "We haven't talked about your good news."

Penny beams. "Ms. Tristan Auerbach wants the privilege of selling *Rapture on Black Sand* to the highest bidder."

She could be a published author before her seventieth birthday. And if this manuscript sells, the other eight she's written could follow.

"I'm happy for you."

"Listen, honey, you should send Tristan *your* book. I'll recommend you personally."

She should have congratulated Penny sooner—it's been weeks. Mired in her own sludge, she's been avoiding the lounge, begging off Masterpiece mystery nights. Had the biographer found an agent for *Mínervudottír: A Life,* Penny would have baked her a cake the same day.

"I'm not sure a romance agent would be interested in a book with no romance."

"The romance of crushed ships!" says Penny. "The romance of gangrene."

Penny loved her now-dead husband. Loves her little house. Loves writing her entertainments. Didn't have kids because she never felt like it. When the biographer compares such fulfillment with her own sticky craving, it is tempting to despair.

"I apologize, Pen."

"What for?"

"Being a bad friend."

Penny nods. "You've had better years."

"I'm really sorry."

She starts buttoning her turquoise cardigan. "I forgive you. But you better not miss my book party."

"Won't, swear."

"And I think you should apply for Fivey's job."

"Hardy har."

"I do not happen to be joking. You're a good candidate."

The biographer laughs anyway, spewing blue bits of muffin across the lounge.

Climbs to the top of the east stairwell. Sits down against a wall.

The excitement she once felt about a nineteen-year-old biology major's sperm, her willingness to drink a foul but magical tea, her wild hope on that run to Mattie's house—

Gone.

She picks at the laces of her sneakers.

All the doors have closed.

The ones, at least, she tried to open.

How much of her ferocious longing is cellular instinct, and how much is socially installed? Whose urges is she listening to?

Her life, like anyone's, could go a way she never wanted, never planned, and turn out marvelous.

Fingering her shoelaces, she hears the first bell.

Thinks of her brother getting accepted into his first-choice college and gloating, "I'm set."

WE NEED COP WATCHERS! said the flyer at the Polyphonte Collective.

The second bell.

By walking, she tells her students, is how you make the road.

The morning after Portland, Mattie pointed to the photo on her dresser. "He's cute. Who is he?"

"My favorite and only brother," she said.

He wore that skull T-shirt for years, she told Mattie. It was the shirt of a band he loved; she forgets which one. The biographer never had a head for band names or song titles or the music itself, which worried her when she was younger—was she missing something crucial?

She did not tell Mattie that even though Archie graduated with honors from his first-choice college, he was not set.

She did not tell Mattie about finding him, eight years ago, in the kitchen of his apartment. He wore black jeans and no shirt. Lips blue, cheeks flat and white. On the counter was a half-eaten bowl of cereal, bearful of honey, burnt spoon, lighter, glassine packet. The needle lay on the floor beside him.

"Hey, kiddo," says her father. "To what do I owe?"

"Spring break is soon," she says, "and I was thinking of visiting."

"Visiting whom?"

"*You,* genius."

"The Duke of Denturetown? The King of Hemorrhoidia?"

"Can't you just say 'Daughter, I'd love to see you'?"

"I'd love to see you. But bear in mind that spring break in Orlando is a hellscape."

"I'll bear it," she says.

Ice too heavy to proceed. Crew hammering at the pack to save the lead. We are more than a hundred kilometers from Fort Conger, where Greely's expedition is believed to be.

Lead gone. Food and gear dragged onto a floe, tents pitched by the sledges. Cook fills mugs with pea soup and boiled bacon.

We woke to the floes rafting up around the ship. Massive blue-white shelves, thrust vertical by wind and tide, jumped roaring out of the water and smashed at the keel. To my hoard of knowledge I may now add the sound ice makes when it destroys a ship. Booming gun cracks, then a smaller yelping; and from the vibration the ship's bells began ghoulishly to ring. Within hours, says the captain, *Khione* will be sunk.

# THE MENDER

After her motionless weeks in jail, the walk to town feels awful. Her knees are buckling by the time she reaches the Acme.

She keeps her head down against the lights, the stares. One box of licorice nibs. One bottle of sesame oil. Is she inventing the stares? Maybe her mind is buckling too. She hasn't been sleeping well; the memory of bleach keeps waking her.

When they released her, the lawyer was there to take her home. "Hold on to my arm, okay?" he said. "Don't let go." They came out of County Corrections into a chattering snarl of cameras and microphones, and all the microphones were being pushed into her face. Some of them hit her face.

"How's it feel to be free, Ms. Percival?"

"Are you angry at your accusers?"

The lawyer put his mouth on her ear: "Don't say a word."

"Do you plan to sue Dolores Fivey?"

Clicks and flashes.

"What's the next step for you?"

"Any opinion on the local seaweed infestation and the economic losses it's caused?"

"Have you ever provided an abortion?"

Click flash click flash click flash.

"At your accusers?"

"To be free?"

Click. Flash.

"Hello? Gin?" A bright voice behind her.

The mender stops in the aisle. Canned tomatoes make loud red suns across her vision.

"It's me—Mattie."

She turns and blinks at the girl, who is steering a shopping cart; and her mother, who has long gray hair, big teeth when she smiles. The mender has watched them together on Lupatia Street.

"Mom, this is Gin. Gin, this is my mom."

"Pleased to meet you," says the astonished mother. She holds out her hand and the mender shakes it; the skin is dry. "How do you two...?"

"We met at the library," says Mattie Matilda.

"Oh." The mother's eyes relax a little. Kind brown eyes. She has kept the girl safe and well.

"Hello," says the mender stiffly.

She glances at the girl's midsection: flat in a close-fitting sweater. Her hair: less lustrous. Her skin: no darkening patches. How and where did she take care of it? She managed not to get caught. She went a different path. She won't be wondering and forgetting, forgetting and wondering again. Or she will wonder—but not the same way the mender did.

"I'm so glad about your verdict," says Mattie Matilda.

The green of her irises is not the same green as the mender's.

Mine and not mine.

"What a terrible thing to go through," says the mother.

The mender nods.

"They fired Principal Fivey," says Mattie Matilda.

The mender nods.

"We should be on our way," says the mother, "but it was nice to meet you, Ms. Percival." Her cart starts rolling.

"Bye!" The girl waves.

The mender waves back.

Soon it will be February fifteenth: the Roman festival of Lupercalia. And the girl's birthday.

\*     \*     \*

She and Cotter started the girl. The mender, with her body, continued the girl. For a time her clock was full of water and blood and a kicking fish. Which is both important and not important.

He may figure it out himself, once he sees her enough times in town. But he may not. Should she tell him? All that Cotter does for her. The bread on her step each week; the nutmeg pie at Christmas. Hauling Temple's plastic-wrapped body in his truck bed to the harbor, hoisting the body onto a borrowed boat, maneuvering the boat in darkness out of the slip and past the breakwater and into open ocean. Without hesitation he did these things.

The girl is continuing herself. Has no need of Cotter, or of the mender.

But if she ever returns to the cabin of her own accord, she will be welcomed in. Given tea that tastes good. Introduced to Hans and Pinka and the halt hen. (She is already acquainted with Malky.)

The mender pays for the nibs and sesame oil.

Walks back to the forest.

When the track narrows to a footpath, canopied by chain fern and rhododendron and Oregon manroot, she looks for the silver fir with the hourglass resin blister.

*Hello, Temple.*

Alive in the women who've swallowed mixtures made with her skin, her hairs, her eyelashes.

Buried in the sea.

\*     \*     \*

The mender rubs leopard's-bane salve into her burning calves. Lies in the dark with the cat on her chest. No more human voices the rest of the day. She wants only Malky's growl and the *mehhh* of Hans and Pinka. The bleat of the owl, chirp of the bat, squeak of the ghost of the varying hare. This is how Percivals do.

She packed her rucksack with the anemometer and aneroid barometer, a flask of tea, two biscuits. Informed a tentful of card-playing crew she would be back in a few hours.

"If not, we'll whistle for you," said the boatswain, to groggy laughter.

She hadn't been walking long when the fog flew in.

There are many names for fog. Pogonip. Brume. Ground clouds. Gloom. Mínervudottír had written every name in her brown leather notebook. She stood now in a dense, creamy mist, the worst ice fog she'd ever known.

Was her compass damaged? Had she forgotten to bring it?

Bells and sledgehammer = fog signal

She shouted "Help" in three languages.

When her legs were too numb and trembling to lift themselves, she sat down.

No reindeer bag to crawl into.

She thought she heard the ship's bells, but couldn't place their direction.

She drank ten sips of tea.

It was like sitting in a cloud.

*Brother, where are the bells?*

Eivør tried walking again but could see nothing in front of her except whiteness. She was afraid of stepping in a crack in the ice and dropping into the sea.

She sat down again.

Slit lambs hung in the shed, throats red.

*I know which hillside.*

She had no reindeer bag.

*This lamb fed from.*

Survival was not assured. Her eyes were closing. She lay down ~~and slept until~~. She tasted milk-boiled puffin—she was chewing her own cheeks.

*Brother Gunni, bells are the where?*

If she didn't move, her blood would stop.

*Persist,* Eivør told herself.

She stood and staggered on.

# THE DAUGHTER

Dearest Yasmine,

I'm writing this letter from the Math Academy. It's not as amazing as we envisioned, but it's good.

I miss you. Always wondering how you are. What kind of school situation do they have there? Do you still want to do pre-med? My plan is marine biology. I touched a whale's eye on the beach.

Please believe me, Yas: I didn't want to tell anyone. I thought you were going to die so I called them. That was the only reason.

Also: I had ~~a procedure~~ something happen. Three months ago.

When you get out of Bolt River, can we be friends again?

Love,
MATTS

Mínervudottír was found under a pane of ice. They saw her face first, as if pressed up to glass, one cheek flat and white. The blacksmith wrote later, to his wife: *I have never seen an eye opened wider.* She had removed her coat to free herself to fight the current and break the ice. Her fingernails, from scratching, were almost gone.

The search party did not chop open the water to claim the explorer's corpse. They may have crossed themselves, or said prayers, or simply been relieved that one less mouth was alive to feed. *It is odious to lose a woman's body to this wilderness,* wrote the blacksmith to his wife, *but we hadn't the strength to retrieve it.*

# THE BIOGRAPHER

Where does the book end?
It has to stop somewhere.
She has to step out of it.
*Mínervudottír: A Hole.*

Most whales, when they die, don't wash up on beaches. Their carcasses fall to the ocean floor, where they are consumed over time by foragers big and small. A deep-sea whale fall can feed scavengers for fifty years or more.

*Osedax,* types the biographer into her computer, *is a bone-eating worm.*

She peers through the slatted blinds at the heat-slicked lawns and palmettos and fire bush. The air-conditioning is jacked so high she shivers. Dad's condo is a stucco box fastened to a row of other boxes, each with a tiny lanai overlooking the community center. It's not all bad, he says. The community center has a barbershop and shows movies. Every Fourth of July, they serve a decent whiskey punch.

Archie never set foot in Florida. The idea of a retirement village appalled him, and Ambrosia Ridge sounded like a porn name. One of their last arguments was about his refusal to visit. The biographer didn't love retirement villages either, but Dad was here now. Archie called her a pious bureaucrat and hung up.

She calls toward the bedroom: "I'm turning down the AC, okay?"

"Be out in a sec." His bedsprings jounce.

"Don't rush. Breakfast is still in progress."

It will take him time to emerge. When he walks, his pain is conspicuous—the hunched-over shuffling, the pausing every few feet. He waves off the biographer's questions about treatment options. She needs to call his doctor herself.

\*　　\*　　\*

Once her father has shambled in, she explains the Faroese meal laid out on the coral-laminate countertop: boiled puffin eggs (chicken eggs), wind-dried whale blubber (pork bacon), and Shrovetide buns (canned-dough biscuits).

"My doctor says I can't have bacon"—he crams a strip into his mouth—"but blubber is allowed."

"Why can't you?"

"When you're old, they like to prohibit things. How else are they going to fill up those twelve-minute appointments? No bacon, no sugar. And no amorous exertion."

"*Dad.*"

"Oh, relax."

The biographer chews and stares out at the man-made pond. Like many things at Ambrosia Ridge, the pond is depressing and soothing in equal measure. The aerator generates a round-the-clock fountain, proof of fraudulence; yet the little fountain, throwing beads of green sunlight, is actually kind of pretty.

"Let's toast to your mother."

She lifts her cup. "To Mama."

Dad lifts his. "To my dear heart."

The refrigerator whirs. A distant lawnmower revs its motor.

"Should we also," says the biographer.

He nods.

"To Archie," she says.

"To Archer, who was the sweetest little boy." Clears his throat. "To go from such sweetness to—"

Pawning their dead mother's jewelry.

Pushing a steak knife into the fat of Dad's upper arm.

"Peace," says the biographer.

They raise their cups.

Dad eases himself down off the high stool. "This goddamn chair is hell on my back. I'll just stand."

She really needs to call his doctor.

"So today is my birthday," she says.

He slaps his forehead. "What? Jesus, did I forget?"

"We don't need to celebrate, I just—"

"Answer: I did *not*." He takes a folded envelope from his shirt pocket. "Happy birthday, sweetheart."

"Wow, Dad, thank you!"

Inside the envelope is a gift certificate for Rose City Singles, good for two months of online membership and three speed-dating evenings. MEET SINGLES IN OREGON AGES 40+.

"Okay." She takes a long sip of coffee.

"An unconventional gift, I realize, but it might prove useful?"

He lives at Ambrosia Ridge. He's in acute physical pain much of the time. She says mildly, "Thanks," and sets the certificate next to her plate.

"I am a fan of the Shrovetide bun," says Dad, buttering his third.

"I'll buy more dough before I leave. You just twist open the canister and they bake themselves."

"I wish you could stay longer, kiddo."

"Me too." Despite the gift certificate, this isn't a lie.

Reasons I can't:

1. Job

The school term ends in June. But she might apply for Fivey's position. There are some changes she wouldn't mind making. Fewer bubble tests, more music classes. Social-justice and meditation curricula. *Principal Stephens.* A good job for a pious bureaucrat?

Or she could work outside the apparatus, as the Polyphontes do.

After the body of Eivør Mínervudottír sank to the bottom of Baffin Bay, west of Greenland, it entered into many other bodies.

348

\*   \*   \*

She is menstruating when she dies. Strips of burlap wadded into her crotch unfurl in the water, making a brief red cloud. A Greenland shark smells the blood from two miles off; turns in a slow, silent arc; and aims his sleek bulk in the blood's direction.

Crumbs of her skin drift up into the brine channels. Reindeer fur and flannel threads catch on ice dendrites reaching down from the undershelf.

After the apex predators have had their fill, the smaller ones feast: hagfish, lobsters, limpets, clams, brittle stars. Then the amphipods, the bone-eating worms, the bacteria.

A narwhal hunting for air holes drags its shadow across her.

Krill gnaw green blooms of algae off the ceiling of ice.

The explorer comes, over time, apart.

Weeks after digesting Mínervudottír's flesh, the Greenland shark is caught near the western coast of Iceland. The fishermen lop off his head and bury his body in gravel and sand, heap it with stones that press out the shark's natural poisons (urea and trimethylamine oxide). After two or three months, the fish—by now fermented—is sliced and hung in a shed to dry. The pieces grow a brown crust, a shocking smell. When citizens of Reykjavík eat the shark on December 25, 1885, they are eating Eivør Mínervudottír.

She did not leave behind money or property or a book or a child, but her corpse kept alive creatures who, in turn, kept other creatures alive.

Into other bodies she went, but also other brains. The people who read "On the Contours and Tendencies of Arctic Sea Ice" in *Philosophical*

*Transactions of the Royal Society of London* were changed by the explorer. The English translator of her notebooks was changed by her. Mattie, hearing her tell of the *grindadráp,* was changed. The biographer, of course. And if her book has any readers, Mínervudottír will persist in them.

She brought in research that helped pirate ships penetrate the North, guns cocked, drills whetted.

And she brought: *If wrecked in this vessel, we wreck together.*

And she brought: *The name I like best is "pack."*

Instead of applying for the principal job, the biographer could spend the summer at Ambrosia Ridge baking Shrovetide buns, calling doctors, and starting her next book. Go as Dad's date to the Fourth of July picnic.

She could stay in the fog-smoked mountains, applying or not applying, breathing in the Douglas-fir and Scotch pine. The waves thumping, spilling, sucking back.

She wants more than one thing.

To write the last sentence of *Mínervudottír.*
    To write the first sentence of something else.
    To be courteous but fierce with her father's doctors.
    To be a foster mom.
    To be the next principal.
    To be neither.
    She wants to stretch her mind wider than "to have one."
    Wider than "not to have one."
    To quit shrinking life to a checked box, a calendar square.
    To quit shaking her head.

To go to the protest in May.
To do more than go to a protest.
To be okay with not knowing.
*Keep your legs, Stephens.*
To see what is. And to see what is possible.

# ACKNOWLEDGMENTS

I am grateful beyond measure to Lee Boudreaux, whose brilliant editing pushed this book into bolder, deeper territory, and to the phenomenal Meredith Kaffel Simonoff, who is my dream agent in every way.

I've been lucky to work with a magnificent team at Little, Brown. Much gratitude to Carina Guiterman for taking the helm so deftly; to Katharine Myers, Sabrina Callahan, Julie Ertl, and Jenny Shaffer for publicity magic; to Lauren Harms for the stunning cover; to marketing wizards Ashley Marudas and Lauren Passell (clap, clap!); to executive production editor Karen Landry and copyeditor Dianna Stirpe; and to the wonderful Reagan Arthur.

This book's journey through the world owes a great deal to Suzie Dooré, my superb editor in the UK; to Emilie Chambeyron, Charlotte Cray, and Ore Agbaje-Williams at The Borough Press / HarperCollins; to Linda Kaplan, Reiko Davis, Colin Farstad, and Gabbie Piraino at DeFiore and Company; and to Alice Lawson and Katie Robbins. Thank you all.

Thanks to the Money for Women / Barbara Deming Memorial Fund, the Regional Arts and Culture Council, and Portland State University for financial support during the writing of *Red Clocks,* and to the editors of *Tin House, Lenny Letter, Columbia,* and *Winged: New Writing on Bees,* where excerpts from the novel appeared, in different form.

I'm grateful for the generosity and inspiration of Emily Fridlund, Noy Holland, Sam Irby, Miranda July, Kelly Link, Maggie Nelson, Alissa Nutting, Karen Russell, Christine Schutt, Joy Williams, and Lidia Yuknavitch.

For their encouragement, support, and suggestions, I thank Heather Abel, John Beer, Liz Ceppi, Paul Collins, Sarah Ensor, Brian Evenson, Jennifer Firestone, Michele Glazer, Adria Goodness, Amy Eliza Greenstadt, Alastair Hunt, Amanda Huron, Michelle Latiolais, Janice Lee, Nanci McCloskey, Tony Perez, Ruthie Prasil, Peter Robbins, Pete Rock, Shauna

# ACKNOWLEDGMENTS

Seliy, Sophia Shalmiyev, Roger Smith, Anna Joy Springer, Laura Stanfill, Rachel Strasler, Gabe Urza, and Adam Zucker. Special thanks to the early readers of the manuscript: Zelda Alpern, Kate Blackwell, Eugene Lim, and Diana Zumas.

Thank you to my family: Kate, Felix, Diana, Casey, Bridget, Greg, and little Charles. E grazie alla mia famiglia in Italia: Lucia Bertagnolli; Piero, Mauro, e Michele Dipierro; Chiara Berattino; e Federico Zanatta.

Most of all, thank you to Luca, for his fierce and marvelous love, and to Nicholas, for being exactly himself.

# NOTES

Some details of European animal trials are taken from E. P. Evans's *The Criminal Prosecution and Capital Punishment of Animals* (London: William Heinemann, 1906).

"City born of the terror of the vastness of space": W. G. Sebald, "And If I Remained by the Outermost Sea," in *After Nature,* translated by Michael Hamburger (New York: Random House, 2003; first published in German by Eichborn AG [Frankfurt am Main], 1988).

Details of blindness curing and drum shattering are taken from Francesco Maria Guazzo's *Compendium Maleficarum,* translated by E. A. Ashwin (London: John Rodker, 1929; first published in Latin by Apud Haeredes August [Milan], 1608).

"Of all divers, thou hast dived the deepest...And not one syllable is thine"; "Has moved amid this world's foundations...when tossed by pirates from the midnight deck": Herman Melville, *Moby-Dick; or, The Whale* (London: Richard Bentley, 1851).

"When I lay with my bouncing Nell, I gave her an inch, but she took an Ell: But...it was damnable hard, When I gave her an inch, she'd want more than a Yard": John Davies of Hereford, "Wits Bedlam" (1617), in *A Dictionary of Sexual Language and Imagery in Shakespearean and Stuart Literature,* vol. 1, by Gordon Williams (London: Athlone Press, 1994).

"They rob the poor under the cover of law...and we plunder the rich under the protection of our own courage": Captain Samuel Bellamy, as recorded in *A General History of the Robberies and Murders of the Most Notorious Pyrates,* by Captain Charles Johnson [pseud.] (Guilford, CT: Lyons Press, 2010; originally published in 1724).

"I love the old way best, the simple way / Of poison, where we too are strong as men": *The Medea of Euripides,* translated by Gilbert Murray (New York: Oxford University Press [American Branch], 1907; first performed in 431 BC).

# NOTES

"Geography has made us neighbors.... Those whom nature hath so joined together, let no man put asunder": John F. Kennedy, "Address Before the Canadian Parliament in Ottawa" [speech], May 17, 1961, online transcript, The American Presidency Project website, http://www.presidency.ucsb.edu/ws/?pid=8136.

"The red morn betoken'd wreck...to herdmen and to herds": William Shakespeare, "Venus and Adonis," in *The Works of William Shakespeare*, vol. 2, edited by Charles Knight (London: George Routledge and Sons, 1875), ebook.

*"We are the dinosaurs, marching, marching...We are the dinosaurs. We make the earth flat!":* Laurie Berkner Band, "We Are the Dinosaurs," *Whaddaya Think of That?* (New York: Two Tomatoes Records, 1997).

"I have been lifted off the earth to sit on the ocean..." borrows from a line in Virginia Woolf's *The Voyage Out* (London: Duckworth, 1915): "how strangely they had been lifted off the earth to sit next each other in mid ocean..."

"Warm as toast, smaller than most": Margaret Wise Brown, *Little Fur Family* (New York: Harper Brothers, 1946).

Some particulars of Mínervudottír's ice research are taken from Adolphus Washington Greely's *Handbook of Arctic Discoveries* (Boston: Roberts Brothers, 1896).

## ABOUT THE AUTHOR

Leni Zumas is the author of the story collection *Farewell Navigator* and the novel *The Listeners,* which was a finalist for the Oregon Book Award. She teaches in the MFA program in creative writing at Portland State University.

# THE PSEUDONYMS OF GOD

# THE
# PSEUDONYMS
# OF GOD

## by ROBERT McAFEE BROWN

THE WESTMINSTER PRESS
Philadelphia

ISBN 0-664-20930-0 (CLOTH)
ISBN 0-664-24948-5 (PAPER)

LIBRARY OF CONGRESS CATALOG CARD No. 77-178813

PUBLISHED BY THE WESTMINSTER PRESS
PHILADELPHIA, PENNSYLVANIA ®

PRINTED IN THE UNITED STATES OF AMERICA

# Contents

# Introduction: "Christianity And..."

The early working title for this collection of essays, "Christianity And . . . ," was meant to convey that Christianity cannot be understood in a vacuum, but only in relation to other aspects of human existence. The theme, if not the title, has persisted in spite of the warning of C. S. Lewis' senior devil, Screwtape, that such thinking serves only to encourage the demonic hierarchy below:

> What we want [Screwtape writes to Wormwood], if men become Christians at all, is to keep them in the state of mind I call "Christianity And." You know—Christianity and the Crisis, Christianity and the New Psychology, Christianity and the New Order, Christianity and Faith Healing, Christianity and Psychical Research, Christianity and Vegetarianism, Christianity and Spelling Reform. If they must be Christians, let them at least be Christians with a difference. Substitute for the faith itself some Fashion with a Christian colouring. Work on their horror of the Same Old Thing.[1]

The present title, THE PSEUDONYMS OF GOD, was finally chosen because it better describes the intent of the essays, even though it may initially sound less clear. (When I queried the publisher about the possible esoteric nature of the word "pseudonyms," I got the reply that in the present climate of opinion the word "God" might seem even more esoteric.) As the essays in Part II make clear, the theme is borrowed from the writings of the Italian novelist Ignazio Silone, who repeatedly suggests that God is found in unexpected places today, assuming strange or false names (e.g., pseudo names) and confronting us where we least anticipate his presence.

Example: On the day on which this introduction was completed, the San Francisco *Chronicle* carried two front-page stories side by side. In one of them, Daniel Ellsberg was surrendering himself to the federal authorities and facing a prison sentence of up to ten years for releasing "the Pentagon papers" to the public, because of his conscientious conviction that Americans need to know how their Government misled them into a needless war that has killed hundreds of thousands of innocent people. In the adjoining column, Billy Graham, a Christian evangelist who has never publicly opposed the expansion of the Vietnam war, was exhorting his followers to affirm the bumper-sticker slogan "America: Love It or Leave It," and insisting that we should be praising our nation rather than criticizing it. In which column was the prophetic word of God being spoken? It seems to me patently clear that on this occasion God was speaking through Mr. Ellsberg rather than through Mr. Graham. The theme of the "pseudonyms of God" insists that God cannot be confined to our churches, our theologies, or our "religious" actions, and may be working more through "secular" communities, "secular" thought, and "secular" actions than we care to admit. To acknowledge this is, of course, to acknowledge that the traditional "sacred-secular" dichotomy has to go by the boards, and to insist, as a result, that God can work wherever he chooses to do so.

Since the essays in this volume attempt to illustrate various facets of the overall theme, they should be able to stand on their own feet, and a brief rationale for their grouping and ordering will suffice.

Part I, "Adventures in Theological Self-awareness," attempts to trace my increasing recognition that Christians must listen to the world as well as speak to it. The first essay offers a fairly solid 1960 theological statement, and the subsequent essays show how that position, although basically unchanged, has been subjected to remolding and reshaping by the events of the ensuing decade.

Part II, "The Pseudonyms of God," develops the specific theme of the book in more detail, setting it in the context of other attempts to account for the remoteness of God from modern life. It also indicates some of the more explicitly Biblical and Christian overtones of the theme.

Part III, "Discovering God's Pseudonyms Today," offers a variety of specific examples of the pseudonyms I believe God is using today. These essays attempt to show how God is working on the educational scene, in the political arena, and in such unlikely experiences as death, imprisonment, and civil disobedience.

The final section of Part III, "Vietnam and the Exercise of Dissent: A Fragment of History," is slightly different in tone and intention. From about 1964 to the present, my theological life has been dominated by the conviction that the American presence in Southeast Asia represents an almost unmitigated horror. This book is not the place to spell out the reasons for that conviction,[2] but it is the place to illustrate some of the ways in which that conviction has been expressed. I have tried to show how my theological convictions about war, the state, and dissent were gradually sharpened and directed by the course of outer events. My basic position on dissent was clear long before Vietnam was an issue, but Vietnam forced me into more specific expression of that concern than would otherwise have been the case. I offer these papers as a fragmentary case study of how the world informs and transforms a theological position, to illustrate my belief that theology is forged through engagement instead of detachment, on pavements more than in libraries, and in the midst of ambiguities rather than clarities.

Since most of these essays originated in response to specific situations, the source and date of original publication is indicated at the beginning of each one. Minor changes have been made to eliminate overlapping, and to remove slight anachronisms resulting from the interval between original composition and present publication.

If there is any personal debt these pages seek to repay, it is to the one who taught me most about "Christianity and the world," Reinhold Niebuhr. His death, during the time this book was being prepared for the press, has reminded me once again of how permanent is the imprint of this truly great man upon the American—and world—scene. In him, God assumed no pseudonym, but was directly and marvelously present.

## NOTES

1. C. S. Lewis, *The Screwtape Letters* (The Macmillan Company, 1943), p. 126.

2. For a more detailed accounting, cf. "Vietnam: Crisis of Conscience," *The Catholic World*, Oct., 1967, reprinted in M. E. Marty and D. G. Peerman (eds.), *New Theology, No. 6* (The Macmillan Company, 1969), pp. 229-242; "Why I Oppose Our Policy in Vietnam," *Presbyterian Life*, Jan. 15, 1968, pp. 14-17, 38-39; and more fully, *Vietnam: Crisis of Conscience* (with Michael Novak and Abraham Heschel) (Association Press, Behrman House, Herder & Herder, Inc., 1967), esp. pp. 7-9 and 62-106.

# I
## ADVENTURES
## IN THEOLOGICAL SELF-AWARENESS

# Theology as an Act of Gratitude

## GRATITUDE AND GRACE

In the years that I have taught theology, it has become increasingly clear to me that the distinctive word in the Christian vocabulary is the word "grace." That God is gracious to us, that he loves us no matter how unlovable we may be, that he visits us in the midst of our distresses when we have no claim whatsoever upon his attentions, that he identifies himself wholly with us, that he changes our situation by what he does—all of this is the heart and center of the Christian gospel, and all of it may be conveniently summed up under the word "grace." God as revealed in Jesus Christ is a gracious God. This is the gospel we preach. It is also the gospel we teach.

And if grace is the distinctive word to describe God's attitude toward us, there is also a word that describes the nature of the response we are called upon to make. That word is "gratitude." Gratitude is what must characterize our dealings with God because grace is what characterizes God's dealings with us.

If the real test of a theological affirmation is whether or not

Inaugural address as Auburn Professor of Systematic Theology at Union Theological Seminary, given in Oct., 1960, and subsequently published in the *Union Seminary Quarterly Review,* Special Issue, Dec., 1960. Used by permission.

it can be sung—and that may be the most important test—then the affirmation of gratitude is a particularly resonant Protestant affirmation. And there is one hymn that, more than any other, expresses this stance of gratitude. It is a hymn that seems to be the appropriate one for every occasion of worship. I find myself wanting to use it at the conclusion of every sermon I preach, so that it will confirm the fact of the good news, in case my own proclamation has been faulty. It is the hymn that seems most appropriate after a baptism. It is the hymn that gathers up our sense of gratitude after a wedding. It is the hymn par excellence to be sung after we have celebrated the Sacrament of the Lord's Supper, the Eucharist, the very service of thanksgiving and gratitude. It is the appropriate hymn to sing before or after a meal, and was in fact originally written to be sung as a grace. It is the hymn that I fervently hope will be sung at my funeral. It is the hymn that sums up what our reaction to the gospel must be, and describes what kind of people we must be because of the gospel. It is the hymn "Now Thank We All Our God."

Now thank we all our God with heart and hands and voices,
Who wondrous things hath done, in whom his world rejoices;
Who, from our mothers' arms, hath blessed us on our way
With countless gifts of love, and still is ours today.

O may this bounteous God through all our life be near us,
With ever joyful hearts and blessed peace to cheer us;
And keep us in his grace, and guide us when perplexed,
And free us from all ills in this world and the next.

All praise and thanks to God the Father now be given,
The Son, and him who reigns with them in highest heaven,
The one eternal God, whom earth and heaven adore;
For thus it was, is now, and shall be evermore.

Why are we people who must be grateful? Simply because God is the gracious God; because, as the hymn puts it, he has done "wondrous things"; because in Jesus Christ he has visited and redeemed his people; because "God was in Christ reconciling the world unto himself"; because the world, this sorry world of ours, is a world into which God has come, a world that he has transformed, a world that is the scene of the victory he wrought over the powers of evil in the cross and resurrection. This seems to me truer and truer every day. The more I read the New Testament, the more I find this the presupposition without which the New Testament would never have been written. The more I read the daily paper, the more I realize that this is the only way in which the chaos and frightful ugliness and terror of modern life can be understood apart from bleak despair.

Now I am quite aware that to say that we live in a redeemed world, or that God in Christ has wrought a cosmic victory over the powers of evil, or that Jesus really meant it when he said not only, "In the world you have tribulation," but also really meant it when he went on to say, "But be of good cheer, I have overcome the world"—I am aware that to say these things is not only to sound naïve but also to involve oneself with a lot of tough theological problems: Why doesn't the world look more redeemed? Why is God's activity so hidden? How can we really believe that "the Lord our God is good, his mercy is forever sure," when all, or at least most, of the evidence seems to point in precisely the opposite direction? All I will say to this at the moment is that I would rather be saddled with problems of that sort, which arise because the gospel evokes confident affirmation, than be saddled with the dilemma of having no more to offer than the hesitant postulate that it may turn out that God will somehow possibly swing the balance of things in his favor more or less, though of course we're not yet sure. On those terms, it seems to me, there would be no gospel to preach. Consequently, the gospel I affirm is the good news that we live in God's world, a world which in Christ he has invaded and conquered. In this world we will surely have tribulation, but we can be of good cheer, for he has overcome the world.

Since this has happened, we can be grateful. All we really can do is to live lives of gratitude. Because God is gracious, we are to be grateful.

> *Charis* always demands the answer of *eucharistia* [writes Karl Barth, i.e., grace always demands the answer of gratitude]. Grace and gratitude belong together like heaven and earth. Grace evokes gratitude like the voice an echo. Gratitude follows grace like thunder [follows] lightning.[1]

Now, there are many ways in which we can be grateful. We can pray. We can engage in politics. We can love our families. We can build buildings. We can be theologians. My particular way of trying to be grateful is to be a theologian. This is what it seems to me the grace of God calls upon me to do—to show my gratitude by trying to think out loud, as it were, about what his grace means. I hasten to add that these ways of being grateful are not mutually exclusive ways. Theology is not an alternative to praying; the more I theologize, the more I am convinced that it is hollow if it does not grow out of the attempt to pray. Theology is not an alternative to loving one's family, though I must add that it often seems to cut into time that rightfully belongs to one's family. Nor does theology exempt one from trying to build buildings to the glory of God. So there are many ways of being grateful.

What attitudes, then, must be brought to the theological task if theology is indeed a response of gratitude for the gift of grace? Let me suggest four things that flow from the basic consideration that theology is an act of gratitude.

## 1. *Christian Theology as a Confessional Theology*

First of all, Christian theology will be a *confessional theology*. The one who speaks is himself grateful. Better, I who speak am myself grateful. I do not as a theologian merely describe why other people are grateful. I also try to tell other people why I am grateful. As a Christian theologian, I am a believing theologian, a confessing theologian. I am not so much reporting at arm's length what "they" out there believe, as I am confessing where I stand. And I ought to be able to do this in such a way that the listener could at least respond, "Well of course if I could believe *that,* I would be grateful too." I may not be able to convince him that it is true—and nobody ever argued anybody else into the Kingdom of God— but at least he ought to be able to see why I am grateful, and realize that if grace is real, gratitude is every bit as real, and that both are real to me.

Now this first point may seem very obvious, but I stress it because it seems to be far from obvious to many people of my own theological generation, who apparently feel that it is cheating with the evidence and distorting its academic integrity to indicate one's own involvement in it. Consequently, I feel compelled to take issue with those who say that the theologian can legitimately disengage himself from his subject matter. I am dubious of the approach that says: "Where I stand theologically doesn't matter. I simply lay out the various options for the students." No, this is really to say that the subject matter of theology, while it may be very interesting stuff, isn't really a life and death matter for me, and therefore need not be a life and death matter for anyone else. The alternative is not to sell a particular theological line—a point to which I shall return in a moment. The alternative is to make the student aware that the subject matter of theology really makes a difference. If theology is an act of gratitude, then it must be a confessing theology, a theology with which I as a theologian proclaim my own involvement and therefore my own gratitude.

## 2. Christian Theology as a Church Theology

But to say this is not enough. For the faith I confess in gratitude is not a faith I have invented, but a faith I have received; not a faith that is the response of my intellect, but a faith to which my intellect must make response. Theology as an act of gratitude is not my solitary act of gratitude, but an expression of the gratitude of the entire Christian community. Theology is not only confessional theology, it is also a *church theology.*

I have no right to teach a faith that is simply *my* faith, but I have every right and duty to teach a faith that is the church's faith, a faith that I have received and appropriated as the gift of God to me through his church. Schleiermacher makes the point in the Prolegomenon to *The Christian Faith*:

> Since Dogmatics is a theological discipline, and thus pertains solely to the Christian Church, we can only explain what it is when we have become clear as to the conception of the Christian Church. . . . The present work entirely disclaims the task of establishing on a foundation of general principles a Doctrine of God, or an Anthropology or Eschatology either, which should be used in the Christian Church though it did not really originate there, or which should prove the propositions of the Christian Faith to be consonant with reason.[2]

The point is that theology is not some self-sufficient discipline of some self-sufficient individual, i.e., me; theology is an activity of the church, an expression of the faith of the church, and therefore—no more but no less—the servant of the church. It is the church being grateful. The church's theology is not an end in itself, but merely a tool to help the church do its job better. So when I speak as a theologian, I am not speaking just for myself, though I must always take responsibility for what I say and for the fact that I may have corrupted what needs to be said because of my own deficiencies as a theologian. What I am called upon to do is to articulate the faith by which the communion of saints has lived, lives, and will continue to live. Since God has been gracious to his community, his community must live in grateful response, and theology is one of the niches within the total life of the church where this grateful response is expressed.

I spent Pentecost in 1960 in East Berlin. On that day, a German-speaking Swiss pastor and I conducted the service of

Holy Communion in a Lutheran parish church behind the Iron Curtain. It fell to me to say before the bread was distributed to people living deep in the East Zone, "Take and eat this bread in the sure and certain faith that Christ died for you, and feed on him in your heart by faith *with thanksgiving*." In gratitude! How could I, R. M. Brown, comfortable, well-fed, much-too-complacent Westerner, tell East Germans who live in constant danger of life and livelihood because they do such reckless things as coming to Communion services, how could I tell them to be grateful? I, of course, as R. M. Brown, could tell them no such thing, but I, as an ordained minister of the church of Jesus Christ, was the appointed means through whom they could be told that because the promises of God are true, and Christ did die for them, they could live in the East Zone—in the East Zone!—with a song of gratitude on their lips. I had no right to say, "I tell you on my authority to be full of gratitude." But I had every right, as the proclaimer and transmitter to them of the bread of life, to tell them that because it *was* the bread of life, they not only could and should, but must, be grateful. In a very special way I know, because of that celebration of the Eucharist, that *charis* is answered by *eucharistia,* that grace is answered by gratitude. But this was not my insight; it was, and is, the very lifeblood of the church.

## 3. *Christian Theology as a Listening Theology*

Since neither I nor the church invented the faith we are called upon to share, Christian theology is not only a confessional theology and a church theology, it is also a *listening* theology. The theologian earns the right to speak only when he has subjected himself to the discipline of listening. There are at least three directions in which the theologian must listen if he is to be a faithful listener.

a. The theologian must listen first of all *to the Bible.* If we believe that God has acted decisively in Jesus Christ, then our starting point must surely be the place where we learn most directly that this is so. We always seem ready to admit that Christ is the Omega, the last, and that all sorts of theological and even philosophical trails can lead to him, however deviously they may wind before they get there. But we must also be more courageous about affirming that he is the Alpha as well, the first as well as the last, and that if theology is to be *Christ*-ian theology, it must not only end with Christ but also start with him. This means, the minute we try to be the least bit specific, that we start with the Bible, since all other materials about Christ are derivative from the Biblical materials. The Biblical listening may be very sophisticated, and it will surely make use of all the cultural and hermeneutical tools at our disposal, but it will remain central to our task, unless we want to end up in a subjectivist morass.

b. In addition to listening to the Bible, the theologian must also listen *to the church*, or, just to make it sound very suspicious, to tradition. We must simply face the fact that we read the Bible in the light of various traditions—Lutheran, Reformed, sectarian, liberal, orthodox, or whatever—and recognize that we can never entirely disassociate ourselves from them. We can no more leapfrog over nineteen centuries to the New Testament, as though the intervening centuries had not occurred and conditioned the way we understand the Biblical materials, than we can be in two places at once. We do *not* start from scratch in every theological generation. We start as recipients of all that has come before, and we must examine *critically* all that has come before. Our forefathers could be wrong and frequently were. Sometimes they were brilliantly wrong, sometimes obstinately so—as useful a distinction as any, I suppose, between heretics and schismatics. But before we dismiss them as wrong we must listen to them gratefully, for at many points they were right. Before we dismiss them as wrong we must appropriate from them what was right. The burden of proof is not first of all upon the Christian heritage to prove itself to me, the burden of proof is first of all upon me when I reject some part of the Christian heritage that has con-

sistently commended itself to others. This is merely an elabo-
rate way of saying that the corporate convictions of the communion of saints over two thousand years are probably a little
more mature than the individual convictions of this particular
"saint" after forty years of sporadic reflection.

c. But in addition to listening to the Bible and the church,
the theologian must also listen *to the world*. Now to say just
how we are to listen to the world would be the subject for another book. I would almost settle here for an overlooked passage in Calvin's *Institutes,* in which he says:

> Whenever, therefore, we meet with heathen writers, let
> us learn from that light of truth which is admirably dis-
> played in their works, that the human mind, fallen as it
> is, and corrupted from its integrity, is yet invested and
> adorned by God with excellent talents. If we believe that
> the Spirit of God is the only fountain of truth, we shall
> neither reject nor despise the truth itself, wherever it
> shall appear, unless we wish to insult the Spirit of God.[3]

We must listen to the world, then, for at least two reasons.
First of all, whatever else we are, we are men of the world,
and do not cease being men of the world when we become
theologians. If I ever have any minimal success in trying to
communicate the gospel to twentieth-century man, it will be
in part at least because I too am a twentieth-century man, because I too live with the doubts of my contemporaries, because I too keep being amazed at the incredible character of
the Christian claim and have to fight the battle of unbelief
within myself just as other men do. But this is not the most
important reason why the theologian must listen to the world.
The most important reason is simply because the world is God's
world. Because he has been pleased to act within it in a life and
a death and a resurrection, we must be confident that having
set his mark upon it, he may also be acting within it at many
other places too. Since we have seen him at work in the world
of Jesus Christ, we must be prepared to see him at work in

other places in the world that Jesus Christ redeemed. We must listen to the world because it is the world that God loved so much that he sent his only begotten Son into it. Our theology does not separate us from the world. It ties us more closely than ever to it.

## 4. Christian Theology as a Modest Theology

Finally, theology must be a *modest theology,* a theology always subject to correction. Because it is so overwhelmed by the magnitude of what it has heard, it must be humble in its own report of what it has heard. I am aware that there is nothing more arrogant than a statement in praise of humility. But at the risk of inverted arrogance, I must stress the point. Theology must never claim too much for itself. It is not the real thing. It is only the faintest echo of the real thing. Commenting on all the fuss that has been made about his *Church Dogmatics,* Karl Barth says:

> The angels laugh at old Karl. They laugh at him because he tries to grasp the truth about God in a book of Dogmatics. They laugh at the fact that volume follows volume and each is thicker than the previous one. As they laugh, they say to one another, "Look! Here he comes now with his little pushcart full of volumes of the Dogmatics!" And they laugh about the men who write so much about Karl Barth instead of writing about the things he is trying to write about. Truly, the angels laugh.[4]

Thus no Protestant theologian has a right to be too impressed by his own theologizing.[5] There is something comic, if not downright absurd, about the claim that a human creature can penetrate the veil of holiness surrounding the transcendent God, or describe with accuracy the events that took place when God penetrated that veil himself in the incarnation of his Son.

Rule One for every theologian ought therefore to be, "Don't take yourself too seriously." This is a very different thing from saying, "Don't take your faith seriously." It means that all our attempts to express our faith must include an echo of laughter. In this case it will not merely be the heavenly laughter of Barth's angels, but our own very human laughter as well. It will sometimes be the laughter of self-mockery at the notion that our fleshly words can encompass the Word made flesh. But it can also be the laughter of delight and pure joy that through the disclosure of his Word in Jesus Christ, God has seen fit to allow his creatures the audacity of forming words about him.

Authentic religious language is finally not the language of the classroom or the lecture hall, but the language of liturgy and prayer. Singing one of Luther's hymns is usually a deeper act of gratitude than reading *The Bondage of the Will*. Praying one of Calvin's prayers is usually a deeper act of gratitude than reading his *Letter to Cardinal Sadolet*. And Protestants, when all is said and done, express their gratitude more adequately in their hymns and prayers than in their theologizing. But if theology can help us to be grateful by teaching us to sing and pray, it will not have been in vain.

## NOTES

1. Karl Barth, *Church Dogmatics*, Vol. IV, Part 1, ed. by G. W. Bromiley and T. F. Torrance (Charles Scribner's Sons, 1956), p. 41.

2. Friedrich Schleiermacher, *The Christian Faith* (Edinburgh: T. & T. Clark, 1928), Ch. 1, para. 2, p. 3.

3. John Calvin, *Institutes of the Christian Religion* (The Westminster Press, n.d.) II, ii, xv; cf. further on this point, "Assyrians in Modern Dress."

4. *Antwort, Karl Barth sum siebzigsten Geburtstag* (Zollikon-Zurich: Evangelischer Verlag AG, 1956), p. 895, my translation.

5. In what follows I have slightly adapted material from the Foreword to R. M. Brown, *The Spirit of Protestantism* (Oxford University Press, 1961).

# A Campaign on Many Fronts:
# A Report on "How I Am
# Making Up My Mind"

*How* one makes up his mind is partly conditioned by *where* he makes it up, and my locale has recently shifted. Geographically, the move has been a move from Union Theological Seminary to Stanford University. Theologically, the move has been from Jerusalem to Athens. But the move was undertaken out of a conviction that if the theological venture is really justified, it must be able to sustain itself not only in the supportive atmosphere of a seminary community but in the indifferent atmosphere of a secular university. This does not mean that there are not devoted Christians among the Stanford faculty and student body, but it does mean that they—and we—constitute a small minority indeed, and that my contacts from day to day and even hour to hour are chiefly with those who simply aren't involved in many of the things about which I care deeply.

Theologically, I have come to terms with the fact that I nevertheless share many things with these people. Their passion and devotion to politics and civil rights puts mine to shame. We can make common cause on many fronts. We are upset at injustice. We want peace. We believe in the right of dissent. Sometimes we occupy different sides of the hyphen that sepa-

Originally published in *The Christian Century,* May 5, 1965, in the series "How I Am Making Up My Mind," and subsequently reprinted in Dean Peerman (ed.), *Frontline Theology* (John Knox Press, 1967). Copyright 1965 by The Christian Century Foundation. Reprinted by permission.

rates "Judeo-Christian." More frequently we simply share a common humanity.

How does the Christian faith fit into this sort of situation? Plenty of people are obviously living good, decent, even compassionate lives without it. Many are, of course, filled with a sense of emptiness (no contradiction, that) but I have gotten past the point of trying to convince happy and committed persons how unhappy they *really* are if they would only take the time and trouble to find out. If this is a description of Bonhoeffer's elusive "world come of age," then I know what he was writing about. To be sure, some of this contentment is veneer, and the veneer wears thin when a President is assassinated or a student commits suicide. But to a great number of these people, friends of mine, it would never remotely cross their consciousness that Christianity had something important to say to them, either in the crises or in the day-to-day routines. What more can we say than Camus to them hath said?

This is the background against which I am "making up my mind." The picture isn't complete without those members of the community (both students and faculty) who *do* care, who *are* disturbed, whose skepticism is always tinged with wistfulness, and whose faith has been purged of sentimentality. But they, and I, are a remnant, and I get the increasing feeling that for *our* day, Christianity must be the religion of the remnant, and that the true household of believers will not be distinguished by its numbers or its outward strength. I see no evidence that we are on the threshhold of a new Age of Faith. So I am "making up my mind" as part of a remnant, amid a vast company of colleagues, the great majority of whom couldn't care less.

## A HERITAGE TO TRANSMIT—CRITICALLY

My stance in this situation is that of genus Protestant, species Presbyterian. My roots are here, not of my own choosing, but because this is the tradition in which I have been nurtured, and I would find no reason to desert it for other ecclesiastical pastures that might occasionally seem greener, unless and until it should seem to me a sin to remain where I am.

I do not, from this stance, re-create the Christian faith for myself from day to day. I have received an inheritance—a faith with a tradition extending back from myself to the apostles (even though the lines of connection aren't quite as tidy in my tradition as they are claimed to be in some others). I am reluctant to jettison this heritage with the ease that some of my Protestant contemporaries appear to be in process of jettisoning theirs. The tradition is not so much called upon to commend itself to me, as I am called upon to be receptive to it. I must first learn before I presume to judge. This does not make me particularly "orthodox," and I would find myself in trouble with a good many presbyteries. But it does give me a responsibility to be faithful to that heritage. Fidelity may involve reinterpretation. Indeed, I am sure it does. But I must always be sure that what gives me difficulty is not simply the result of my own faulty vision. If I turn my back on "Scripture and the Fathers," I am not sure that my resultant message can be commended to others for any reason save the fact that it is *my* message, and since I find it exceedingly difficult to take myself that seriously, I must acknowledge that others would find it even more so. I preach not myself.

I stand, then, in a relationship to a heritage. It may be a critical relationship, but it is a relationship nonetheless to which I must be faithful. I am not about to sue for a divorce, even though I occasionally need the help of a marriage counselor.

## Two Directions of Concern

As I try to communicate what I hear in that tradition, I find myself now doing so in relation to two other and very different factors. Let one of them be described simply as that bent, doubting, questioning entity, *the world*. I cannot theologize in a vacuum, or in exclusively ecclesiastical surroundings (the vacuous content of which I leave for the moment unexplored). I must theologize in terms of the world of modern man. If I could sometimes forget that world in the seminary community, I can never forget it in the university community. It is where I live, work, eat, lecture, argue, hang my hat, and marvel. It is not simply "over there" somewhere, confronting me—it is in me, and I am in it. Its doubts are my doubts. Its sins are my sins. If I ever communicate to this world, it is because I know its accents. Students are sometimes surprised that I speak as highly as I do of Albert Camus. What I have to tell them is that there is a part of me to which Camus speaks, a part of me that utters a hearty "Amen" to what I hear from him, a part of me that is not concerned to "refute" him, but rather wants to take up arms with him against the foes we both despise, even though we get our orders to do so through different chains of command. So I will neither scorn nor condemn this world, nor act condescendingly toward it, even though I cannot find my final peace within it.

The other factor that guides my attempt to rearticulate the Protestant faith is *Roman Catholicism*. And I am thus in something of a bind. For it is quite a trick to look upon the unbelieving world and relate to it, and simultaneously to look upon the believing Catholic Church and relate to it. If my common cause with the world is my doubt, my common cause with the Catholic is my faith. The things I can most easily assert to either one are the things most difficult to assert to the other.

It takes a certain dexterity to move from the realm where all things must be doubted to the realm where most things can be presupposed. [It should be obvious that these lines were written before the recent radical self-questioning within Roman Catholicism had surfaced.] But I have no option apart from trying to develop that dexterity, for if I cannot make up my mind oblivious to the world, no more can I make up my mind oblivious to Roman Catholicism. I have learned much about the Christian faith from my associations with Roman Catholics in

the last five years, and there are few things I would less willingly forgo for the next five, than that ongoing relationship. I
am quite as ready now to read Karl Rahner as John Calvin,
and to learn from Hans Küng as from Martin Luther. In doing
so, I feel a sense not of betrayal, but rather of enrichment.
Withal, I do not secretly wish I were a Roman Catholic, nor do
I nurse a deep desire to become one, whatever doubt some of
my militant party-line Protestant friends may have on that
score. If I am to see the Christian faith afresh today I cannot
make up my mind without trying to see—nay, feel—its Catholic as well as it Protestant nuances.

## THE CATALYST OF DOUBT

As if a simultaneous concern for the unbelieving world and
the believing Catholic Church were not complication enough,
a dialectic of faith and doubt also informs the way I am making up my mind. I am aware that Calvin has some remarkable
passages on doubt, but I am also aware that this problem did
not ruffle his theological beard unduly. But for many of us
today, however, doubt has become an important ingredient of
faith. I would not have chosen this to be the way, and I do not
cherish doubt or love it, but I would be surprised, and even
disturbed, I think, if it were suddenly whisked away. For it is
not merely a descriptive fact about my life, but even one of
the tools of my trade, in the sense that the presence of doubt
keeps theology from being stagnant. I, at least, am never at
the place where thinking can cease because the problems have
all been solved. I am always at the place where thinking must
continue because old problems have a pesky way of reappear-
ing, and old answers have a disconcerting way of losing
power. This place, I would like to believe, is the location of
any live theology. So I must acknowledge the reality of doubt,
not simply to make common cause with modern man, but be-

cause doubt is the price that must be paid for theological growth. Faith without doubt is dead.

But I must also confess (and thereby risk some of that cherished rapport with modern man) that, save in the low moments, doubt does not have for me quite the terror it once did. I would naturally prefer less of it rather than more, but even when the "more" is oppressively upon me, I find myself able to draw increasing comfort from a fact so obvious that I do not know why its obviousness was hidden from me for so many years: to say that I doubt the reality of God is to say something about *myself*, but not necessarily to say anything about God. That his reality should depend on how I happen to feel about him, strikes me as ludicrous in the extreme, and I can usually gain a restoration of perspective by reflecting on that fact. There are long periods of time when I am existentially unaware of God's presence, and at such times I find no particular reason, in my own "feelings" or convictions or theological reflections, to continue believing in him. But I am willing to believe that this is a manifestation of the dimness of my own sight rather than a manifestation of his unreality. The fact that I do not, at a given moment, "see" the sun, does not mean that the sun is not there. My eyes may be closed. There may be a heavy layer of clouds. I may be looking in the wrong direction. It may be nighttime. *Mutatis mutandis* . . .

This is one of my difficulties in trying to relate to the "God is dead" theology. Its adherents seem to me finally to be saying, "We are no longer aware of the reality of God, nor are most of our fellowmen. Therefore, God is dead." That these are accurate autobiographical statements I do not doubt. That they describe the temper of modern man is beyond dispute. But that they say very much about the reality or unreality of God seems to me more dubious. Autobiographical statements and descriptions of modern unbelief are not necessarily *theological* statements. And here lies my other difficulty with the "God is dead" approach. For the assertion that God is dead has been with us for a long time in Western history. The new factor is simply that many who make the statement now make it from within the Christian conviction about the meaning of life and death and God and man.

Is it so very perverse and old-fashioned to identify these statements as bits of information about the state of mind of the speakers but not bits of information about the object of the speaker's speech? The temptation in this "new" theological approach seems to me the temptation that faces every theological generation. It was put with clarity by Msgr. Ronald Knox, when he said of the book *Foundations* that it seemed to be framed as an answer to the question: How much can Jones be persuaded to swallow? How little, in other words, can one believe, and still be a Christian? Which is a bit like asking, How little is it permissible to love one's wife?

That the gospel should be a scandal and a stumbling block is nothing new. We had better not glory—or rather, wallow—in the scandal as though that exempted us from the task of communication, but we had also better not take for granted that the task of communication is simply to remove the scandal, to settle for whatever Jones will, in fact, swallow. When I try to explain some area of Christian faith to one of the *pagani* and he finally responds with, "Oh well, if *that's* all it means, of course I can accept that," I am left with the uneasy feeling that I have been an unfaithful transmitter. Christian faith is not just sanctified despair nor ethics tinged with concern. Nor, when we shout *"man!"* in italics with an exclamation point or two, have we necessarily whispered "God."

As I continue to make up my mind, then, I feel a particular responsibility not to transform the faith into something no longer discernible from a noble humanism. If it is indeed no more than that, let us have the courage to say so directly, and stop clothing it with trappings from the past. If it is, however, more than that, then the price for saying so must be paid, even if this means losing some of the precious identification we have so amply succeeded in establishing with our contemporaries, and appearing the fool. But as Reinhold Niebuhr, my dearest theological mentor, once remarked, there is a considerable difference between being a fool for Christ and being a damn fool.

## THROUGH THE VALLEY—AND BEYOND

But I must not end with too cavalier a dismissal. If doubt is truly real for our generation—and it is—we must not side too easily away from its disturbing implications, or dispose of it by what may look like a trick. For there is a real sense in which I, as modern man *and* theologian, must not shrink from bearing myself the weight of unbelief I see about me. I too must know what it is like to enter into the valley of the shadow of death, if I am to know, let alone communicate, the resurrection that lies beyond the shadow of death. If our theological generation is to speak to godless modern man, it will indeed be in part because we too are godless modern men, or have at one time been so. Our hosannas, like Dostoevsky's, will have been forged out of the crucible of doubt. Our affirmations will have been wrested out of the reality of our negations, and only as the negations have been threateningly real will the affirmations we make beyond them bear the stamp of authenticity. Only if we have borne the weight of unbelief can we also bear the weight of glory.

I continue to believe that only the one who can affirm as well as deny has claim on the title "theologian." To have walked through the valley of the shadow of death is one thing, and no man can evade that route. Indeed, he will traverse it frequently in a single lifetime. But to have walked through the valley of the shadow of death *fearing no evil,* is another and more important thing. We can do so, finally, only as we realize that we do not walk alone and are therefore able to affirm, "I will fear no evil, for thou art with me." The strength to do this and to affirm this is not finally ours. For the rod and the staff belong to another, and the table at which we receive our sustenance has not been set by us.

To affirm these latter things in the Age of Unbelief is not easy. But, then, it never was.

# A Decade of Discoveries and Dangers: How My Mind Has Changed, 1960-1970

Once upon a time there was a theologian who, after his mind had changed a number of times, said on the eve of his fiftieth birthday, "Go to, now, my mind has changed long enough. Henceforth my mind shall change no more." Thereafter what he wrote and spoke only confirmed and underlined what he had previously written and spoken. At age eighty he departed this life in wondrous fashion, suddenly disintegrating into dust. A physician, after microscopic examination of the remains, reported, "This was to be expected. The man had already been dead for thirty years."

An accounting of past change must not imply the attainment of a vantage point that precludes future change, and all that is contained below must be embraced by the more precise rubric, "How My Mind Keeps Changing." On the one hand, "Jesus Christ *is* the same yesterday, today, and forever" (italics added), but on the other hand "we always have this treasure in frail, earthen vessels ("always" added). I see theology as a venture doomed to perpetual but creative frustration, since the test of theology's integrity must be its stubborn unwillingness to confuse its own utterances with the one about whom it

A contribution to the series "How My Mind Has Changed," in *The Christian Century*, Jan. 14, 1970, and reprinted in Geyer and Peerman (eds.), *Theological Crossings* (Wm. B. Eerdmans Publishing Company, 1971). Copyright 1970 by The Christian Century Foundation. Reprinted by permission.

is speaking. Here I neither seek nor expect a continuing city. (My most important theological contribution is surely *The Collect'd Writings of St. Hereticus,* an attempt to lampoon the whole venture from within—a book long since remaindered as if in gentle vindication of the fact that attempts to show the transitory nature of theology are themselves transitory.)

I write this essay in France where, in addition to teaching, I am trying to get some perspective on both the past decade and the next. And I can most easily conceptualize the shifts in my thinking by recalling what I was doing exactly ten years ago on a sabbatical leave in Scotland, although this involves the pretentious gesture of referring to my own books—a type of self-advertisement I feel one generally resorts to only in moments of extreme self-doubt, when in need of the psychic shoring up others have denied one. But the books can provide useful shorthand devices for describing the changes. The sabbatical in St. Andrews was devoted to three tasks: (1) writing a book on ecumenism with Fr. Gustave Weigel, S.J., entitled *An American Dialogue,* (2) finishing a book on *The Spirit of Protestantism,* and (3) reading all the then extant volumes of Barth's *Church Dogmatics.* These exercises illustrate two of the three areas with which I was largely involved in the subsequent decade—e.g., ecumenism and theological methodology. (A third area, theology and politics, will be touched on later, and was symbolized during the sabbatical by an unexpected trip to East Berlin.) In each of these areas "my mind has changed," and the end is not yet.

## METHODOLOGICAL CHANGES—THE DISCOVERY OF A TWO-WAY STREET

My decision to expose myself in detail to Karl Barth represented a certain decision at that time about theological methodology. While I had not become a "Barthian," I was powerfully attracted by Barth's rediscovery of a gospel that was really "gospel"—i.e., the good news that "God is for us" and has demonstrated this affirmation by coming to us in Jesus Christ. I learned from Barth how easy it is for us to cut God down to our size, to fit him into our systems, to take the cost and sting out of believing in him, and that therefore God supplies his own criteria for the appropriation of his reality, rather than fitting into ours. We start with his self-definition in the incarnation, and everything else follows from that.

Barth I found wonderful in clarifying the faith of the believing community. But the fact that two years later I moved from a theological seminary to a secular university meant that I had to do more than give an accounting of the faith of the believing community; I had to operate largely outside its walls, dealing with religion's cultured despisers. Basically I learned that while I might have something to say to them, they also had important things to say to me. Ten years ago I had pretty well worked out my own understanding of the gospel, and I saw my task as one of finding ways to communicate that gospel to those around me. Now I see much more clearly that the traffic between the gospel and the world travels on a two-way street. The gospel helps to inform and define the world, but *the world helps to inform and define the gospel.* I need more than the resources of Bible, theological tradition, and my own commitments if I am to understand my faith and the world in which it is set; I also need the ethical insights of my secular colleagues, the political and psychological analyses of my friends and foes, and the prophetic jab of nonchurchmen whose degree of commitment so often puts my own to shame.

In other words, I have come to believe very much in "the pseudonyms of God," the strange names he uses in the world to accomplish his purposes when his self-proclaimed servants let him down—an insight, incidentally, that I got not from a theologian but from a novelist, Ignazio Silone. To some, this will seem like a return to the natural theology or general revelation that so upset Barth. I prefer to understand it as a recognition that God is at work in an infinitely wider arena of activities than I had earlier believed—which might not be a bad way to start defining a doctrine of grace. To others it may seem as though this shift is the beginning of the gradual but inevitable erosion of a once-firm faith. I don't think so, and one reason I don't is that I was not in the least attracted by the "death of God" movement and its assertion that the hallmark of the modern theologian is his denial of the *theos* that had heretofore been the whole point of his discipline. I remain unconvinced that *my* difficulty in believing in God says very much about God. It may say a great deal about me, but I cannot seriously entertain the notion that the reality of any God worthy of the name depends on how vividly I am able to conceive of him at a given moment. Charles Williams, in *Descent Into Hell,* puts my question: "Shall our tremors measure the Omnipotence?" The question is rhetorical, and Williams' implied answer is also mine: "Of course not."

None of this means that we can build from man to God, or destroy the infinitely qualitative distinction between the two, so dear to Koheleth, Kierkegaard, and Karl of Basel. But it does mean that it is out of the stuff of human life and experience that we get the pointers and hints to suggest, however faintly, something of the reality of the divine. It means that if I ever write a systematic theology, I will start with man and not God. The order of knowing, as the medievalists had discovered, need not be the same as the order of being.

In my teaching, as a result of all this, I am less and less comfortable beginning with traditional theological vocabulary. Words such as salvation, repentance, revelation, eternal life, are so devoid of power for contemporary man that I continually seek for analogies out of human experience that may hint, however imperfectly and haltingly, at what those words are trying to describe—namely, realities that are far from being devoid of power. Example: Students today know a great deal about the immensely healing and binding quality of a common meal, particularly when shared under duress (ongoing hunger, a sit-in, jail), and this provides a starting point for talking about the Eucharist. Example: A girl who has been wronged by a boy, has suffered, has been able to absorb the suffering creatively and heal the alienation by her outgoing love, is not far from being able to appropriate something of the mystery of the atonement. Example: Last spring, teaching theology during a campus sit-in, I discovered that the experiences students were having were replete with analogies relevant to our scheduled discussion of revelation. They understood that a particular moment in time could become revelatory for the meaning of their past as preparation for the event, and could also inform what they would do with their future as a result of the event—a *kairos*-moment if there ever was one, analogous, however faintly, to what Exodus-Sinai means to Judaism, and Golgotha-Garden to Christianity. They also understood some of the perils of attaching themselves to an event that might turn out to be a pseudo-*kairos*, and the disillusionment that could follow.

"We must hear the voice of God in the voice of the times," said the fathers at Vatican II. *Nihil obstat.*

### ECUMENICAL CHANGES—THE DISCOVERY OF SHARED COMMITMENTS

*Nihil obstat,* indeed. My theological antennae are increasingly sensitive to the whole range of Roman Catholic experience, and a happy by-product of my involvement in the 1952 campaign of a young Roman Catholic congressman from Minnesota named Eugene McCarthy was that it initiated contacts with Roman Catholics during a time when the ecumenical climate was frigid if not destructive. These concerns led to the publication of the above-mentioned book with Father Weigel, in which each of us examined the faith of the other. Now, a scant ten years later, the book has no more than historical interest, so rapidly has the climate changed. (Indeed, when I decided to "update" my half of it in 1967 I had to give up and write a new book, *The Ecumenical Revolution*; and when it in turn had to be updated two years later for a paperback edition, so much had happened even in that short interval that the fundamental thesis of the book had to be shifted.)

During the first half of 1960-1970 I gave my major time to the Protestant-Catholic dialogue, making friends across formerly impenetrable barriers, and discovering that to do so was to be accused by some in my own backyard of being "soft on Catholicism." I have no regrets. Those years enabled me to learn that we share infinitely more than divides us, and that the primary attention must be devoted to shoring up bridges of understanding, so that from those vantage points we may build new bridges across the misunderstandings. This conviction was reinforced during my presence at the Second Vatican Council, reported on informally in *Observer in Rome*. The friendships made there, both in coffee bars in the mornings at St. Peter's and in other bars in other parts of Rome in the evenings, transformed me, to my great surprise, from official "observer" to unofficial "participant." I became convinced that all Christians had a tremendous stake in the council, and that a disaster for Roman Catholicism, rather than something over which Protestants could derive ex post facto satisfaction, would be a disaster for all of us. I became a diligent lobbyist.

And this, I think, measures my ecumenical shift of mind during the rest of the decade. *An American Dialogue* had represented an "outsider" looking at Catholicism, sometimes approvingly, sometimes disapprovingly, but always in terms of "we" vs. "they." But through increasing ecumenical experiences I came to feel a wonderful kinship with priests and nuns, a realization that underneath all differences we were embarked on a common venture. I remember the precise moment this awareness surfaced in my consciousness. I had lectured to a Catholic audience in Kansas City, and after the lecture a group of priests and I talked informally until about two A.M. As I went to bed it suddenly came over me that we had not once talked about "Catholic-Protestant differences," the staple of dialogue in those years. We had been talking simply *as fellow Christians* about the problem of communicating our commonly held faith to an unbelieving world. Since then I have ceased to engage in ecumenical head-counting. I feel closer to many Jesuits and Benedictines than to many Protestant ministers. I do not say that to exalt the former and demean the latter, but to describe the increasing irrelevance of such distinctions.

I think that in 1960 there was need for a book on *The Spirit of Protestantism*. If there is such a need in 1970, I must now define it differently. For I no longer see Protestantism as something opposed to Catholicism; I see Protestantism as a stance necessary within the whole church catholic, a stance I find wonderfully portrayed in many Roman Catholic friends and lacking in some Protestant friends. I think I could now comfortably write a book on the spirit of Protestantism called *The Spirit of Catholicism*, and still be faithful to the spirit of that grand old Augustinian monk, Blessed Martin of Wittenberg.

I am disturbed that the revolution going on within Roman Catholicism has ground down many friends, both priests and sisters, many of whom have had to leave the church in order to preserve their integrity. It is a desperate situation when integrity has to be sought outside rather than inside what we call the church. But the ferment, one hopes, may force us to redefine what we call "the church." I can no longer define it institutionally, for I experience it too often with priests and nuns (within or without "church," or wavering) where some of our past differences are overcome and some of our future hopes realized—around a dining room table whereon are bread and wine, and whereat the presence first known in the upper room is once again a real presence.

The ecumenical dialogue has moved me in yet another direction. Through my reading of Martin Buber and my friendship with Abraham Heschel, I have come to an appreciation of Judaism that I did not begin to approach a decade ago. This awareness has been further enhanced by relationships with large numbers of Jewish students in my classes, even classes on Christian theology. I am amazed at how much of Christian faith can be expressed in Jewish terms, and I am wounded daily by the kinds of barriers to understanding and real sharing that have been (almost ineradicably) impressed upon Jewish and Christian psyches by two thousand years of Christian intolerance. And if for me "the hallowing of the every day" is now best focused in a christological framework, I will not try to deny that Hasidism gave me the impetus to begin exploring the question.

## POLITICAL CHANGES—THE DISCOVERY OF NEW COMPLEXITIES

Originally I learned about the relation of theology and ethics from Reinhold Niebuhr, and the lesson has been reconfirmed by a recent interest in Teilhard de Chardin: "By virtue of the Creation, and still more of the Incarnation, nothing here below is profane for those who know how to see" (*The Divine Milieu*, p. 35).

The thesis of the revised edition of *The Ecumenical Revolution* is that the "revolution" is the shift from internal ecclesiastical concerns (intercommunion, apostolic succession, etc.) to extramural worldly concerns (economic development, war, racism, etc.). In the latter areas there is simply nothing that divides me from most of my Catholic friends nor—in the further extension of the dialogue referred to above—from most of my Jewish friends. We make common cause together. (Abraham Heschel, Michael Novak, and I tried to symbolize this fact by jointly writing a book, *Vietnam: Crisis of Conscience*, which was jointly published by Protestant, Catholic, and Jewish publishing houses.) I have already indicated my indebtedness in this area to my secular friends.

A kaleidoscope of memories whirls when I recall the past decade in relation to the body politic—the fearful yet liberating "Freedom Ride" through the South in early summer, 1961, leading to two stretches in a Florida jail, a three-year legal hassle in the courts, and a permanent criminal record; the initial encouragement of the March on Washington and the later shifts made necessary by the rise of Black Power; the fears and hopes of being at Selma and other towns in the Deep South; the struggles against the real estate interests in the "Proposition 14" battle over fair housing in California; the ongoing strike of the farm workers at Delano and my increasing realization that in César Chavez we have been given the closest thing to a modern saint we are likely to see; the increasingly difficult experience of being in the midst of student controversy at a time when one is clearly "over thirty"; and, of course, Vietnam.

I tried to avoid Vietnam, but since the military escalation in early 1965 and my conviction that Johnson and Humphrey had betrayed the nation, it has become the dominant reality of my life. Vietnam has forced me slowly along a path that might be called "reluctant radicalization," though the term is relative since in the eyes of "radicals" I am no more than a (adjective deleted) "liberal." True, in 1961 I had engaged in selective law-breaking, defying a local Florida ordinance on segregation on the ground of its unconstitutionality, but I saw this as a very exceptional activity, to be indulged in only when all other strategies were clearly proved bankrupt. Consequently, when Vietnam became a burning issue, I kept trying, along with other liberals, to apply the working-through-the-law-to-bring-about-change tactic.

We had no effect whatever on national policy, which steadily deteriorated, and I found myself pushed inch by inch, and then yard by yard, along the road to civil disobedience, simply by the patent ineffectiveness of other alternatives. I crossed the line in the summer of 1967, and since then have engaged in illegally "counseling, aiding and abetting" those who feel they cannot serve in the army or cooperate with Selective Service, both in private and in many public events involving the receiving of draft cards for transmission to General Hershey in Washington. The mood of the country being what it was up to a few months ago, I expected to be indicted, tried, and convicted. I had done the jail bit earlier and it had no romantic or martyr-complex allure, but along with many others I was prepared if necessary to go to jail, both to indicate my unwillingness to obey an immoral law and to show my solidarity with draft resisters. That likelihood seems now to have diminished to the vanishing point, but the entire experience has left me with an as yet unresolved dilemma.

The dilemma is this: If the "system" remains as resistant to change in other areas as it has proved to be on Vietnam, if genteel protest fails to produce change, and if one believes (as I think one must) that Vietnam is a symptom of a much deeper malaise in our American way of life, is one not called upon to escalate the number and intensity of his political acts, including civil disobedience—to move, in other words, from the liberal toward the radical camp, recognizing that what is at fault is not just little inadequacies in the system that can be eliminated by tinkering, but the system itself?

The dilemma is compounded by the new dimension of violence in social protest. I have been in what radicals call, scornfully, "the Martin Luther King bag," and I expect to remain there, for I have seen too many students slide down the slippery slope from nonviolence to violence-against-property-but-not-against-people, to violence-against-whatever-is-necessary-to-produce-the-desired-end; and they illustrate, quite tragically, Silone's thesis that the persecuted end up becoming the persecutors. However, on the other hand, as I have met Christians from the Third World (particularly at the Uppsala assembly), or as I talk to American blacks, I am forced to acknowledge that in *some* situations nonviolence seems a luxury the destitute cannot afford. How can minimal justice come to some Latin American countries without violent overthrow of a dictatorship? How indeed? But I am not yet ready to extrapolate from that situation and argue that the situation in the United States is so similar as to call for a similar tactic here. If I were a black, however, I might legitimately feel that the two situations are indeed commensurate, and that covert violence here is just as destructive of human potential as overt violence elsewhere. Perhaps there must be different answers and different strategies for different groups. Martin Luther King told blacks in the '60s to respond nonviolently to angry whites. Perhaps his message in the '70s is to tell whites to respond nonviolently to angry blacks.

This, then, is the area of my greatest theological difficulty. I can no longer rest with the easier, simpler view I had in 1960, that an occasional extraordinary pressure will move our Government in the right direction. Lyndon Johnson contributed mightily to curing me of that beautiful but illusory hope, and Richard Nixon has completed the process.

## The Dangers in the Changes

And now to turn to the dangers in the changes. I sometimes wonder if my *methodological changes* have transformed my theology into a kind of will-o'-the-wisp, tossed to and fro by every wind of doctrine. Where are the long-range goals, the lifetime projects, slowly being completed? I have given up any hope, or even desire, to live that kind of theological life. I do not think it is given to many in my generation to have the luxury of long-range theological planning, and a recent event in my own experience has confirmed this thought. In the winter and spring of 1967 I received a grant that allowed me to fulfill the long-cherished dream of trying to relate a Christian doctrine of man to the revolution in cybernetics and biology. I had kept my calendar completely free for those six months of research. But when the time came, our nation was in the throes of the Vietnam war. The pressures for Vietnam protest were so strong, and the need for people with mobility was so great, that I felt I had no choice but to devote the six months to speaking, writing, and otherwise helping to mobilize protest against the war.

I cite the example not to try to score points, either pro or con, but to illustrate that for me the theological task is now defined by readiness to respond to needs that arise in areas we have not anticipated. The pressure of future world events will define the directions of my theological endeavor quite as much as, and probably more than, any built-in set of professional expectations I bring to the next decade. I cannot conceive of doing theology in a vacuum, and doing it in the context of contemporary history means responding to the unexpected rather than seeking detachment. This means, inevitably, a measure of theological dilettantism. I think I have made my peace with this. Some men must do the long-range reflective thinking that will mold the theological future. Others will be something like theological journalists, trying to bring theological analysis to bear on contemporary events, and vice versa. A few (perhaps only those named Martin Marty) can do both. But it seems clear to me, in a way it didn't ten years ago, that I have chosen the second path, or that it has been chosen for me. So be it.

The danger in my *ecumenical changes* is the blurring of distinctions that are still real. I agree. But I also find that the distinctions really *do* begin to blur. Who would seriously entertain the notion any more that Protestantism and Roman Catholicism are divided over justification by faith vs. justification by works, or over the theme of *ecclesia semper reformanda?* Who would seriously charge any more that Judaism lacks a concept of grace or that Christianity is automatically purged of legalism? I shall not surrender my convictions, but I shall insist that they may be found in different lexicons of experience, in many more areas than I used to believe possible, and that insights not granted to me through my own tradition may become available to me through others.

The danger in my *political changes* is, of course, always the danger of reducing the faith to a humanistic ethic. But I don't think that will be my temptation. My temptation, which besets ethicists as well, will be to forget the dimensions of life not covered by ethics. Camus has written: "There is beauty and there are the humiliated. Whatever difficulties the enterprise may present, I would like never to be unfaithful either to the one or the other" (*Lyrical and Critical Essays*, pp. 169-170). Yes, there is beauty, there is mystery, there is love, and no political sophistication can create them or maintain them in the hearts of men. There is the recognition that "whether we live or whether we die we are the Lord's"—a conviction I really believe and one that has carried me through a number of tense moments in the past decade. There is the community that is the church, and I really believe in that too. Having had my own share of disillusionment with the church, I find myself believing in it more than ever now; and with whatever radical restructuring is in store, and with whatever accompanying pain, I am sure that the gates of hell will not prevail against it, even if it sometimes looks as though the indifference of man or the obtuseness of the curia will.

In other words, I feel as though my own attempts to justify Christian involvement in the secular movements of the time are getting nailed down, and that from that base we must explore again the whole dimension of the gospel that centers on mystery, grace, transcendence, and "a rumor of angels," for I need continual warning that the minute we Christians begin to sound just like everybody else, we've lost the ball game.

The "death of God" theologians said that faith and hope were gone, and all that was left was a theology of love. Then the Germans told us that the big task was to recover a theology of hope. Maybe tomorrow's job will be to recover a theology of faith, and indeed the more I think about it, the more it seems to me that this line of investigation . . .

But that will have to be another book.

# Ecumenism and the Secular Order

Ecumenism is moving in a new direction in our day, the direction of increasing involvement in the secular order. Unless it continues to do this, it will become increasingly precious and ingrown; if it does continue to do this, it can become increasingly creative and forward-looking.

Until recently, discussions of ecumenism have concentrated on the problem of unity, a noble theme in the light of the tragic disunity that has so blunted the witness of the church as a healing and redemptive force in the lives of men. Quite rightly, the conciliar decree *De Oecumenismo* highlights this concern:

> The "ecumenical movement" means those activities and enterprises which, according to various needs of the Church and opportune occasions, are started and organized for the fostering of unity among Christians.[1]

Concern for unity has also been a major thrust in Protestant and Orthodox ecumenical activity, particularly through the stream called "Faith and Order," one of the tributaries leading to the formation of the World Council of Churches. Here also the goal was the restoration of the unity of the body of Christ

Originally given as the Robert Cardinal Bellarmine Lecture at St. Louis University in Oct., 1967, subsequently printed in *Theology Digest*, Winter, 1967, and in J. O'Connor (ed.), *American Catholic Exodus* (Corpus Publications, 1968). Used by permission.

throughout the whole of the *oikoumene,* or "inhabited world."

But there is another meaning attached to the various words derived from *oikoumene,* so that when we speak of "ecumenism" today we ought also to be speaking of mission, of the task of the church to reach out to the entire *oikoumene.* It is not unimportant that the original impetus toward the unity of divided Christians, symbolized by the Edinburgh Missionary Conference of 1910, received its propelling force from the mission field, and from the missionary societies even more than from the denominations. This second meaning of ecumenism, the task of mission to the world, is one on which increasing attention should be focused. Very early in its history, the World Council of Churches discovered that concern for unity seemed to be absorbing much of the attention that likewise needed to be directed toward concern for mission. The minutes of the Central Committee in 1951 point to the need for retaining an emphasis on both concerns:

> We would especially draw attention to the recent confusion in the use of the word "ecumenical." It is important to insist that this word, which comes from the Greek word for the whole inhabited earth, is properly used to describe everything that relates to the whole task of the whole Church to bring the Gospel to the whole world. *It therefore covers equally the missionary movement and the movement toward unity,* and must not be used to describe the latter in contradistinction to the former . . . Every attempt to separate these two tasks violates the wholeness of Christ's ministry to the world.[2]

I believe we can presuppose widespread concern about ecumenism as unity, and need to highlight concern about *ecumenism as mission.* To those who are wary even of a temporary disjunction, I would point out that not only do these two understandings of ecumenism need each other if we are to do full justice to ecumenical concern, but that either one, carried through in any kind of significant way, sooner or later embraces the other.

This point is important enough to illustrate by an interesting example out of ecumenical history. After the 1910 Edinburgh Missionary Conference, two subsequent conferences were held on the theme of "Life and Work," i.e., the ways in which Christians could register the impact of the gospel in their daily activities both individual and corporate. These conferences (at Stockholm in 1925 and Oxford in 1937) pursued themes dealing with the economic order, political responsibility of the churches, education, the state, and so on. At the beginning of Life and Work, doctrinal concerns were rigorously eschewed, for, as the slogan went, "Doctrine divides, service unites." But it soon became apparent that the slogan was a half truth at best, and that theological considerations inevitably intruded; to raise a question about the nature of the church's responsibility in the political order, for example, was to raise the previous question about the nature of the church itself, and to be led into the theological arena of questions about unity, ministry, and sacraments.

During the same period, and also growing out of the Edinburgh Missionary Conference, two further conferences were held, focusing precisely on the theological issues of the church, unity, ministry, and sacraments. These conferences on "Faith and Order" (at Lausanne in 1925 and Edinburgh in 1937) dealt with ecumenism in terms of the search for unity. But those in Faith and Order made the obverse discovery of those in Life and Work; they discovered that they could not do their theological task properly if they were not also concerned about the outreach and mission of the church. To raise a question about the nature of the church itself was also, from their perspective, to raise a question about the nature of the church's responsibility in the political order. Thus Life and Work (concerned with mission) discovered that it needed Faith and Order (concerned with unity), while Faith and Order (concerned with unity) discovered that it needed Life and Work (concerned with mission). Each presupposed the other; neither could adequately define itself without the other. And it was the marriage of these two partners, each unfulfilled without the other, that produced the World Council of Churches.

Subsequent assemblies of the World Council of Churches have therefore addressed themselves to the themes of both unity and mission. Amsterdam (1948) dealt not only with "The Universal Church in God's Design" but also with "The Church and International Disorder"; Evanston (1954) dealt not only with "Our Oneness in Christ and Our Disunity as Churches" but also with "The Responsible Society in a World Perspective" and "The Church Amid Racial and Ethnic Tensions"; New Delhi (1961) dealt not only with "Unity" but also with "Service," and Uppsala (1968), in addition to dealing with themes related to unity, also discussed the mission of the church to the world, the church in economic and social change, international affairs, worship in a secular age, and the nature of a Christian "style of life."

It is my own belief that this theme of concern for the secular order is the direction in which the next ecumenical steps are going to be most creatively taken, and that the watershed in this development was the Geneva Conference of 1966 on the theme, "Christians in the Social and Technical Revolutions of Our Time," which concentrated its attention almost exclusively in this direction, dealing with "Economic Development in a World Perspective," "The Nature and Function of the State in a Revolutionary Age," "Structures of International Cooperation—Living Together in Peace in a Pluralistic World Society," and "Man and Community in Changing Societies."

It is important to notice another aspect of the ecumenical development here. At the Geneva conference, Roman Catholic theologians were not only present, but participated actively in the discussions, and two of the major papers were given by Roman Catholics, Canon Charles Moeller and Lady Jackson (Barbara Ward). It is also important to realize that at Uppsala fifteen Catholic observers were present, not merely to observe, but to have the privilege of the floor, if not yet the privilege of the ballot.

Let us briefly examine what has been happening from the Roman Catholic side in this area of ecumenism. One need only recall the earlier "social encyclicals" from Leo XIII on, to realize that concern for the secular order has been a part of Catholic teaching to Catholics for many decades. *Rerum Novarum* and *Quadragesimo Anno* are landmarks on this road, as is the more recent *Mater et Magistra*, which consciously attempts to stand in their succession. But with the ecumenically-minded Pope John, something new emerged. *Pacem in Terris*, while still a papal encyclical, was addressed not only to Catholics but also to "all men of good will," indicating that a decision had been made to deal ecumenically with the most pressing problem of the saeculum, world peace.[3]

This tradition was continued at Vatican II. The pastoral constitution on *The Church and the World Today*, dealing specifically with issues such as marriage, economics, politics, war, and world peace, was one of the two Council documents likewise addressed not only to Roman Catholics and other Christians but to the whole of humanity. In like fashion, the encyclical of Pope Paul, *Populorum Progressio*, dealing once again with matters of concern to all men, particularly in the economic order, was addressed not only to Catholics but likewise to all men of good will.

What this brief history suggests is that from both sides, our concerns about the *world* have led us closer to *one another*, and we have discovered in the process that we cannot properly concern ourselves about the secular order save ecumenically, save in close concert, working together. When talking about such issues, pope and council no longer address a Catholic constituency exclusively; they address all their fellow Christians and, indeed, all men. Similarly, Protestants and Orthodox in the World Council of Churches do not only consult among themselves when dealing with such issues; they reach out to an ever-deepening Roman Catholic involvement in their own concerns. Ecumenism as concern for the world has gained a substantial foothold.

To concentrate on ecumenism as outreach to, concern for, and involvement in, the secular order is not to eschew the importance of ecumenism as a quest for unity. I believe, indeed, that it may be only through the concern for ecumenism as mission that we will break some of the theological binds that constrict us in our present concern for ecumenism as unity, and that a pursuit today of what were, in an earlier day, the concerns of "Life and Work," will help us see more incisively the ongoing concerns of "Faith and Order."

## 1. THE DIASPORA SITUATION—AND SOME CONSEQUENCES

Fr. Avery Dulles, S.J., sets the context for where we must go from here:

> Ecumenism has become too exclusively taken up with religious questions—with matters of doctrine and worship. . . . From many quarters therefore one hears the call for a new ecumenism—one less committed to historical theological controversies and more in touch with contemporary secular man; one less turned in upon itself, more open to the world and its concerns. The greatest decisions affecting man's future are being made in the sphere of the secular, and Christianity does not seem to be there.[4]

This is both a description and an indictment, and I have an increasing feeling that unless we are truly found in the saeculum, the things we do elsewhere are going to amount to no more than trivial irrelevancies. I therefore accept *both* the description and the indictment. We have not sufficiently concerned ourselves with this arena of the secular in the past, and we must do so in the future. We no longer confront a "Catholic" problem or a "Protestant" problem, we confront a "human" problem. Men are in desperate need. Time is running out. How shall we respond?

The most seductive response, and the most fatal, is the one to which we almost instinctively turn: Let us shore up the crumbling walls of the church, regroup our scattered forces, and assault the enemy as we have done in the past; let us, in other words, recapture our lost territory, let us restore Christendom.

Now I shall not take long to respond to this (as I regard it) highly mistaken plea. There can be no simple return to the past; we cannot restore Christendom, whether of the thirteenth-century variety or the sixteenth-century varieties. The church is not going to dominate our society, and even if it could, to attempt to do so would be to misconceive its role. After centuries of both Catholic and Protestant triumphalism, we have begun to see that the proper stance for the church is not as lord but as servant, since its own Lord was a servant. It would be hard to overstress the importance of the fact that the servant imagery was prominent in Vatican II, even if a lot of the old triumphalist language still lingers on. The church's task is not to assume power from the state, but to offer itself so that the state can use its own power more responsibly. In our time the church will represent at best a tiny minority that might, by the grace of God, become what Toynbee describes as a "creative minority."

The Biblical image for this stance is an image that Karl Rahner, Stephen Neill, Thomas Merton, Richard Schall, Hans Reudi-Weber, and others have recently been expounding—the image of diaspora. The church is scattered, dispersed, to the ends of the earth. It no longer has terrestrial power, nor should it seek it once again. It is that band of people, here and there, united along the conduits of power mysteriously supplied by the Holy Spirit, who, wherever they are, offer themselves and the resources of their institution in the service of all men, and not just in the service of those who happen to belong to the institution. Richard Schall describes the situation:

Christendom is rapidly dissolving around us. . . . Without our going into exile, the non-Christian world has engulfed us as modern means of communication create one world in which we are a small minority, and as the population explosion indicates that each year the percentage of Christians decreases. We are thus in a situation similar to that of the Jews of the diaspora, scattered among people whose culture, mores and thought patterns are not like ours nor will they become so; our cathedrals and temples are no longer in the center of life nor do they bring the whole community together under God. If we hope to reach modern man, it will not be so much in terms of gathering him into the church as of going to him in the midst of our dispersion.[5]

In such a situation Karl Rahner reminds us not to yearn wistfully for an earlier era but to accept the present era joyfully. The diaspora situation is no cause for despair. It is the situation in which God has placed us today, and we must live the diaspora-life affirmatively, rather than seeking to restore the Christendom-life frantically. The church need not, as Thomas Merton and Hans Küng have pointed out, speak in the language of victory communiqués.

I am not sure how much we have really understood what a radically new set of outlooks and postures would be required if we took this description seriously. And I am not sure how many of us, if we did come to such a realization, would be willing to cope with it. For such a discovery would be very threatening and very risky, even at the level of our accustomed ways of doing things and our ordinary day-to-day structures.

The geographically isolated seminary, for example, is a structure reflecting the old Christendom mentality. Earlier prescription: Isolate your shock troops for sufficient years to insulate them thoroughly against contamination from the world, and then set them loose to regain all that lost territory for the Queen of Heaven. The new prescription would read:

Educate your shock troops right along with the enlisted men (for which read "in the context of an urban university") so that they are completely at home in secular culture and can share in its best while offering a fresh alternative to replace its worst.

Seminary education, however, is hardly the key to secular man's redemption. We are going to find that many of the other things we have taken most for granted, most associated with the "fullness" of the faith, are going to have to be put up for grabs. The religious orders furnish a further example. Is it right, in the diaspora situation, that whole communities should live together in isolation, even on a university campus? Should not members of such communities be dispersed through the dormitories, through the surrounding area, in the apartments and the slums, sharing fully in what it means to be a modern man, rather than being protected from the political, social, and economic problems that beset ordinary mortals?

The plight of many Protestant ministers extends the problem. Selective Service exempts from military duty the physically unfit, the mentally incompetent, and the clergy. Why should ministers have exemption? Why should they not be full men, either fighting if they so choose, or declaring their conscientious objection if they so choose, like other men? Why, to press another point, should they be professional holy men, exempted from the task their parishioners face of earning a living day by day? Why not, after the manner of Paul, earn their living at a "secular job," and thereby be freed from being beholden to those who ante up the salary check? If the criterion is *diakonia*, service, involvement in the affairs of men in today's world, is the structure of a "kept clergy" really defensible any more?

What about the very physical structures in which we worship? Are they not also a reflection of the Christendom mentality. The medieval cathedral *dominated* the town. The New England meetinghouse *dominated* the village green. We like

our church spires to be higher than surrounding structures—
though the fate of St. Patrick's Cathedral, dwarfed for decades
by Radio City, symbolizes the fate of such ecclesiastical *hu-
bris*. The rank and file still insist that a church must "look like
a church," by which they mean, I discover, what John Betje-
man calls the "ghastly good taste" of nineteenth-century Christians who decided that pseudo Gothic was ordained by God at
the moment of creation in an irreformable ex cathedra decree.
Does not all this still create the impression that God is somewhere else than where people normally are, and that if we
want to find him we must go apart to find him, withdrawing
from the saeculum into the holy?

I am always baffled by the high degree of initial Catholic
resistance to having the Mass elsewhere than in a church,
since on historical grounds alone the precedent of having
Mass on the second floor of somebody's house would seem
most Scripturally fitting. I suggest that if we take the diaspora
situation seriously, we are going to be far less concerned about
church buildings in the future (save for concern that we probably have too many of them), and will find that in our scattered existence, wherever we happen to find ourselves may be
the ideal spot in which to worship the Lord of all creation,
since it will be precisely in the midst of his creation. Jesus did
not choose a very religious spot on which to be crucified—in
fact, it was chosen for him by the secular authorities and it
turned out to be the city dump heap. Perhaps today a sanita-
tion project would be a more appropriate place to celebrate
Good Friday than before a high altar.

But we must not linger overmuch with such matters, which
are merely illustrations of the fact that if we take seriously our
new situation in the saeculum, as the scattered and dispersed
people of God, many things are going to be up for grabs, and
everything will have to be rethought in the light of our new
situation. The posture in that new situation must be one of *diakonia,* and it must not be *self*-regarding, i.e., for the sake of

the church, but *other*-regarding, i.e., for the sake of the neighbor in need, whether in the church or not.

## 2. INVOLVEMENT IN POWER STRUCTURES

Now such a possibility, unfortunately, can become hopelessly romantic and unrealistic. If we really want to minister to the neighbor in need, it will not be enough to do so merely on a personal, individualistic scale, important or rewarding as such an action may be to all concerned. Nine Jesuits, let us say, moving to the slums of St. Louis and living among the people, sharing their hardships, being there as humane individuals, can engage in genuine ministries of healing and compassion, but they are still likely to remain "Band-Aid ministries," i.e., effective only in repairing damage that has already been done. But nine Jesuits, in concert with some ministers and rabbis and informed lay people, moving in on city hall to demand new rent control commissions, or helping people organize to fight corrupt landlords, or setting up precinct caucus groups to force politicians to do something about ambulance service or price gouging—such groups could begin to have an impact on the whole structure of the city, and on the basic structure of human lives. Apart from such action, both structures will remain pretty much the same, for there is a clear axiom of modern life (which the doctrine of original sin corroborates), that those with power do not voluntarily surrender it. What I am saying is that the Christian, living in diaspora, who does want to serve his fellowmen must, whatever else he may do, act politically. He must gather others together, form groups that can exercise power, and work from some kind of power base, with all the temptations and abuses to which he thereby becomes liable.

There are those who become very nervous in the face of such suggestions, and who feel that overnight the church will reduce itself merely to the level of another secular social-service agency. I concede that we would be in difficulty if the church in fact were nothing but a kind of equivalent of the AFL-CIO sprinkled with holy water, or if the church became no more than one pressure group among other pressure groups. But I passionately insist that this is not our problem, that it is not likely to be our problem for at least half a century, and that in the interval we can count on the inertia of good Christian folk to keep us from rushing pell-mell into the secular arena leaving everything else behind us. Surely the thing we need to fear is not overinvolvement in the world of contemporary politics; if there is to be an indictment of the church today it will not come from our overinvolvement but because we are so pathetically underinvolved.

What have we been doing, we church people, for the last few decades, that the painfully obvious conditions in our cities, with their inevitable (I repeat, inevitable) outbreak into riots and violence, simply were not acknowledged by us until too late? What have we been doing, that our nation can become involved in the wrong war at the wrong time in the wrong place, and we church people engage in only pitifully feeble protests of a foreign policy that is killing thousands of Americans and hundreds of thousands of Asians in an exercise of demonic futility? Do not let anyone say that racism and Vietnam are political rather than theological issues—they are both, but they are fundamentally human issues, which means that they are also fundamentally theological issues, for any issue that involves the life and death of the children of God is a theological issue, whether the proper theological formulations are pronounced or not.

### 3. A SAMPLING OF PROBLEMS

What I am saying is that if modern ecumenical history demonstrates that Christians are now beginning to attack contemporary problems together, modern world history demonstrates that the kinds of problems we must now attack together are problems like racism and Vietnam. This raises baffling predicaments for many churchmen.

The period of recent church history by which I am most instructed in facing the task of the church in the early '70s in America, is the period of the early '30s in Germany. The German church, Catholic and Protestant, faced the rise of a monstrous evil, Nazism, and was unable to speak an effective word against it, or do an effective deed to counter it. Either because it felt that politics was not its business (part of the legacy of a Lutheran "two-realms" doctrine of church and state) or because it kept waiting for the "right" moment to speak and act (part of the legacy of a Catholic heritage that overemphasized the virtue of prudence), the time passed when the church could speak and act. There was left to it nothing but the individual voice from the prison cell. The voice from the prison cell counts—perhaps it speaks to us across three decades more powerfully than it did contemporaneously—but it comes too late to affect the immediate situation, which in this case was the build-up of Hitler's demonic power, the systematic slaughter of six million Jews, and the death in warfare of many more millions.

And my great fear today is that those looking back at the churches in the late '60s and early '70s will pronounce upon them the same indictment pronounced upon the church in the early '30s—"too little and too late." Let me therefore single out four kinds of problems that usually inhibit us from acting ecumenically in the secular arena and attempt to speak to them, using Vietnam as a way of making the discussion concrete.

1. There are those who say that the issues are too complex for the church to be able to speak. Some issues are morally clear-cut, we are told, but other issues, such as Vietnam, are perplexing and ambiguous, demanding a degree of political, historical, and military expertise the church cannot claim to have.

But recognizing the complexity and ambiguity of a problem

will simply not get us off the hook. Every social issue is complex, full of implications we may not have grasped. To favor a minimum wage for migrant farm workers may be a matter of simple justice, but it does indeed jeopardize the profits of the owners of the farms on which the migrants work. To vote for any candidate for public office is to support policies of the candidate of which one does not approve, as well as supporting the policies of which one does approve.

But there is nevertheless a point to the complaint, and the point is that churchmen must never let piety go bail for expertise. In this much advertised "age of the laity," we must call upon our laity who are experts in Southeast Asia, or Sino-Russian relations, or international diplomacy, and learn from them. We must not presume to a political or military expertise we do not possess. But even a decent humility in the face of the immensity of the problem does not permit uninvolvement—silence is merely complicity with existing policy. The church need not say everything, but it can say some things, and say them well. One example: In Vietnam we have been bombing civilian areas without apology as a matter of "military necessity." Hanoi aside, we bomb, strafe, napalm, and bulldoze whole towns and villages, utterly destroying them, also as a matter of "military necessity." Can such things go unchallenged by the church? Father John Sheerin has pointed out that our daily military actions are almost perfectly described in the Vatican Council document on *The Church and the World Today*:

> Any act of war aimed indiscriminately at the destruction of entire cities or of extensive areas along with their populations is a crime against God and man himself. It merits unequivocal and unhesitating condemnation (article 80).

Splendid. But where is the "unequivocal and unhesitating condemnation" that should be on the lips of every churchman today? If, in solemn council, we are willing to speak strongly, but then not apply such speech to particular situations, it would be better not to have spoken at all.

As far as the danger of making wrong judgments is concerned, we can be sure in this secular day and age that if churchmen make mistakes they will be so informed by their fellowmen. (I speak from the vantage point of considerable personal experience, that the day when clerical statements had sanctuary from critical dissection has passed.) What is called for, in this situation, is not reserve and timidity, but a certain daring and even brashness. A statement by Karl Barth in the last volume of his *Church Dogmatics* might well be the charter for such a day: "Better something doubtful or overbold, and therefore in need of correction and forgiveness, than nothing at all." [6] So let us do our homework, on Vietnam or whatever, and not let complexity become a device for avoiding involvement at risk.

2. A second problem involves the degree of specificity we should give to our statements or actions. Can we advocate specific programs, specific actions, specific candidates? Doing so involves many risks, not all of them wise. The great danger is in creating the impression that a given policy or candidate is the "Christian" one, and that others are, by the rules of logic, anti-Christian, or at least sub-Christian. There is a great danger in claiming too much for our insights, illustrated by the remark of that great Missouri theologian Harry S Truman, that American foreign policy during his administration was based squarely on the Sermon on the Mount. What I am pleading for is considerably to the right of such a claim, but it is also considerably to the left of those who would permit us only to utter platitudes. Our danger is more from platitudes than from particularities.

Let me illustrate once again in terms of Vietnam. I have felt for several years that we cannot discharge our prophetic duty simply by saying earnestly that we are for peace in Vietnam, or that the love commandment should be implemented in Southeast Asia. I have advocated that the churches, as churches, must at least back such proposals as U Thant's Three Points. In a book recently published with a Catholic lay theologian and a Jewish rabbi (by which format we were trying to demonstrate the need for secular involvement in ecumenical terms), I repeated these and other suggestions, such as greater use of international agencies to initiate negotiations, and made some less than cordial remarks about Mr. Johnson, Mr. Rusk, and Mr. Humphrey. One critic, however, faulted my portion of the book on the ground that I was too specific. While sharing many of my concerns about the war, he did not feel the churches should so unqualifiedly back certain political actions designed to bring the struggle to a conclusion. Similarly, in sharing a platform with another theologian in Washington, I discovered that he agreed that the churches should urge our country to find ways of ending the war, but disagreed that we had any right to recommend a bombing pause as a way to achieve this end.

To propose a specific alternative to present policy, however, is at least to call upon the policy makers to justify their present course of action. Nothing in the public debate thus far has persuaded me that the Government's response is adequate. In such a situation, I would insist that rather than being silent, the churches should become more vocal than ever, forcing the experts to constant scrutiny of our policy. And when we discover, as we have, that the experts themselves do not agree, and that most Asian experts, as a matter of fact, feel our policy is wrong, we have an even greater responsibility to keep such issues alive and on the conscience of our nation.

3. A third problem is tactical as well as theological. To what degree do we make common cause, in the public arena, with those whose presuppositions we do not accept? The old fear was always that to espouse anything to the left meant being manipulated by the Communists. (In California there is a new fear that if you espouse anything at all you will be manipulated by the Birchers.) But let us not surrender too quickly. We need not be embarrassed if some of the convictions of

Christian faith are shared by Marxists. To be for social justice is not wrong just because people with beards are also its champions. Opposition to Vietnam is not evil because others couple their oppositions with disenchantment over the procedures and traditions of Western democratic culture.

Let me illustrate concretely. I was asked (by the editor of *Ramparts*, if truth be told) to speak at the April, 1967, Mobilization Against the War in Vietnam. It was clear that the planning for the mobilization was in the hands of what would be called the far left, that anybody could appear under whatever presuppositions appealed to him provided he was against the war, that Vietcong flags would be flying, and that almost all of the church groups had officially forsworn support. I was engaged at the time in a pretty intensive tour of speaking and writing on Vietnam aimed at the middle class, which is where I figured the votes and the power were. So I declined the invitation, fearing that I would become "tainted" by such an appearance, and would be written off by those I most wanted to reach, as a tool or pawn of the left. But the more I reflected, the more it seemed to me that this was a very superior and condescending attitude to take, so I changed my mind and did appear on the program.[7] And while there were a couple of speeches that made me cringe, by and large the affair was an amazing display of concern, outrage, and moral protest, 62,000 strong—in which the churches were virtually unrepresented. The absence that day of the religious community was a very conspicuous absence since all other segments of the community—doctors, union officials, public entertainers, professors, whatever—were present. But we churchmen had been afraid to sully ourselves by contact with those outside our ranks. We insisted on a privilege one doesn't get—the privilege of fighting on a battleground solely of our own choosing.

I hope the religious bodies of San Francisco learned a lesson from that day. I think I did. It is that we must not be so concerned about our own purity that we forget about human need. If Pope Paul and the Vatican Council address their concerns to "all men of good will," we had better be willing to associate with such people and make common cause with them.

4. A final complaint against church involvement in the secular arena goes: "But if we take a stand, we'll divide our membership." The statement is true. We will. But the question is whether this is such a bad thing. I am persuaded that people are going to leave the church in droves in the next decade or two, and that they are going to do so for one of two reasons: either (*a*) because the church takes too clear a stand on social issues and they disagree with that stand, or (*b*) because the church doesn't take a stand on anything and they figure it's not worth the bother. I'd much prefer to be caught on the initial horn of that dilemma. The question is not, "Can we avoid offending people?" but rather, "Can we relate the offense of the gospel to the contemporary scene?"

It seems to me inconceivable that in the name of the Christian gospel our churches could condone a public policy stating that we must achieve a military victory in Vietnam at any cost, even if it means risking the involvement of China and thus triggering World War III, the direction in which our present policy seems irretrievably to be taking us. And if we cannot condone such a policy, then we must oppose it, however unhappy that fact makes some churchmen.

And if there is going to be too much institutional lethargy for us to move as far as many would like to move in opposition to Vietnam, then at the very least the church must give massive support to those within its ranks who are constrained to move beyond the present ecclesiastical consensus. There is a witness of conscience that many individuals within our fellowship feel constrained to make about racism or Vietnam, based on the attitude of that old ex-Augustinian monk who said, "Here I stand, I can do no other, God help me." The witness is not only for the sake of conscience, but also for the sake of the church, offered in an effort to move it from timidity to venturesomeness. A time comes when one must oppose evil even if he cannot prevent it.

That time always comes sooner for individuals within the church than for the church itself, and yet it seems to me quite conceivable that Vietnam is forcing such a choice even upon the institution. And we always run a danger of being institutionally insensitive to those prophetic spirits within our midst who summon us to a higher degree of commitment and risk than we might otherwise be prepared collectively to take.

### 4. CONCLUSION: THE NEED FOR RISK

What I plead for, therefore, in conclusion, is the willingness of the church in our day to take immense risks in the arena of involvement in the secular order. Let us be prepared to fail a few times, if only that we may learn by those failures how not to fail the next time, if only that we may persuade the suffering race of men that we desire to stand at their side, sharing their burdens, working on their behalf, bearing their cross.

If the church is to err in our day, let it err on the side of overinvolvement rather than underinvolvement. Let it be specific rather than general, making mistakes of commission rather than of omission. Let it be too far to the left rather than too far to the right, or (as is its usual posture) comfortably and complacently in the middle. Let it be too radical rather than too conservative. Let it spend itself now for a bleeding and bent world, rather than conserving itself for a future it may never have. Let it, finally, trust not in its own wisdom, much as it must employ its own wisdom, but let it trust rather in the resource of the divine wisdom that can overrule human folly, even ecclesiastical folly, for its own ends. Let it trust not in its own power, but in the grace of God, who can turn our weakness into his strength, and out of our faltering footsteps erect a clearer highway for the pilgrims who follow us.

### NOTES

1. W. M. Abbott (ed.), *Documents of Vatican II* (Association Press, 1966), p. 347.

2. Cited in Lukas Vischer (ed.), *A Documentary History of the Faith and Order Movement, 1927-1963* (The Bethany Press, 1963), pp. 177-179. Italics added.

3. The only earlier encyclical I recall that was similarly directed to non-Catholics as well as Catholics was Pius XI's *Mit brennender Sorge* (1937), addressed to the German nation and dealing, albeit cautiously, with the issue of Nazism. In this case, even the customary Latin form was forgone. Unfortunately, the message did not get through to non-Catholics. Cf. Albert Camus's critique in *Resistance, Rebellion and Death* (Alfred A. Knopf, Inc., 1961).

4. Cited in *Convergence,* The Gustave Weigel Society, Vol. I, No. 1, pp. 4-5.

5. Cited in M. E. Marty and D. G. Peerman (eds.), *New Theology, No. 2* (The Macmillan Company, 1965), p. 271.

6. Karl Barth, *Church Dogmatics,* Vol. IV, Part 2, ed. by G. W. Bromiley and T. F. Torrance (Charles Scribner's Sons, 1958), p. 780.

7. Cf. below, "Protest for the Sake of Persuasion," for the text of the speech.

# II

## THE PSEUDONYMS OF GOD

# The Pseudonyms of God

The language about God these days tends to be a curious combination of modesty and extravagance—modesty at how little some people claim to know about him, extravagance at the degree of assurance with which others claim we can know little or nothing.

To some, of course, God is still totally and triumphantly *present*, and a noted evangelist can rebut the charge that God is dead by countering, "I know that God is alive, because I talked with him this morning," a response that effectively stops further discussion.

But the mood generally is more chastened. Ever since the time of Isaiah, and probably before him, men have spoken of God as *hidden*, and Pascal was not the only one to echo Isaiah's plaintive cry, "Truly, thou art a God who hidest thyself." [1]

Martin Buber has spoken of the *eclipse* of God, another dramatic image, and has insisted that in spite of this eclipse, brought about in part at least by man's sin, we must seek to redeem the word that has fallen into such disrepute. "We cannot cleanse the word 'God' and we cannot make it whole," he writes, "but, defiled and mutilated as it is, we can raise it from the ground and set it over an hour of great care." [2]

Originally published in C. F. Mooney (ed.), *The Presence and Absence of God* (Fordham University Press, 1969), Ch. 7, with a final section that is now incorporated in the next essay. Used by permission.

In our day, the notion of the *absence* of God has gained much currency: there may be a God, but if so the evidence of his presence is so agonizingly slim that we must discount the possibility that he will reappear in our time. Until he does, we must, in Gabriel Vahanian's words, "Wait without idols." [3] This theme seems new and rather daring, but it may in fact be little more than a refinement of the deistic notion, not of the absent God, but of the absentee God, the one who was once around but has now retired to the sidelines, leaving the universe to run its own course, virtually independent of him.

Even more extravagant than these images, of course, is the contemporary theme of the *death* of God, although it is not always clear what the proponents of this theme mean. Sometimes they mean that the idea of God, as a theme of human contemplation and commitment, has died, and that the term is thus a description of our cultural situation rather than a metaphysical or ontological statement.[4] Many of them find the news curiously liberating and seem unimpressed with Rabbi Richard Rubenstein's disavowal of such optimism: "The death of God as a cultural phenomenon is undeniable," he comments, "but this is no reason to dance at the funeral." Others, however, press beyond this phenomenological statement to the assertion that God really and truly has died, that this death is a historical event, and that it took a so-called Christian civilization about nineteen centuries to catch up with the truth. But even those who most buoyantly proclaim God's death go on to insist that there has been a kind of resurrection of God in a new form, as the epiphany of new possibilities for a humanity now liberated from false and outworn beliefs.[5]

In connection with this last position, I happen to be among those who believe that reports of God's death, like the initial reports of Mark Twain's, have been somewhat exaggerated, and I agree with the editors of *New Theology, No. 4* that the so-called "death of God theology" was a phenomenon already passing from the theological scene when it was belatedly discovered by *Time, Newsweek, Playboy,* and other representatives of the mass media.[6] I do not therefore intend in what follows to flail a dead horse, let alone a dead God.

These modes of speech in our day which speak of God as present, hidden, eclipsed, absent, or dead, are, I suggest, extravagant modes of speech. I do not use the term pejoratively but descriptively, and partly as a means of setting off by contrast the more modest and less extravagant task with which this essay is concerned. For I want to deal with the more circumscribed theme of the *pseudonyms* of God, the "strange names" I believe him to be using in our time, the unexpected ways in which he is at work.

This theme suggests that to the degree that God is *present,* he is present in strange ways, and that the usual criteria for measuring his presence have to be revised. To the degree that God is *hidden,* he has chosen to hide himself (as Isaiah suspected) so that we are forced to search him out in unlikely places. To the degree that he is in *eclipse,* the shadows bringing about that eclipse can force us to survey the once-familiar terrain from new perspectives, and finally see that terrain with greater clarity than was possible when it was fully bathed in the sunshine of an undisturbed faith. To the degree that God is *absent,* such absence is his self-imposed catalyst to force us into acknowledging fresh modes for his apprehension. And to the degree that he is *dead*—but here, of course, the comparative mode of speech breaks down, for it is not possible to speak of degrees of "deadness." The death of God as a description of a cultural phenomenon, however, can be so described, and to the degree that our notion of God has suffered mortal blows, this may in fact be precisely the prerequisite for a genuine resurrection in our experience of the true God, purged of some of the confining and distorting notions we have tried to attach to him.

And it is for this task of trying to make ourselves open once again to the reality of one whose dimensions we cannot measure, and whom eye cannot see nor ear hear, that the imagery of the *pseudonym* may be of some use.

## SILONE'S USE OF PSEUDONYMS

The theme was first suggested to me in the very moving novel of Ignazio Silone, *Bread and Wine*.[7] The novel tells the story of Pietro Spina, a communist revolutionary in Italy in the 1930's, during the rise of Italian fascism, and the period in which Mussolini waged his savage war against Ethiopia. Spina is concerned to discern the signs of the times, and an elderly priest, Don Benedetto, who had been his teacher, makes the rather startling remark to him:

> In times of conspiratorial and secret struggle, the Lord is obliged to hide Himself and assume pseudonyms. Besides, and you know it, He does not attach very much importance to His name. . . . Might not the ideal of social justice that animates the masses today be one of the pseudonyms the Lord is using to free Himself from the control of the churches and the banks?[8]

To get the full force of this statement, it must be realized that "the ideal of social justice that animates the masses" in Italy in the 1930's, to which the priest was referring, was Italian Communism. Don Benedetto was saying, in other words, that the hand of God might be more clearly discerned among the Italian Communists than among the Italian priests or bankers.

Initially this seems a strange idea, perhaps even a demonic idea. It seems strange that a God who presumably wants to enter into fellowship with his children should show himself not directly but indirectly, and it seems demonic that the vehicle through which he should indirectly show himself— the pseudonym or false name he should use—would be something so apparently antithetical to his purposes as Communism. But Don Benedetto, as he pursues his theme, makes clear that there is nothing new in this idea. It has, in fact, a long history.

This would not be the first time that the Eternal Father felt obligated to hide Himself and take a pseudonym. As you know, He has never taken the first name and the last name men have fastened on Him very seriously; quite to the contrary, He has warned men not to name Him in vain as His first commandment. And then, the Scriptures are full of clandestine life. Have you ever considered the real meaning of the flight into Egypt? And later, when he was an adult, was not Jesus forced several times to hide himself and flee from the Judaeans? [9]

Silone is so caught up with this theme that in his stage version of *Bread and Wine* he renames the story, *And He Did Hide Himself,*[10] developing even more prominently the notion that Jesus himself had to assume pseudonyms.

We may push the matter a bit farther, therefore, not only in terms of Silone's use of the theme but also in terms of his insistence that this is not a new theme but an old one, and that it is indeed a consistent Biblical theme as well.

## BIBLICAL EXAMPLES OF THE PSEUDONYMOUS GOD

Three Old Testament examples of the theme of God's use of pseudonyms may be suggested as the foundation for a further consideration of its possible contemporary usefulness.

The *first* of these occurs in Gen. 28:10-17. Jacob is en route from Beersheba to Haran. Night comes, and so he camps along the road, stopping at what is described as "a certain place." There is nothing special about this place at all. It is not a shrine, it is not a holy place, it is not the goal of the day's journey. It is simply where Jacob happens to be when the sun goes down. During the night he has a dream about a ladder set from earth to heaven, upon which angels are ascending and descending. What is important for our present purposes is neither the dream nor the content of the dream, but the comment that Jacob makes when he awakes, since it becomes almost a paradigm of the experience of the pseudonymity of

God. The next morning Jacob makes two statements, both of which are very true: first, "Surely the Lord is in this place," as indeed he was; second, "I did not know it," as indeed he did not (cf. Gen. 28:16). God's presence was not dependent upon Jacob's perception of that presence—a fact from which we can derive some comfort when we today too readily identify the reality or existence of God with our own degree of perception of his reality or existence.

But even more important was the fact that the reality of that presence came home to Jacob in a quite unexpected place and set of circumstances. Jacob did not discover God in a shrine or place of worship, but far from any such place. He did not discover him in the midst of any cultic exercise or act of mercy. He did not suddenly in the midst of prayer experience the healing reality of God's presence. No, it was in the totally unexpected event of setting up camp in the desert, in the midst of a tedious journey, that God manifested himself in a strange way. How strange and irregular it was to Jacob's experience is rather perversely attested to by the fact that Jacob's reaction was precisely to build a shrine on that spot, to try to regularize the unexpected experience, to divest the experience of its pseudonymity and make it predictable, calculable, and manageable.

A *second* Biblical example of God's use of pseudonyms is one to which Don Benedetto himself makes oblique reference in his conversation with Spina, and one that is recounted in I Kings 19:1-12. A little later in Israel's history Elijah is also leaving Beersheba, only this time the journey is not a calculated one; Elijah is fleeing to the wilderness to escape from that very domineering queen named Jezebel, who is after his neck. Yahweh pursues him and orders him to stand upon the mount before the Lord. "Before the Lord": but how will Elijah know of the presence of the Lord? The account continues:

> And behold, the LORD passed by, and a great and strong wind rent the mountains, and broke in pieces the rocks before the LORD, but the LORD was not in the wind; and

after the wind an earthquake, but the LORD was not in the earthquake; and after the earthquake a fire, but the LORD was not in the fire; and after the fire a still small voice.[11]

The Lord strong and mighty was not in the wind. The Lord of heaven and earth was not in the earthquake. The Lord of all power was not in the fire. Recall that these means—earthquake, wind, and fire—were the normal ways through which a man in Elijah's time would have expected a theophany of the divine presence. But no, after these usual manifestations of the divine comes "a still small voice," or as one translator has put it, "the sound of a soft stillness." [12] And it was in "the sound of a soft stillness" that the God of earthquake, wind, and fire was present—the last place on earth in which Elijah would have expected to find him. Once again, God is working through the unexpected, and confronting man not in the normal way but in a strange way, through pseudonymous activity.

A *third* example of this strange activity of God occurs still later in Israel's history, recounted in that curious and disturbing passage in Isa. 10:5-19.[13] Isaiah is rightly worried because Israel is paying no attention to Yahweh's demands. He feels that Yahweh is about to engage in a mighty manifestation of his sovereign power. And he links this with the fact that Assyria, a great "secular" world power, is poised on the northern borders about to invade the land of God's people, the Jews. Isaiah feels that the power of Yahweh will be manifested in the ensuing battle.

Now the customary thing to assume in such situations was that God would, of course, work through his chosen people. They who were to be "a light unto the Gentiles" would surely be the vehicle through which the strong right arm of Yahweh would be manifest to the Gentiles. But Isaiah did not say that at all. Instead, he said the scandalous and shocking thing that God's instrument would be the pagan Assyria, and that it would be through Assyria's power that God would show forth his will. Assyria, of course, did not know that it was being used by God, and did not even acknowledge the existence of God. Indeed, Assyria would later claim that it had won the victory by the power of its own strong arm, and would scoff at the notion that it was the instrument of Yahweh. But nevertheless, so Isaiah asserts, it will be by means of Assyria that God will declare his will to his people Israel.

Once again, God uses a strange name. He does not use the name of his people Israel, he uses the name of a pagan people, Assyria. Assyria, not Israel, becomes "the rod of his anger, the staff of his fury," and the "godless people" against whom Assyria is sent is, paradoxically, the very people of God.

These are three instances, taken almost at random, of a theme that could be reproduced many times over from the Old Testament. They illustrate that God can use whatever means he chooses, whatever means are to hand—a rest stop on a trip, the calm after a storm, the hosts of the pagans—in order to communicate his will to his people. His ways of working are not limited to the ways people expect him to work, and he clearly refuses to be bound by man's ideas of how he ought to behave.

There is a further interesting thing about these examples. They illustrate three classic ways in which men have claimed to "find God"—through *personal experience* (in the case of Jacob), through *nature* (in the case of Elijah), and through *history* (in the case of Isaiah). In each case, indeed, a confrontation takes place between man and God, but in each case it takes place in an unexpected way. The personal experience is not the personal experience of worship or some other conventional means of encountering God. The confrontation in nature is through the vehicle of nature least expected to produce such a confrontation. The lesson read from history is the lesson least expected and the hardest to accept. In each case, God uses a pseudonym, a strange name, and upsets all human calculations.

## God's Pseudonyms Today

Let us accept, then, Don Benedetto's theme that God is sometimes obliged to hide himself and assume pseudonyms, and that he does not attach very much importance to his name. The name men conventionally attach to him may now be an empty name, the place men look for him may now be the place he is not, and the places men fail to look may be precisely the locations in which his hidden activity is most apparent to those who look with eyes of faith.

Where, then, do we find signs of his pseudonymous activity today? Are we to look for him *only* in strange places? I do not believe so. To say that he acts pseudonymously does not mean he can never be found in his church, but it surely means that he is not confined to his church. To say that he acts pseudonymously does not mean that his light no longer shines through the saints, but it surely means that his saints are more numerous, and are found in more unlikely places than we are usually inclined to acknowledge. To say that he acts pseudonymously does not mean that Scripture is no longer useful in discerning his hidden ways, but it surely means that other literature as well is a vehicle for discerning his veiled presence, not only in Silone, who knows the lineaments of a Christian faith he cannot directly profess himself, but in a host of other writers who plumb the depths of the human predicament with a sensitivity not found in most contemporary pulpits.[14]

To try to discern the signs of the presence of the pseudonymous God in the world today is surely a risky business, but the risk must be taken, if we are not to leave the thesis of this essay irrelevantly suspended in midair. I therefore offer two examples of places where I see signs of his activity more compelling to me than the conventional modes of his expression theologians normally delight to trace.

The *first* example of this pseudonymous activity of God in

our present age is in the agitation and demonstration in which
our country has been engaged in the field of civil rights for
minority groups, whether through cries for "Freedom Now" or
for "Black Power." The white church, to its shame, has not
been very active in this struggle. One does not look to those
who call themselves "God's own people" for leadership in this
matter. There has been little significant indication that many
white Christians have really been concerned about the indig-
nities that they and other white people have visited upon the
black people of this country for the last three hundred years.
If we are to be honest, we must acknowledge that the real battle has been carried on by the secular groups, or by the black
church groups, but not by the white church groups. Whatever
advances have been won in the cause of social justice have
been won either in the face of white Christian apathy or white
Christian opposition. As Martin Luther King has forcefully and
correctly put it, "What is disturbing is not the appalling actions of the bad people, but the appalling silence of the good
people."

We do not usually expect to see the hand of the Lord in secular groups, in public demonstrations, in picket lines, in sit-ins,
in civil disobedience, in people being herded off to jail, in
court rooms, and all the rest. But can we escape the fact that
those are the places and activities through which concern for
the fact that *all* men are God's children is being expressed today? And that the same fact is not expressed, but denied, in the
white communities with written or unwritten covenants of
closed occupancy, or the white churches with the token black
tenor prominently displayed in the choir? No, the Lord is in
those strange places, and like Jacob, we have not known it.

The tragedy has been that we have not learned it soon
enough, and that because of our blindness and callousness and
indifference, the incredible patience of nonviolent black discipline has turned to violence. The white community, holding
all the power, has done too little, too late, and forced the despairing outcry that finally has exhausted any hope of working

through the white-dominated political process, and turns in total frustration to all that is left—the brick, the stick, the fire, the bullet.[15]

To me the most haunting line in contemporary literature occurs in the exchange between Msimangu and Kumalo, the two black priests in Alan Paton's book *Cry the Beloved Country*. They are talking about the white man. And Msimangu says to Kumalo, "I have one great fear in my heart, that one day when they are turned to loving they will find we are turned to hating." [16] So insistent is the theme that Paton has Kumalo recall it a second time at the very end of the book: "When they turn to loving they will find we are turned to hating." [17] It is already possible that this could become the epitaph of our nation. And the question is: Can we hear that as the insistent clamor of the pseudonymous God in our day, addressed to us, warning us, "Do not look for me just in the sanctuaries, or in the precise words of theologians, or in the calm of the countryside; look for me in the place where men are struggling for their very survival as human beings, where they are heaving off the load of centuries of degradation, where they are insisting that the rights of the children of God are the rights of all my children and not just some; and if you will not find me there, expect to find me acting in more heavy-handed fashion elsewhere."

There is a *second* place where I see the pseudonymous God at work in our nation today. I believe that he is using his "strange name" in trying to tell us something desperately important through the rising voice of protest about American involvement in Vietnam.[18]

That there is something wrong about the most powerful nation on earth systematically destroying a tiny nation ought long ago to have been crystal clear to everyone—but it has not been. Dropping napalm on women and children and the aged so that peoples' chins melt into their chests, ought long ago to have aroused in us the height of moral indignation—but it has not. That we justify our presence in Vietnam in the name of opposing a monolithic "world communism" that began to crumble over a decade ago, ought long ago to have made us demand a stern accounting of our leaders—but it has not. That we are entitled to impose our will wherever we wish in the world, supporting military dictatorships that do not represent their people, ought long ago to have made us cry out in protest—but it has not. "Destroying a city in order to save it," as an American officer recently described our destruction of Ben Tre, ought to impress us as a hideous example of Orwellian doublethink—but it does not.

Where did the prophetic denunciation of this sort of thing begin? Not in the churches, not in the business world, not in the labor unions. No, it began with the students, who on this issue have displayed considerably greater moral sensitivity than their elders. They have helped to remind the rest of us that national pride and arrogance are things in which they take no pride, and for which their generation is not willing to kill dark-skinned peoples thousands of miles away. The gradual escalation of moral protest in response to the escalation of military power came as students across the land began to tell the older generation that the war we are fighting is both futile and immoral. Many from both generations may not like some of the stridency of voice and action that accompanies the protest, but it has been our deafness that has made the stridency necessary, and woe to those of any generation who do not hear in this anguished protest a strong note of moral urgency.[19]

That the manner of contemporary protest against the war—or anything else—is disquieting, is no sign that God is absent. Indeed, we can expect that God's presence in whatever form will be disquieting. We will find him not just where there is peace, but where there is turmoil; not just where things are calm, but where things are stirred up; not just where things are satisfactory, but where dross and gold are being separated. For, as the prophet told us long ago, "He is like a refiner's fire."

## Notes

1. Isa. 45:15. Pascal picks up the theme in *Pensées,* 194, 242.

2. Martin Buber, *Eclipse of God* (Harper & Brothers, 1952), p. 18. Cf. also the very perceptive pursuit of this theme in Emil L. Fackenheim, *Quest for Past and Future: Essays in Jewish Theology* (Indiana University Press, 1968), esp. pp. 229-243.

3. Gabriel Vahanian, *Wait Without Idols* (George Braziller, Inc., 1964).

4. Cf. Gabriel Vahanian, *The Death of God* (George Braziller, Inc., 1961), and writings from William Hamilton's "middle period," such as *The New Essence of Christianity* (Association Press, 1961).

5. The literature is endless. Cf. *inter alia,* T. J. J. Altizer and W. Hamilton, *Radical Theology and the Death of God* (Bobbs-Merrill Company, Inc., 1966), and T. J. J. Altizer, *The Gospel of Christian Atheism* (The Westminster Press, 1966), for firsthand expositions.

6. Cf. M. E. Marty and D. G. Peerman (eds.), *New Theology, No. 4* (The Macmillan Company, 1967), esp. pp. 9-15.

7. Ignazio Silone, *Bread and Wine* (Atheneum Publishers, 1962), a revision of an earlier form of the novel published in America by Penguin Books, Inc., 1946. I have pursued this theme further in "Ignazio Silone and the Pseudonyms of God," in H. J. Mooney, Jr., and T. F. Staley (eds.), *The Shapeless God* (University of Pittsburgh Press, 1968).

8. Silone, *op. cit.* (Penguin), pp. 247-248. Silone's later revision does not contain the quotation in this precise form.

9. Silone, *op. cit.* (Atheneum), p. 274.

10. Ignazio Silone, *And He Did Hide Himself* (London: Jonathan Cape, 1946).

11. I Kings 19:11-12.

12. J. A. Bewer, *The Literature of the Old Testament* (Columbia University Press, 1938), p. 48.

13. Cf. further below, "Assyrians in Modern Dress."

14. On this theme, cf. *inter alia* such recent writings from diverse viewpoints as N. A. Scott, *The Broken Center* (Yale University Press, 1965); S. M. TeSelle, *Literature and the Christian Life* (Yale University Press, 1966); and Peter M. Axthelm, *The Modern Confessional Novel* (Yale University Press, 1967).

15. The above words were initially written before the release of the Presidential Advisory Commission's Report on Civil Disorders. This "secular" document insists, in hard-hitting terms, that the

reason for the riots is not black conspiracy but "white racism." Cf. *Report of the National Advisory Commission on Civil Disorders,* with an introduction by Tom Wicker (Bantam Books, Inc., 1968). The document is a splendid example of the voice of the pseudonymous God speaking in our time.

16. Alan Paton, *Cry the Beloved Country* (Charles Scribner's Sons, 1948), pp. 39-40.

17. *Ibid,* p. 272.

18. Cf. further below, the section on "Vietnam and the Exercise of Dissent."

19. Cf. further below, " 'Those Revolting Students.' "

# The Supreme Pseudonym

The previous examination of the pseudonyms of God has brought us to a point at which it might be argued that the case has been made: God can work in unexpected ways, employing pseudonyms, and we have illustrated the theme with examples drawn from both Biblical and contemporary history. Q.E.D. It is a temptation to stop right there.

But one must not succumb to the temptation to stop right there. For out of a number of further questions that could be raised, there is one at least that must be faced, whatever others are omitted. This is the question: How can one be so sure that it is *God* who is working in these various ways, and not someone or something else? Isn't this whole approach likely to make God simply capricious, not really trustworthy or knowable, to be looked for merely in the bizarre or curious circumstance? Or, to focus the question even more bluntly: Don't we simply pick our own pet social hobbies and try to invest them with ultimate moral worth by saying that they are the activities through which God is working? Aren't we simply trying to enlist God on our side?

---

The first section of this essay was originally included in the preceding one. The latter portion has been written expressly for the present volume.

### THE CRITERION FOR PSEUDONYMOUS ACTIVITY

That is a fair question. The guidelines for an answer involve, for me at any rate, a shift from the Old Testament to the New, though I think an answer congruent to the one I shall suggest is possible on Old Testament terms as well.

If we want a criterion by means of which to discern where God is employing pseudonyms today, I think we find it in relation to the time and place where God did show us most clearly who he is and how he makes himself known to us. Other attempts to trace his activity must be tested against how adequately they reflect what we know of him from that central event. The time, of course, is the first thirty years of what we now call the Christian era, though it presupposes the many generations of Jewish history preceding it. The place is that tiny little strip of land known as Palestine, tucked off in a corner of the Roman Empire. And the important thing for our present concern is that this event likewise underlines the unexpectedness of the divine activity, the sense in which *here too God used a pseudonym,* the sense in which here too his activity was just as strange and unexpected as in the case of Jacob, Elijah, or Isaiah, the sense in which all that came to fulfillment in the life of Jeshua bar Josef is simply contrary to the way any of us would have written the script.

Let us seek to drive the point home by the following device: Suppose we were waiting now for some tremendous manifestation of God's activity. Suppose that it had been promised that God would intervene in our human situation, and that it was now clear that the time was at hand. Where would we look for him?

Surely, the answer would be, in one of the great nations, where as many people as possible would be exposed to this important fact; surely in a well-established family with much influence; surely in such a way that all the resources of public opinion and mass media could be used to acquaint people with what had happened; surely it would be the most public and open and widely accessible event possible.

But in terms of the way the New Testament reports it happening back then, if it were to happen today, it would be more like this: A child would be born into a backward South African tribe, the child of poor parents with almost no education. He would grow up under a government that would not acknowledge his right to citizenship. During his entire lifetime he would travel no more than about fifty miles from the village of his birth, and would spend most of that lifetime simply following his father's trade—a hunter, perhaps, or a primitive farmer. Toward the end he would begin to gather a few followers together, talking about things that sounded so dangerous to the authorities that the police would finally move in and arrest him, at which point his following would collapse and his friends would fade back into their former jobs and situations. After a short time in prison and a rigged trial he would be shot by the prison guards as an enemy of the state.

Most of us would find it hard to take seriously the claim that such an event was God's supreme manifestation of himself. The whole episode would indeed appear to be a pseudonymous act, with the emphasis on the "pseudo," inflected this time as "false." And yet that is precisely what the attitude of almost any first-century person must have been to the assertion that the Son of God had been born in a cowstall in tiny Bethlehem and that he was, of all things, a lower class Jew, whose parents became refugees, and who himself had to go into hiding on several occasions. If on some occasions "the common people heard him gladly," when it came to the showdown and there was a public "demonstration" in the streets of Jerusalem, they quickly shifted their "hosannas" to cries of "Crucify him." [1]

And yet those episodes and others like them are the very stuff out of which the Christian claim has come. Jesus of Nazareth becomes God's unexpected way of acting, God's pseudonym, and he becomes the norm or pattern in terms of which

we are to believe that God will continue to act. So if it strikes
us as strange today that God should be working through
blacks in cities, or through students who for reasons of conscience defy a law, or through groups that are not part of the
religious establishment, such assertions are at least consistent
with the strange way God acted back then through one who
was looked upon as a criminal, spat upon and despised, and
finally strung up on the city dump heap.

Since he was an outcast, we must not be surprised to find
contemporary reflections of his presence among the outcast.
Since he was a servant, we must look for signs of his presence
today among those who serve. Since he was part of an oppressed minority, we must expect to hear the echo of his voice
today among those who are oppressed. Since two thirds of the
world goes to bed hungry each night, we must recall that he
made available not only spiritual comfort but solid and tangible loaves and fishes. Since he became man, we must acknowledge that in every man there is one who can be served in his
name, just as he served all men in his Father's name. Since he
lived very much in the world, we will look for him not only in
holy places or by means of holy words, but we will look for
him also in the very common, ordinary things of life for which
he gave himself: bread (whether broken around a kitchen
table or at an altar), carpentry, men in need, even tax collec-
tors.

In a time when men suffer, we will not be surprised to discover that he suffered also, nor will we flinch when Bonhoeffer
pronounces the initially disturbing words, "Only the suffering
God can help," [2] even though it is probably the ultimate in the
pseudonymous activity of God that he could be acquainted
with grief. And yet in this grief-stricken world that appears to
be one of the chief places where we must look for him today.
In his parable of the king and the maiden, Kierkegaard responds to the claim that in Jesus the incarnate God is present:

> The servant-form is no mere outer garment, and there-
> fore God must suffer all things, endure all things, make

experience of all things. He must suffer hunger in the desert, he must thirst in the time of his agony, he must be forsaken in death, absolutely like the humblest—behold the man! His suffering is not that of his death, but his entire life is a story of suffering; and it is love that suffers, the love which gives all is itself in want.[3]

So the point of greatest clarity is the point of greatest incongruity and surprise. Jesus himself is the grand pseudonym, the supreme instance of God acting in ways contrary to our expectation, the point at which we are offered the criterion in terms of which the action of God elsewhere can be measured. And if we miss his presence in the world, it will not be because he is not there, but simply because we have been looking for him in the wrong places.

## IMAGES FOR THE SUPREME PSEUDONYM

It is not only an interesting cultural fact, but a matter of theological importance, that the person of Jesus has been rediscovered by the youth of our era. Whether one is listening to *Jesus Christ Superstar* on the radio, encountering Jesus Freaks in a public park, or reading the latest popular rewriting of the New Testament story, one cannot help being struck by the widespread acceptance of at least certain parts of the message that originally transformed a bunch of case-hardened skeptics in Palestine into devoted followers who were willing both to live and to die for their leader.

Such people today still seem to have a good deal of difficulty with the notion of the church, and if there is a single recurring indictment on their lips it focuses in the question to churchmen, "Why don't you follow your leader?" There is a feeling that Jesus put a great deal of himself on the line, and that the trouble with his followers is that they're unwilling to do the same. So there is a new mood of openness to asking the question about the ongoing importance and significance of this Jesus of Nazareth.

If we are to deal with this question in a meaningful way today, we must begin by seeing Jesus first of all as a man, as someone who entered into and fully shared our human creaturehood. He is not a kind of "reverse astronaut," of whom it could be said, "We men have sent an earthly creature into the heavens and brought him back down, so why should not God be able to send a heavenly creature down to earth and take him back up?" The trouble with such a position (long implicit in certain kinds of orthodoxy) is that it makes virtually impossible an appreciation of Jesus as a flesh and blood creature like ourselves. No—the Jesus with whom we must start is a Jesus who really walked along dusty roads, was hungry, tired, and disillusioned; who on one occasion is reported to have wept, and on another was described as "a wine-bibber and a glutton." When he spoke in a synagogue he was thrown out; when he went to a wedding it was not to officiate at the ceremony but to provide the wine for the last round of drinks; when he appeared to his followers on a lakeside after his resurrection it was to invite them to a fish fry. If we can start with this fact of the humanness firmly established, then we can go on to employ a variety of images that will illustrate the point and also carry us beyond it. Here is a sampling of images, ranging from clown to fish, with a few more in between for good measure.[4]

1. *Christ the clown.*[5] A number of the paintings of Rouault depict the face of a clown, and a number of his other paintings depict the face of Christ. It is often hard to distinguish between the two. There is an instructive point in that fact. If we think about the face of the clown, we discover that he is not only comic, he is also tragic. He not only makes us laugh, he makes us want to cry. The laughter he evokes from us is not far from tears. When he takes a broom and tries to brush away the spot of light that is focused on the circus floor, we know very well that the light will always elude him and move beyond his reach just as he gets to it. We are amused at his efforts to catch up with the spot of light, but we are also

troubled because we know that he never will. He shows us the gap between how he looks at the world, and the way the world really is, and he enables us to enter vicariously into his own experience and discover that the way *we* see things is not the way things really are. He calls into question our perception of things.

This is likewise one of the functions that Jesus has fulfilled in the history of man. He too calls into question our perception of things. No matter how we look at the world, he challenges our viewpoint. If we believe that the world is an evil place, we are confronted by the fact that he embodied love within it in such a way as to suggest that love is at the very heart of things. If we believe that the world is a beautiful place, we are confronted by the fact that when Jesus gave expression to that beauty the world could not fit him in, and very quickly did away with him. There is no stance we can take about ourselves or our world that is not challenged when we confront Christ the clown.

2. *Jesus the revolutionary.*[6] In this age of revolution it is not surprising that revolutionaries have been claiming Jesus as a revolutionary. At the very least, this is an important counterbalance to a traditional Sunday school picture of "gentle Jesus, meek and mild." But it is much more than that, for if one reads the Gospels with any kind of openness, it is clear that Jesus was a constant challenger and disturber of the established order. The religious establishment took its lumps from him, and so did the political establishment, from Herod ("that fox") on down. We forget too easily that he came to bring not peace but a sword (a disturbing thought even if no more than a metaphor), or that when he took on the establishment directly it turned massively against him, so that the Roman Empire found a convenient way to get rid of him within a couple of years of the beginning of his public ministry. When we look at the nature of his teaching and the quality of his actions it is not at all surprising that the authorities should have been upset, or that as men look at him today they should continue

to be upset, for this man was a "convicted criminal" who was put to death by the state and we do not usually look to convicted criminals for insights into the meaning of life.

When religious people decide that it is centrally important to observe the Sabbath, he issues the rude rejoinder that the Sabbath was made for man, not man for the Sabbath. When we decide that piety and proper belief and membership in the church are the criteria of Christianity, he reminds us, in a disturbing story about sheep and goats, that it is not piety or proper belief or church attendance that count, but whether or not we have been concerned with the neighbor in need. This is indeed revolutionary stuff, and many a *status quo* has foundered on less severe challenges. And when we temporize with indecision or inaction, he confronts us with his assessment of the church at Laodicea: "How I wish you were either hot or cold! But because you are lukewarm, neither hot nor cold, I will spit you out of my mouth." (Rev. 3:16, NEB.)

3. *Jeshua bar Josef,* the teacher. Much of Jesus' revolutionary challenge comes through his teaching, for although he is a first-century man, the son of a carpenter, he spoke words that we cannot avoid or evade. Many people go so far as to say, "I can't take seriously the claim that Jesus was divine, but I'm willing to admit that his teachings were sublime."

Kierkegaard had an appropriate response to the point. He applauded his reader for having made this acknowledgment and suggested that the reader illustrate his commitment by the simple act of living out Jesus' teachings. He predicted, however, that the reader would find himself with a difficult task on his hands, since the teachings are not easy and comfortable, but make extraordinary demands upon us, culminating in the imperative, "Be ye therefore perfect, as your Father in heaven is perfect."

Furthermore, if one tries to build a case for the uniqueness of Jesus on the basis of his teachings, one is in for trouble, since there is nothing in Jesus' teachings that is not found somewhere in the Hebrew Scriptures or in Jewish commentaries on them. To be sure, he sifted out the best in the tradition that was his, but on the level of teacher alone the most we can finally say is that he provided a useful verbal anthology of rabbinic insights.

4. *"The man for others."* The real value of Jesus' teaching, then, is that he embodied what he said. And the message he spoke—and lived—had to do with a love that put others before self. Dietrich Bonhoeffer described Jesus as "the man for others," the one who is the model of a love that is available for all men.[7] This love, as expressed in Jesus' life, and not just in his words, has at least two significant qualities. First, it is *love for the unlovable,* not merely love that is offered to those who appear worthy of it. It is love that reaches out across all boundaries, whether of class, creed, race, or nation. It is an all-inclusive love. Second, it is *suffering love,* a love that is willing to take on the burden of the other, willing to stand in the place of the other—what Bonhoeffer described as "deputyship."

There is a corollary to this contention: if Jesus is "the man for others," then the church that describes itself as his body must carry on that function today by being "the church for others."[8]

5. *Christ the offense.* All these demands begin to get to us. Instead of soothing us, they make us uncomfortable. If we are honest, our response is liable to be like that of Peter, who, when first confronted by Jesus, did not respond positively at all. Instead, he said, "Get away from me, leave me alone!" (A modern version of "Lord, depart from me for I am a sinful man.") And on a number of occasions Jesus himself suggested that no one could really understand him unless he had gone through the possibility of being offended by him. Kierkegaard says there are at least three ways in which Christ becomes an offense to us.[9] First of all we are offended that a mere man should make such demands on us—the demand that we sell all that we have and give to the poor, that we pray for our enemies, and so on. Who is this man that he should ask so much

of us? Secondly, we are offended that this man should claim to
be the Son of God. Kierkegaard feels that it is not the nature
of the claim, but the nature of the claimant, that is so
offensive, for this particular man is from the lower working
class; he is a Jew, a member of a minority group; he is not
educated, cosmopolitan, or sophisticated. That *this* man
should claim to be the Son of God is simply not entertainable.
Thirdly, we are offended by the fact that the one who claims
to be the Son of God should come to the end that he did, that
the one who is God in the flesh should end up hanging on a
cross in a dump heap, with flies buzzing about his putrefying
body. That is not the way we expect God to be at work on the
human scene. And Kierkegaard concludes that we must at
least go through the *possibility* of being offended by Christ on
all these scores, if we are ever to be able to take him seriously.

6. *Healer and feeder.* There is obviously more to the New
Testament picture of Jesus. He is not only the one who
offends, challenges, and tears down. He is a positive reinforc-
ing presence as well as a threatening and challenging one. It is
clearly recorded that "the common people heard him gladly,"
even if they did fail him in the pinch. Many people were in
fact drawn to him. Many of those who encountered him received salvation, which is simply our word for "health" or
wholeness. People in his presence not only felt condemned,
they also felt accepted. People who were sick became well. If
Peter's initial reaction to Jesus was to want to get away from
him, at the end of his life he realized that only Jesus' healing
forgiveness could make life tolerable once more. Those who
were hungry when he was in their midst were fed, whether
they were nourished by the bread of the earth or the spiritual
bread of his nourishing presence. Indeed, it was in the sharing
of an evening meal at Emmaus that some of Jesus' followers
recognized that it was he who had been with them all afternoon. We can never say that he was unconcerned with the
body or the things of this earth. His healing and sustaining

power was not only spiritual but also physical—thereby showing that the two cannot be separated.

7. *The clue to the cosmos, or, the picture in the empty
picture frame.* Most people when confronted by the word
"God" are unable to give much content to the term. It is as
though they had a picture frame with the title "God" beneath
it, but had no idea what kind of picture ought to go within the
frame.

The only materials we have to work with are those drawn
from our own human experience, and if we want to picture
what is ultimate for us, then we must point to that which is
closest, in our human experience, to ultimacy. And here is
where the images we have thus far invoked begin to coalesce
into an image we might put into the picture frame. For when
we point to the one who challenges all our perceptions, who
lives a life of suffering love as "the man for others," and whose
presence is not only disturbing but also healing, then we are
moving toward a human description of what ultimate reality
might be like.

This is what the early Christian community was talking
about when it developed the first and shortest of all Christian
confessional statements, *Kurios Christos,* Christ is Lord, since
the word *kurios,* or "lord," was the word for the highest allegiance to which one could be committed. Those early Christians were saying by such a declaration, "The highest loyalty
which we can pledge is given by us to this man, who represents for us in human terms who God is." In him they found
God defined, but they also found themselves defined, which is
why—much later—their descendants could write a much
longer creedal statement that included a definition of Jesus as
"true God and true man."

8. *Christ the fish.* The whole thing is brought together in
one of the early Christian symbols. In those first decades, during a time of repression and persecution, Christians needed secret code words and symbols by means of which to communi-

cate with one another. One of the symbols that was early adopted was the fish, since the Greek word for fish, *ichthus*, was an acronym for the Greek words *Iesus Christos Theos Uius Soter*, meaning, "Jesus Christ, Son of God, Savior."

"Savior" is a word that first-century people used more easily than most twentieth-century people do. "Liberator" would be our closest equivalent. When we talk about being "liberated" from self-preoccupation or white power structures, we are talking about being "saved" from them, released from them, no longer dependent on them. Similarly, when we talk about being "liberated" for new opportunities or a new society, we are talking about being "saved" for something. And it was just this experience of being liberated or freed that the early Christians associated with Jesus. Just how free they were is indicated by the fact that they were not only willing to live, but also to die, on his behalf.

Eight images do not exhaust the meaning of Jesus as the supreme pseudonym for God's activity in the world. But they may in their turn suggest others, which in their turn may cause us to see God working in even stranger ways, and to say, first in perplexity, "There too?" and then, with more assurance, "Why not?"

## NOTES

1. Cf. the shift between Matt. 21:9 and Matt. 27:22-23.

2. Dietrich Bonhoeffer, *Letters and Papers from Prison* (The Macmillan Company, 1967), p. 197.

3. Søren Kierkegaard, *Philosophical Fragments* (Princeton University Press, 1962), p. 40.

4. For a fuller treatment of the theme of contemporary images of Jesus, cf. Geoffrey Ainger, *Jesus Our Contemporary* (Seabury Press, 1967) and *Which Jesus?* by John Wick Bowman (The Westminster Press, 1970).

5. A fuller, though somewhat different, treatment of this theme is contained in Harvey Cox, *The Feast of Fools* (Harvard University Press, 1969), Ch. 10, "Christ the Harlequin."

6. On this theme, cf. the two contradictory estimates in S. G. Brandon, *Jesus and the Zealots* (Charles Scribner's Sons, 1968), and Oscar Cullmann, *Jesus and the Revolutionaries* (Harper & Row, Publishers, Inc., 1970).

7. Cf. Bonhoeffer, *op. cit.,* esp. pp. 209-210, foreshadowed in his earlier lectures, *Christ the Center* (Harper & Row, Publishers, Inc., 1966).

8. For some of the implications of this contention, see below, Part III, "Discovering God's Pseudonyms Today."

9. Cf. Kierkegaard, *Training in Christianity* (Princeton University Press, 1941), esp. Part II, pp. 79-144.

# Assyrians in Modern Dress

The annual catalog of a religious publishing house recently contained several pages of book titles under the heading "Christian Fiction." This was followed by a shorter section of book titles under the heading "Interesting Fiction."

Some religious-minded people seem content to keep the divorce permanent, for they feel that somehow a book that is not a work of "Christian fiction" is suspect, even if it is interesting. Unfortunately there is no necessary connection between a writer's being a Christian and being a good writer. Some good writers *are* Christians (people like T. S. Eliot, W. H. Auden, Alan Paton, and Graham Greene come immediately to mind), but there are many more good writers who are not, and any Christian who proposes to live responsibly in the twentieth-century world must take the latter into account as well as the former.

To what degree, then, is it possible for the Christian to see the hand of God at work in non-Christian writers? What is there to be learned from the Salingers and the Steinbecks, who cannot be dismissed as unimportant, since they tell us important things about ourselves and the world in which we live? Indeed, the claim for the Salingers and the Steinbecks can be put more strongly: They do not merely tell us "interesting" things, they tell us true things; and they do so with greater

Originally published in *Presbyterian Life,* May 1, 1962. Used by permission.

sensitivity and accuracy than many so-called "Christian writers." How, then, are we to understand the way in which non-Christians can operate as God's pseudonyms?

## 1. CHRISTIANITY'S CULTURAL IMPACT

An initial answer to this question (and a very inviting gambit it is) is to assert that such writers are simply the unconscious inheritors of the Christian faith and culture within which they were nurtured. They reflect and transmit much more of the Christian perspective than they are themselves aware of doing.

To say this is to say that our culture has been nourished by Christian roots. The affirmation that man has particular significance, for example, is an affirmation that was originally made because of an underlying affirmation that man is a child of God and therefore of eternal worth. But for the last several hundred years the affirmation of man's significance has increasingly been made without reference to the underlying affirmation of his dependence on God. The fruit of the Christian perspective is still with us, but it is a blossom that has been severed from the roots that originally gave it life. And Salinger, Steinbeck, and Company still regard man with tenderness and even reverence. Salinger, in fact, has been accused by John Updike of loving his characters more than God loves them. And Steinbeck, for all the demonry he sees at work in human beings, obviously has a deep and abiding love for what one of his characters calls "that glittering creature, man." In other words, these writers covertly confirm much of the Christian perspective that they overtly disavow.

But we must not claim too much for this contention. It can be a cheap and easy victory, with the Christian sitting on the sidelines and claiming that the Christian faith gets credit for everything good that a modern writer says, while it bears no responsibility for the places where the writer doesn't quite ring true. Furthermore, one can legitimately ask whether the

Christian faith is really as pervasive as this view suggests. It is quite possible that the glimpses of truth these writers have are not nurtured by Christian faith at all, but simply by honest examination and reflection of the world they see about them— which is a far cry from a Christian world. Any claims, therefore, that Christians make about the cultural or social impact of the faith must be modest claims.

## 2. THE GENERAL AVAILABILITY OF TRUTH

There is a second way of relating the theological insights of contemporary writers to the Christian faith. This attitude can be found clear back in the second century. The early Christian apologists had to come to terms with the fact that the pagans had said a lot of true things without benefit of Christian revelation. So Justin Martyr said, "Whatever has been well said anywhere or by anyone belongs to us Christians" (*Apology,* II, 13). Presumably he meant that since all truth was one, and all truth came from God, therefore any manifestation of the truth was a manifestation of God at work. This means that truth is to be welcomed wherever it is found, whether in Christian or non-Christian garb.

The late Archbishop Temple came to much the same conclusion after an examination of the Prologue to John's Gospel. The Prologue deals with the Word of God, the logos, the creative power of God, the Word that has become flesh and dwelt among us, so that God's creative activity is now manifest in the life of men. That Christ is the agent of all creativity made it possible for Archbishop Temple to put a high value, therefore, on every expression of creativity: "By the Word of God— that is to say, by Jesus Christ—Isaiah, and Plato, and Zoroaster, and Buddha, and Confucius conceived and uttered such truths as they declared. There is only one divine light; and every man is in his measure enlightened by it." (William Temple, *Readings in St. John's Gospel,* p. 10.)

The implication of such a statement for the realm of creative literature is obvious. It can be indicated by revising the sentences quoted above so that they read: "By the Word of God . . . Salinger, and Steinbeck, and Faulkner, and Kafka, and Carson McCullers conceived and uttered such truths as they declared. There is only one divine light; and every author in his measure is enlightened by it." (William Temple, revised.)

The conclusion to be drawn is not that the existence of Salinger, Steinbeck, and Company proves that Christianity is really on the ball after all, but rather that Christians must listen to Salinger, Steinbeck, and Company more sympathetically than they sometimes do. God does not limit himself solely to "Christian thinkers" or people within the church, and there must be proper humility on the part of Christians in the face of this fact. Non-Christians can be vehicles of God's truth too.

But the solution has a difficulty. The danger is that the Christian appropriation of non-Christian literature will be no more than a patchwork affair. Rather than hearing the author on his own terms, the Christian lifts from a given author only those things that are congenial to a Christian view, and thus mutilates the author's message. In this way a kind of man-made gospel is created: a slice of life from Nathanael West, a dash of despair from Franz Kafka, a note of compassion from J. D. Salinger, a bit of realism from Robert Penn Warren, some bright battlements of hope from John Steinbeck, possibly even a bit of raucous mysticism from Jack Kerouac—the Christian mixes all these together, tops them over with a thin Christian icing, and then says, "See? This is what I have been talking about all along!"

That these various voices may all, in their various ways, be witnessing to a part of the truth, or even a part of the Christian gospel, need not be doubted. But to pick and choose this way is to end with a synthetic product and to fail to do justice to the integrity of the author's own point of view.

### 3. ASSYRIANS IN MODERN DRESS

Is there a way to avoid these difficulties? If there is, it would seem to come by recognizing more than the cultural impact that Christianity may make on writers, or even the general availability of truthful insights to all men, who try to write honestly. It would come by affirming that God can use *all* things for his purposes—the forces of truth, to be sure, but also the forces of untruth. Modern writers can, in other words, be understood as "Assyrians in modern dress."

The figure of the Assyrian is meant to conjure up a remarkable passage in the Old Testament, Isa. 10:5-11. Israel, understood by Isaiah to be God's people, is being besieged by the pagan Assyrians, who are definitely *not* God's people. The usual pattern in such situations is for the prophet to call down God's judgment upon the pagans and to gird Israel for the task of being the agent through whom God's power and might can be displayed to the pagans. But in Isa., ch. 10, precisely the opposite conclusion is drawn: God uses the Assyrians to make his way known to Israel. It is an astonishing notion— "pagan" Assyria is God's vehicle of revelation to "believing" Israel.

Such a perspective is a useful one for understanding a Christian approach to "pagan" writers. The Christian need not claim that the non-Christian writers are covert Christians, nor need he appropriate from their writings only those things that are congruent with a Christian witness. For the thing that makes Assyria so forceful a witness against Israel is precisely its unbelief. Isaiah never says that Assyria is to be taken seriously only at those points where Israel and Assyria agree. Assyria must be listened to and reckoned with as Assyria, as nonbeliever. Assyria must be seen on Assyria's terms.

And this is the stance from which the Christian can most profitably look upon Salinger, Steinbeck, and Company as "Assyrians in modern dress." They must first of all be allowed to speak as themselves, with their own full voices, to be heard first of all and basically *on their own terms.* That they should be vehicles of God's revelation to Christians may sound surprising to the Christian, but it is no more surprising than the original notion that Assyria was a vehicle of God's revelation to the Israelites. The Assyrians in modern dress can likewise speak their word to us.

But it will not only be their word. It will also be God's word. To some, perhaps not least to the writers themselves, this will sound preposterous. To clarify it, another look must be taken at the Isaiah passage. After asserting that God makes use of pagan Assyria to effect his will in Israel, Isaiah goes on realistically to assert that it never enters Assyria's mind that it is being so used by God, and that the Assyrian king would probably have been either amused at, or contemptuous of, such a suggestion. For, as Isaiah says, "he does not so intend, and his mind does not so think" (Isa. 10:7).

But to whatever degree it is proper to assert that the Assyrian is the unconscious, or even unwilling, instrument of a God in whom he does not believe, to just that degree it is proper to assert that the modern Assyrians can be the unconscious, or even unwilling, instruments of a God in whom they do not believe either. It may be true of Arthur Miller, as it was of the Assyrian king, that "Arthur Miller does not so intend, and his mind does not so think" (Isa. 10:7, revised).

The modern writer, then, can be used by God without his willingness to be so used, or even his consciousness of being so used. He too may find himself amused at, or contemptuous of, such a description of himself. But this does not lessen the effectiveness of what he is and says. It may even heighten it. His very disbelief may be the one thing needful to disturb the contemporary complacent Israelite from his shallow and inadequate belief. All of which may mean that the writer will be speaking more significantly and effectively and challengingly today than many of the theologians who overtly and too glibly pronounce the name of God.

There are at least two other ways in which the modern Assyrians can speak to the modern Israelites who are ourselves. *First* of all, they can show us what a world without God is really like, and set forth in all its starkness the world as seen through eyes of disbelief. Tennessee Williams starts out to talk about pity and love, but before he is through he has to talk about fear and evasion:

> Men pity and love each other more deeply than they permit themselves to know. The moment after the phone has been hung up, the hand reaches for a scratch pad and scrawls a notation: "Funeral Tuesday at five, Church of the Holy Redeemer, don't forget flowers." And the same hand is only a little shakier than usual as it reaches, some minutes later, for a high-ball glass that will pour a stupefaction over the kindled nerves. Fear and evasion are the two little beasts that chase each other's tail in the revolving wirecage of our nervous world. They distract us from feeling too much about things. Time rushes toward us with its hospital tray of infinitely varied narcotics, even while it is preparing us for its inevitably fatal operation. (Preface to *The Rose Tattoo*.)

This is the world apart from grace, a world in which the promises of the gospel, the good news, have not been heard. And it may be part of the purpose of God that men be reminded, by his unknowing servants, just what his world is really like if men exclude him from it.

But it is not enough to describe the modern Assyrian as depicting a world that the Christian need not inhabit. For their *second* contribution can be that of forcing Christians to recast their complacent forms of faith. It may be that modern men cannot really come to mature faith today until they have gone through the depths of disbelief with Tennessee Williams or Albert Camus or (for all their overtones of gentleness) John Steinbeck and J. D. Salinger.

It may be that such men must be our guides in the contemporary *descensus ad infernos*, the descent into hell, which, in the hell the modern world has become, must be gone through if there is ever to be a resurrection. We are called upon to entertain their vision, to run the risk of standing with them, so that we may see everything they see (the bad along with the good) and receive no prior assurances that there is more to see than they describe for us. We can be sure that faith will not emerge unscathed from such a venture. But a faith fearful of attack is hardly a faith worth having, and better that it be demolished than that it fortify a world of illusion. Commenting on the artistic achievement of T. S. Eliot, Amos Wilder writes:

> Dante traverses all the circles of Hell to know what Paradise means, and this Hell was not a private one alone, but the inferno of a whole age and of many cities and courts. T. S. Eliot's great achievement rests on the fact that he has himself been initiated into the furies and stagnations of our age and its cities. (*Otherworldiness and the New Testament,* p. 31.)

An initiation into the "furies and stagnations of our age and its cities" is what is promised us by the modern Assyrians. Some, indeed, offer us much more, but if they do, it is only because they too have accepted that bitter initiation. Faith undergoes attack at the hand of the modern Assyrians, but the faith that enters the fray with openness and courage has the possibility of emerging a stronger faith, dignifying rather than debasing the name of faith. The Assyrian who forces us to this extremity can be God's instrument, and is God's instrument, whether he wills it or not. He must not be expected to carry us over the great gulf that separates belief from nonbelief. But he can take us to the brink of that gulf and show it to us. He may not be the bearer of grace, but he may at least be the preparer for it.

And who knows but what the one who prepares the way may also, in the mysterious providence of God, participate himself in that which is to come?

# III

## DISCOVERING
## GOD'S PSEUDONYMS TODAY

# 1. EDUCATION

# No Promise Without Agony:
# An Address to Educators

In the old days, the preacher spent most of his time telling good, decent people what a terrible state the world was in, and how they'd better hop to it before Satan got a stranglehold on the future. Both preacher and analyst could afford the luxury of announcing doom. But that's not news anymore. We do not need to be reminded that next year might be worse than last. Our most extravagant hope is simply that it will not be too much worse. Furthermore, no educator has to feel guilty any more that he has fled from the "real world" to the "ivory towers of the university." Everybody knows about the agony. We do not need a description of that. The real question is: Is there any promise? Can we believe in more than the agony?

I am going to suggest that if there is any promise for America, it will be only as we go through, and not try to circumvent, the agony. President Nixon, in a curiously contradictory metaphor in his inaugural address, said, "The American dream will not come to those who sleep." Somewhat intoxicated by that figure of speech, I respond that the American nightmare will be creatively appropriated only by those who are wide

Originally given as an address to the Twenty-fourth Annual Conference of the American Association for Higher Education, and published in G. Kerry Smith (ed.), *Agony and Promise: Current Issues in Higher Education* (Jossey-Bass, Inc., Publishers, 1969). Used by permission.

awake, and who can see from within it some pointers to hope. No promise, then, without agony.

Let me suggest some shifts of perspective through which we must go if we are to discover signs of promise in the midst of the agony, centering on the words *violence, power, materialism,* and *compassion,* and keeping two further prescriptive words up my sleeve for the conclusion.

## 1. FROM THE FEAR OF OVERT VIOLENCE TO THE ACKNOWLEDGMENT OF COVERT VIOLENCE

The first shift involves a deeper analysis than we usually make of the quality of contemporary life that scares us most. Our fear of overt violence must be countered by our acknowledgment of covert violence.

When I refer to "the fear of overt violence" I am pointing to something all too real to the middle-class white American. If he has not yet been the victim of violence, he fears that he soon will be. If he is on a campus, he fears a sit-in, maybe in his office, during which his files will be destroyed. If he is in a computer center, he fears what might be called a smash-in. If he is in a classroom, he fears a disruptive teach-in. If he is white, he is scared silly when he sees as many as three blacks with Afro hair styles, black jackets, and dark glasses, moving in his direction. When he hears angry rhetoric by members of any minority group, he is sure that the verbal overkill is just about to escalate into the unveiling of hitherto hidden knives, clubs, and guns.

And this is not just a white middle-class hang-up. The protesting student cannot but fear the stock-in-trade of his opposition—mace, billy clubs, and tear gas, used to put down what the student thinks are the legitimate concerns for which he is protesting—fearing the kind of treatment his fellow students got in Chicago, in August, 1968, or in Berkeley, in May, 1969. The black or the Puerto Rican or the Mexican-American has every reason to fear the violence that may be perpetrated against him if a cop or a white gang happens to catch him in a secluded spot.

But I suggest that we will not advance from agony to promise, until we recognize that such an analysis of violence is superficial. Our fear of overt violence must be countered by our acknowledgment of covert violence. By *covert violence* I mean something more subtle and destructive than physical violence, terrible as that is, and the common threat that links together the two kinds of violence I am describing is the denial of personhood. The violence manifested when Sirhan Sirhan squeezes the trigger, and the violence manifested when a white man denies a job to a black man, are finally cut from the same cloth. In each case, the perpetrator of the violence is saying, "You don't count. I will get you out of the way." When a city rezones its school districts to make sure the black students will not get into the good schools and thus "lower standards," that is covert violence. When landlords pile up tremendous profits from rat-infested slums, that is covert violence. When society gives a dole to minority members but will not restructure itself to provide jobs for them, that is covert violence. When we send an eighteen-year-old to jail for five years because he says, "I refuse to kill Vietnamese peasants," that is covert violence.

The report of the World Council of Churches Geneva Conference commented, "Violence is very much a reality in our world, both the overt use of force to suppress and the invisible violence (*violencia blanca*) perpetrated on people who by the millions have been or still are the victims of repression and unjust social systems . . . the violence which, though bloodless, condemns whole populations to perennial despair." That unfortunately describes America. We are not only committing overt violence in Vietnam, but we are committing covert violence in Oakland, Chicago, Memphis, Detroit, Seattle, Jackson, and Boston.

What has come to be called "institutional racism" is a particularly telling example of covert violence, illustrating that even though as individuals we may be very open and understanding and unbigoted, we participate in institutions whose very structures guarantee that they will perpetuate the things we think we are opposing. Individually as educators, we believe in a fair shake for all students, regardless of race, color, or creed, but our entrance examinations have tended to cater to middle-class, white, suburban Americans, so that *de facto* it has been exceedingly difficult for members of minority groups to gain admission by our "normal" standards. That is covert violence. In principle, we believe that military service should not exempt certain classes of people, and yet we condone a selective service system that *de facto* discriminates in favor of white middle-class kids who lived in good enough parts of town to get good enough high school educations to get into colleges, and whose parents can pay the tariff to keep them there, so that those who actually get drafted are more likely to be the disadvantaged who do not have enough education to get a II-S deferment that will enable them to dodge the draft for four years. That is covert violence.

Until we see the agony in such terms as these, we will be in no position even to begin to look toward any promise.

## 2. FROM THE ABUSE OF POWER
### TO THE CREATIVE USE OF POWER

Let nobody in this day and age try to argue that power per se is evil—or good. Power is what we make of it, and the choice is in our hands. And it is the abuse of power that has led not only to the overt, but also to the covert, violence we have been examining.

Why are students so turned off by the older generation? Surely a major reason is their feeling that we of the older generation have engaged in a monstrous abuse of power. Without turning this talk into a panegyric against the American presence in Vietnam, let me use that simply as the most glaring example of the point, since it is the event most responsible, I

believe, for the great disaffection the young presently feel for
the old (and for "old" read "anyone over twenty-six," which is
when you become nondraftable). How does the student view
our presence in Vietnam? He sees the most powerful nation on
earth using overwhelming force to pummel one of the tiniest
nations on earth. He sees incredible technological resources
being used almost solely for destruction—pellet bombs timed
to go off sporadically and destroy civilians, napalm melting
the flesh indiscriminately of young and old alike, biological in-
genuity being used to defoliate tens of thousands of acres of
verdant jungle, half a million men being deployed eleven
thousand miles (40 percent of whom have been injured),
more explosives being used in a single day than were used in
the entire North African campaign of World War II, political
and economic and military resources being used to shore up
an oppressive dictatorial regime in Saigon, the verbal overkill
of the President and Vice-President being used to justify it all
in the name of "moral commitments"—the student sees all this
and he cannot help thinking, "Here is power, all right, and it is
power that is being terribly abused."

And then he looks back over the last half decade and asks,
"Who was opposing all this? Were the Catholic bishops? Or
the Protestant preachers? Or the businessmen? Or the congressmen? Or the trade unions? Or the educators?" And after
citing the few brilliant exceptions—the Bishop Shannons, the
William Sloane Coffins, the Eugene McCarthys, and the William Fulbrights—he has to say that the older generation has
*not* been opposing all this. And the student verdict, justifiably,
has become: America has abused its power, and become so intoxicated by the exercise of it that America has lost all sense of
proportion and moral value.

The answer is not to disavow power, though some, students
included, tend at least temporarily to think so. But "flower
power" will not feed starving peoples. No, the answer is to
move from the abuse of power to the creative use of power.
To some, such talk may sound utopian, but wearing both of

my hats—that of educator and that of clergyman—I respond that if between them the universities and the churches and synagogues cannot begin to work toward the creative use of power, we might as well throw in the sponge.

What would this involve? It would involve setting some new priorities, saying in effect: Very well, we *do* have the most power in the world. How are we going to use it? It would involve recognizing that the most important use of power in which we could engage would be the sharing of it. Suppose that instead of using our foreign aid to shore up corrupt dictators in Southeast Asia and South America and the Caribbean, we were to use our resources to help the economies of younger nations get on their feet? Suppose we took seriously the very minimal goal that the Pontifical Commission for Justice and Peace, and the World Council of Churches, have recommended—the contribution of 1 percent of our gross national product to an international monetary fund, the resultant pool to be available to developing nations for use in making their own economies more self-sufficient? Suppose we did that? We would at least be making the first beginning steps toward using power responsibly and creatively. Suppose that instead of spending eighty-seven billion dollars a year on the military budget, and thirty billion dollars a year on Vietnam alone, we rethought our sense of priorities and realized how grotesque it sounds to the black man when in the face of those expenditures we tell him that we cannot find six billion dollars a year to implement the Kerner Commission Report? When our own increase in gross national product in one year is more in dollars than the total budgets of all the countries of South America combined, do we have any right to expect the South Americans to look at us in any but the most distrustful terms? Is it a creative use of power to be spending billions of dollars on moon shots and space exploration of other planets— exciting though those may be—when on this particular planet two thirds of the peoples of the world will go to bed hungry this very night?

And I submit to you that if educators and churchmen are not willing to dedicate the finest hours of their lives to emphasizing the incredible reallocation of priorities that is called for by our present abuse of power, we have no reason to believe that anything less than holocaust and revolution will result. We either shift from the abuse of power to the creative use of power, or we face Armageddon—and possibly in our own lifetimes.

### 3. FROM MISPLACED MATERIALISM TO TRANSFORMED MATERIALISM

It is a cliché both political and clerical that we have lost our sense of "eternal values" and that we must "recover the spiritual." I have nothing against eternal values, but my point just now is that they are expressed in and through the material. Thus if somebody talks about "the eternal value of the human soul," I want to remind him that in both Judaism and Christianity, persons are not viewed as having eternal souls and transitory bodies, but as possessing a kind of psychosomatic unity of body and soul, indivisible. This means that if you talk about a human being as having eternal or infinite worth, you are cheating on the evidence unless you are just as concerned with whether he has enough to eat as you are with whether he has experienced a presence that disturbs him with the joy of elevated thoughts. We have no right to be more concerned with a person's soul than we are with whether or not he has soles on his shoes. Our neighbors' material concerns, if we may so put it, are our religious obligation.

And for reasons hard to fathom, an incredible proportion of the material goods of this world has been entrusted to the United States of America. For the first time in the history of the world, we now have the technological know-how to see to it that nobody in the world needs to starve or be cold. For the first time in history! And if you want a job as an educator, if you want a challenge, look for ways to put all that information and technique to work. Let us train scientists who will increase our technological expertise to grow food and thus get greater productivity per acre; let us train economists who will find better ways to make capital available to underdeveloped nations; let us train political scientists who will help to develop regional economic and political alliances to increase trade within the Third World and between the Third World and us; let us train teachers who will instill the vision of the one family of man in our young; let us train politicians who will lead us rather than simply follow where the latest poll suggests the rank and file want to go. Let us do these things so that, as the richest nation on earth, we can shift from a misplaced materialism, dedicated to providing luxury items we do not need (complete with built-in obsolescence), into a transformed materialism dedicated to the task of sharing the goods of this earth with the two thirds of the world that is ill-fed, ill-housed, ill-clothed, so that such clichés remain clichés no longer, but merely epitaphs of a world we refused to accept and were determined to transform.

## 4. From Academic Detachment to Moral Compassion

In the light of such needs, it is high time that, self-consciously and determinedly, we address ourselves to the question, "Education for what?" and indeed "Education for whom?" and that we take careful stock of the ends to which our knowledge is being put. I take my cue for the moment not from the humanists and theologians but from the scientists. On Tuesday, March 4, 1969, scientists participated in a Day of Concern. By the hundreds, they left their classrooms, laboratories, and field assignments to ask the question, "For what and for whom are we doing this work?" They were rightly disturbed that biologists are being paid by the Government to do research in germ warfare, that physicists are hired to provide us with more efficient antiballistic missile systems, that money that could be going into cancer research is being diverted into poison gas research, that medical expertise that could be ministering to a ghetto is being hired to research more hideous forms of napalm. They were saying, "It is time we took a long, hard look at what society is telling us to do with our knowledge."

I hope their example will force the rest of us to take a similar look at what we are doing with our knowledge. There is a moral question to be asked of political scientists who devote their energies to devising new methods of counterinsurgency, when those methods will be used to stifle peoples' revolutions against tyrannical regimes. There is a moral question to be asked of educators who promote a school system in which students come to believe that the right of dissent must be stifled when it goes against the *status quo*.

Do not misunderstand me. I am not making the specious plea for "instant relevance," which says that I need not complete a book if it does not immediately turn me on, or says that history is a waste of time because only the twentieth century is important, or claims that every experiment, every discussion, every lecture, must equip me instantly to go outside the classroom or the laboratory and cope. Rather, I am pleading for the breadth of vision that can enable us to see that any study of any significant body of material will make us more usefully equipped citizens to cope with a world that continues to multiply problems even as we study. It is particularly true in our day that those who ignore history are doomed to repeat it. I am pleading for study that is infused with moral compassion—and I remind you that that word *compassion* means "to suffer with," to be alongside the other, in his misery as well as in his joy, in his terror as well as in his triumphs, in his agony as well as in his promise. Let us not be embarrassed by this concern; let us rather see the nobility of it, and realize that it is the sense of compassion that makes us human, that makes us brothers, that separates us from the animals and from the machines.

All well and good, but how do we get from here to there? Let me suggest two qualities that could help us in that transition.

The *first* of these qualities is conveyed by the Greek word *metanoia*. This means an about-face, a turning in an opposite direction, or, as theology has translated the word, a conversion. Do not be turned off by the word, I beg you. For nothing less drastic will suffice. It will simply not do to say to rich, contented, and unconcerned Americans, "Just go on being more of the same." No, what is called for is a change of direction, a fresh start. It means, "Take a fresh look at *violence*. You are so afraid somebody will beat you up that you don't realize that you are beating people up all the time." It means, "Take a fresh look at *power*. If you continue using it so destructively it will destroy you as well." It means, "Take a fresh look at *materialism*. As long as you keep goods only for yourself you build up a head of steam that will soon explode and destroy us all." It means, "Take a fresh look at *education*. You are so busy describing life that you are stifling peoples' power to live." And at this point at least, we could afford to take a leaf from Karl Marx, appropriate his final thesis on Feuerbach, and see it as an indictment of ourselves: "Philosophers [for which now let us read 'educators'] have interpreted the world in various ways; the point, however, is to change it."

To all of this, the plea for *metanoia* means, "You are on the wrong track, or at least you are going the wrong way, a way that leads only to mounting agony. You may be fooling yourself, America, but you are fooling nobody else. The rest of the world sees through your rhetoric, your self-justifying talk, your cloaking of your own vested interests in the name of pious double-talk."

Can education demand conversion or force it? Of course not. But what education *can* do is to force people to confront choices, to point out the consequences of given courses of action, so that a decision can be made to turn about, to begin again, to make a fresh start, to undergo (and I do not apologize for the phrase) a conversion experience. Will we learn from Vietnam that backing a dictator is no way to liberate a people, and that destroying a city is no way to save it, so that we do not make the same mistakes in Latin America? Only as we become wiser than we were before Vietnam. Will we learn from the escalating race riots in this country that white people cannot indefinitely coerce and maim and destroy black people without a day of reckoning finally coming? Only as the lessons of Watts, Detroit, Newark, and a dozen other brutal realities are learned more quickly than we have learned our lessons in the past. Can we move from agony to promise? Only by measuring the agony full scale, with no illusions and no sentimentalities, and then committing ourselves to a new direction, again with no illusions and no sentimentalities, recognizing that we undertake great risks, but that they are risks infinitely worth taking, for they commit us not to narrow nationalism, but turn us about to the whole family of man.

And where do we find the vision and power to do that? Here I suggest a *second* quality. Let me sneak up on it by suggesting that perhaps the opposite of agony is not promise, but (as the title of Irving Stone's biography of Michelangelo suggests) ecstasy. Ecstasy is a situation in which one is in *ex-stasis,* or "standing outside oneself." That is to say, it is the situation of having perspective on oneself, of seeing oneself in relation to whatever is beyond oneself. It is the quality—to employ another theological word—of transcendence. By this I am not insisting upon the image of a Great Big Being off somewhere in the sky, and I immediately remind you that Herbert Marcuse, whom nobody is about to accuse of being a theologian, can use the word to describe engaging in what he calls "the great refusal," the unwillingness to accept things simply as they are, the repudiation of one-dimensionality, the recognition that we make a judgment about the present in terms of something that is not in and of the present.

Perhaps this could be described simply by saying that we are called upon to have a sense of humor about ourselves, to apply to ourselves the reminder Kierkegaard wished he could have suggested to Hegel, namely the comic fact that he who thought himself the infinite surveyor of all that is, had occasionally to turn aside from his manuscript to sneeze. The thing that most frightens me about the New Left, or the radical right, is not that they threaten middle-class values. Middle-class values need to be threatened. What frightens me about them is the absolute humorlessness of their crusade. There is something terrifying about the crusader who is never for a moment aware of his own shortcomings, the partiality of his insights, the finitudes of his being, the actual narrowness of his angle of vision—for he has no resources to guard him against the fanaticism of taking himself with such utmost seriousness that it would be beyond his capacity to admit that in any particular instance he had been wrong. This ability to laugh at ourselves, to see something slightly comic in our pretensions, is a blessed gift, for it is an acknowledgment of some standard of judgment or value, beyond ourselves, in the light of which we can cut ourselves down to size.

And when we can do that, then we can experience *metanoia,* turning about, conversion. People describe this over-againstness, this "other" that judges them, in many ways. I am not saying you have to be a Christian or a Jew to experience it, though I have found that in my case it helps. But I am saying that this sense is what makes one a human being—a person—and that only because of it, only because we feel confronted by it, can we know either agony or promise—or ecstasy.

# "Those Revolting Students"

The way a reader inflects the word "revolting students" will indicate his underlying attitude toward present-day undergraduates. If his instinctive reflex is verbal ("Today's students are revolting against society"), he may or may not have a high regard for them; but at least he recognizes that they are doing something. If the reflex is adjectival ("How revolting those students are!"), then he has clearly made a value judgment, and a negative one at that.

Many people share a sense of revulsion at what is happening on the campuses. The words "Berkeley" and "sit-in" are likely to render the middle-aged apoplectic. It is not hard to find four-square Americans who feel that the solution to such campus unrest is simple: "Kick out the commies, kooks, and perverts." Dr. Max Rafferty, formerly the highest official in the California educational system, describes an education at Berkeley as "a four year course in sex, drugs and treason."

As one who teaches on a campus that has its fair share of "revolting students" (and I opt for the verbal rather than the adjectival reflex), and who has talked to some, listened to more, and read a fair number of pages both by and about them, I cannot help feeling that the new breed has hardly

Originally published in *Presbyterian Life,* Nov. 15, 1966, and subsequently printed in *Church and Home, The Episcopalian, The Lutheran, Presbyterian Survey, Together,* and *United Church Herald.* Used by permission.

gotten a fair hearing in the mass media. These students are saying some things to which the rest of us need to listen; and we are not entitled to cover our ears simply because we object to the stridency of an occasional voice or the length of an occasional beard.

What, then, is their word to us? Why is there such a widespread attitude of revolt on the part of today's students? Let us examine the dissatisfactions, the remedies, the motivations, and the problems.

## THE DISSATISFACTIONS

1. One big gripe surely centers around the theme of *depersonalization*. The IBM card is a symbol of what disturbs students in our culture. "I am a person," a placard at a student rally will often read, "do not fold, spindle, or mutilate me." And they feel that the university fosters rather than diminishes depersonalization. Part of this is because of the sheer size of so many institutions of higher learning. Clark Kerr, president of the University of California, coined the term "multiversity" long before the outbursts began. Classes today are too large and the term "mass education" is just that—education of masses rather than persons. The university is an assembly-line factory in which a student (reduced to a number) is processed through a diploma mill, seldom meeting faculty, and all too frequently knowing the top professors only by hearing their lectures over closed-circuit television.

If it isn't that bad everywhere (and it isn't), that is nevertheless the direction in which the revolting student sees the university moving. It can only get bigger and more impersonal, and nobody seems to be doing anything about it. So he protests. Let it be added that he protests rightly. It is wrong for education to move in this direction, and if nobody else is crying "Stop!" more power to the student when he does so.

The new concern could be symbolized by asking the question, "Where is the center of the university?" In the medieval university, the answer was clear: the center was the chapel, a fact emphasized both in the architecture and the curriculum. Somewhere along the way, the center shifted to the classroom, in which the professor imparted (paternalistically) the insights of his research. A case could be made for saying that the center of the university is now the library, for the invention of movable type has rendered the lecture method outmoded, even if the lecturers have not yet caught up with the ugly truth.

But it would not be accurate to say that for the revolting student the center of the university is any of these things. The new center might be symbolized by the student's place of residence—not necessarily a campus dormitory, since these tend to be rejected as impersonal and confining. The new center is a place for talk, discussion, informality, and exchange of ideas; where hypocrisy can be disavowed, and in which a connection can be made between thought and action, from which the student might go to a lecture but might also go to tutor a ghetto child, and from which either activity would be equally appropriate.

2. The protest is lodged against the university, because that is where the student is. But the protest is more deeply lodged than that. The protest is actually against the *whole of contemporary society*. The Byrne Report to the Regents of the University of California grasped this fact succinctly: "We conclude that the basic cause of unrest on the Berkeley campus was the dissatisfaction of a large number of students with many features of the society they were about to enter." The university is seen as a microcosm of the whole culture, a culture characterized by impersonality in business, in living arrangements, even in social life, a culture in which nobody dares to be himself and everybody wears a mask for fear he may be found deviating at some point from timid conformity.

The revolting student rejects this whole conception of life as phony. Part, indeed, of the adult restiveness in the face of student revolt is surely based on the disturbing accuracy with

which the younger generation has unmasked the pretentious-
ness and insecurity of the older. The indictment against the
older generation goes: "You set off the atomic bomb. You were
complacent until Dachau. Your Depression wasn't so great.
You got trapped in Korea. Now, you want to threaten my life
in some place like Vietnam. You assassinated Kennedy and
gave me in his place a professional politician from Texas. Your
generation has failed us and yourselves utterly" (in Katope
and Zollrod, eds., *Beyond Berkeley*, p. 233). Here is part of
the reason for the campus slogan, "Never trust anyone over
thirty."

This disillusionment cannot be understood apart from a
word often on the lips of undergraduates: Vietnam. Virtually
all the revolting students place Vietnam high on the list of
what is wrong with the Great Society. They are unimpressed
by White House propaganda, disenchanted with the President, shocked by napalm, and unwilling, many of them, to
serve in a war that seems to them morally indefensible. In
1964, most of them worked for Johnson's election (or at least
against Goldwater's election), and they then found the President doing in Vietnam precisely what he promised them
during the campaign he would not do. Next time around they
wanted a peace candidate and got Nixon, whom they see as a
rerun of the Johnson duplicity. So they doubt the sincerity
and even the integrity of the decision makers. The "Pentagon
Papers" do not surprise them, but merely confirm their suspi-
cions. They are therefore the more upset when they discover
how much of a university budget is supplied by Government
funds that support research related to the military, and how
silently the university establishment appears to acquiesce in
being "used" by what they feel is an immoral national policy.

So the wheel comes full circle. The university is a part of
the Establishment the student rejects. He sees too many
trustees and administrators and faculty members working
hand in glove with a society dedicated to human destruction
and the denial of the meaning of personhood. Or, at the other

end of the spectrum, the student sees the university training him to be an uncomplaining middle-class person, adjusted to all the proper middle-class mores, doing nothing to jar the well-oiled machinery called the Great Society. He sees his father caught in society's rat race, and he wants no part of it: "So you win the rat race. You're still a rat."

3. The student also feels that the university has adopted *an ambivalent and inconsistent attitude* toward him. On the one hand, the university tells him that he is mature enough to discuss all ideas in the classroom; on the other hand, the university tells him he is not mature enough to order his own social life, and fights a rearguard battle for "social regulations." On the one hand, the university urges him to think for himself and arrive at his own conclusions; on the other hand, if the student thinks his way through to a negative assessment of our Vietnam policy, or opposes some generally accepted pattern of moral behavior, he is likely to find himself in trouble with the trustees. On the one hand, the university tells him that he is bright, and that he must make a responsible contribution to society; on the other hand, when he tries to improve the society of which he is presently a part, namely the university, he finds himself reproved for his audacity. To press the latter point: on the one hand, the university tells him that the decision-making process is a precious part of the democratic heritage; on the other hand, it excludes him from any significant role in the decision-making process of the university, save for a relatively powerless student government system or token membership on committees.

So goes the complaint. Overstated? Perhaps. But not so overstated that it can be ignored. For there is an uncomfortably large dose of truth behind each item on the complaint sheet, focusing on the last point. The revolting student feels that as a part of the university, he should have some share in the decisions the university makes, particularly since the decisions are bound to affect him. He wants to share in making the decisions that determine his future.

4. This suggests another note to the protest, the note of *impatience*. A given student has only four years. He is not willing to wait five years for gradual change in the direction of curriculum reform—a pace that would strike most administration officials or faculty committees as breathtakingly rapid. Just as the black does not want his dignity to be a reality only in the next century, and cries "Freedom *now!*"—so the student does not want the university to become what it ought to be only when his grandchildren matriculate. He wants a true community of learning, and he wants it now. He wants curriculum reform that will liberate him from dull courses and foolish requirements. He wants to become acquainted with his professors before his twenty-fifth reunion. He wants to be treated as a person rather than a number during the current semester, and not only when he has acquired the means to endow a new physics building.

## THE REMEDIES

So what does the revolting student propose, and how does he expect to achieve his ends? As Martin Meyerson said, in reviewing the events at Berkeley, "The protesting students are more sophisticated in their condemnations than in their proposals." To indicate that this is not merely the jaundiced view of one over thirty, a letter from a group of undergraduates, seeking radical change in the university, can be cited: "What kind of activities do we envisage? To be frank, at this point our intentions outstrip a clear understanding of how best to achieve them. One of the greatest problems we have with planning is that we do not believe there should be too much of it—at least, not beforehand."

This refreshing candor illustrates the mentality of much of the revolt. The students feel that they have been the victims of overplanning. They want education to be a little more *ad hoc,* to play it by ear, to let a structure evolve from new relationships that will develop when impersonality has been rooted out, rather than to impose a structure in advance that will depersonalize those who submit to it.

Certainly the dominant concern is with the importance—one could even say the sanctity—of the person. If present structures don't enhance that, so much the worse for the structures. Some students live in open disdain of the present structures, but have a resigned willingness to try to bend them a bit. A few, the ones who get the headlines, have given up on the structures as archaic beyond hope of redemption, and are ready, in the words of Mario Savio during the earliest Berkeley difficulties, to do whatever is necessary "to bring the university to a grinding halt." Others have decided to experiment with parallel structures. Staying within the university, they are trying to create experimental courses, in which the goals they desire—small classes, give-and-take, informality, less rigidity, relevant subject matter—can create an atmosphere in which true learning will proceed, and provide the type of education they feel the university is not now providing for them.

Although some revolting students have given up, a great many really do believe that things can be changed. What gives them the feeling that change can be brought about, even in so recalcitrant a body as a university community? The reason for the early optimism, at least, is clear. It was founded in the remarkable success in the middle 1960's of the civil rights movement, however much that movement may now have lost its initial momentum. Many of the early revolting students had had active involvement in the civil rights movement and were determined to apply that experience back on the campus. As the movement developed, the early emphasis on nonviolence gave way to a willingness to engage in violence for certain ends and this has widely divided the ranks of student leaders.

When the elders protest such pressures, the students reply that if injustice exists (as they are sure it does in their case), they have the right, indeed the moral right, for a redress of grievances, and if they are not listened to, to move to stronger measures. The university is entitled to expel students who break its rules, and it sometimes does. But it must be said that the results of student pressure—however much some may deplore it—have in fact often brought confrontations between students and administration that have sometimes led to change. A great deal depends on whether an administration can see through angry rhetoric to justified demands for change, or whether it remains defensively "up tight" at the least sign of trouble. Most administrators would rather solve problems around a conference table than have to request local police to remove students forcibly from the university administration building.

## The Motivations

Why do the revolting students occasionally go to such extremes? What are their motivations? It is not sufficient to write them off as "commies, kooks, and perverts." The Rafferty analysis is doomed from the start. Indeed, I cannot discern any clear ideological center to the movement, Marxist, anarchist, or otherwise. Many of the students are confused and not all are involved from similar motivations. There are surely some for whom marching in protest against Vietnam has been a convenient way of kicking the old man in the teeth. But for others, the motivation has been a high commitment and idealism, an almost desperate assertion that society need not remain the way it always has been. It is these same students, it must be remembered, who initially responded in droves to the idealism of the Peace Corps.

Pervading the whole, it seems to me, is a high degree of idealism mixed with impatience at the lethargic rate of society's adjustment to the revolution of our time.

To see the point, one must compare the students of the late '60s with the students of the early '50s. The latter were the "silent generation," the students who wanted to play it safe. They lived in the era when "speaking out," or espousing causes, meant trouble with Congressman Velde or Senator Joseph McCarthy. It meant getting one's name on the wrong list in Washington, or being labeled "too controversial" to be a good employment risk. By contrast, the emancipation of university students from that kind of cowering conformity is to be understood not as a sign of moral degeneration, but of moral health.

Education, after all, has left its mark. A truly educated person must be a dissatisfied person. If he has been exposed to enough of the greatness of the past and the possibilities of the future, he must remain permanently dissatisfied with the present. His vision may have come from the Old Testament prophets, or from the moral passion of Albert Camus, or from that social critic least honored in America, Karl Marx. He may have learned of the true, the good, and the beautiful from Greek philosophy, or of sin and grace from Paul and Augustine. But wherever he has gotten it, such exposure cannot help but give the student a perspective in terms of which he must endure a state of permanent dissatisfaction. And the task of the university is not to keep such a student separated from the world, but to enable him to involve himself more responsibly in it. The real cause for worry is not student action but student apathy.

## The Problems

But new problems ride into history on the back of every advance. What are the problems the revolting student faces?

One criticism has already been implied. It is clear that students oppose depersonalization, and it is clear that they want a new respect for the person as person. But it is not nearly as clear how they propose to get it. They disdain structures without realizing that, particularly when large numbers of people are involved, structures can enhance personal freedom as well as destroy it. The alternative to bad structures is not lack of structure but better structures, structures that are designed to maximize the creative interplay of freedom and order.

In coping with this problem, there is a danger that the idealism of the revolting student may turn sour. By next spring some of the dreams of last fall will have turned out to be impractical, if not impossible. Leaders in experimental courses will have found that objectives must be more clearly defined, that in the process of such definition clashes of opinion will emerge, that factions and cliques will develop, that programs will have to be scaled down to fit existing financial resources, that not every student will be highly motivated to work without being graded. In short, most of the traditional problems of the traditional university, having been shoved out the front door, will unhappily and inevitably reenter from the rear. And while some will be impelled to work harder to resist the old patterns, others will become disillusioned. A precursor of such disillusionment is the ease with which revolting students cry "sellout" when someone in the midst of a crisis suggests a modification of tactics or a scaling down of immediate demands.

Another problem centers on the students' vision of the university. Their cry goes, "The university belongs to the students." However true this may be, it is only part of the truth. The students are not the whole of the university. One can imagine the uproar on the part of the students if any other segment within the university made such a sweeping claim, viz.: "The university belongs to the faculty." The university is not only a place students inhabit, but a place where research is conducted, where writing is done, where scholarly resources are collected, even when undergraduates are not on the scene. The university, furthermore, is responsible to future students as well as present ones, and it is not self-evident that those who inhabit the university for a four-year period should write all the ground rules that may have as much as a twenty-year series of implications.

Coupled with this less-than-total vision of a university is a tendency to downgrade those dimensions of education that are not strictly in the realm of interpersonal relations. The university is more than one vast experience in sensitivity training, and education is more than human exchange of points of view "in depth." There is a content, a subject matter, to master, and some of it has to be gotten from methods as old-fashioned as reading books and engaging from time to time in writing down, on pieces of paper, in sequential fashion, and by a certain date, one's thoughts about a subject, either in the form of a blue book or a term paper. If one wrote a paper only when he felt like it, it is a safe guess that not many papers would get written. This does not mean that writing papers is the goal of the educated man, but it does mean that certain disciplines (of which writing papers is one) are essential to some kinds of ordering of one's mind, however passionately the revolting student may demean them.

In recent times student revolt has come up against the ancient problem of the relationship of ends and means. In search of ends that enhance personhood, students have sometimes been willing to use means that violate personhood. The escalation of violence on campus is the best example. There is a certain inconsistency in claiming to be against violence abroad while engaging in violence at home. And there is no clear line between violence-against-property and violence-against-persons. In a recent case of arson at Stanford, a fire was started at two A.M. so that no persons would be harmed. But the fire destroyed twenty years of research of a visiting professor from India, thus doing irreparable violence to the personhood of that professor. The widespread "trashing" on campuses after the United States invasion of Cambodia in the spring of 1970 made the nation aware of student revulsion at Mr. Nixon's action. But it also turned off many other students, who did not find throwing rocks through the nearest available window a very creative way either to mobilize support or to counter what they considered a grossly immoral action by the Administration in Washington. Thus there have been significant attempts to find new means of lodging protests. But the means will remain creative only if those with power listen and respond creatively.

There is another side to student revolt that has received insufficient attention above, although it has gotten inordinate attention in the public press. This is the revolution in personal mores and ethical choices. The concern of the student not to conform to a middle-class image of what society expects him to be leads to the beards, the long hair, or the sandals—which, after all, are extraordinarily harmless ways of revolting. But in the search for self, and in revolt against the moral codes of the society they reject, some students go much farther. In the name of freedom, they experiment with drugs, particularly marijuana and LSD, and insist that their sexual activities are their own business and nobody else's.

There is a danger here. It is the danger, not to be scorned by those who express devotion to personhood, that people will be badly hurt. LSD can enslave and destroy as well as occasionally liberate. Promiscuous sex can do immense psychic harm, and the presumably casual liaison may have far-reaching and damaging effects beyond what can be anticipated at the time. There is, in other words, an unrecognized inconsistency in the attitude of many revolting students. They risk irreparable harm, not just to themselves but their friends, in areas of experimentation that are too dangerous to be treated lightly and cavalierly. Furthermore, the increasing preoccupation among a segment of the revolting students with drugs and sex can actually be an expression of a withdrawal from the problems and pressures of society by retreat into a private and presumably more easily managed world that turns out, in fact, to be very public and not so easily managed after all.

These are all areas, then, in which the revolting students will need to do more thinking. But the conclusions they reach will have to be their own rather than those of their elders. After all, we're over thirty.

## 2. POLITICS

# The Faces of Patriotism

A Los Angeles businessman protests the use of a certain textbook in a high school American history course, because it contains "controversial" opinions. He concludes his plea with the words, "It just confuses our young people today to be exposed to both sides of a question."

A prominent theologian warns that we must not assume that God is automatically on our side in the cold war, and reminds us that much of the appeal of Communism has sprung from the indifference of Western nations to those in need. A South Carolina newspaper calls this a "coward's religion," and replies that of course God is on our side, while a columnist for a national weekly attacks "downgrading ourselves" and asserts that we must "upgrade" ourselves instead.

School children find themselves being exposed to the famous oath of Stephen Decatur, "Our country! . . . may she always be in the right; but our country, right or wrong!" and urged to emulate the attitude.

A pastor in a western city says that we are too concerned about ourselves, and that we should be sending more money, materials, and personnel to underdeveloped areas of the world. The local paper accuses him of being "communist-inspired"; his children are hooted off the school yards as "un-American"; and his wife receives abusive phone calls whenever he is out of the house. It is still an open question whether his church board will support him or ask for his resignation.

Incidents like these are not hard to come by. They could be multiplied a hundred times over. The papers are full of them. And there is a common thread running through such incidents and holding them together despite their apparent diversity. The common thread is an attitude that goes something like this: America is right. America is God's nation. To criticize America is unpatriotic and un-Christian. The good citizen doesn't criticize his country. Rather, he defends it against all attacks, whether military or verbal.

*A group of displaced persons, still catching their breath after their flight from a totalitarian and despotic government, huddle near a mountain in a desert. The word comes to them from the one they are called to serve, "You shall have no other gods before me."*

*Another group of people, living under a regime of far-reaching power and state control, a tiny minority in the midst of those who do not share its beliefs, gathers once a week and utters a simple and apparently innocuous affirmation, a two-word creed that goes, "Kurios Christos," meaning "Christ is Lord."*

*A third group, living in a country just taken over by a new political party whose members wear swastika armbands, meets in a church synod at Barmen, and in the face of the new political threats, declares to the world, "Jesus Christ, as He is attested to us in Holy Scripture, is*

*the one Word of God, whom we have to hear and whom
we have to trust and obey in life and in death."*

Incidents like these—of the Hebrews returning to Israel,
and Christians living under the Roman Empire and the Nazis
—are a little harder to come by. But with diligent searching
they too could be multiplied a hundred times over, even
though the papers are not full of them.

What do the two sets of incidents have in common? At first
sight, apparently nothing. The first incidents seem to have all
sorts of political overtones, while the second seem to be devoid of any political consequences at all. The first incidents
occurred in a democracy, the second in areas under totalitarian rule.

But perhaps all these incidents speak to a common problem
more clearly than seems apparent on the surface. Are the latter incidents really as "nonpolitical" as they appear to be?
They deserve more careful scrutiny.

The people huddled in the shadow of Mt. Sinai were not
being given lofty and irrelevant advice. For the commandment "You shall have no other gods before me" is at least as
down-to-earth and relevant as the commandment "You shall
not steal," or "You shall not commit adultery." It exposes what
was the constant temptation of Israel, and what has been the
constant temptation of people ever since—the temptation to
worship gods other than the one true God, to worship idols or
deities of their own creation. This means that the alternative
to the worship of the living God is not, as we usually assume,
the temptation to atheism, but rather to idolatry.

And the truth contained in that observation is not limited to
wandering Israelites at the foot of Sinai. Today, for example,
Communism is to be feared not because it is so atheistic, but
precisely because it is so "religious," because it makes such a
total demand upon the individual, because it demands total
commitment from him, a total giving of the self to the cause,
in response to the invitation, "Sell all that thou hast, and give

to the poor, and come, follow the dialectic." If the Gospel according to Mark demands total allegiance to God, the gospel according to Marx likewise demands total allegiance to another god, the god of the party, the god of the system.

So there are gods many and lords many. Our problem is not atheism but polytheism, that is to say, not that there is no God but that there are too many gods. The temptation to "follow the dialectic" may not entice many Americans today, but other temptations do entice us. If we do not serve this god, we are serving some other god. It may be the God of Sinai—or Calvary—but it may also be the god of successful suburban living, or the god known today as The Organization, or the god (at whose demands we must presently look) of Americanism and superpatriotism.

Turn to the group whose creed was *"Kurios Christos."* These people derisively called "Christians," who met in the first-century Roman Empire, were more political than their simple formula of commitment might suggest. For they lived in a world where everyone was required to assert, once a year, *"Kurios Caesar,"* meaning "Caesar, the state, is lord." Ultimate allegiance, in other words, had to be given to the state, and the state could tolerate no higher allegiance given elsewhere. So when the Christians said *"Kurios Christos,"* they were not only saying "Christ is Lord," they were also saying, "The state is *not* lord." They were affirming a higher loyalty than their loyalty to the state. They were saying in the new Christian context what their Jewish forebears had said at Sinai, "We will have no other gods before God." This got them into considerable difficulty, from which difficulty the hungry lions in the Roman arena were the chief beneficiaries.

The German churchmen, meeting together at Barmen in the shadow of Hitler's rise to power, appeared to be ducking the political issue and making an innocuous and irrelevant theological statement. Was that the best they could manage in the face of the Nazi menace?

It was, in fact, the very best thing they could possibly have said. For when they asserted that "Jesus Christ . . . is the one Word of God, whom we have to hear and whom we have to trust and obey in life and in death," they too were saying that no one else, nothing else, could usurp the place of that one Word of God, and claim an allegiance more binding than allegiance to Him.

"We condemn the false doctrine," they went on, "that the church can and must recognize as God's revelation other events and powers." The implication was clear: Since Jesus Christ is the one Word of God, "other events and powers" such as Nazism, anti-semitism, allegiance to Hitler, must be repudiated. This got them into considerable difficulty, too, and many who started talking this way at Barmen stopped talking at Buchenwald, paying with their lives for their refusal to bend the knee to the new idols.

"But even if the second set of incidents *is* more political than appears on the surface," the complaint would run, "What has all this got to do with America? These incidents all took place in totalitarian countries where the proper thing was to oppose the regime in power. That kind of attitude would be unpatriotic and subversive in a democracy like the United States."

Is the complaint a proper one? Is it unpatriotic to be critical of one's country? Does it undermine democracy to raise questions about how adequately it is working in a given place? Surely the answer to these questions must be "No." It is *not* unpatriotic to be critical of one's country; this is rather the true and proper kind of patriotism. It does *not* undermine democracy to call attention to places where it needs to be improved; this is the only true way to strengthen it. The very fact that some people would question the legitimacy of the two previous sentences is a sure indication that they need to be said loudly and with increasing frequency today. For the lifeblood of a true democracy lies in the right of dissent, the privilege of the public forum, the inherent correctness of questions to those holding power. If these things are denied, then in principle the totalitarian mentality has already conquered. For it is the essence of the totalitarian mentality precisely to deny to its members the right of dissent, the privilege of the public forum, the inherent correctness of questions to those holding power.

And it can always "happen here." It is a curious fact about the present American scene that those who must blatantly shout about their "Americanism" are precisely those most determined to deny the right of dissent to those who disagree with them. They believe in the right of dissent for themselves, but not for those who disagree with them. In the name of "patriotism," another word they abuse, they insist that all Americans must think alike, namely the way *they* do, for their point of view is (*a*) American, (*b*) right, and (*c*) Christian. This means that anyone disagreeing with them is (*a*) un-American, (*b*) wrong, and (*c*) un-Christian. Q.E.D.

Now this type of mentality does not just threaten the outermost political processes; it also threatens the innermost souls of men. For it is nothing but the most current form of idolatry, the worship of a false god, the same idolatry that was condemned at Sinai, in the first-century Roman Empire, and at Barmen. It is an attitude that says, against Sinai, "You *shall* have another god before the living God, the god of our ideology." It says, against the first-century Christians, "Our point of view, our way of conceiving what is good for men, is lord, and claims our absolute allegiance. Let no one disagree." It says, against Barmen, that "other events and powers"—namely, *our* reading of events, our program—are the "one Word of God" who must be obeyed in life and in death.

This is not an extreme or melodramatic way of putting it. This is merely the logic of the position when held up for examination. And what it means is that uncritical patriotism is no true patriotism at all. It is no service to one's country to hide its faults as the only way of extolling its virtues. And it is no true service to God, to identify him and his will with one nation, and assert that anyone who has reservations about making the nation an idol is unpatriotic. The true patriot will recognize that to say "This nation under God" is not to say something bland and comforting, but to say something revolutionary and disturbing, for "This nation under God" must mean, "This nation under the *judgment* of God, as well as under his protection." No nation can be worthy of the protection if it is unwilling first to submit to the judgment.

When Americans spend increasing millions each year on luxury items they don't need, while millions of other people go to bed homeless and starving, then the nation stands under the judgment of God. When advertisers deliberately falsify their claims, when churches remain segregated, when businesses put a premium on dishonesty, when tax evasion is a favorite indoor sport, then the nation stands under the judgment of God. And when young people should not be exposed to both sides of a question, when it is a "coward's religion" to assert that God may not be unambiguously pleased with us, when Stephen Decatur's oath is the grade school password, when concern for underdeveloped nations is "un-American," then, too, the nation stands under the judgment of God.

It is not "unpatriotic" to say such things. It is, in fact, an act of patriotism. For the only patriotism worth talking about is the patriotism of the one who loves his country enough to criticize it, who extends the same privilege to all who love their country, and who does not set himself up as the one to decide who may and who may not speak. Another way of putting it is to say that the one who loves God can properly love his country, because he is saved from the danger of making his country into God and can thus avoid the temptation of the new idolatry. It is not "this nation, which is God," or "this nation, alongside of God," but "this nation, *under* God," that expresses the true context for patriotism.

A number of years ago in Britain, G. K. Chesterton wrote some lines that are astonishingly descriptive of our situation in America today:

> The walls of gold entomb us,
> The swords of scorn divide;
> Take not Thy thunder from us,
> But take away our pride.

In a later verse, he proposed a further remedy, in typically Chestertonian terms, appealing to God to "Smite us and save us all." The super-patriots today want to be saved without being smitten. On the other hand, the complete defeatists have decided that we will be smitten and not saved. But the person who takes patriotism seriously, patriotism "under God," will realize that smiting and salvation are always mysteriously intertwined.

# An Open Letter to Spiro T. Agnew

Dear Mr. Agnew:

I do not know how many of your letters you read, let alone answer, and since I would like you to read this one I send it as an "open letter."

I write out of deep concern about the divisiveness that both your rhetoric and your ideas are creating in our country—a divisiveness that may well destroy us as McCarthyism threatened to destroy us in the 1950's, unless you are willing to hear the case of those who are disturbed by what you say. I want to try to make that case to you.

I have no right to insist that you change your ideas, though I hope I will persuade you to rethink some of them. But I have every right to insist (the verb is carefully chosen) that you change your method of proclaiming them. You do not escape responsibility simply by accusing your critics of "hot, wild rhetoric," for it is by "hot, wild rhetoric" that you have made your name a household word. You have indeed won instant fame, but at a price—a price higher for the nation than for yourself: the phenomenon of a Vice-President spreading fear and invective across the land reflects a country being urged by its elected leadership to abandon thought and rationality at a

Written in May, 1970, shortly after the invasion of Cambodia and published in *The Christian Century*, Oct. 14, 1970. Copyright 1970 by The Christian Century Foundation. Reprinted by permission.

time when we have special need of the ability to understand one another rather than to hate.

In so addressing you I wear a number of hats, and they are all hats that you have made the object of your scorn. To avoid pretense, I will describe them at the outset. On the most immediately human level, I am the father of draft-age sons—sons who love their country and are not going to tarnish its image further by participating in a war they believe to be immoral; some of your choicest epithets have been reserved for such young men. Second, I am a university professor; I work for one of the institutions of our society against which you have leveled sweeping accusations of social irresponsibility, and I represent a profession you have repeatedly accused of corrupting our young. Third, I am a clergyman, committed to the ecumenical attempt of groups like the National Council of Churches to relate religion to life; and these are groups for which you have expressed contempt. Finally, I am an American; but I am not the kind of American you approve of, since I express disagreement with many of the domestic and international policies of the administration you represent.

On all four counts, then, I am what you have described as one of the rotten apples you would like to clean out of the barrel. Can you listen to a reasoned plea from such a person? Before you throw me out of the barrel, let me try to explain to you what the concerns of these four groups are, and why members of them feel so strongly that you are doing a disservice to our country.

I

First, as *the parent of sons of draft age,* I plead with you to make another attempt to understand that youth can oppose this war for honorable reasons. I shall not speak in the name of my own sons, who are quite capable of representing their own position, but I must try to speak in the name of the hundreds of young men I have talked with over the past four or five years. As I hear your scathing descriptions of American youth who oppose the war, I wonder if you have ever actually listened to a nineteen-year-old pouring out the anguish of his soul as he decides that he cannot obey the command of his Government that he kill. I have listened to many of them. They are not the "effete snobs" or the cowards and moral degenerates you describe at fund-raising banquets. They simply believe (along with increasing numbers of older citizens who are beginning to catch up with their ideas) that the American military presence in Vietnam is *wrong*. They see America backing a corrupt military dictatorship that does not represent the South Vietnamese. They see us inflicting appalling destruction on a country and a people. They know that civilians —women, children, and old people—are slaughtered day after day whether by bombs from 50,000 feet, napalm from 5,000 feet or rifles from 5 feet. They know that the Vietcong are ruthless, but they are unimpressed by the argument that our moral posture should be dictated by the enemy. They reject the rhetoric of "victory" and the theory that the way to end a war is to widen it.

In the face of this, what do they do? They say, "No." They say, "I will not fight in such a war." They say, "I will choose prison or exile before I will do such things." Do you have any idea, Mr. Vice-President, what goes through the mind and heart and soul of a nineteen-year-old who decides, out of the most honorable of motives, that he must follow his conscience, and then discovers that his country offers him only the dishonorable alternatives of five years in jail or a lifetime of exile? I wish that just once you would seriously entertain the possibility that such youths do in fact represent an immense source of moral health for our nation, rather than being rotten apples.

If you did so, you might not be won over to their position. But you might come to realize that young men in this nation can oppose a particular war for reasons other than the cowardice, malice, or stupidity you attribute to them, and that they have a right to expect the Vice-President of a nation such as ours to be the advocate of the rights of conscience rather than the prosecutor.

Consider further what your rhetoric does to these young men once their consciences have been formed. Many of them are still too young to vote. Denied that course of action, they have written letters, they have spoken, they have pleaded, they have marched. To no avail. So finally, last fall, they organized peaceful demonstrations on a national scale, to express their moral convictions. And what happened? They were told beforehand by their President that he would ignore them, and afterward that while they had been expressing their moral concern, he had been watching a televised football game. And these demonstrations became the occasion for your now-famous attack on the "effete snobs" who engaged in such activities and led to your suggestion that such rotten apples be thrown out of the barrel.

Such was the response of our *two highest officials* to the anguished voice of youth. What did you expect them to do after that? Resume "business as usual" and thus betray their consciences? Go back to touch football and junior proms while their nation continued to destroy civilians half a world away? Can you not see that your language, which has only escalated in intensity since that first speech, made students despair of being heard without speaking more bluntly and acting more determinedly? I weigh my words with most sober care when I say that it was not only cartoonists, columnists, and commentators, but also countless American parents who saw in the Kent State massacre the culminating logic of your rhetoric. You have not disposed of a problem that must lie on your conscience simply by accusing such people of "sick invective." For Kent State tragically juxtaposed students totally frustrated by your scorn, and guardsmen confirmed in all their negative views of students by your reiterated contempt for them. Many other things contributed to that senseless slaughter, to be sure. Yet there must be some moment when, deep in the inner recesses of a decency all men share, you have to confront the fact that rhetoric such as yours—the rhetoric not of an ordinary citizen but of the Vice-President of the nation—helped cause those bullets to fly.

## II

In referring to students, I am already putting on my second hat, that of a *university professor*. I believe that education is the prerequisite of responsible democracy, and therefore that your attacks on our colleges and universities are destructive not only of education but of democracy as well. It may be that your polemic against universities desiring to admit members of disadvantaged minority groups (read "blacks," "Mexican-Americans," "Puerto Ricans," etc.) is based on a lack of understanding of how higher education is trying to democratize itself and overcome the social elitism of what have heretofore been predominantly white middle-class preserves. Since you are an infrequent visitor to our campuses, you can perhaps be excused for having a less than comprehensive picture of what is happening there—though by the same token you might also be urged not to express such confident assurance that you know how to cure all the ills you claim have invaded those campuses.

But there is one point at which I must try to make you see how your prescriptions, far from curing educational ills, would simply destroy the educational process. You have made it very clear that you would like to impose a kind of political loyalty oath on everybody in the universities, from the president down through the faculty and students. Let me illustrate that charge. At a time when university presidents have been notably tardy in standing up and being counted, you have urged the firing of the president of Yale University, Kingman Brewster. The sins of which you have convicted him are (1) raising questions about the adequacy of our present electoral process and (2) voicing skepticism about how fair a trial black men can get in our courts today. And not only do you want Mr.

Brewster fired; you have urged that a "hard core of faculty and students" be dismissed from our colleges and universities —an updated version of the apple-barrel metaphor. Even if one were to grant you your self-appointed role as ideological censor of American higher education, what criteria would you employ to single out the "hard core" you want to purge? Would you begin by dismissing all who agree with Kingman Brewster that we should improve our electoral and judicial processes?

Can you not see why the very suggestion of an ideological purge such as you advocate—let alone the criteria you could be expected to employ—denies everything that a university should be? Let me try to tell you why. In a democracy, universities must be the places where *all* ideas can get a hearing, whether they are good or bad, dangerous or innocuous. Universities must be the places where truth can make it against error without having to cheat; in other words, the places where we can believe that truth is not so frail that it can win only when error is refused a hearing. Your speeches make clear that you want to deny that free exchange. Were we to follow your advice, we could not build the intellectual muscle that can be developed only by the exercise of comparing good ideas with bad; we would be turning out flabby minds unable to cope with challenge. I cannot think of a more effective way to destroy democracy. But according to your scenario, it is unthinkable that a student should be allowed to listen to Kingman Brewster, or that having listened he could be trusted to make up his mind one way or the other about what Kingman Brewster had said.

Beyond that, the thing you seem to fear most is that the universities not only will foster an exchange of opinion among themselves but will become the seedbeds of dissent throughout our society. You do not want either the Kingman Brewsters or the "hard core of faculty and students" challenging our society. But those of us in the universities look upon them as among the few institutions left in America where the right of criticism is built into their very existence. Educated people help society precisely by refusing to let society—any society—become complacent about itself, by raising awkward questions about where foreign policy is leading, by asking why housing is so low on our list of national priorities, by insistently reminding us that those who ignore history are doomed to repeat it. Not only is the right of dissent the condition of the university's staying healthy; it is the university's task to keep insisting that the right of dissent is the condition of the nation's staying healthy.

And you misread the situation very badly when you can assume—as late as May 22, 1970 (three weeks after the Cambodian invasion)—that the advocates of such concerns are no more than the small "hard core" you propose to dismiss. No, the group that is now speaking up in opposition to what America is doing in Southeast Asia is large and widespread; it has united students and professors, squares and dissidents, administrators and sophomores, secretaries and Nobel prize-winners. If you realize your desire to "dismiss" those responsible for the hue and cry, you will have to dismantle and destroy the universities—and if that is your aim, let us have no further pretense. As long as you insist that there is no place in higher education for a Kingman Brewster or for faculty and students with unpopular ideas, then the universities must more than ever be seedbeds of dissent, not only to preserve themselves but to preserve society from such repressive ways of thinking. Demagogues used to burn books; you would fire educators. The difference is imperceptible.

So we are deeply alarmed when we hear you urging the destruction of the things that can protect a free society. In the name of such things—truth, rational inquiry, freedom of expression, willingness to hear other points of view, the right of dissent—we see it as our task to keep the light of reason alive in a land frighteningly bewitched by the unreasoned and emotional rhetoric of which you have become the chief propounder. No longer are we reassured by your occasional lip-service tributes to the right of dissent, for unfailingly, when the chips were down, we have seen you fall back upon the insistence that those who disagree must be removed.

### III

And now, of course, I am putting on my third hat, that of *clergyman,* for I am beginning to preach a sermon. But I shall resist the temptation even though there will not be another occasion for you to hear me in the pulpit, since I am not one of those clergymen who will be invited to preach at the White House. You have been very caustic in your comments about preachers who say, for example, that pollution might be a moral problem, and about church organizations that recommend recognizing mainland China so that we can begin talking together before we are reduced to the alternative of bombing each other. You want us to talk about "evil" rather than about contemporary issues.

Can you not understand how false that dichotomy is? Can you not understand that those of us who believe in God as the father of all men are by that very belief forced to concern ourselves precisely with *all* men and not just with white Americans? Can you not understand that when we protest the use of napalm in Vietnam, it is not because we are secret agents of the ghost of Uncle Ho but because we deplore burning the flesh of innocent villagers who are created in God's image? Can you not understand our conviction that help for black people who are destroyed in our cities might be a higher moral priority than sending a man to Mars? Can you not understand our own indignation when you indignantly attack people who want to cut the space program and, as you so graphically put it, pour the money down the drain of the nearest slum?

It is part of a clergyman's appointed task to look at political decisions and ask what they do to *people.* It is part of our task to press the question of whether the whole family of man is helped or hindered by what a single nation does. I thank God that for increasing numbers of clergymen America's pollution of the atmosphere *is* a moral problem, even if for you it is not. If such destruction of this good earth is not a moral problem, I would like to know what is. If the destruction of a small defenseless country is not a moral problem, I would like to know what is. If nominating mediocre men for the highest court in the land is not a moral problem, I would like to know what is. If an excessive use of executive power to enlarge a war (to the almost total disregard of legislative power) is not a moral problem, I would like to know what is.

These are some of the things with which clergymen today are concerning themselves. Such concerns are not a flight from the gospel; they are an attempt to say that the gospel means something here and now in the total life of all men. I hope you can begin to understand that American clergy are not going to follow your advice and tune out on such issues. There is, for example, a group today called Clergy and Laymen Concerned About Vietnam. It includes Catholics, Protestants, and Jews. Its mandate now has widened to include Cambodia. In the future it will turn to Laos or Guatemala or Baltimore slums or whatever next presents itself as a threat to the dignity of dispossessed peoples.

I take heart in the company of such men, for we have a peculiar and wonderful kind of freedom. We have an allegiance to our country, but we also have a more ultimate allegiance, for we have been told on the highest authority that whenever it comes to a showdown, "we must obey God rather than men" (Acts 5:29). And I hope you will begin to understand that in the light of such a commitment increasing numbers of us clergymen will endure not only your verbal wrath (if it continues); we will endure whatever implementations of that wrath the Attorney General may devise, before we succumb to that most dangerous of all creeds, "My country, right or wrong."

## IV

Such a statement may sound to you as though I have forfeited the right to wear my fourth and final hat, that of an *American.* But can you not see that I am unhappy with America today not because I hate it but because I love it so much? Can you not see that *for that reason* I fear an America in which you say it is wrong for Congress to object when the President nominates a mediocre judge to the Supreme Court, an America in which you insist that Congress should give an automatic rubber stamp to a unilateral Presidential decision to invade a neutral country, an America in which you state that those with ideas you dislike should be excluded from university life, an America in which you want the churches to stay out of the arena of politics, an America in which you become wrathful when the mass media criticize the decisions that Republican officeholders make?

In contrast to all that, I want an America in which the "checks and balances" the Founding Fathers created between the executive and legislative branches of government are honored rather than impugned; an America in which the best men possible sit on the Supreme Court bench; an America in which there is a stern review of decisions that threaten to widen wars nobody wants; an America that is not afraid that its youth will crumble if exposed to new ideas on a university campus; an America in which churchmen can offer their best to the body politic, like everybody else; an America whose leaders do not simply name-call in the face of criticism but are willing to learn from criticism. And most of all, right now, I want an America whose elected officials will set an example of moral leadership rather than fan sectional hatreds, and who will unite us in the pursuit of justice for minorities rather than divide us by playing upon our fears of one another.

As the second-highest official of our country, you had an unparalleled opportunity to provide some of that badly needed moral leadership. You have rejected the opportunity. After the tragedies of Cambodia and Kent State and Augusta and Jackson, some of us hoped that Mr. Nixon had learned that part of the task of governing is to listen, and that he would communicate that truth to you. Either he did not or you chose not to hear, for you have specifically stated since those tragic events that you will up rather than lower the ante of inflamed rhetoric.

I grieve. In a time when we have the greatest need in our history for elected leaders who will set a responsible style of public discussion, I grieve at your petulant insistence that you will not cool your words until your critics cool theirs, and that you see no responsibility, imposed upon you by your high office, to set a high tone for public discourse. I not only grieve; I come close to despair. For if I take you at your word, I can only anticipate an America in which the Vice-President himself continues to take the lead in dividing, inflaming, wounding, and so destroying our country.

## V

But *must* I "take you at your word" in this matter? I wonder if you might still realize how grievously you are dividing America with your recently invented oratorical style. I wonder if you might still understand how the office of Vice-President has lost dignity at home and abroad by the use to which you have put it.

I hope you might. I hope it is not so late in the day that you have become the prisoner of a style from which you cannot shake loose. I want to believe that you could still "cool it," lower your voice, delete your ripest adjectives, try to draw men closer together rather than pushing them farther apart. Then you could still set an example, as Vice-President, that would elevate political discussion rather than continue to degrade it. I am afraid that not even a radical rhetorical change of pace could win you back the trust of the millions you have alienated. But you still could, if you chose, lessen the flow of divisiveness and harm that has followed in the wake of almost every speech you have made. And you could decide even at this late hour not to add further to the harm you have already done. For that we could thank you, and then get back to the task of restoring reason and understanding to political discourse.

But if you do not so choose—if you continue to pierce us with the rhetoric that divides, the hyperbole that inflames, the excesses that challenge the very freedom to challenge you— what then? I know that I myself shall do two things, and I hope my fellow Americans will do them too. First, I shall draw my own conclusions about a President who lets your destructive rhetoric continue to speak for him, and then I shall summon all my willpower to ignore you henceforth, to realize that I have heard a hundred times over all you have to say, to resolve that Spiro T. Agnew is no longer news.

# ABC—Assy, Bonhoeffer, Carswell

The twenty-fifth anniversary of the death of Dietrich Bonhoeffer (April 9, 1970) involved a cluster of events that were centrally related to the way I heard about the congressional refusal to ratify Judge Carswell's nomination to the Supreme Court—an action my family and I learned about when we were four thousand miles and six time zones away from Washington, on the border between France and Switzerland.

During the fall and winter quarters of the 1969-1970 academic year I taught theology to a group of eighty Stanford University students at the university's overseas campus in Tours. Toward the end of March we all dispersed—most of the students to return to the California campus, my family and I to go to Geneva where I was to have a spring-quarter sabbatical. As expatriates of six months' standing, we had endured together the rise to instant fame of Spiro T. Agnew, smarting collectively under the strident proclamations of the second-highest official in our native land, though we had held our heads a bit higher when the Senate refused to ratify the nomination of Judge Haynsworth to the Supreme Court. But when Carswell's nomination was announced, we took it as a foregone conclusion that the Senate could never pull off a defeat of a Nixon Supreme Court appointee twice in a row. So we parted, discouraged about our country and wondering how

Originally published in *The Christian Century*, March 24, 1971. Copyright 1971 by The Christian Century Foundation. Reprinted by permission.

it and the rest of the world would survive both Agnew and Carswell. (This was before Cambodia broke and gave us bigger things to worry about.)

## I

I settled down in Geneva to continue work on a translation of a book about Dietrich Bonhoeffer, the German theologian who was martyred by the Nazis on April 9, 1945, for his part in the plot against Hitler's life. Since I had been closely studying his life and thought over a number of months, the approach of the twenty-fifth anniversary of his death had special meaning for me. And it was that anniversary that brought together three most unlikely items in my life—items that arranged themselves, I noted in retrospect, as an ABC: Assy, Bonhoeffer, Carswell. In good theological fashion, rather than starting at the beginning I shall begin in the middle.

By a strange—I am even willing to say "providential"—coincidence, the early morning post on the anniversary of Bonhoeffer's martyrdom brought me a copy of the huge book on Bonhoeffer's life by Eberhard Bethge, the friend to whom Bonhoeffer sent most of his famous *Letters and Papers from Prison*. There seemed no more appropriate way to spend that particular morning than with that particular book. So, putting my translation aside, I read the sections in which Bethge describes Bonhoeffer's decision not to remain in the safe refuge he had found in America in the summer of 1939, but to return to Germany, knowing full well that he had, as he said, to work and pray for the defeat of his country, and having a pretty good inkling that it might cost him his life. I followed Bonhoeffer through his increasing activity in the resistance movement, his deeper and deeper involvement in the plot against Hitler, his arrest, his eighteen-month imprisonment, his lengthy interrogation, and finally his hasty trial and quick death, just a week before the Americans liberated the Flossenburg concentration camp where he had been held.

Bonhoeffer's story belongs, as Reinhold Niebuhr said, to "the modern acts of the apostles." For me it has had increasing meaning as I have come to believe (1) that churchmen today must be willing to put a great deal on the line to oppose evil policies of evil governments and (2) that the evil policy of our own Government in Southeast Asia makes it an evil government. I have tried to resist making facile comparisons between Nazi Germany and the United States, but as the Vietnam war has mounted in intensity, the Bonhoeffer experience has seemed more and more relevant to the American experience. We too have undergone the exclusion, one after another, of viable political alternatives to bring about change, and we find ourselves forced to contemplate "resistance" activities as the only means of sensitizing the conscience of the nation.

## II

Such uncomfortable thoughts were the net result of my reliving of the Bonhoeffer story, with Bethge's help, on the anniversary of the day when he paid the full price for his convictions. April 9 was a Thursday, and since our children had a half-holiday from the Geneva school on Thursday afternoons, we were taking advantage of this weekly opportunity to see the surrounding country before our ten-week sabbatical ran out. We had decided to drive over to Haute-Savoie in France that Thursday, to visit the church of Notre Dame de Toute Grâce at Plateau d'Assy. This remarkable building is one of the first modern churches to incorporate the work of contemporary "secular" artists: Léger—brilliant mosaics on the exterior; Matisse—a painting of St. Dominic on tile; Chagall—the baptistery; Rouault—two stained-glass windows; and Jean Lurçat—a magnificent woven tapestry hung in the chancel.

It was that tapestry which caught my eye and kept my attention. I was both fascinated and repelled by it, and I found myself returning to it again and again. It is a huge and brilliantly colored depiction of scenes in the Biblical drama, drawn particularly from the twelfth chapter of Revelation, which deals with the struggle between a woman (presumably the church) and a beast (presumably Satan). In harsh tone and line, Lurçat portrays the ongoing battle between good and evil, a battle that, as the book of Revelation indicates, will mount in intensity until the last days—a theological notion whose accuracy I would judge to be among the most empirically evident in today's world.

At first, as I looked at the tapestry, it seemed pretty clear to me that the forces of evil were in the saddle and that the huge beast would make short work of the maiden. However, the printed description of the tapestry that is handed all visitors instructed viewers to hold on to the ultimate truth that the final outcome of the battle, to be decided at some eschatological moment, is already assured: Satan will be defeated and evil overthrown, the virgin will be victorious over the beast, St. Michael will conquer the dragon. But the victory, to say the least, is veiled. Lurçat has not tried to provide a central focal point for his tapestry, since this is given by the crucifix on the altar below—another sign that victories, if they come, are indeed veiled; for to see "victory" in the cross is surely to find it in the face of a fairly obvious kind of historical defeat.

I could not help juxtaposing the scene on the tapestry with the scene at the Flossenburg concentration camp twenty-five years earlier to the day. And although I left the church buoyed up eschatologically by the claim that good would triumph on the last day, I was contemporaneously much depressed by the apparent evidence that good was bound to get it in the neck right up to the last day itself. It occurred to me that we were indeed living in what Bonhoeffer's contemporaries in Germany described as *zwischen den Zeiten,* between the times—between the disclosure of some partial meanings in history and an ultimate fulfillment of history. But I felt that the time between those disclosures was a sorry business in which the Bonhoeffers were sure to lose and the Carswells sure to win.

My mood was temporarily lifted—enough so that for a few moments I forgot all about Carswell, whose confirmation was then being debated in the Senate—by an exchange with a wonderful Dominican priest in a T-shirt whom we met in the presbytery behind the church just as we were leaving Assy. I told him that I was a Protestant theologian, that I had been an observer at Vatican II, that I wanted to buy some of the postcards he had on display to use in my classes at Stanford, and that I would like to know what they cost. "My dear friend," he told me, "this is not a den of robbers, but a house of prayer"; he refused any money and gave us all his blessing.

### III

Down the mountain we went, blessed indeed and needing it badly, for we went into a fearful storm, in the midst of which almost with the force of a lightning bolt, my wife uttered the word "Carswell!" She was suggesting that the vote must have been taken by now. We switched on the car radio, resolved to believe that a fairly close vote to confirm would represent some kind of moral victory. After much dial-turning we did get a fragment of a sentence: ". . . phoned him from the White House urging him to remain on the bench." It wasn't enough to satisfy the mind, but it did boggle the mind. For the first time in weeks we were confronted with the possibility, the unbelievable possibility, that the Senate had twice in a row voted its conscience. By the time we got back to Geneva the storm was over, and we could begin to pick up enough consecutive sentences to be sure that the impossible had happened. There was a rainbow in the firmament, even though nobody saw it but us.

Having spent the morning immersed in the Bonhoeffer experience of the futility of trying to transform governments, and the afternoon at Assy being reminded that evil is going to continue winning some pretty impressive triumphs—having, in short, come to a very gloomy conclusion about what could be done on the human scene, I found a modicum of hope restored to me through the action of the United States Senate: hope that there can, after all, be some frail but important victories, and that one is never entitled to give up on the fresh possibilities that even an unpromising day may bring.

Before this becomes a simplistic homily of hope, I should report that virtually everything Mr. Nixon has done since last April 9 has served to make my straw of hope seem an ever more slender reed. But even in the midst of growing despair about the future of our nation and increasing frustration about how its policies can be effectively opposed, I am sustained by that word out of a thunderstorm that all is not always lost, that though there may be new setbacks forcing us to go down with the Bonhoeffers, we can at least go down in the company of good men, supported by the fact that there are just causes which are worth any sacrifice and that even out of apparent defeats new hopes occasionally materialize. And so I remain grateful for the rekindling of faith that was given me in the way those courageous U.S. senators faced their very lonely, and very public, moment of truth.

## 3. LIGHT IN THICK DARKNESS

# Meditation on a Particular Death:
# A Fragmentary Adventure in Grace

I believe in . . . the communion of saints.
                                        —The Apostles' Creed
Neither shall there be any more pain . . .
                                        —Rev. 21:4
Greater love hath no man than this, that a man lay down
his life for his friends.
                                        —John 15:13
The peace of God, which passeth all understanding . . .
                                        —Phil. 4:7

This is an inadequate labor of love. It is an attempt to set
down, while the experience is still fresh with me, something of
the impact which a particular death, D.'s death, has had upon
me. It is a rather personal testimony, but it somehow seems
terribly important to try to record it, in the faith that it may
be an act of love to share what one has learned, even though,
or perhaps particularly because, the learning has been very
painful. I want to try to capture something of what has been
going through my heart, so that others who have been affected
by D.'s death may perhaps be able to say, "Yes, I felt that
too!" or more important, "There was more to it than that!" and

Written one week after the death of David E. Roberts at Union Theological Seminary in Jan., 1955, and published anonymously in *Religion
in Life*, Vol. XXVI, No. 4 (Autumn, 1957). Copyright 1957 by Abingdon
Press. Reprinted by permission.

then be empowered in the Spirit to continue the process of sharing in the community of faith.

D. taught me many things by living, and these I shall presuppose. It is the things he taught me by dying that I shall describe here. I need say of his life only that I had heard him laugh, I had seen him in pain, I had sought his counsel, I had looked forward to a lifetime of work with him—so that it is clearly the case that it is *who* D. was in his lifetime that makes his death so important for me. It is not death in general, then, or the death of *x*, which has touched me. Something much more intimate, much more precious than that is involved. It is his particular death which has helped me to know that many things, which heretofore were only words, are triumphantly real, and for these things I must give thanks.

# I

The most significant thing D. has done for me by dying has been to make real for me the meaning of the affirmation, "*I believe in . . . the communion of saints.*" Other deaths in the past gave me resources of faith; I can believe in "the resurrection of the body, and the life everlasting." These I could muster to meet the shock of D.'s death. But never before he died had I been truly aware of the almost incredible depth and splendor of the affirmation, "I believe in the communion of saints." This, more than anything else, has taken away the sting of D.'s death, insofar as that is possible. I do no more than record my newfound conviction, given me by the grace of God and by D., that the occasional sense of communion I had with D. in his former life has been replaced by an almost piercing sense of his nearness in his new life. The fact that we are no longer related at particular points in time somehow means now that we can be related at every point, at all times. I used to be conscious of him in his office, or his classroom, or as he sat in chapel—now I am conscious of him in my office, in my classroom, as I sit in chapel. I do not mean this in any ghostly sense; I lay claim to no visions. I do mean that my relationship with D. has incredible new dimensions.

This I have discovered to be both a terrible and a wonderful thing. It is terrible in the sense of the poignancy and bereftness with which it invests almost every moment of the day and night, since this new relationship is (at least so far) too intangible to have the same kind of total meaning as was possessed by the relationship we used to have. But it is a wonderful thing also, and in this very important sense, that it invests every moment of time with a sense of the dimension of eternity. I am simply not alone. I am surrounded by "a cloud of witnesses," D. most preeminently among them. D.'s death brings me into an awareness of eternity that makes eternity (for the moment at least) wonderfully real. This is true on several levels.

On one level it means that certain specific times and places will always have special meaning—here a joke was told, here a pipe was lighted, here Berdyaev was explained, here a child was kissed. But it means much more than that. For it also means, on another level, that when another joke is told, another pipe lighted, another philosopher explained, another child kissed, this is somehow related to, and done in the presence of, eternity. D. is now "present" in a way he never was before. I have the strange and wonderful feeling that I get to know him better each day, and that far from his death diminishing his influence over my life, his death means that his true and lasting influence has just begun to be felt. So that whatever the communion of saints means, it means at least this—that the fellowship of believers in Christ is not limited to time and space, nor do those believers in time commune only with believers in time, and those believers beyond time commune only with those beyond time. For me such distinctions have now become quite inadequate—a new dimension has entered into my life, making every moment momentous with sacramental quality.

I am told that this sense of the immediacy of the presence of one who has died will fade or diminish with the passage of time. And I rather imagine that the *intensity* of the experience will suffer some diminution. But if in any really significant way I lose, or become dulled to, the dimension of eternity in my heart which D. by his very act of dying has introduced, then, hard as it is to say it, I will have to ask God through some other experience of pain to make me aware once more of his "terrible goodness," and I will have to look upon that pain, as I have tried so desperately to look upon D.'s death, as "the pain God is allowed to guide."

What I am so gropingly trying to express has been put in better words by C. S. Lewis in an essay in which he describes the impact that the death of Charles Williams had upon him. (Williams, like D., cast his influence over many lives; he was the kind of gay, sparkling conversationalist that D. was. And I am just unsophisticated enough to rejoice in what I feel sure is the joyous acclaim with which Charles Williams and D. have recently "discovered" one another.) Lewis talks about "the ubiquitous presence of a dead man," of whom one is constantly reminded by almost everything that happens, with whom in a real sense one shares everything that happens; and he concludes: "No event has so corroborated my faith in the next world as Williams did simply by dying. When the idea of death and the idea of Williams thus met in my mind, it was the idea of death that was changed." [1]

I first read those words five years ago. I thought they were very interesting, and rather stirring. Now, substituting for "Williams" the name "D.," I know that they are true. No event has so corroborated my faith in the next world as D. did simply by dying. When the idea of death and the idea of D. thus met in my mind, it was the idea of death that was changed. He, by dying, has taught me that.

There is another level still. The "communion of saints" is now real for me not only as something that bridges and in fact destroys the distinction between eternity and time, or to put it another way, invests every moment of time with the splendor of eternity. The communion of saints has come alive for me in the sense of the new bonds of sheer love and tenderness that D.'s death has forged among those who loved him. Never again can I be satisfied to describe this community as a "community of scholars," or "an institution of higher learning." D.'s death has brought to me a realization of the wondrous concern that men and women can have for one another, of the devotion which can spring to the surface in the most unexpected places. When I think of the "bands of love" that I have felt surrounding D.'s family, D.'s friends, D.'s students, my final response, even in the midst of pain, must be one of gratitude to God.

## II

A second phrase has come home to me with particular meaning during these days when D.'s presence has been almost as heartrendingly real as his absence. And these words have, by virtue simply of who D. was and what he had been through, helped me greatly to come to honest terms with his death. These are words at the end of the Apocalypse, describing the new heaven and the new earth, *"Neither shall there be any more pain."* (Rev. 21:4.) This was the thing for which I could be grateful, in the first stunned moments when I learned of D.'s death and knew that in a few moments I was going to have to force myself to go downstairs and give a lecture. "Neither shall there be any more pain"—these words told me that the last and most significant word about a human being is always *God's* word. God knows D. had suffered pain of an intense physical sort for almost the last two years of his life. And there had been other pain too, at other times—pain of doubt, pain of tragedy, pain of despair. And D.'s death could be a blessing at least to this extent, that the pain was gone.

It may be that other parts of the total verse are more important: "And God shall wipe away all tears from their eyes; and there shall be no more death, neither sorrow, nor crying, neither shall there be any more pain: for the former things are passed away." But in terms of D.'s particular death, I must assert that the pain he bore became sacramental for me, as his death shouted forth to me the assurance that the writer of the Apocalypse was speaking truth, and that D.'s pain has at last been given up to God, taken away by God, and healed by God. It will always remain a sorrowful mystery to me why the pain could not have been taken away on this side of death, but I will accept that mystery as one that God in his own good time will make plain; and rather than looking in self-pity at my loss, I will try to rejoice with D. in the fullness and freshness of his newfound life.

I must make one comment about the place of pain in D.'s *life*—a fact of which his death helped to remind me. I am sure that one of the reasons why D. was so extraordinarily effective as a pastor and counselor to this community, was because of the pain which he himself had known. I think, for example, of the pain of doubt. At one time, at least, during the years I knew him, this was very real. And it was precisely because he had known for himself in such an agonizingly real way what doubt was, that he helped so many students to work through their own doubts. One friend of mine, after consulting several people about a particularly baffling problem, made the comment later, "D. was the only one who really understood the questions." Of course he understood the questions. For at one time, at least, in his own life, they had been *his* questions.

### III

D.'s death has opened up for me another meaning of the gospel. Even to state it may seem to verge upon the sentimental or the idolatrous, but I mean it in a way that I think is safely removed from either of those sins. During the reading of the Scripture lesson at the funeral service, it hit me with almost physical force, that in the most literal sense of the words it was true that D. had *"laid down his life for his friends."* It was precisely because he had given himself so totally and so lavishly to generations of students and faculty, that his body was broken. To the extent that I made demands upon him, D. died for me. One remembers, with a kind of wistful sadness, his efforts finally to guard some time for his family and for a margin of health, and how he was yet always being battered upon from without, as person after person made claims upon his energies. And so the truth that there is no greater love than to lay down one's life for one's friends comes home with a peculiar poignancy in the fact of D.'s death.

I realize that the full significance of this phrase of our Lord's should have long since come home to me as I contemplated and tried to involve myself in the event of his crucifixion. But I shall always owe to D., by virtue of the very fact of his dying, the immediacy for my own faith of this truth which his own life and death incarnated. And I do not fancy that God is ill pleased, if through one of his children we come to see more clearly than we had before, the meaning of what happened to his own Son. In making me aware of the depth of the greatest love, D., by his death, has opened for me one further window into eternity.

## IV

Finally, D.'s death has helped to transform from a phrase to a reality *"the peace of God, which passeth all understanding."* Until his death I had always known that there were many things about God which passed particularly *my* understanding, but I did not know the extent to which this peace of God, even though it passed understanding, could be real. And D.'s death has illumined for me at least two aspects of the peace of God.

One of these I have hinted at in writing about his pain. It is clear to me that D. now knows the peace of God in a full and ultimate way. For him the ambiguities are passed, the paradoxes are resolved. He can, perhaps, say, "Why, of course! I should have known all along it was this way!"

But there must surely be more to the peace of God than that. That which D. knows in its fullness must in some measure be a possibility for us as well as for him. There is no thing for which I have prayed more earnestly for those close to D., than that somehow the peace of God which he knows can be increasingly real for them.

And I now know that this *can* be real. I know it, to be sure, only fragmentarily, and I doubt that it is given to many people fully to experience it in this life. The peace is not an easy peace, or a static peace, but it *is* a kind of peace. It is a peace that we find not in the absence of pain but in the midst of pain; not in pure joy but in a joy that is embedded in sorrow; not in unruffled calm but in a calm that rests secure in the center of enormous turmoil. These are not "dialectical statements" for a technical discourse on "the peace of God"—they are only descriptive, *merely* descriptive (one might say) of what D.'s death has taught me about how the peace of God comes to us. It is a peace for which a heavy price is paid; it has cost me D.'s death to find it. To know resurrection, it is quite clear, one must first know death.

And I am quite sure that God somehow also knows *this* kind of peace which he grants *us*, as well as the peace he has granted D. For the most adequate description of it would be found by pointing to the figure of the Crucified One in all his agony, saying in perfect serenity, "Father, into thy hands I commit my spirit." If that is truly the peace of God as men experience it in history, then I have discovered what it is only since, and because of, D.'s death.

> Man was made for Joy and Woe;
> And when this we rightly know
> Thro' the World we safely go.
> Joy and Woe are woven fine,
> A Clothing for the Soul divine.[2]

I am sure that "the peace of God," in the sense in which I know that D. knows it, will gradually become more real for those who love him, and that even though joy and woe will remain "woven fine," some of the woe will be suffused by the deeper joy which D. now has.

## V

It may be that in time I will be able to make an act of thanksgiving to God for D.'s death, in this sense at least—that he permitted D. by his very death to bring me closer to God, by dying, than anyone else has or could, by living. I have the strange feeling that the things I learned from D. in his lifetime, important as they are, are not worthy to be compared to the things that he has taught me in the space of one long, terrible, and wonderful week since his death. And I know too that the things he has helped me to learn in that one week are only the beginning of the things which I shall continue to learn from him.

I could never say that this "justifies" D.'s death. But I do say that in these ways, his death, which at first seemed to me totally bad, has become a sacramental means of grace for me, and in that sense at least has shown forth the love and the goodness and the mercy of God, so that I can be filled with gratitude to God for D.'s life, short as it was, and also be filled with gratitude to him that in the midst of the deepest sorrow I have yet known in this life, God has been pleased to reveal to me something of his love and grace.

The moments when I can say this with utter conviction come and go, to be sure, but I know at least that *they* are the real moments, and I can live between them in faith that they will return. I know in an unutterably real way, how true are the words that were sung at D.'s funeral, to the almost unearthly beauty of Bach's music, words that go like this:

My faith is still secure
And still I love my God,
For all my pains and fears
Are chastenings of His rod.
With God I am at peace:
No more will I repine.
God is my strength and shield
Protecting me and mine.

Whate'er my God ordains,
Though I the cup must drink,
That bitter seems to my faint heart,
I will not faint nor shrink.
My tears shall pass away
When dawns again the day,
Sweet comfort then shall fill my heart
And care and pain depart.

And so my God I thank
And love Him truly still.
On earth the only law
Is to obey His will.
In Him I put my trust,
In His I place my hand.
Thru pastures green I'm led
Unto the promised land.

### Notes

1. In C. S. Lewis' introductory article to *Essays Presented to Charles Williams* (Oxford University Press, 1947).
2. William Blake, *Auguries of Innocence*.

# Ecumenism Behind Bars

*Leon County Jail*
*Tallahassee, Florida*
*August 5, 1964*

. . . Probably the most difficult thing to cope with is the uncertainty. You unfasten your seat belt to get off the plane and have no idea what will happen when you have gotten to the bottom of the ramp. A rumor is out that you are to be rearrested immediately. If so, will you be allowed to contact counsel? Will you be able to maintain outward calm, no matter how much your stomach is churning inwardly?

There are no policemen at the foot of the ramp but, to your surprise, there are reporters. How did they know you were coming back to face jail sentence? Can you talk to them without committing your fellow ministers and rabbis to some attitude or reaction of yours they may not share?

You walk into the airport terminal, the same terminal where three years before a mob had gathered in the darkness intending to beat you up for being a "nigger-lover"; the same terminal where three years before the city officials had finally arrested you—not the mob—for "unlawful assembly with incitement to riot."

---

Originally published in *Presbyterian Life,* Sept. 15, 1964. Used by permission.

Much is still the same. The rabbis and the black and the white ministers with whom you had come to test the airport facilities are there. Even some of the reporters who were covering the story three years ago are back. The murals on the wall, though slightly faded, are the same murals.

But there is one important difference. The restaurant, which three years before had refused to serve you because some of your group were black, is now integrated. The issue that had brought you here three years ago is no longer an issue. That battle has been won. But the city officials, three years later, are stubbornly insisting, on a legal and procedural technicality, that you return to face imprisonment.

It is now late at night. You have missed the airport bus into town, six long, dark miles away. Every time you made that trip three years ago you had a police escort, so that the rednecks waiting to get you would be thwarted, even in the dark in which they love to work. A reporter offers you a ride back to town, where you have been told that you will be able to stay in an integrated hotel—a miracle beyond all your anticipations.

You thank the reporter, climb in, and drive off. As you leave, another car pulls out of the parking lot behind you and follows you into the dark void of that six miles of country road to town. The car's headlights stay a measured distance behind you, and once again the involuntary pang of fear makes its way up to your throat. You wonder who is in that car, and how long they will wait before they gun their motor, pull up alongside, and force you off the road.

And then you catch yourself. This is pure fantasy, induced by a sleepless night and a hectic day. That sort of thing might have happened three years ago, but this is 1964, and the civil rights bill has been passed. Things have changed.

You relax, and you do get to your hotel without incident. But you can't help remembering that not so far away, in Mississippi, cars *are* pulling up and forcing other cars off the road, and "nigger-lovers" are being beaten up and killed, and it is still 1964, and the civil rights bill has been passed. Only things have not changed.

The next day you go to court, are given brusque and contemptuous treatment by the city judge, and find yourself once again in the same jail you inhabited three years ago—a step that had to be taken so that the lawyers could start the long, weary fight up through the courts again.

Once more, there is uncertainty; though now you are safely behind bars, the uncertainty is no longer tinged with fear. You may find your case reinstated and be out on bail in a few hours. Or a number of appeals may be necessary, and you may be here a few days. Or, though it is hard to conceive, you may lose the whole case on a technicality and face the prospect of a full sixty-day incarceration . . .

What has all this got to do with ecumenism? A number of things. And the word is one you begin to appreciate in a new way when you are behind bars. For you discover very soon that, although the law can keep you in jail, the law can't keep the church out of jail. You realize that you are not alone. You do not have a heightened mystical sense of the presence of God, but you do have a heightened tangible sense of the presence of the communion of saints. The telegrams of support begin to come—from a Catholic layman in California; from a white southern Presbyterian couple in Arkansas; from a group of priests, nuns, lay people, and Protestant ministers on joint retreat; from a Catholic seminary professor; from members of the rabbis' congregations; from your own denominational officials; and, most humbling of all, from Martin Luther King —humbling because he has been in jail dozens of times more than you have, and how many telegrams did you think to send to him?

It's not just the telegrams. It's the fact that almost all the telegrams remind you that the senders are praying for you and have groups of people praying for you. And you realize as you sit in jail that Protestants in Hot Springs, Catholics in Menlo

Park, Jews in Springfield, blacks in Newark, "WASPs" in New York City, and many others you know not of are upholding and supporting all of you by a great web of love and concern and intercession.

When one of the rabbis gets a telegram that goes *"Baruch ata adonai matir assurim"* (and how the prison censors must have puzzled over that one), you know as a Protestant that you too are being included in the ancient prayer of the Jewish liturgy that goes, "Blessed art thou, O Lord, who freest the captives." When a priest wires you of "the prayers and penances of many for your group," you are strengthened at the picture of Catholics gathered to pray exclusively for Protestants and Jews.

Not only are there ecumenical "prayers and penances," there is joint ecumenical action as well. The chairman of the social action commission and the vice-president of the Synagogue Council of America join with the director and associate director of the Commission on Religion and Race of the National Council of Churches of Christ in sending telegrams of protest to the city officials. Another official of the National Council of Churches of Christ wires your group that he is willing to enlist clergymen to picket the jail (and that one does rock the prison censors). A Presbyterian denominational official flies down from Nashville just to visit you in prison. Another comes from New York. Later a large basket of fruit arrives in their name. The local Jewish rabbi visits the jail every evening. The black clergy of Tallahassee continue the marvelous public support they gave you three years ago, visiting the jail, bringing writing materials (on which this is being written), reading matter, shaving equipment—vehicles all of an *agapē* that transcends denominational boundaries, and encompasses and destroys interfaith boundaries. For the first time, local white Protestant ministers visit the "nigger-lovers" in jail—three of them, all told, in an act that defies the local mores and brings a further sense of local support to the inmates.

Finally, after a few days of this, one of the rabbis says to you, "It's the black who has brought us all together. Until the civil rights movement, I hardly knew any Protestants, and I certainly didn't know any Catholics." And he is right. You discover that you still have theological differences with the rabbis inside the jail who are living with you, and with the Catholics outside the jail who are praying for you. But you make the even more important discovery that on this particular issue—equal rights for all men—you have absolutely no differences whatsoever. Here you are totally and unequivocally one. Catholics and Jews are not less concerned about civil rights than Protestants. Protestants and Jews do not see the *imago Dei* in the black any less clearly than Catholics. Catholics and Protestants do not have insights into the civil rights struggle that are denied to the Jews—though Catholics and Protestants still have a lot to learn from the Jews about how Catholic and Protestant abuse of the Jews in the past has given the lie to Catholic and Protestant lip-service concern for them.

As you share a deepening ecumenical fellowship in jail—the Jews joining with you when you pray, you learning from the rabbis a grace before meat from the Jewish liturgy—you wish that a priest also were in your midst. In 1961, the occasion of the incident that has prompted your present plight, it was not possible to work out procedures whereby a Catholic priest could accompany you on a Freedom Ride, though you know some who would like to have done so. Would it have been so hard, you wonder, in 1964, when so much has happened to the church and the world in the interval? And you wonder if in another three years, under similar circumstances, a Catholic priest from the locale of the arrest might find his way clear to visit the jail and pray with his Protestant and Jewish brethren.

Ecumenism, you recall, specifically involves the renewal of bonds between members of divided Christendom, with a special concern beyond that arena for the Jews, who are so deeply and uniquely your spiritual brothers. But the concern to draw together, which ecumenism represents, must finally extend beyond ecclesiastical boundaries to relationship with all men, whether ecclesiastically affiliated or not. You discover foretastes, even of this, behind bars. You share the bullpen with a number of men picked up for drunkenness. Early on, one of them makes a disparaging remark about "kikes." Your rabbi friends endure it in silence, but you learn very soon that another of your cell mates, still suffering from the shakes of acute alcoholism, has gone to the offender and threatened, in no uncertain terms, to bash his head in if he repeats the word. The most humbling reaching out across all barriers comes from another inmate, a southerner who has had experience in a good many jails across the land, and who after a meal, shakes hands with you and says, "This is one time I'm proud to be in jail."

Prison walls are high and thick and hard. But they are not impenetrable to love on the wings of prayer. Denominational walls are high and thick and hard too. But they are not impenetrable either. And you realize that it may be a special gift of grace to have lived behind both kinds of walls, in order to make the discovery that neither one is as formidable as you once thought.

Postscript: Released a few days later, our last act as a group was to go to the airport restaurant that had refused to serve us three years earlier, enter it in company with a number of local black clergymen, and have a cup of coffee together—as close to a sacramental experience as I ever expect to have away from the communion table.

When I add up the bus fares, plane fares, taxi fares, and food bills that it took to get that cup, I'm sure no past cup of coffee ever cost as much as that one did. But I'm equally sure that no future cup of coffee will ever taste as good.

# The Berrigans: Sign or Model?

Most people writing about the Berrigans make a big point of the closeness of their own relationship to one or both of the men who have become such important symbols of war protest, and who will continue to occupy that role even through their years in prison. I had better begin, therefore, by admitting that I can't score many points that way, much as I would like to claim them as close friends. On a few occasions, I appeared on antiwar programs and platforms with one or both of them; I had the privilege of introducing Dan at his last appearance before the Stanford University student body; I also had the privilege of speaking on a program with Phil one summer at Emory University in Atlanta, and exchanged some letters with him after he was first arrested. Since both of them spoke and wrote so much, however, and spoke and wrote with such unforgettable vigor and moral passion, those of us whose personal acquaintance with them has not been of long duration nevertheless feel that we know them very well. By all accounts, this has been true also of those who have only known the Berrigans through books or television. Since both of them have such skill in communicating, Dan through quiet but com-

Originally published in a fuller version in the *Holy Cross Quarterly,* Jan., 1971, and subsequently reprinted in William VanEtten Casey, S.J., and Philip Nobile (eds.), *The Berrigans* (Avon Books, 1971). Used by permission.

pelling poetic imagery and Phil through his fact-filled and powerful arguments against war, their impact in personal terms has surely been much wider than either of them is aware.

## THE POWER OF THEIR WITNESS

Why is this so? Why has the witness of these two men been so widespread and so profound? I think the fundamental reason is because they have served in our war-wracked society as *signs* pointing to some truths we would otherwise forget (and might indeed prefer to ignore) even when they have not always served as *models* whom people have directly imitated. This point came home to me with great vividness after Dan spoke to the Stanford student body shortly after he had been tried and convicted for dropping napalm on draft board records and was awaiting sentence. He described in a very quiet and persuasive way the reasons that led him to take that action, an action that seemed rather strange and perhaps even grotesque to much of his audience. But the morning after his speech, two students with their fiancées appeared in my office, stating that while they were not yet ready to drop napalm on draft board records, they did feel, as one of them put it, that "Father Berrigan has raised the ante for all of us." Both students had been considering requesting classification from their draft boards as conscientious objectors to the war. But after hearing Dan Berrigan, they had to ask themselves whether they could comply even to that extent with a structure that was supplying the manpower to prolong the war. Subsequently, both students decided that they must turn in their draft cards and refuse to be part of the Selective Service System; at this writing they await the inevitable arrest and imprisonment that will come. Dan Berrigan was to them a *sign* if not a model—a sign that things are not well in our society, a sign that each of us is called to move from ordinary to extraordinary action in order to force our society to realign its moral priorities.

Another way in which the Berrigans have served as signs to our society has been by the highly symbolic character of what they have done, creating pictorial images that are uncomfortably difficult to erase from our minds. If their action at Catonsville seemed "grotesque" to some, it also served to dramatize, in unforgettable fashion, the grotesque moral priorities that have been erected in our country: we give medals to men who drop napalm on civilians in Southeast Asia, but imprison men who drop napalm on pieces of paper in southeast United States. If such a statement seems oversimplified, it is nevertheless a vivid and poignant reminder of what has happened to the collective conscience of our nation: we are outraged when paper is burned, and we are not outraged when children are burned. So when people respond that the action of the Berrigans was "extreme," I think the Berrigans are justified in responding that extreme moral insensitivity on a national scale calls for extreme action on an individual scale to challenge such moral insensitivity: "Our apologies, good friends, for the fracture of good order, the burning of paper instead of children, the angering of the orderlies in the front parlor of the charnel house. We could not, so help us God, do otherwise. For we are sick at heart, our hearts give us no rest from thinking of the Land of Burning Children." So wrote Daniel in the preface to *Night Flight to Hanoi.*

I do not think the Berrigans have suggested that their action at Catonsville was a *model* for everyone else. But I think they have demonstrated that their action is a *sign* to everyone else, namely, a sign that our country has dislocated its sense of right and wrong, and that when the rest of us remain insensitive to that dislocation, ways must be found to bring us to our senses and restore our moral sensibilities. If we do not drop napalm, then we must find *our own ways* to get the message across to others. Until we do, the Berrigans will give us no rest.

Another way in which the Berrigans have been a sign to our society is epitomized by the astonishing photograph that ap-

peared in the national press on the morning after Dan's arrest.
It was the epitome of the nature of our contemporary society.
For here were two men, one of them smiling, free, and clearly
liberated, the other scowling, uptight, and clearly in bondage.
But it was not the FBI agent who was free; the free man was
Daniel. And it was not Daniel who was in bondage; the man
in bondage was the FBI agent. So one looked at this picture
and asked, "Who is truly free?" And the answer was that the
man who was going to prison was the man who was truly free,
while the man who was sending him to prison was the man
who was truly bound. All the normal assessments of our society were challenged by the spontaneous gaiety of a man about
to spend three and one half years in jail.

Let us press the point. What is the power of their witness?
Why have we continued to listen to them? Why have we felt
a strange wistfulness that they have been doing things that
needed to be done even if we ourselves were not doing them?
Why is it likely to be the case that when the history of the
twentieth-century church is written, the Berrigans, both of
them "criminals" in the ordinary sense of the word, may be remembered as the truly prophetic witnesses of our time? I
think the answer is found in the remarkably high degree of
consistency between their words and their deeds. They said
what many of us said, but they then went on to do what few
of us were willing to do, putting themselves in total jeopardy
for the sake of their convictions. And each acted in his own
style. Dan, as many have commented, has something of the
pixie in him, and he is a poet, whatever else he may be as a
politician and an activist. Phil is strong on well-documented
sledgehammer analysis, and yet he does not let analysis go
bail for action. Both of them, in other words, converged from
different perspectives on the need to do and not merely to say.
And it is surely the nature of the prophet that he acts out what
he believes, and does not merely talk about it, even when the
action will entail the payment of a heavy price. Such commitment is the more compelling when seen within the framework

of other commitments already made. I am impressed, for example, by their mutual pledge to one another that they would not leave the Roman Catholic priesthood. It has become far too easy for Christians, and especially Catholics, to "write off" the more *avant-garde* social witness of those Catholics who have subsequently left the church. But the Berrigans are not going to give us such an easy out, and they will be around to haunt those of us who are part of the Christian community for many years to come.

A further factor that gives power to their witness is the fact that their minds—and deeds—have not remained static. Both of them have moved long strides from where they originally started, one step at a time, and each advance a decisive one. They have not been content to "do their thing" in ordinary, conventional fashion, do it over and over again, complain about not being heard, and let it go at that. This, I fear, has been the route for most of the rest of us. Instead, as they have seen one level of protest after another fail to make an impact on the American conscience, they have been willing to move to new forms of protest. As they have moved to higher degrees of protest, they have had a smaller constituency following them in every detail. But each advance in their thinking and acting has forced the rest of us to reexamine our own thinking and acting. They have made it impossible for the rest of us to be content with where we are. They continue, as my student commented, "to raise the ante for all of us." Voices of protest like the Berrigans' have made it necessary for the rest of us to reexamine previously held positions. It is patently clear to me that if the rest of us had been protesting the war with vigor four or five years ago, there would have been no need for the kinds of actions to which the Berrigans were finally forced. It is because the rest of us were not quick enough to recognize the immorality of the war, and because our voices were too muted and our actions too genteel, that the public conscience was *not* aroused until very late in the day. If the Catholic bishops had said forcefully in 1965 what they finally said timidly in 1968, and if we had been listening to voices like Gordon Zahn's a little more carefully than to voices like Cardinal Spellman's, then perhaps napalm would have ceased being dropped on Vietnamese children and napalm would never have had to be dropped on Catonsville Selective Service records.

A final point that must be stressed, perhaps above all others, is that the Berrigans' witness has remained consistently nonviolent. All who were present at the time of the trial in Baltimore will testify that both brothers spent inordinate amounts of time outside of court urging their supporters to cool it, to avoid inciting violence or provoking it, insisting at every turn that the way to make a witness against violence in Southeast Asia was hardly to practice violence in southeast America. Any attempt to equate the Berrigans with the violence-prone activities of the militant far left is surely stretching the facts further than the truth will bear. And if there has been any single point at which the sign-model analysis is to be faulted, it is surely at this point—that nonviolence is an increasingly compelling *model* for producing social change, thanks particularly to the Berrigans, as well as Martin Luther King, César Chavez, Archbishop Helder Camera and a few others. There is a difference between the revolutionary who wants to bomb, burn, and destroy, and the revolutionary who proposes to bring about change through means other than bombing, burning, and destroying. The latter is the vocation the Berrigan brothers have taken upon themselves, and one must hope that even from their pulpits in prison, they can continue to make us hear the reality that, at least for those of us who are white middle-class Americans, a peculiar burden of witness is placed upon us to engage in the changing of our society by means that are nonviolent.

### Some Problems the Berrigans Bequeath to Us

A variety of questions can be raised about the place of the Berrigans on the American scene.

1. We must continually ask ourselves why we are so attracted to them when we hear what they say and do not the things they do. There is a terrible temptation to let them go bail for us, to say in effect that because they have done what they did, we need do nothing more. We are tempted to take refuge in the fact that because they have been a sign, we need not be, or to be content with the fact that since they are in jail, the witness has been made (by somebody else, thank God) and we are thus let off the hook. It may be that we are attracted to them precisely because the level of their commitment is so much deeper than ours that we never feel really threatened by their presence into doing deeds that could bring similar unfortunate consequences upon ourselves.

2. Their actions highlight an ongoing perplexity in the realm of ethics: (a) do we act as we do simply because we must, whatever the consequences, or (b) are we called upon to weigh the consequences in deciding what we will do? There comes a point when we simply must act on the basis of the principle, "Here I stand, I can do no other." Dan and Phil clearly reached that point long ago, and they clearly believe also that the consequences of their actions will help, rather than hinder, the cause of peace. But what if this assessment turns out to be incorrect? What if the consequences should turn out to be (as the saying now goes) counterproductive? Some of their critics argue that in doing what they did the Berrigans have made it more difficult to end the war, by stirring up protest not against the war but against the protestors against the war.

The difficulty with this argument is that since one can never be sure of all the consequences, and since baleful ones can always be projected, one may be reduced to such a vapid kind of moderation that no significant prophetic stance is ever taken. No one would be happier than Mr. Agnew or Mr. Mitchell if all those against the war never acted in a way that could produce counterreactions in "middle America." If one does not risk stirring up antagonism, one simply allows apathy or injustice to reign unchallenged. When one recalls the statements that Mr. Nixon, Mr. Agnew, and Mr. Mitchell have made about protest and dissent in the last twelve months, it is clear that they are prepared to allow any kind of "dissent" that does not threaten their own policy in Southeast Asia. Any significant action will carry within it the risk of stirring up antagonism, but it can also carry within it the possibility of creating new centers of support, and (even through the antagonism) helping to join the issue in a way that would have been impossible otherwise. So against the charge that certain types of actions may have unfortunate consequences can be offered the countercharge that inaction may have the most unfortunate consequences of all.

3. An even tougher question raised by the Berrigans' activities is that of the degree of allegiance one is called upon to give to a structural fabric of our society. (I use the words "structural fabric" as a rather awkward circumlocution for "law and order," since the latter has come to be such a code word for right-wing oppression.) When the Berrigans first burned the draft board records, they waited for the police to arrest them, submitted to trial, and indicated that they would go to jail if convicted. But somewhere along the line, they came to the conclusion that it was no longer proper to play ball with the system, and that a corrupt society had no claim over their consciences.

Now *any* Christian must affirm that a point may come when he must refuse to play ball with the system. Many of us who have been far less vigorous in our war-protest activities than the Berrigans have asserted that at certain points we are willing to break the law, but very few of us have challenged the whole legal system to the extent exemplified by the Berrigans' evasion of surrender to the authorities for imprisonment. A sick society needs some kind of order and structure, and one must analyze the social structures very carefully before deciding that a given society is beyond repair from within. Such a point of total defiance clearly arrived for Dietrich Bonhoeffer and his collaborators in their resistance against Nazi Germany, and it has always been a part of Christian belief that in the final analysis "we must obey God rather than men." (Acts 5:29.) Whether we can maintain the minimal structures necessary for social life without allegiance to some system of law, and without courts and punishment for the breaking of law, is a question that the Berrigans force us to consider afresh, and their actions provide a disturbing sign that we must take seriously, particularly if those actions are not yet the model most of us are prepared to imitate. (My existential confusion is symbolized by the fact that I took a kind of unholy glee in the fact that Daniel Berrigan was able to elude the oh-so-efficient FBI for four months, even though I would not be inclined to take that course of action if I myself were arrested, convicted, and sentenced to jail. Perhaps my glee was irresponsibly romantic, the comfortable glee of one who enjoys seeing *somebody else* demythologize an omnipotent power, and is willing to let somebody else pay the price for one's own greater sense of freedom. But Dan has reminded me by his action that there is a kind of freedom that is possible even when one is bound, a kind of liberty that can be exercised even by those who are being hunted and pursued. And in this very up-tight age, that is a lesson all of us need to learn.)

Sign or model? The Berrigans are a legitimate prophetic sign to us so long as we do not let their actions go bail for our inactions, and they will remain an ongoing prophetic sign by continually keeping us off balance, as their very absence from our immediate midst forces us continually to reevaluate the kind of society that brands them criminals. But if they *free* us to make our own protests in our own ways, they also *bind* us to make those protests more sharply tomorrow than we did yesterday, and to face the uncomfortable possibility that what we may be called upon to do next week is of a magnitude we would not even have considered last month.

## 4. VIETNAM AND THE EXERCISE OF DISSENT: A FRAGMENT OF HISTORY

# The Last Judgment Is Now

The parable of the Last Judgment has been put to many uses. I shall not endeavor to extract from it a detailed account of what American foreign policy in Vietnam should be. Let me, however, highlight three things from this parable that furnish a backdrop for our concern about Vietnam. And although the parable deals with the nations, let us not evade its direct word to us as individuals, but hear it rather as addressed to each of us.

1. In terms of this parable, *How is it that we shall be judged?* Let us not worry about imagery or detail or rhetoric. Let us simply ask the hard, clean question, "How is the worth of a man determined?" And we discover that the question before which we will be held accountable is not: "Were you baptized?" or "Did you tithe?" or "Can you distinguish between true and false doctrine?" Those questions may, in various contexts, be important, but they are not, either individually or collectively, the all-important question. The all-important question, according to this parable, is simply: *"What did you do for those in need?"* What did you do for the hungry, the thirsty, the lonesome, the ill-clad, the sick, the imprisoned?

Where are such people today—those in terms of whom the

A speech given at the National Mobilization of Clergy and Laymen Concerned About Vietnam in Washington, D.C., Feb. 1, 1967.

authenticity of our lives will be judged? We have them, to be sure, in Washington, Cleveland, Topeka, Birmingham, Albuquerque, San Diego, and Portland. But we have them also in a special way in Vietnam, and there our responsibility is the greater.

It is our presence that has made them hungry, by defoliating their crops.

It is our presence that has made them thirsty, by befouling their springs and rivers.

It is our presence that has made them lonesome by killing their children with napalm.

It is our presence that has made them naked by destroying their production capacity.

It is our presence that has made them sick by bombing their supply routes.

It is our presence that has imprisoned them by evacuating their civilians to relocation centers and destroying their villages for our military convenience.

The question stands: "What did you do for those in need?"

2. A second emphasis of this parable is surprising and threatening to conventionally religious people. We have been taught that religion deals with our spiritual needs; the constant criticism we hear leveled at our churches and synagogues is that we are meddling where we don't belong: "Reverend, don't talk politics, preach the gospel"; "Rabbi, let's have a little less about acts of charity and a little more about Judaism."

But in the parable, the terms of accountability are not "spiritual" at all. The question is not: "Did you give them spiritual nourishment?" but "Did you give them soup?" Not: "Did you give them peace of mind or peace of soul?" but "Did you give them a piece of bread?" Not: "Did you clothe their spiritual nakedness with sound theology?" but "Did you cover their shivering bodies with warm clothing?" The parable tells us that our concern for those in need will be measured in the *most materialistic down-to-earth terms imaginable:* we are to deal specifically with hunger, thirst, loneliness, lack of clothing, illness, imprisonment.

We are not allowed to pretend that all that is someone else's job, that those are "secular" enterprises, and that we are to deal exclusively with "spiritual" enterprises.

The parable demolishes that pious evasion. For it puts in blunt pictorial terms the truth that is embedded in both Christianity and Judaism—that the two great commandments (which we Christians had better have the grace to acknowledge are no Christian invention but come from the Hebrew Bible) these commandments, to love God and love the neighbor, are one and the same. The parable translates that from the abstract to the concrete: for the Christian to feed the hungry is to feed Christ; for the Jew to feed the hungry is to give honor to God.

Where, then, is God found? Not necessarily in our cathedrals or churches, not in our closed-off religious sectors—but in the halls of Congress where issues of hunger and thirst and illness are debated; in our State Department where men determine who will live and who will die; in the efforts of humble citizens who seek to mobilize their outcry on behalf of those who suffer nakedness and want. We clergy do not "take God" to those places, but if we *go* to those places, it is *there* that we will find him. And if through those places we minister *not* to those in need, we neither minister to God nor in his name.

3. The third thing we learn from this parable is something religious leaders in particular need to hear. For when we ask who are those in this story who have done the will of their Father, we learn a surprising and important thing: *the righteous do not know that they are righteous.* "Lord, when did we see thee hungry and feed thee, or thirsty and give thee drink? And when did we see thee a stranger and welcome thee, or naked and clothe thee? And when did we see thee sick or in prison and visit thee?" (Matt. 26:37-39.) The righteous do not ap-

proach the moment of judgment confident and secure, loaded down with a whole bagful of good works to be dumped on the scale of judgment. They do not say, "We of all people have earned the divine favor." No, confronted by the terms of judgment they feel themselves empty and defenseless. They say in effect, "On the terms you dictate, we have nothing to offer, there is nothing to commend ourselves to you."

These are surely the only terms on which we can face God —not in self-confidence, but in abasement. Let us not presume as clergy that we are righteous because we oppose a foreign policy we believe to be unrighteous; let us not presume as a nation that we are righteous because we oppose an ideology we believe to be unrighteous. Let us put aside the terms "righteousness" and "unrighteousness," which means putting aside any kind of human presumption, leaving to God the disposition of what we offer up to him.

The parable is very harsh. It rises to a crescendo of judgment, with only a grace note of mercy. It can be argued that it is not the whole story of our faith, that it is "one-sided," that it must be seen "in context," and all the rest. So be it. But there are times when we do not deserve a balanced picture, where we need to isolate one harsh note and blare it forth. To many in our suffering world today, the note most needed is the note of grace and compassion. But that is not the note *we* need to hear. The note we need to hear is the note of judgment, the reminder that by what we have done and continue to do, the word that may be spoken to us is simply the word of judgment: "Depart from me, you cursed." Our hope, in the face of that possibility, cannot be that we presume on "cheap grace," or count on benign divine indifference to our deeds, but that we seek, before it is too late, a fresh direction.

If we do not do so, we can be sure that God will judge us harshly, and will hold us accountable for the horror we continue to unleash. But if we turn about, if we seek to undo whatever measure we can of the wrong that has been done, then we can also be sure that as we walk that long and hard and often discouraging road, God himself will be with us, to guide and chasten and sustain us, and that he will deign to use even us in restoring some portion of the divine creation we have so grievously misused.

# Protest for the Sake of Persuasion

While I speak only in my own name today, I do speak as a churchman, and I hope there are many within the churches and synagogues who will affirm my words.

I am haunted by the memory of German Nazism in the '30s, and the failure of the church to speak and act until it was too late. I am haunted by the ongoing reality of American racism in the '60s, and the failure of the churches and synagogues to involve themselves until the eleventh hour. But I am even more haunted by the escalating evil of this war, and the timidity of the American religious community in condemning it. In combating those three evils of our day—totalitarianism, racism, and war—we of the religious communities have been tardy opponents, and for that we must first of all ask forgiveness of those who have been manning the battlements of our absence.

But breast-beating is cheap. What is demanded of the religious communities is involvement. Both the pledge and the reality of that involvement have been wonderfully symbolized in recent days by Martin Luther King. His was the probing and disturbing voice of conscience in the battle against racial injustice at home, and his has now become that voice in the battle against international injustice abroad. I only pray that this time we will follow him more swiftly than we did before,

A speech given at the Spring Mobilization Against the War, Kezar Stadium, San Francisco, April 15, 1967.

so that his voice and the voice of his courageous wife will be transformed from a duet into a mighty chorus of concern that American honor is stained by the Vietnamese blood we shed.

You and I share that concern today, whatever the theology or ideology that has brought us here. We may disagree about the tactics of protest—but we agree that this war is immoral. We may disagree about how or why we stumbled into this war—but we agree that there is no problem of greater urgency than finding a way to stop it. We may disagree about the specifics of a negotiated peace—whether it should be based on U Thant's three points or Martin Luther King's five points or Senator Fulbright's eight points—but we agree that there is something brutalizing about using military escalation to solve political problems.

We therefore share a deepening sense of moral indignation and moral outrage, and we must give voice to it. We do so not because we hate our country, but rather because we love our country so much that we cannot remain silent when our leaders commit us to policies of devastation and destruction. We make our protest not only out of love for our nation, but in the name of an allegiance higher than allegiance to our nation. We give that higher allegiance different names. For some, it is allegiance to truth. For others, it is a witness to the inviolability of conscience. Some hearken to it in response to Yahweh's word from Sinai, "You shall have no other gods before me." Others respond with Peter and the apostles, "We must obey God rather than men." Usually when we obey truth or conscience or God, we can also obey our nation. But when allegiance to truth or conscience or God conflicts with allegiance to our nation, then we have no choice—we must follow that higher allegiance whatever the cost. And Vietnam has posed that choice for us.

The cost is not yet great for most of us, although it may become so. Some, indeed, may court the joy of cost too quickly. If you are among them, I beg of you, do not seek a premature martyrdom. Martyrdom is never to be sought for its own sake.

It is only to be accepted if it comes. The immediate need, while we still have a democratic process, while we still have instruments of protest, is not for martyrs but for statesmen. We need to do more than get on record. We need to do more than salve our consciences. We need to change our nation's policy. *Protest must be for the sake of persuasion,* for the sake of swelling the ranks of those who feel this monstrous war must end.

Why does the Government so consistently ignore the petitions, the marches, the letters, the advertisements, the demonstrations? Because it is convinced that we speak only for a handful. Not until we have made clear to our Government that we who oppose the war speak for vast numbers across the land, and not just for the dedicated few, will our voice be heard. And if that sounds hopelessly square, I remind you of one elementary fact of political life—squares have votes.

This means that stemming from our common witness today, different ones of us will have different tasks tomorrow. It means that Republicans must persuade their party to overcome its instinctive death wish in wooing the right wing, and offer the voters a choice in '68—not a Nixon or a Reagan or a Romney, but a candidate who will have the courage to oppose our present policy, and thereby give us a choice. It means that all of us must give every support—moral, spiritual, and legal —to men of draft age who apply for conscientious objection, supporting to the uttermost everyone who says, "No matter what you do to me, I will not kill my fellowman." It means asking our ministers, priests, and rabbis of draft age to forgo their clergy exemption, and request conscientious objector status, and make their witness count more visibly. It means supporting the congressmen who are already on record against our present policy, so that they will be bolder, persuaded that they speak for millions and not a handful. It means most of all creating a climate of opinion in this country so strong, and so articulate, that it will not only be politically feasible for our own government to end the war, but politically suicidal for it *not* to. That, I fear, is the only language the White House presently understands.

I no longer believe we can get the message through unaided. Perhaps only before the bar of world opinion can our leaders be persuaded of the folly to which they increasingly commit us. We must ask the other nations of the world to save us from ourselves. Many nations, ourselves included, daily express outrage at what goes on in Rhodesia or South Africa. Surely the time has come when the searchlight of that sort of international judgment must come to focus on us. So I would plead with the other nations of mankind that through their press, their UN delegates, their trade policies, they remind us of how we look to them.

Let them remind us that when we poison the wells of Vietnamese villages, we also poison the wells of international understanding; that when we drop napalm we not only burn the flesh of women and children in Vietnam, we also incinerate the tissue of human dignity everywhere; that when we support despotic regimes by the force of our arms, we make a mockery of justice; that when we destroy a people in the name of liberating them, we also destroy what little remaining trust the rest of the world can have in us; that when we rewrite history to justify our policies, we debase the word "truth" of all meaning; that when we press for military victory at whatever cost, we not only destroy a basis for negotiation, but also destroy our country's honor; that when we measure progress by "body count" and rejoice in news reports of enemy deaths, we dehumanize ourselves and kill the dream of love.

Let us ask the rest of the world to say these things to us, and let us have the courage to say them to ourselves. Perhaps thereby we may be shocked into repentance and redirection, so that one day it will again be possible for an American to stand within the community of nations, and utter with integrity such words as truth and honor, justice, trust and love.

# "We Must Obey God Rather than Men":
## The Case for Dissent

In the early summer of 1960, I had the privilege of hearing Bishop Dibelius in East Berlin describe the proof-text game he had to play against the Nazis in the early '30s and against the Communists in the late '50s. Whenever the church refused to follow an edict of the state, the authorities would quote Rom., ch. 13: "Let every person be subject to the governing authorities. For there is no authority except from God, and those that exist have been instituted by God. Therefore, he who resists the authorities resists what God has appointed, and those who resist will incur judgment." (Rom. 13:1-2.) On such occasions, the pastor or the bishop or the congregation under attack would respond with the words of Peter, words that became very familiar to their adversaries: "We must obey God rather than men." (Acts 5:29.)

There is no part of our Christian heritage more in need of proclamation today, no part that more clearly defines contemporary Christian responsibility, than the words, "We must obey God rather than men."

The shadow of the war in Vietnam lengthens over the lives of all of us and of the entire world—a war that by deliberate policy our own Government every day makes larger and therefore more brutal and more immoral, and which that same

Originally given as the commencement address at Pacific School of Religion in June, 1967, subsequently published in *Humanity: Critique and Commitment,* Feb., 1968. Used by permission.

Government simultaneously calls upon us to support more and more unequivocally. Those who find themselves unable to give that support must agree that some hard choices are very soon going to be faced. As I survey the almost tragically inevitable direction of our present foreign policy, it becomes clear to me that we must be prepared for a situation in which our freedom to speak a prophetic word may become more and more circumscribed, and that we must take realistic stock of what this means for the future of the church and our own place in it.

I deliberately invoke the analogy to the German situation, for I think there is no period in recent Christian history that says more to us about the American Church in the early '70s, than the situation of the German Church in the early '30s. Germany confronted a monstrous evil, Nazism, and with a few significant exceptions, churchmen did not rise to the challenge by denouncing that evil until it was too late, until the only witness that could be made was the witness of martyrdom. Any speech or action that might have checked the rising tide of Nazi power was muted for too long. Either people did not really comprehend what was happening around them, or else they waited for the "right time" to speak and act—and found out, too late, that they had waited too long. Since the church did not act, the Dietrich Bonhoeffers, the Fr. Alfred Delps, the Franz Jaegerstetters, had to speak their word from prison. And they, though dead, speak to us now, and they tell us, in the face of the evil of our day, which is an immoral war: "Do not wait too long to speak or you will lose the possibility of speaking effectively; do not wait too long to act or you will discover that there is nothing you can do."

In saying this I am not comparing Mr. Johnson to Adolf Hitler, or the Democratic administration to the Nazis. But I am, let it be clear, saying that as the German churches remained silent in the face of the burning evil of their day, totalitarianism, so too the American churches are remaining silent in the face of the burning evil of our day, an unjust war that threatens to engulf the entire world. Let us learn from the

German experience that the sins of silence and inaction are sins for which we too, in our day, may be held accountable.

To some that comparison may sound more hysterical than historical, but I am deadly sober about it, and I suggest two things for the Christian church today that are underlined by the words "We must obey God rather than men."

## 1. THE RIGHT OF DISSENT

The first of these is the church's responsibility to maintain for itself and for others the right of dissent. Note that I do not say the *privilege* of dissent, but the *right* of dissent. The positive and theological way of putting this is to affirm the sovereignty of God, to indicate that in affirming his sovereignty we are denying similar sovereignty to everyone and everything else save him.

Why belabor such an obvious point? Because it appears more and more likely that the greatest domestic casualty of the struggle in Vietnam is going to be the right of dissent. Although I think that Mr. McNamara and Mr. Goldberg do genuinely believe in the right of dissent, let me be very blunt, in order to focus the problem. I no longer believe Mr. Johnson, Mr. Humphrey, and Mr. Rusk when they give lip service to the right of dissent. Each of them, after paying the expected lip service, goes on to say, "but" and what follows the "but" cancels out what precedes it. Dissent, they say, is costing the lives of American servicemen, or it is encouraging Hanoi to resist and thus prolonging the war, or it is playing into the hands of the Communists, or something of the sort. Dissent in their book always ends up as something unpatriotic. General Westmoreland has virtually equated dissent with disloyalty. Last year Congressman Hébert of the House Armed Services Committee argued that we should, as he put it, "forget the First Amendment," so that people like Martin Luther King and Stokely Carmichael could be put in jail—and not one member of the congressional committee disagreed with him. From more and more quarters we hear the statement, "My country, right or wrong." Whether uttered by churchman or politician, the statement is a blasphemy and must be denounced by the church as such. Any plea for uncritical nationalism is idolatry, and at whatever cost, the church, and churchmen, must insist that dissent is not only possible but honorable; not a mere privilege but a basic right. We must be willing to die for that right before we surrender it up as hostage to a war we cannot support. If we cannot stand up and be counted on this fundamental point, then we have no reason to expect that anything else we say is going to count for much.

With that as foreground, let me now supply briefly the theological background, the positive affirmation, out of which such a claim emerges. To me the evidence is cumulative and overwhelming.

The first commandment is our touchstone: "You shall have no other gods before me." The ultimate loyalty must be to God alone. It cannot be to false gods, whether of nation, church, or ideology. Nothing can be allowed to usurp the final loyalty which we can give only to God. That fundamental affirmation we share with the Jews.

The early Christian community worked its way through to the same affirmation. When the members of the Sanhedrin summoned the apostles and told them to stop this nonsense of preaching about a resurrection from the dead, Peter, speaking for the others, replied, "We must obey God rather than men." If there is a conflict between what men call upon us to do, and what God calls upon us to do, then for the Christian the priority is clear and unequivocal: We must obey God rather than men, whether the men are the Sanhedrin, the local draft board, the House Armed Services Committee, or the White House.

The point is clearly focused in the earliest creedal affirmation of the Christian community. The creed was both theological and political. It was simply: "Christ is Lord"—"lord" being the one to whom I give my ultimate and unqualified allegiance, the one before whom all other allegiances are second-ary and conditional. Theological to the hilt.

But political also, for in the first century each citizen of the Roman Empire had to reaffirm every year a contrary creed, "Caesar, the state, is Lord"; it is to the state that I give my final and unconditional allegiance. So to affirm that "Christ is Lord" was also to affirm that "the state is not Lord," to say "I do not give my highest allegiance to the state, I give it only to the God made known in Christ."

Sixteen centuries later the Westminster Assembly reaffirmed the principle in its Form of Government, with the ringing words, "God alone is lord of the conscience." The ultimate loyalty of the Christian is not to the king (the seventeenth-century symbol of power), nor is it to the President (the twentieth-century symbol of power), it is to God and him alone. All other loyalties are subordinate, all other loyalties are conditional, in relation to that absolute and final loyalty to God.

The shoe begins to pinch as we get closer to home. My own denomination has recently adopted a new confession of faith which makes the point as follows: "Although nations may serve God's purposes in history, the church which identifies the sovereignty of any one nation or any one way of life with the cause of God denies the Lordship of Christ and betrays its calling." Fair enough. But the confession also spells it out in even more immediate terms. It calls upon the church to for-give its enemies and commends "to the nations as practical politics the search for cooperation and peace. This requires the pursuit of fresh and responsible relations across every line of conflict, even at risk to national security, to reduce areas of strife and to broaden international understanding." It was that phrase, "even at risk to national security" that continues to upset a small but vocal minority.

But actually, of course, that is only twentieth-century lan-guage for an age-old Christian conviction. Yahweh did *not* say on Sinai, "You shall have no other gods before me, except your

own national security as Jews." Peter did *not* say to the Sanhedrin, "On the whole, we prefer to obey God rather than men,
but if you're really insistent we'll make an exception this time."
The creedal affirmation of the early church did *not* go, "Christ
is Lord except when the state insists that *it* be Lord." The
Westminster divines did *not* say, "God is lord of the conscience most of the time, but if the state wants to be lord of
the conscience then, of course, we'll bow to its request."

No—we cannot admire first-century Christians for putting
loyalty to God above loyalty to the state, and then say that we
don't have to do likewise. We cannot praise Martin Luther for
saying in the face of demands of both church and state, "Here
I stand, I can do no other," and then revise it in our era to
read, "Here I stand, more or less, until things get too hot."

With all that, I would insist, there can be no substantive
disagreement among Christians. We are called upon to maintain for ourselves and for others the right of dissent because
we place loyalty to God above every other loyalty.

## 2. THE PRACTICE OF DISSENT

But in addition to championing the *right* of dissent, I believe we are now called upon to be the *practitioners* of dissent.

Dissent exists on many levels. I am concerned that it continue to exist on all those levels, and that each person, within
the church and without, find that level of dissent at which his
conscience insists that he operate, and then operate there with
all his might.

For some people this will mean working within one of the
two major parties for a genuine choice. For others it will mean
trying to launch a protest candidate, serving notice on
whoever is elected, that there is a sizable minority within the
country that insists that we work more actively for peace. Still
others will feel that such goals are far too remote—people are
dying today, and we cannot wait for an election year. These
persons will push for such political alternatives as a cessation

of the bombing, an overall de-escalation, willingness of the United States to recognize the Vietcong at any negotiating table, a greater reliance by our Government on the United Nations and other international instrumentalities of negotiation, and so on.

My own concerns were once almost exclusively of the latter sort. I came away from the Washington clergy mobilization in January, 1967, convinced that our task as churchmen was to articulate the massive unrest among the broad middle group of citizens—those who are not "extremists" but who are increasingly disturbed, and who, since they have the votes, Washington cannot afford to ignore. It had been my feeling that Washington is quite prepared to put up with, and be unmoved by, a minority of dissent from the far left, or from pacifist groups, writing off such protest as a tolerable nuisance. I felt that the voice of the perturbed middle was growing, that it could not be written off, and that what was previously the timid and cowering silence of the religious community was at least growing into a louder and louder whisper of concern.

But I now fear that whispers or even agonized speeches may be too little and too late. For the past year, all we have seen from our policy makers is a harder and harder line of military action, an increasing response from those in high places that dissent is disloyal, a disregarding of peace feelers from the other side, and a sabotaging of their efforts to enter into negotiations, a progressive hardening of the terms on which *we* are willing to negotiate from our side, a series of deliberate acts of military escalation designed on the theory that if we turn the screw a little tighter the increased pain will cause the other side to capitulate, a consequent willingness to risk drawing China and Russia into an Asian land war, a national ethos that is increasingly ready to condone the use of atomic weapons "to get the war over."

I think that this policy of military escalation is a policy of folly and utter madness, that we have become so enamored of our power, so captivated by our own propaganda, that our administration has now committed itself to the belief that a military victory is not only possible but necessary, and is deluding our people into the monstrous conclusion that by destroying a tiny nation we are somehow striking a blow for human freedom.

### 3. A TIME FOR CIVIL DISOBEDIENCE

Now even if you accept only a part of that analysis, then the issue is posed: What are we to do? What, in the name of God, is to be the posture of that body of Americans committed to the Prince of Peace, committed to the God who is Lord not only of the Americans but also of the Vietcong, committed to the God who is judge not only of North Vietnam but also of our own State Department? The genteel protests, I have become convinced, are not going to register where they need to register—at the White House. Let me repeat that even so they must be continued, and that each of us must find his own level of activity and protest and concern. A year ago I would have been content to stop there.

But the time has arrived when some within the churches are being called upon to pay a higher price in order to record indelibly our moral abhorrence of the policy of our nation. It is not a role for all. But it is a necessary role for some.

In the past I have always been timid about civil disobedience, not only because I am as chicken as the next fellow, but also because it has often been strategically ineffective and morally dubious. In the early years of the civil rights struggle, the term "civil disobedience" was usually a misnomer, for it was possible when breaking a local or a state law, to do so in the name of the federal law, to appeal, in other words, to the forces of law and order to bring about the overthrow of unconstitutional laws and insist upon the enforcement of already existing laws.

But the issue isn't that tidy in relation to Vietnam, and the extremity of the present situation means that if we are to obey God rather than men, we must now live with something less than spick-and-span tidiness. I do not think that civil disobedience simply for its own sake is likely to be anything but negative and disruptive. But I do think there are certain things the church may be called upon to do, which, although they may be classed as "civil disobedience," will have a positive moral content, and represent our committed attempt at the present time to respond to the demand that "we must obey God rather than men."

Let me use as an example the kind of pastoral problem churchmen are encountering. A young man comes to his pastor and says, "I simply cannot in conscience fight in this war." The pastor explores with him the position of conscientious objection. But it turns out that he does not qualify. The c.o. form requires him to swear that he is opposed to "participation in war in any form." And he says: "I can't honestly say that. I might have fought against Hitler, but I don't know, I wasn't born then. I might fight in some future war, but I don't know, it hasn't confronted me yet. All I *do* know is that I cannot and will not fight in this particular war. I think it is immoral and wrong, and for me to participate in it would be a violation of all I hold sacred and precious. If this means going to jail, then I'll have to go to jail."

And that is precisely what it does mean. To honor his conscience, such a person must break the law. He must refuse induction, be arrested, and face five years in prison.

Now I think the time has come when Christian ministers and congregations and denominations must stand beside such individuals—at equal risk. It is not enough to warn them, "If you follow your conscience you will break the law and have to pay the consequences." We must also say: "If that is the price you are willing to pay to obey God rather than men, then we will pay that price too. Just as it is against the law for you to refuse induction, so too it is against the law for us to 'counsel, aid or abet' you in a decision to refuse service in the Armed Forces. But since God alone is lord of the conscience, and not the state, we *do* counsel, aid and abet you in your stand."

I have worded that response very carefully so that it violates the terms of the present Selective Service Act and opens the one who utters it to the possibility of up to five years in prison and up to ten thousand dollars in fines. If Congress should, at the behest of President Johnson, declare war on North Vietnam, such a response would not only be illegal, it would also be considered an act of treason.

That nevertheless seems to me a type of action that the times and our faith are calling upon some of us to risk. I believe that rather than being merely negative and disruptive, it has a positive moral content, and that it says and does something affirmative. I am sure that there are other acts by means of which we could individually and collectively demonstrate that we have a loyalty higher than loyalty to the state when the state demands that we act contrary to conscience, and that if we are not to deny the whole heritage of our faith, summed up in the statement, "We must obey God rather than men," we must be prepared to move in such directions, even when they are called "civil disobedience."

I realize that to many, perhaps most, the notion that the church not only condone but encourage what are defined as illegal acts (and may later be defined as treasonable acts) sounds like the height of betrayal. But if we believe that what we are presently doing in Southeast Asia is wrong, can we permit ourselves the luxury of escaping from that dilemma by silence or by more token gestures of disapproval? Can we turn our backs while our Government brings us closer and closer to the threshold of World War III? Can we ignore the fact that every day not only are the lives of Americans being lost, but also the lives of North Vietnamese, lives of South Vietnamese, lives of Buddhists, lives of people who are one and all children of God? I believe we are now at one of those crucial if exceedingly uncomfortable points of human history, where God is forcing upon us some kind of ultimate choice—where he is saying to us, "Either by your silence and inaction you condone terrible evil and thereby assume responsibility for its continuance, or, at whatever cost to yourself, by speaking and acting, you try to arouse people to stop that evil."

Let us face the further possibility that even these alternatives may be too hopeful. It may be too late to arouse enough people so that the evil is stopped. It may be that all that is really left to us is the obligation to get on record; to speak—knowing that it may make no apparent difference; to act—knowing that it may have no discernible consequence; to risk the charge of disloyalty in the name of a higher loyalty to which we are bound; to risk the charge of treason in the name of a divine constraint placed upon us; to risk the loss of job, prestige, comfort, security, and personal safety, in the belief that when the choice is forced we have no choice but to obey God rather than men.

The German Church waited too long. Perhaps if it had spoken sooner it could have averted the death of six million Jews and countless other Europeans, Americans, and Asians. It finally had only the voice from the prison cell. The American Church has waited too long. Perhaps if we had spoken sooner we could have averted the death of thousands of Americans and hundreds of thousands of Asians. If we do not speak and act decisively, we too may finally have left only the voice from the prison cell.

Difficult times, hard choices, and agonizing decisions face the church—but times, choices, and decisions that are likewise glorious because they offer us the chance to respond with our whole being to the divine mandate, "You shall have no other gods before me," with the word and the deed that says, "We must obey God rather than men."

The late Alexander Miller, reflecting on times in his own life when he had to make difficult choices, wrote: "I . . . regret

. . . the times when I failed to meet a challenge because the risk was too great, or to meet a need because the cost was too great. I don't regret any of the times I stuck my neck out for what I then thought was right; I do regret the times I kept it in."

# In Conscience, I Must Break the Law

"Vietnam? I've got other things to worry about." There was a time when it was easy for me to say that. I was worried about the California battle over Proposition 14, in which the real estate interests were trying to palm off on the California voters legislation designed to discriminate against minority groups, a measure later declared unconstitutional by the United States Supreme Court. I was worried about the plight of the migrant workers in the San Joaquin Valley, who were striking for the right to bargain collectively. I was also, if truth be told, worried about other things as well: getting tomorrow's lecture finished, scrounging up the extra dollars I was going to need when state income-tax time rolled around, finding time to get acquainted with my kids, recouping some of the losses on the writing project on which I was currently so far behind.

In this, I was like many millions of Americans. In addition, also like many millions of Americans, I was probably afraid to face the issue of Vietnam, afraid that if I learned enough about it, I would have to join those radical, far-out types who two or three years ago were saying in such lonely fashion what many middle-class people are saying now: That our pol-

Originally published in the Oct. 31, 1967, issue of *Look* magazine. Copyright, 1967, by Cowles Communications, Inc. Used by permission. Reprinted in Frederick Crews and Orville Schell (eds.), *Starting Over: A College Reader* (Random House, Inc., 1970). Written shortly after the adoption of the Selective Service Act of 1967.

icy in Vietnam is wrong, that it is callous and brutalizing to those who must implement it, that it cannot be supported by thinking or humane people and that if one comes to feel this way, he has to engage in the uncomfortable and annoying and possibly threatening posture of putting his body where his words are.

In the interval since I discovered that I couldn't duck Vietnam any longer, I have tried to do my homework, read some history, examine the Administration's position, listen to its critics and come to a stand of my own. I've come to a stand, all right. And I only regret, not just for the sake of my own conscience, but for the sake of the thousands of Americans and the hundreds of thousands of Asians who have died in Vietnam, that I did not come to it with much greater speed. For I have now gone the full route—from unconcern

to curiosity
to study
to mild concern
to deep concern
to signing statements
to genteel protest
to marching
to moral outrage
to increasingly vigorous protest
to . . . civil disobedience.

The last step, of course, is the crucial one, the one where I part company with most of my friends in the liberal groups where I politic, with most of my friends in the academic community where I work, and with most of my friends in the church where I worship. And since I am a reasonable man, not given to emotive decisions, one who by no stretch of the imagination could be called far-out, one who is not active in the New Left, one who still shaves and wears a necktie—a typical Establishment-type middle-class American WASP—I feel it important to record why it is that such a person as myself finds it impossible to stop merely at the level of vigorous protest of our policy in Vietnam and feels compelled to step over the line into civil disobedience.

My basic reason is also my most judgmental: I have utterly lost confidence in the Johnson Administration. Those who do not share that premise may shrink from the consequences I draw from it. All I can say by way of reply is that I tried for many months to work from the presupposition that the Administration was genuinely seeking peace and that it was trying to conduct foreign policy in honorable terms. But the record now makes patently clear to me that our Government is not willing to negotiate seriously save on terms overwhelmingly favorable to it and that it has refused to respond to many feelers that have come from the other side. I can no longer trust the spokesmen for the Administration when they engage in their customary platitudes about a desire to negotiate. What they do belies what they say, and at the moment they express willingness to talk with Hanoi, they engage in further frantic acts of escalation that bring us closer to the brink of World War III and a nuclear holocaust. I do not believe that they are any longer reachable in terms of modifying their senseless policy of systematically destroying a small nation of dark-skinned people so that American prestige can emerge unscathed. All of us who have written, spoken, marched, petitioned, reasoned, and organized must surely see that in the moments when Mr. Johnson is not calling us unpatriotic, he is simply ignoring a mounting chorus of moral horror with benign disdain and proceeding day by day, week by week, month by month, to escalate the war far past the point of no return.

This means that if one believes that what we are doing in Southeast Asia is immoral, he has no effective way of seeking to change such a policy, for the policy, in the face of two or three years of increasing criticism, is only becoming more hard-nosed, more irrational, more insane. The procedures through which change can normally be brought about in a democracy are increasingly futile. Mr. Johnson emasculated

Congress in August, 1964, with the Gulf of Tonkin agreement, which he now uses to justify air war over China. Public protests are written off as examples of lack of patriotism or lack of fidelity to the Americans now in Vietnam or even, by members of the House Armed Services Committee, as treasonable. With each act of military escalation, the moral horror of the war is escalated. We have been killing women and children all along; now, we kill more of them. We have been destroying the villages of civilians all along; now, we destroy more of them. We have been breaking almost every one of the rules that civilized men have agreed constitute the minimal standards of decency men must maintain even in the indecency of war; now, we break them more often.

This escalation of military power demands the escalation of moral protest. Those of us who condemn this war, who are repulsed by it, and who realize that history is going to judge our nation very harshly for its part in it, must see more and more clearly that it is not enough any longer to sign another advertisement or send another telegram or give another speech—or write another article. The ways of genteel, legal protest have shown themselves to be ineffective. During the time of their impact, escalation has not lessened, it has increased. (I leave as a purely academic matter the question of whether escalation would have been worse without the genteel protests. Undoubtedly, it would have been. But it is too easy a rationalization to argue that we might have killed 500,000 Vietnamese, whereas, thanks to the protests, we may have only killed 100,000. Howard Zinn has remarked that World War II furnished us with a very convenient moral calculus: it is not permitted to kill six million Jews, but anything short of that number can be justified in comparison.)

Military escalation has become our Government's stock response to every problem, and in its exercise, our leaders have demonstrated themselves incapable of change. Their only response, now no more than a conditioned reflex, is to hit a little harder. They have become prisoners of their own propaganda.

Their rationalizations of their policy become more frantic, their attacks on their critics more strident, their defense of their actions more removed from the realm of reality. In justifying the decision to bomb within ten miles of the China border, Mr. Johnson, in a not untypical burst of omniscience, assured us that he knew the mind of the Peking government and that the Peking government would not interpret our action as a widening of the war. But who, even in Peking, can predict how that government will respond? Such acts and gestures and declarations on our part indicate the awful temptation of using power irresponsibly and the way in which our blithe self-confidence may sow the seeds of our own—and everybody else's—destruction. I do not know which is more terrifying to contemplate: the possibility that Administration leaders really believe the reasons they give to defend their policy or the possibility that behind their public reasons, there lies another set of motivations and justifications that they dare not share with the rest of us. On either count, their right to lead the most powerful nation on earth is faulted.

I have already suggested that history will judge them harshly. But such a statement is a little too smug, however true it may be. History will judge *us* harshly, that is to say, those of us who continue to support our present policy makers, either overtly by echoing their tattered clichés or covertly by our silence. He who is not against them is for them.

In the face of such conclusions, one is counseled, "Work for '68. Wait for '68." I will, of course, work for '68, just as, inevitably, being a child of time, I must wait for it. But I am no longer content to throw all my energies in that direction, and for the following reasons: (1) It seems clear that no Democrat will have either the courage or the power to challenge Mr. Johnson. In the face of his virtually certain nomination, it is important that millions of persons like myself get on record as indicating that under no circumstances whatsoever would we vote for him. (2) There is little indication that the Republican

Party will offer a real choice. Nixon and Reagan are more hawkish than Johnson, and Romney has displayed an indecisiveness about Vietnam seldom matched in the history of American politics. (3) The vacuum within the two major parties leaves voters opposed to our Vietnam policy with rather bleak alternatives. The decision to cast no vote at all cannot be justified by those who believe in the democratic process. All that is left, then, is to vote for a protest candidate who will not win. Several million voters so acting might serve notice on whoever wins that there is a body of opposition that cannot be discounted. But serving notice is a far cry from influencing policy. (4) All of this remains desperately abstract, however, because 1968 is a full year off. What is not in the least abstract is that in the meantime, men and women and children are dying. They are dying horrible deaths, inflicted not only by the Vietcong but also by our own soldiers. As our casualty rate increases in the next twelve months, the casualty rate of the enemy will increase perhaps ten times as fast. Meanwhile, our escalation will be bringing us closer and closer to war with China and possibly with Russia.

In the face of such facts, an informed conscience does not have the luxury of waiting twelve months to see what the political machinery may or may not produce. Therefore, I find myself forced, by the exclusion of alternatives as well as by an increasing sense of moral imperative, to escalate my own protest to the level of civil disobedience. The war is so wrong, and ways of registering concern about it have become so limited, that civil disobedience seems to me the only honorable route left.

I make this judgment, foreseeing two possible consequences.

First, there is always the remote possibility (on which it is not wise to count too heavily) that civil disobedience might make a significant enough impact on the nation as a whole that the policy makers could not any longer ignore the voice and act of protest. If engaged in by significant enough numbers of people (and significant enough people), it could conceivably shock the nation and the world into a recognition that our actions in Vietnam are so intolerable that a drastic shift in our policy could no longer be avoided. There is the further remote possibility that others, not yet ready to escalate their protest to civil disobedience, might at least escalate somewhere in the spectrum and thus produce a total yield noticeably higher than in the past.

I would like to believe that such things might happen. I see little likelihood that they will. Why, then, protest by breaking the law, if such protest is not going to do any discernible good? Because there comes a time when the issues are so clear and so crucial that a man does not have the choice of waiting until all the possible consequences can be charted. There comes a time when a man must simply say, "Here I stand, I can do no other, God help me." There comes a time when it is important for the future of a nation that it be recorded that in an era of great folly, there were at least some within that nation who recognized the folly for what it was and were willing, at personal cost, to stand against it. There comes a time when, in the words of Fr. Pius-Raymond Régamey, one has to oppose evil even if one cannot prevent it, when one has to choose to be a victim rather than an accomplice. There comes a time when thinking people must give some indication for their children and their children's children that the national conscience was not totally numbed by Washington rhetoric into supporting a policy that is evil, vicious, and morally intolerable.

If such language sounds harsh and judgmental, it is meant precisely to be such. The time is past for gentility, pretty speeches, and coy evasions of blunt truths. Evil deeds must be called evil. Deliberate killing of civilians—by the tens of thousands—must be called murder. Forcible removal of people from their homes must be called inhumane and brutal. A country that permits such things to be done in its name deserves to be condemned, not only by the decent people of other countries but particularly by the decent people who are its citizens, who will call things what they are and who recognize finally and irrevocably that the most evil deed of all is not to do bestial things but to do bestial things and call them humane.

In light of this, I no longer have any choice but to defy those laws of our land which produce such rotten fruits. I believe with Martin Luther King that such civil disobedience as I engage in must be done nonviolently, and that it must be done with a willingness to pay the penalties that society may impose upon me. I recognize the majesty of law and its impregnable quality as a bulwark of a free society, and it is in the name of law that I must defy given laws that are an offense against morality, making this witness wherever need be—in the churches, on the streets, in the assembly halls, in the courts, in jails.

Each person who takes this route must find the level at which his own conscience comes into conflict with laws relating to American presence in Vietnam, and the cardinal rule for those engaging in civil disobedience must be a respect for the consciences of those who choose a different point along the spectrum at which to make their witness; words like "chicken" or "rash" must have no place in their lexicon. Some will refuse to pay that portion of their federal income tax directly supporting the war. Others will engage in "unlawful assembly" in front of induction centers. For myself, it is clear what civil disobedience will involve. I teach. I spend my professional life with American youth of draft age. And while I will not use the classroom for such purposes, I will make clear that from now on my concerns about Vietnam will be explicitly focused on counseling, aiding and abetting all students who declare that out of moral conviction they will not fight in Vietnam. I will "counsel, aid and abet" such students to find whatever level of moral protest is consonant with their consciences, and when for them this means refusing service in the Armed Forces, I will support them in that stand. In doing so, I am committing a federal offense, for the Military Selective Service Act of 1967 specifically states that anyone who "knowingly counsels, aids or abets another to refuse or evade registration or service in the armed forces" opens himself to the same penalties as are visited upon the one he so counsels, aids and abets, namely up to five years in jail or up to ten thousand dollars in fines, or both.

I will continue to do this until I am arrested. As long as I am not arrested, I will do it with increasing intensity, for I am no longer willing that eighteen- or nineteen-year-old boys should pay with their lives for the initially bumbling but now deliberate folly of our national leaders. Nor am I willing to support them in action that may lead them to jail, from a safe preserve of legal inviolability for myself. I must run the same risks as they, and therefore I break the law on their behalf, so that if they are arrested, I too must be arrested. If this means jail, I am willing to go with them, and perhaps we can continue there to think and learn and teach and reflect and emerge with a new set of priorities for American life. If, as is far more likely, this means merely public abuse or ridicule, then perhaps a minority of us can be disciplined, chastened, and strengthened by that kind of adversity.

But whatever it means, the time has come when some of us can no longer afford the luxury of gentility or the luxury of holding "moderate" positions. The issue must be joined. Our country is committing crimes so monstrous that the only thing more monstrous would be continuing silence or inaction in the face of them.

# Draft Card Actions

## A. FROM A MANDATE FOR MURDER
## TO A PLACARD FOR PEACE

What does one preach about on an occasion such as this? Not about Vietnam or the draft, for you already have strongly formed convictions on those matters. Instead, I shall preach about those of you who are turning in your draft cards, and I shall preach about ten minutes.

Originally we had hoped to have this service in Grace Cathedral, and we were disappointed that your request to make an act of highest moral commitment was denied such a clear symbolic setting. But as I reflect upon it, I begin to believe that it is a good thing we are not in a cathedral, that the time has come to take our faith out of buildings and express it in the marketplace, not to confine it within cement walls but to express it on cement plazas. So although the church today would not support you with its buildings, many churchmen today support you with their bodies.

Those of you who are going to turn in your cards are engaging in this act from a variety of presuppositions.

For some of you, the allegiance you express is to Yahweh your God, and you are today responding to his first command-

---

A "sermon" on the steps of the Federal Building, San Francisco, Dec. 4, 1967, in connection with a specific act of civil disobedience.

ment, given to your people on Mt. Sinai, "You shall have no other gods before me," not the god of nation or ideology or war machine or draft.

Others of you are acting out your conviction that, as the earliest Christian confession put it, "Christ is Lord," thereby denying that Caesar is Lord, denying that the state is Lord, denying even that Lyndon is Lord. You are saying by your action, in conformity with another early Christian utterance, "We must obey God rather than men."

Still others of you, who believe neither in the God of Abraham, Isaac, and Jacob, nor in the God and Father of Jesus Christ, nevertheless also affirm your belief in something or someone more ultimate than the whim of General Hershey, or the power of a draft board, or the god of nationalism. You give this allegiance different names—conscience, integrity, honor, decency. It represents for you too an ultimate loyalty you cannot define but which your action affirms, and what you do speaks so loudly that we do not need to hear what you say.

All of you, therefore, are affirming with Martin Luther, "Here I stand, I can do no other," even though many of you may not want to go on to add, as he did, "God help me." Will you be offended if I, from where *I* stand, make that prayer on your behalf and mine?

We have been accused of "anarchy" and "extremism." The President of our land, in tones that border on contempt, calls us disruptive and virtually disloyal. But I believe that we are acting today not because we hate our nation and its processes, or hold them in contempt, but precisely because we love this land, because we love it so much that we cannot remain idle and complacent when we see it destroying its moral fiber, and in the process threatening the destruction of all mankind.

It is because we believe in law that we must challenge a particular law. It is because we trust the body politic that we must on this occasion challenge the body politic. It is because we are committed to justice that we must be prepared to be the recipients of injustice. And if this be "anarchy" and "extremism" then so be it, we must wear that label proudly. But I choose rather to believe that what we do today is not an act of disloyalty but an act of a higher loyalty, an appeal from America ill-informed to America better-informed, an appeal to our national leaders to recover sanity before it is too late, an appeal from the law of conscience, a law that the highest court in the land can never overrule.

Let me address a few pastoral words to those of you who are about to turn in your cards. The deed you do today must be your own. It cannot be a decision someone else has made for you or forced upon you. It must be a deed about the rightness of which you are convinced in your innermost being.

For you make a decision today to endure not only the first event but also the last in a predictible sequence of events—a sequence that will move from turning in the card, to receiving a delinquency notice, to reclassification as I-A, to an induction notice, to arrest, to trial, to conviction, to imprisonment. You must be ready today to follow that course to the end. If you *are* ready, if the decision is yours, then know that your act today is a moral act of the highest consequence and that you make it not alone, but with the support of a community of concern beyond just yourselves—ministers, priests, rabbis, laymen; Catholics, Protestants, Jews, humanists—who by our presence here pledge to you our support, many of us by such action placing ourselves in the same legal jeopardy as you, and, sharing your convictions, offering to share your incarceration for those convictions.

In facing that kind of future, I remind you of the words of a hymn written in a similar situation of great travail, "Ye Fearful Saints" (and I remind you that "saint" does not mean a holy man but simply a believer):

> Ye fearful saints, fresh courage take:
> The clouds ye so much dread

Are big with mercy and shall break
In blessings on your head.

Let's face it. There is no one here today who is not fearful. No
one cavalierly or complacently sets himself against his government, his friends, his family. But let us not only acknowledge fear. Let us also believe that courage comes to the fearful. Let us also believe in the mercy and blessing that the hymn
describes, recognizing that with all the turmoil that precedes
such a decisive step, there can indeed be a strange and wonderful serenity, once the step has been taken.

A newsman asked me a few days ago if it was not sacrile-
gious to use the offering for an act of law-breaking. I could
only remind him that the offering is an offering of the self, and
that it is an offering one makes to the highest he knows. If
there is a conflict between the law and the highest that one
knows, the offering must nevertheless be made, whether to
Yahweh or Christ or conscience, or all three. You are saying
through your act that even though your government orders
you to kill dark-skinned men seven thousand miles away, you
will refuse to do so, whatever the cost to you personally, that
in the face of a terrible evil, America's war abroad, you will
here and now seek to wrest something good out of that evil—
a witness to an ultimate loyalty that no man and no government can coerce.

Your depositing of your draft card in the offering plate can
be a powerfully symbolic expression of wresting good out of
evil. The card you now hold has become for you a symbol of a
system of coercion and force, of killing and destruction. But
the moment you place it on the offering plate it becomes
transformed into something else; it is transformed by that act
from a mandate for murder to a placard for peace. It will immediately go in the mail to General Hershey's office, there to
be transmitted to the FBI, and thence perhaps to your local
draft board. At each stage on that journey it will be a messenger of peace. It will say to Selective Service, to the FBI, to the

local draft board, to the whole country, that there are those who believe that they may not kill their fellowmen, and who are willing to pay a price in order to recall our nation from a policy that forces men to do just that. It will be a messenger proclaiming that a man must follow his highest loyalty, openly, cleanly, and without equivocation. The card remains a card, but your act endows it with a message. It becomes a messenger of peace.

Dietrich Bonhoeffer, the German martyr executed by the Nazis, who once said, "Only he who cries out for the Jews has the right to sing Gregorian chant," thereby tieing religion and politics together indissoluably, also said, in words I likewise wish to make my own:

> One asks: What is to come?
> The other asks: What is right?
> And that is the difference
> Between the slave and the free man.

God be praised that today you are not asking the enslaving question: "What is to come?" but are asking the liberating question: "What is right?" and are offering your own unequivocal answer.

## B. A NATIONAL CALL TO CLERGY IN SUPPORT OF COFFIN, SPOCK, AND COMPANY
### (with Fr. Daniel Berrigan, S.J.)

One of our number, Rev. William Sloane Coffin, along with four other citizens, has been indicted by a federal grand jury, on charges of conspiracy, based on "counseling, aiding and abetting" those who in conscience refuse to fight in Vietnam.

There are many of us who believe that the war in Vietnam is immoral and that men should not be forced to participate in

---

A response to the decision of the United States Government to indict five men for conspiracy.

it. There are many of us who believe that it is therefore a moral act to refuse in conscience to cooperate with the system that involves men in that war. There are many of us who have been engaged in "counseling, aiding and abetting" such men. We have counseled them to find whatever level of moral protest is consonant with their consciences, and when this means refusing service in the Armed Forces we have supported them in that stand.

Now that indictments have been issued against a few of us, no one must conclude that the rest of us are going to be dissuaded from our ongoing pastoral task of giving moral guidance and support to young men who have made the decision of noncooperation.

Therefore, we call upon all clergy—Protestant, Catholic, and Jewish—who in conscience can do so, to join with us and other citizens in acts of public support on January 29, 1968, the day of the arraignment of the five indicted men. On that day we will give our support not only by word, but also by deed, to young men who find that in conscience they can no longer cooperate with the Selective Service System. We will do so by personally receiving their draft cards at an ecumenical service of worship, and transmitting them to the Selective Service office in Washington.

We recognize that this act opens us to the possibility of indictment. While we do not seek indictment for the sake of indictment, we must, however, be willing to risk it for the sake of an ongoing witness to our belief in the integrity of conscience.

By this act, we will demonstrate our support of all the men under indictment, our support of all young men of conscience, and our ongoing belief that the right to give counsel and support and help is a constitutional and moral right we cannot relinquish, even under intimidation, without destroying our own souls and further tarnishing the moral fabric of the nation we love.

## C. WHY ARE WE HERE?

Why are we here?

We are here tonight because five of our fellow citizens were in a federal court this morning—where they ought not to be.

We are here tonight because William Sloane Coffin has said: "The clergy cannot educate young men to be conscientious and then desert them in their hour of conscience"; because Benjamin Spock has laid his body on the line to defend the notion that war is unhealthy for children and other living things; because Marcus Raskin has insisted that what we are doing in Southeast Asia is indefensible; because Michael Ferber has urged that men who oppose the war have a right to oppose it openly and publicly and cleanly; because Mitchell Goodman has had the temerity to suggest to young men of draft age that this is a time to say "no."

We are here tonight because such men must be assured, and the Government that indicted them must be assured, and the country that is watching these proceedings must be assured, that those of us who share their convictions have no intention of going into hiding just because the price of public utterance and action has been upped. We who share their conviction are also prepared to share their vulnerability.

We are here tonight because five of our fellow citizens were in a federal court this morning—where they ought not to be.

We are also here tonight because 500,000 of our fellow citizens are in Vietnam tonight—where they, too, ought not to be. We probably have many different reasons for feeling that they should not be there—political, tactical, moral, and even military. But it should be crystal clear that our action tonight is a

---

A speech given at a rally in Glide Memorial Church, San Francisco, on the evening of the arraignment of "Coffin, Spock, and Company," at which draft cards were received and forwarded to the national office of Selective Service.

supportive action for them also. We feel that they are wrongly there, and that unless our national policy is changed, not only will they remain there to kill and die, but that hundreds of thousands of others will be sent there likewise to kill and die. At the moment, the only way men of draft age can affect our policy is to refuse to go to Vietnam at heavy price—arrest, trial, imprisonment, and fine.

We are here tonight also because thousands of young men on whose behalf five indicted men are charged with conspiracy, must also be assured that if the price of freedom of conscience to protest an immoral war is increasing, there are many of us who are prepared to ride that whole inflationary spiral with them, and who do not propose to be intimidated into leaving them alone in their moment of decisive witness, whether the cost be misunderstanding or ridicule or scorn or contempt or indictment or imprisonment. When our society believes that it can silence dissent by intimidation, then it is very late in the day and the time for speech and deed can no longer be postponed.

We are here tonight because we tremble for what would be happening to our nation if we had been intimidated into *not* being here, and because we fear what is happening to our nation even though we are here—a growing moral paralysis that is content to say to the finest of our youth: "You may have conscientious convictions—just so they do not clash with the convictions of the White House. You may speak publicly—just so long as you say nothing of which we do not approve. You may act as you feel morally bound to act—just so long as we decide that your actions conform to *our* definition of 'the national interest.' You may be for peace—just so long as you do not inhibit us in the waging of war." We are here tonight because notice must be served that we do not accept such limitations as consistent with the American vision or with the moral stature of free human beings.

We are *not* here tonight to act spitefully toward our country, to thumb our noses at the Attorney General of the United

States, saying no more than, "Some of us will now break the law, arrest us if you dare." But we *are* here to serve notice, with desperate earnestness and resolve, that if to stand in full support of the five indicted men, and in full support of all men who in conscience cannot cooperate with the draft—that if to do so means that we are breaking the law of the land, then such a law must indeed be challenged, and we are prepared to do so, and suffer the consequences, with them and for them. Thus our intention tonight is positive; to give witness forthrightly and without dissimulation to our convictions, not for the purpose of seeking legal entanglements, but with the willingness to risk legal entanglements, if that is the price that must be paid, so that, in the words of Albert Camus, our words and deeds will "speak out loud and clear," and that we thus voice our condemnation "in such a way that never a doubt, never the slightest doubt, could rise in the heart of the simplest man." For, as a recent Supreme Court decision put it, "The greatest menace to freedom is an inert people."

# What Kind of "Patriotism"?

In July, 1939, Dietrich Bonhoeffer, having come to the United States to avoid the war that was about to break out in Europe, realized that he had made a mistake. He wrote to Reinhold Niebuhr about his decision to return to Germany:

> Christians in Germany will face the terrible alternative of either willing the defeat of their nation in order that Christian civilization may survive or of willing the victory of their nation and thereby destroying our civilization. I know which of these alternatives I must choose, but I cannot make that choice in security.

Although we may cringe in the face of words like "Christian civilization," we know what was at stake for Bonhoeffer. He returned to Germany and gave himself through the resistance movement to working for the defeat of his nation. It cost him his life.

During a brief visit to Zurich in the autumn of 1941, Bonhoeffer was asked by Visser 't Hooft, "What do you really pray for in the present situation?" Bonhoeffer replied: "If you want to know, I pray for the defeat of my country, for I think that is the only possibility of paying for all the suffering that my country has caused in the world."

Written after the invasion of Cambodia in May, 1970, and published in *Christianity and Crisis*, Vol. XXX, No. 11 (June 23, 1970). Copyright June 23, 1970, by Christianity and Crisis, Inc. Reprinted by permission.

And in the summer of 1970, we American Christians, reacting to the American invasion of Cambodia, have to ask ourselves whether we have not come perilously close to the position in which Bonhoeffer found himself, and whether we, too, may not have to will and to pray for the "defeat" of our country.

There is an irresponsible way of raising this question that assumes in advance that there is nothing worth saving in the American experience and that the sooner the whole thing is destroyed the better. But the question can also be raised in a way that assumes there is still so much potential good in the American experience that it must at all costs be saved from destroying itself, even if the cost of that salvation is now going to be the "defeat," or at least the "humiliation," of America in the President's attempt to extricate us from Southeast Asia under guise of some supposed military "victory."

It is desperately important to avoid irresponsible rhetoric here, but irresponsible rhetoric has surely been employed by Mr. Nixon in justifying our invasion of a neutral nation on the grounds that America must not endure the first defeat in its proud 190 years of history. As long ago as 1967, Robert McNamara, then Secretary of Defense, said that words like "victory" and "defeat" had no meaning in our involvement in Southeast Asia. However, if the terms of discussion are to be those of Mr. Nixon, we begin to wonder if such intoxication with victory can be overcome by anything short of "defeat." If our present foreign policy is going to be predicated on the assumption that our military prestige must remain untarnished, then surely we are called upon, with Bonhoeffer, to will and to pray for the defeat of such a notion.

What Mr. Nixon's rationale demands in the name of "patriotism" must be attacked on precisely the grounds on which he defends it. For it is a diabolical kind of patriotism that is willing to shore up our own national self-esteem at the cost of invading another country and is willing to let the domestic scene go up in smoke to preserve the military image. We must surely insist that the true "patriotic" stance for our time is to insist that we love our country too much to let it escape from Southeast Asia without having learned some very hard and searing lessons. If our pride can be chastened only by humiliation and only by the "defeat" of many things that presently characterize our national and international posture, then surely we must, with Bonhoeffer, will and pray for those things as preconditions for the recovery of national health and sanity.

In these ways, at least, we must will and pray with Bonhoeffer for the following:

the defeat of all in our national life that enables men to make political decisions in the light of military criteria, instead of the other way around;

the defeat of the attitude that says that saving face is more important than saving lives;

the defeat of all verbal tricks that lull us by telling us on the occasion of an invasion that there has been no invasion;

the defeat of the mentality of those in public life who ignore and scorn peaceful protest and then profess to be astonished when subsequent frustration moves the protest to more dramatic expression;

the defeat of those who use "law and order" as code words for repression against minority groups and minority opinions, and cannot tolerate the notion that justice means a radical reordering of our priorities.

Our times will not enjoy many victories for justice; perhaps the most we can hope for is the defeat of certain injustices. But that in itself would be a nobler banner for patriotism than the White House cry for an American victory in Southeast Asia.

# Draft Board Actions

## A. TO SAVE LIFE RATHER THAN DESTROY IT

For over five years my major activities against the war, both as a professor and as a clergyman, have been related to the young men who are drafted to kill and be killed, ordered by their Government to commit crimes against humanity. I have sought through speaking, writing, counseling, petitioning, and marching to raise a voice against that illegal, immoral, and now increasingly racist war, and against the laws and structures that force young men to participate in it.

I have come to the place where the words I have spoken with my mouth must now be spoken more loudly with a deed. I feel that it is wrong for young men to be forced to enter draft board offices and be enrolled in organized murder. I feel that it is wrong for such offices to enroll them. And I now find no other way open to me to say *that*, than to engage in this symbolic act of impeding entrance to the draft board office. I can no longer stand idly by while young men are forced to do things that the consciences of all good men abhor, nor can I stand idly by while members of minority groups are increasingly drafted to take up the burdens of the fighting.

---

A statement read in front of the San Mateo draft board on Ash Wednesday, 1971, prior to linking arms with eight other citizens in an act of civil disobedience.

I can no longer avoid the conviction that I must engage in a small corporate act designed to *save* lives, rather than engage in ongoing complicity in huge national acts designed to *destroy* lives. I do this in a spirit of nonviolent love, hoping thereby to show that the violence we are committing abroad must be stopped by nonviolence at home.

I hope that others will engage in similar acts, or in acts consonant with their own consciences, in order to heighten our nation's awareness of the immoral nature of the war we are forcing our youth to wage, so that our moral abhorrence will be expressed in ways the Administration can no longer ignore.

It is important to me that we engage in this act on Ash Wednesday, since Ash Wednesday is the beginning of a season of penitence. I engage in this act penitent for the weakness of my own protest in the past, and penitent for the sins of my nation against its own sons and against the peoples of Southeast Asia. I do so hoping that for others as well as myself today will mark the beginning of a new direction—a turn toward a world in which "nation shall not lift up sword against nation, neither shall they learn war any more."

## B. THE POWER OF LOVE IS STRONGER THAN THE LOVE OF POWER

I am a citizen, a clergyman, a professor. I am also a father, and on this occasion I am proud to be blocking the entrance to this draft board in the company of my draft-age son. As a clergyman, I choose to preach my Good Friday sermon not in a church but on a pavement, not with words but with a deed. I do so grateful that today is not only Good Friday but also the beginning of the feast of Passover, the time when Jews reenact the liberation God gave his people.

---

A statement read in front of the Berkeley draft board on Good Friday/ Passover, 1971, prior to linking arms with sixteen other citizens in an act of civil disobedience.

The sermon I seek to do instead of say is very simple. It goes like this: "It is wrong for young men to go through these doors and be enrolled to kill. Since it is wrong it must be opposed. And we today are opposing it by blocking these doors in a spirit of nonviolent love."

Nonviolent love didn't work too well against the state that first Good Friday. The state won. Or so it seemed. But Easter turned the apparent defeat into victory, and showed that love can defeat fear and hate, that freedom is not finally held in bondage. At that point the message of Good Friday/Easter and the message of Passover are the same—love is conquering even when it seems to lose.

We, too, will seem to lose today. Once again the state will seem to win; we will be taken off to jail. But we affirm by our presence here that the power of love is stronger than the love of power, that no jail need imprison the human spirit, that Good Fridays can turn into Easters, that Passover triumphs can be repeated, and that as long as good men are being drafted to fight evil wars, we (or others like us) will return to this spot.

## C. THE MORAL NECESSITY
## OF CIVIL DISOBEDIENCE

Your Honor: We appreciate the court's willingness to let us make a statement concerning our reasons for blocking the entrance to the Berkeley draft board on Good Friday/Passover, April 9, 1971.

While the seventeen of us acted for a variety of reasons, we were united in a belief that the war in Southeast Asia is wrong, that Americans should not be destroying Asian lives and Asian countries, and that as long as men go through the doors of draft boards, the manpower for waging that war or

A statement read in the Municipal Court at Berkeley, April 19, 1971, before being sentenced for impeding entrance to the Berkeley draft board.

similar wars is assured. On Good Friday/Passover we chose to engage in a symbolic act of stopping that flow of human lives heading toward destruction. What we have said for years with our words we chose to say this time with our bodies as well. We tried to say that as long as we stand here, no man will be enrolled here to kill or be killed, no work will be done here to widen the war, no one will receive orders here that make him a potential war criminal, no action will emanate from here that will lead to the dropping of napalm on children, the shooting of women, or the destruction of villages.

In doing what we did, we broke a law. We did so knowingly. We did not do so lightly. Before that morning all of us had decided that we must up the ante of our protest, risking whatever charges might be brought against us (whether five years in jail, or five days, or less), believing that the crime we committed pales to insignificance before the crimes our nation orders young men to commit once they have walked through those doors.

Any of us, seeing a defenseless child in Berkeley, and standing between that child and someone ordered to burn the child, would break a law, whether local ordinance or federal statute, in order to save that child from burning. Your Honor, without seeking to be melodramatic, I say as soberly as I can that each of us sees burning children (and many other horrors) as the ultimate end of what begins in a draft board office. So to prevent such deeds, even at the cost of breaking a law, seems to us not only morally defensible but morally necessary, not simply to purge our consciences but to sensitize the consciences of others as well. We hope that our act will force you and others in this court, and those on the street outside, to ask again and again and again, "What am *I* doing to end this war?" We do not say that you must do what we have done, but we do hope that, acting in a spirit of nonviolent love as we have tried to do, and in whatever ways are most consistent with your own consciences, you too will insist that not only must the killing stop, but that it must begin to stop right here.

I think there was a kind of intuitive feeling on the part of those arrested, whatever their religious convictions, that Good Friday/Passover was an appropriate time to do what we did. Good Friday is the day when nonviolent love appeared to be defeated by a powerful state. But for Christians the seeming defeat became a victory on Easter when love rose triumphant out of apparent defeat. The feast of Passover is the time when Jews recall their liberation from the tyranny of a powerful state. Again, the triumph appeared to be a defeat, for there were forty years in the wilderness before the Promised Land was reached. In both cases hope was deferred but not extinguished, and so those two events, Good Friday and Passover, help to illustrate our trust that in the midst of the seeming defeat of our own act of nonviolent love, a victory is being worked out.

For we believe, whether Christian, Jew, Zen, or agnostic, that what we stood for on that pavement will triumph over what the draft board stands for, and we believe that the vulnerable love of a single human person is stronger than the apparently invincible power of an entire state. So we are here not in frustration or anger or resentment, but in hope. For we also believe that no arrests, no police stations, no courts, no governments, and no prisons, will finally prevail against the quiet but growing movement that is the conquering power of love.

# Epilogue: "We Must Love One Another or Die"—A Christmas Meditation for Every Day of the Year

Christmas is a time when we indulge our sentimentalities. We see pictures of the helpless "Babe of Bethlehem" and are charmed, forgetting that the helpless Babe ends up on a cross, the first-century equivalent of an electric chair. We read about "gentle Jesus meek and mild" and forget about what T. S. Eliot called "Christ the tiger." We enjoy the rich pageantry of the visit of the Magi in the first part of Matt., ch. 2, and overlook the sequel, the slaughter of the innocents, in the latter part of Matt., ch. 2, where it is reported that Herod, in a fit of rage, killed all the male children under two years of age, because the Magi had tricked him.

We extend the sentimentalities into the later events of Jesus' life. We become so innoculated by paintings of an effeminate, golden-haired nineteenth-century Nordic Jesus, that it is almost inconceivable to us that such a one used a whip, in a spirit of righteous indignation, to drive loan sharks out of the Temple. We are so used to thinking of him as mild and milquetoast, that we find it hard to think of him excoriating the Pharisees for their hypocrisy, repeatedly referring to them as "blind guides" and "blind fools" (check the handy collection of imprecations in Matt., ch. 23). We move easily to visions of Easter Sunday morning (presented to our minds in widescreen, living Technicolor), forgetting that resurrection is

Published in *California Living,* Dec. 24, 1967. Used by permission.

preceded by death, and that in this particular case the death was a grisly one, enacted on a city dump heap under barbaric conditions that can disturb the stomach even of one who has seen a freeway accident.

But at one point we refuse sentimentality. We never allow it to intrude into our interpretations of Jesus' teaching. At that point, we become hard-nosed. At that point, we remind ourselves that all the love business has to be understood metaphorically, or viewed as an instance of Oriental hyperbole, or pruned away so that it won't make unpleasant demands upon us. At that point, reversing our field, we declare Jesus to be the sentimentalist, and dismiss him as visionary and impractical, so that we can get on with the business of living in the hard world his love commandment fails to understand.

This betrayal of love is the ultimate betrayal. Because of it, men have slaughtered their fellowmen in the name of the Prince of Peace. Walls of unscalable height have been erected between men and between nations. To the early Christians, the cross was a symbol of the love of God for man, but later Christians did things under the sign of that cross that made it to Jews a symbol not of the love of God for man, but of the hatred of man for man. Of the instrument of their own liberation, Christians fashioned an instrument of others' persecution. In the name of the God that cross revealed, German soldiers inscribed "Gott mit uns" on their army uniforms and went into bayonet battle with French soldiers whose priests had assured them God was on their side. A vicar of Christ on earth praised Mussolini for his invasion of helpless Ethiopia. "German Christians" hailed Adolf Hitler as a new messiah and acquiesced in his systematic liquidation of the Jewish people.

These things, and many more, we Christians have done in our disavowal of sentimentality, and yet every Christmas we turn to the trees and the crèches and the carols (tremolo, please, on a Hammond organ), and for that one day become sentimentalists once more, after which we resume the hardheaded role from which our sentimentalized Jesus would presumably lead us, were we not on our guard.

It would appear that we have things exactly backward. For his teaching, which we dismiss as sentimental, is actually the most hardheaded kind of realism. And his life, which we sentimentalize, is almost brutally realistic.

In his *New Year Letter*, W. H. Auden remarks, "We must love one another or die." Surely the options are that stark. Auden wrote his line shortly after the beginning of World War II, when Western man seemed about to enter a new Dark Age. In the 1970's we are, if anything, closer to a Dark Age than even Auden could have supposed in 1939. There is the realistic possibility that this has happened to us not due to an excess of love but due to a deficiency of love. Our history has not been a record of practicing love and thereby showing our sentimentality; it has rather been a refusal to practice love, thereby unmasking our brutality.

All of which, in turn, can be sentimentalized. In a day when churches are accused of becoming "too involved in political issues," it is clear that the charge is not only trivial but inaccurate. If the churches are to be faulted, it is not from overinvolvement in the political arena, but from underinvolvement.

It is one thing to say, as followers of Christ quite glibly say, that love should be operative in human relations, both individual and corporate. This can be said with little pain and produce equally little response. But it becomes desentimentalized when it is spelled out in concrete terms. And we resent such rude intrusions. Love in the abstract, confined to the churches and pulpits, is fine. But let love be translated into a specific attitude toward, let us say, fair housing legislation, and howls of protest result. Or let it be suggested that love must be extended to dark-skinned peoples not only in East Oakland and Watts, but to dark-skinned peoples in Vietnam, and this makes love so specific and so demanding that people wince.

In such situations, love is no longer vague and pious. It is a

crushing demand. Whatever else it may be, it is no longer sentimental.

Is peace on earth just a dream? It will be a dream as long as
people insist that love is just a dream, as long as they insist
that it be kept isolated from where men live their lives and
make their decisions, as long as they pretend that it is only an
"ideal," as long as they are afraid to translate it into justice, as
long as they refuse to understand it as a simple description of
the terms on which life must be lived if men are to survive,
and life is to be more than a way station on the path to self-
destruction.

We have reversed our priorities. Our sentimentalities have
blinded us to the fact that behind the manger lies the shadow
of a cross, and that in front of the love commandment lie a
host of obligations that must be embraced, if we wish to live
in love. For if we refuse to embrace them, we will die in hate.